THE
PURITANS

COMING JANUARY 1995

An American Family Portrait Book Two:
THE COLONISTS

An American Family Portrait

BOOK ONE

The Puritans

Jack Cavanaugh

VICTOR BOOKS

A DIVISION OF SCRIPTURE PRESS PUBLICATIONS INC.
USA CANADA ENGLAND

Copyediting:
Carole Streeter and Barbara Williams

Cover Design:
Paul Higdon

Cover Illustration:
Chris Cocozza

Maps:
Mardelle Ayres

Library of Congress Cataloging-in-Publication Data

Cavanaugh, Jack.
    The puritans / by Jack Cavanaugh.
       p.   cm.
    ISBN 1-56476-440-0
    1. Massachusetts—History—Colonial period, ca.
1600-1775
Fiction. 2. Puritans—Massachusetts—Fiction.
3. Family—Massachusetts—Fiction. I. Title.
PS3553.A965P87 1994
813'54—dc20   93-46112
                                    CIP

2 3 4 5 6 7 8 9 10 Printing/Year 98 97 96 95 94

VICTOR BOOKS,
1825 College Avenue,
Wheaton, Illinois
60187.

This series about an American family is dedicated to my family·

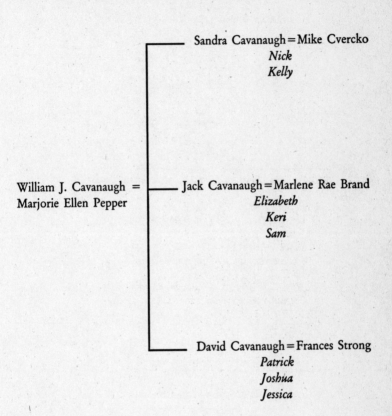

William J. Cavanaugh = Marjorie Ellen Pepper

Sandra Cavanaugh = Mike Cvercko
Nick
Kelly

Jack Cavanaugh = Marlene Rae Brand
Elizabeth
Keri
Sam

David Cavanaugh = Frances Strong
Patrick
Joshua
Jessica

ACKNOWLEDGMENTS

In a work this size, there are always many people to thank:

To Barbara Ring, Carolyn Jensen, Carol Rogers, and John Mueller—your manuscript comments were invaluable; I value your friendship even more.

To Linda Holland—your faith in my ability to produce this series is humbling; thank you for giving me the chance.

To Art Miley—thank you for your enthusiasm for my writing career; you were more excited than anyone else when I was offered a book contract.

To David Malme—your professional counsel has been as priceless as your cover suggestions were humorous.

To Greg Clouse and the staff at Victor Books—I consider you trusted co-laborers in the Lord.

To the loving memory of Linda Schiwitz—the fiction critique groups at your home stung me and inspired me. I look forward to the day when we see each other again, so I can hear your critique of this work.

KEY

A Castle ruins
B Mountains
C Chesterfield Manor
D Chesterfield Road
E Looms
F Meeting house
G Well
H Church
I Matthews house
J Trees
K Stone bridge with
   three arches
L Low stone wall
M Mill
N Corn field

STREAM

WILLIAMS LAKE

TO TIVERTON

HIGH STREET

MARKET STREET

BRIDGE STREET

VILLAGE GREEN

RIVER EXE

TO EXETER

EDENFORD, DEVONSHIRE

c. 1630

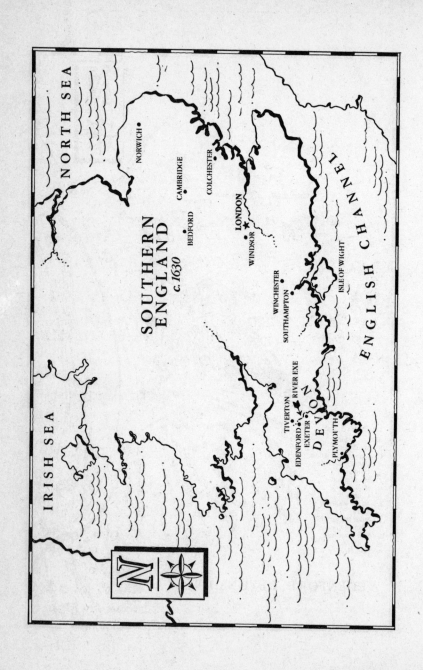

Chapter 1

THE best thing that ever happened to Drew Morgan occurred as a result of the worst thing he ever did in his life. Drew Morgan found love and faith when he caused godly people to suffer.

For most of his life he agonized under the weight of his guilt—even after the people forgave him, even after he married one of them. It wasn't until the last months of his life that he found relief from his torment.

Drew Morgan's feelings of guilt vanished the day he received a revelation from God. It was a simple revelation, comprising a single sentence:

GOD IS AT HIS BEST WHEN MAN IS AT HIS WORST.

As revelations go, it couldn't begin to compare with the one received by John the Apostle on the Isle of Patmos. However, for Drew Morgan it meant the release of a lifelong burden.

For centuries after his death, the descendants of Drew Morgan kept his revelation and his legacy alive. Once each generation the Morgan family held a special ceremony to appoint a new guardian of the family faith. At the ceremony the previous guardian and keeper of the Morgan family Bible would appoint an heir to preserve the family's spiritual heri-

tage, just as Drew Morgan, their founding father, did in 1654.
The heir's name would then be added to the list of former
guardians of the faith in the front of the Bible. It would
become his responsibility to ensure that the faith of the Morgan family survived another generation.

The highlight of the ceremony was the telling of the story
of the Morgan family faith. By tradition, it always began with
the same words, "The story of the Morgan family faith begins
at Windsor Castle, on the day Drew Morgan met Bishop
Laud. For it was on that day that Drew Morgan's life began
its downward direction."

Drew winced as the massive wooden door groaned and
popped on its iron hinges, sounding like an old man's bones
after a long night's sleep. He glanced behind him. Nothing.
The guard with the large jaw was nowhere in sight. Holding
his breath, he tugged again, as if by holding his breath he
could silence the door's complaint. With just enough room to
stick his head through, Drew leaned into the doorway. A long
hallway spread before him. At the far end a floor-to-ceiling
cathedral window stretched proudly where the passageway
split at right angles leading to other parts of the castle.

Nothing stirred. Drew pulled his head out. The vast courtyard that lay between him and the castle walls was clear of
activity. Good. Everyone was still at the reception. He was
sure he'd slipped away without anyone noticing.

Clutching his bundle under one arm, Drew yanked open
the door with the other, leaped across the threshold, and
pulled the door closed behind him, quickly but quietly.

For a long moment he stood with his back against the
rough timber of the door, cradling his cloth bundle against
his chest. The scene before him was magnificent. Exactly
what he was looking for. Drew Morgan found himself standing in a different world.

The scene was one of glorious chivalry, unlike the shallow realm that was currently prancing about in St. George's Hall. They were a fellowship of the self-important—crusaders of flattery, wealth, and status. The world represented in this hallway was of a more noble England—the age of Camelot when men believed in courage, virtue, and honor, and women were beautiful and chaste.

The soft, late afternoon sun streamed through the imposing window, bathing the hall in a sacred light. Drew felt as if he were walking on holy ground.

Artifacts of the Arthurian era were exhibited the length of the hall, interrupted only by a pair of double doors on each side. Mounted shields heralded the past glory of noble families: a moorcock with wings extended represented the family Hallifax; a lion brandishing a battle-ax atop a castle turret announced the family Gilbert; and the Swayne family's griffin raised its sword triumphant in victory. These were crests a man could be proud of, not like the Morgan family crest—a collared reindeer. What evil knight would be intimidated by a collared reindeer? To make matters worse, the reindeer had a sneer on his lips. Who ever heard of a sneering reindeer?

Something on the Gilbert shield caught his eye. He stepped closer to examine it. There were four long indentations on the lower right quadrant. Drew's fingers reverently explored the gouges. *The scars of battle. Did the blow that made these marks fell the warrior? Did the next blow end his life?*

The click of a latch startled Drew. It came from around a corner at the end of the hallway. He heard a door open, then steps and voices. His eyes darted back and forth. Which way should he go? Back out to the courtyard? No, the guard with the large jaw might be out there. The voices grew louder. Drew ran to the hallway door on the left. Locked. The voices grew louder. He dashed across the hallway and tried the other door. The latch yielded. The door swung inward. Drew slipped through the opening and closed the door behind him, but not completely; he didn't want the click of the latch giving him away.

"I will meet her tonight in that little room next to the buttery," one voice said. A young male voice.

"Really?" The second voice sounded younger than the first.

"Of course! She wants me to kiss her."

Drew peeked through the sliver of an opening. The bodies of the voices came into view as they passed the doorway. Two servant boys younger than Drew. Both carried large silver trays covered with silver lids. Each lid had the figure of a stag's head for a handle. The aroma of venison drifted through the sliver in the doorway.

"Did she say she wanted to kiss you?" the younger boy asked.

"Of course not, horsehead!"

"Then how do you know?"

The older boy's voice deepened. "When you get to be my age, you just know when a woman wants to be kissed."

Drew watched as the younger boy balanced his tray with a shaky hand and fumbled for the doorlatch leading outside. The older boy told him to hurry up but offered no help. A moment later, they were gone. Only the smell of the venison remained.

Drew heaved a sigh. Then, turning around, he gasped at what he saw.

The shields in the hallway had inspired him but the contents of this room overwhelmed him. Standing erect against the gold inlaid walls and stretching around the entire perimeter of the room was an army of medieval armor lined elbow to elbow. In awe Drew's gaze glided from one suit to the next all the way around the room. There was armor of many styles from England, France, and Germany. Gazing from suit to suit, Drew moved to the center of the room in circles, like a ballet dancer pirouetting in slow motion.

Drew's bundle fell to the floor with a thud. He was awestruck. It was as if he were surrounded by knights. *So this is what it was like to be King Arthur,* he thought. Suddenly, he became Sir Morgan, knight of the Round Table.

"Fellow knights," he boomed in a voice he was sure King Arthur would use in a similar situation, "thank you for answering my call. I have it on good authority that the location of the Holy Grail has been revealed to us. As you know, the search for the Grail is no ordinary quest; only he whose heart is pure and upright will succeed."

Sir Morgan scanned the armor until he found a French suit. Strutting toward it, he said, "Lancelot, you are without doubt the most accomplished knight among us. However, you failed to control your lust for Guinevere. You are not worthy to make the quest."

"Sir Gawain . . ." Drew scanned the room looking for a Gawain. When his eyes fell on a black suit of German origin, he halted mid-sentence. It was so exquisite that it pulled the imaginary knight to it as to a magnet. Not only could Drew see himself in the highly polished surface, but he could make out the details of the room behind him. The armor was flawless, the legacy of a master craftsman who had died hundreds of years earlier. Drew ran his fingertips lightly across the breastplate and lance rest. He lifted the visor and was almost disappointed not to see the face of a knight staring back at him.

This helmet needs the head of a knight!

Drew solemnly lifted the helmet from the shoulders of the empty suit of armor. It came off with surprising ease. Then he ceremoniously raised the helmet over his head and tried it on. There was a moment of darkness and then Drew viewed the world from the perspective of a knight. With only a small slit in the visor, the view was restricted, but to Drew it was glorious. He laughed with excitement and the sound echoed around his head. He looked at the other knights surrounding him. Looking at the now headless suit of armor, he grinned and thought, *Why not?*

Placing the helmet on the floor he took the suit of armor apart. He stripped down to his underclothes, piling his waistcoat, doublet, and breeches in a heap. Not knowing how to proceed, he decided to work toes to head. First he placed the plate-covered sabaton on his feet, the greaves on his lower legs, and the curved cuisses on his upper legs. He swung the hip defense, the skirt of tasses, around his waist and fastened it on the side. Then he donned the breastplate. He wrapped the upper pauldron and lower vambrace on each arm, joining them at the elbows with small cupped couters. The gorget was placed around his throat like a necklace of small curved plates chained together.

With each piece of armor, Drew felt a transformation taking place. The armor gave him a feeling of authority and courage he had never experienced before. There was no doubt in his mind that if a dragon entered the room, he could slay it. If a maiden was in danger, he could rescue her. Single-handedly he could defeat any enemy who dared challenge king or country.

The transformation was almost complete. All that was lacking was the helmet. The room echoed with the clanking of armor as he reached for the headpiece. To his dismay, he couldn't get past his knees. He straightened up, adjusted the armor and tried again, but he got no closer to the helmet. *Some knight,* he thought. *I can't even dress myself!*

With great effort, Drew got down on his knees, picked up the helmet and placed it over his head. His vision narrowed to a slit. *There. I did it.* Getting up again, however, proved to be an even more difficult task. Steadying himself with his left

hand, he managed to swing his right leg forward. With his
foot planted, he pushed himself up. He gained his footing,
but not his balance. He staggered around the room like a
stunned combatant who had just received a heavy blow. Finally, he was able to steady himself. Sir Morgan the Brave
stood tall and proud in the company of his fellow knights.

Now for a weapon and shield. After all, a knight is naked
without his sword. Drew clanked over to a broadsword
mounted on the wall below a shield bearing the coat of arms
of the Buckingham family.

Just then the outside door slammed. Someone was coming!
He heard voices again, this time much older than the boys
who had passed by earlier. Although the person who was
speaking was without doubt a grown man, there was a noticeable whine in his voice.

The voices grew louder. "Let's go in here," another voice
said. "I don't want anyone overhearing us."

Drew quickly clanked toward the wall and joined the ranks
of his fellow knights lining the perimeter of the room. On
the way he did his best to kick his pile of clothes behind the
armor.

At that instant, the door of the room swung open. Drew
did his best to suppress his breathing and calm his racing
heart. The slightest fidget would cause the armor to creak.

He could hear what the men were saying, but couldn't see
them at first, his vision restricted by the helmet. There were
only two voices. The second voice was pitched higher, but it
had an unmistakable sound of condescending authority in it.

"Are you certain Lord Chesterfield is loyal?" the high-
pitched voice asked.

A moment of silence. Drew guessed the answer to the
question was a nod because of the next question.

"How do you know?"

"I heard him talking to Lord North during Holy Week,"

the whiny voice replied. "They talked about the trouble those . . . those Puritans were causing in Essex. I heard him tell North . . ."

"*Lord* North," the high-pitched voice corrected.

". . . *Lord* North that the Puritans in Devonshire were hard workers and that as long as they produced good quality wool serges he would leave them alone."

The two men entered Drew's field of vision. The man with the whining voice was a commoner; his clothes were clean, but those of a servant. He had huge black eyebrows that bobbed up and down when he spoke. The other was a clergyman. He walked with his hands clasped in front of him, resting on a rather large paunch.

It was then that the cleric noticed the cloth bundle in the middle of the room. Drew suppressed a groan. He'd forgotten about his bundle! With no little effort, the clergyman bent over and picked it up. Turning the bundle over several times, he examined it and then began peeling away the layers of cloth. At the center, he found a book. He flipped the pages. As he did, a wry smile crossed his face.

"What is it, your grace?" the commoner asked.

"Nothing of consequence," replied the cleric. He began to rewrap the book, then stopped, frozen a moment in thought. He scanned the perimeter of the room beginning with the wall opposite Drew. His eyes traveled along the wall to the corner, then down the back wall. Drew leaned his head as far back in the helmet as he could without moving the armor. The cleric's scan traveled down the row toward him. A shiver shot up Drew's spine. Was it his imagination or did the cleric's gaze hesitate when it passed him?

With a sharp intake of air and a slap of the book, the cleric said, "Well, Elkins, we had best get back to the reception before we're missed. Lord Chesterfield's statement isn't enough. I want proof of his loyalty. I'll expect another report when I come to Devonshire for the hunt."

Drew watched the men until they were out of his field of vision. He listened as the door opened and closed. Still, he didn't move until he heard the outer door open and close. All was silent again.

For the second time that afternoon, Drew had escaped detection. He let loose a long sigh and stepped forward to give himself maneuvering room. He'd better get out of the armor and return to the reception. He felt good about himself. He'd handled two near captures with the cool dispatch of a seasoned knight. Actually, not too bad for someone with no real train . . .

"Halt, Sir Knight!"

Drew wheeled to his left and came face to face with the clergyman who was still holding his book. An instant later the door swung open and the man named Elkins charged in, "You was right, your holiness!" he yelled, pointing at Drew.

The two men advanced toward him with unconcealed amusement. Drew backed away, but as he did, his heel caught on a piece of clothing that hadn't been kicked back far enough. With arms flailing Drew tumbled backward, falling against the suit of armor next to him. A series of crashes followed. First Drew, then a cascade of armor crashed to the floor as one suit hit the next in domino fashion. With a single misstep the valiant Sir Morgan was felled, taking a fourth of his fellow knights with him.

Lying on the floor, with the perspective of his visor all Drew could see were the vaults on the ceiling. He struggled unsuccessfully to get up. He was helpless, like a bug on its back.

There was a rustling of cloth before a round red face entered his field of vision. The cleric was on his hands and knees peering into the slit of the visor.

"Now then, let's see if our fallen knight has a face," said the cleric.

The visor on the helmet was raised and Drew came face to face with the clergyman. The man's eyes bulged slightly, but otherwise were clear and sharp. He sported a wide mustache streaked with gray and a fashionable beard, the kind worn by the king, covering only the chin and combed to a point at the tip.

"It's a rather young face, I would say," the cleric said, still amused. "Does the face have a name?"

Drew considered his options. He could make up a name and try to bluff his way out of this predicament. He could take a sudden vow of silence. The problem was, he didn't know how much trouble he was in. Was there a law against masquerading as a knight? Of course, if forced to, he could tell the truth.

"Answer the cleric!" Elkins shouted, kicking Drew's leg. The kick didn't hurt; the armor took the blow as its maker intended.

"I'll take care of this!" the cleric shouted at Elkins. "And keep your limbs to yourself. Do you want to damage the armor?"

Turning back to Drew, he repeated the question, this time more forcefully. "Does the face have a name?"

Drew tried to nod, but pinned to the floor the helmet remained fixed in its position. Consequently, his nose slid up and down in the opening.

"Well, what is it? Tell me your name, boy."

"Drew."

"Drew," the cleric said, almost as if he were tasting the name. "Drew. Drew. Short for Andrew?"

Drew started to nod again, thought better of it, and gave a simple affirmative instead.

"Is that all? Just Drew?"

Drew was hoping to leave his father out of this. Now there was no recourse but to act like a knight and take the consequences of his actions. "Morgan. Drew Morgan."

The cleric was taken aback. "Lord Percy Morgan's boy?"

"Yes."

"I see," said the cleric, obviously displeased. With a grunt and a groan, he raised his bulk off the floor and stood towering over Drew. "Let's get the knight up," he said to Elkins. Then to Drew, "Can you lift your arms, Sir Morgan?"

Drew raised both arms. The cleric grabbed one and the commoner the other. As they lifted him, the knight's visor slammed down, causing a ringing in Drew's ears.

"Elkins," the cleric said, "go to the hall and get Lord Morgan. Bring him to my room at the chapel."

"What about the boy, your holiness? What if he tries to escape?"

The cleric closed his eyes and spoke in a tone usually reserved for children. "The boy isn't going anywhere. In this outfit he can barely walk. I am confident I can keep up with him should he attempt to bolt."

If Elkins was insulted by the cleric's condescending tone, he didn't show it. He dutifully set out to fulfill his mission.

"Take the helmet off," the cleric instructed. "Let me get a better look at you."

Drew obeyed. As the helmet cleared his head Drew's gaze met the cleric's cold stare. Drew lowered his eyes.

"Look at me!" the cleric shouted.

Drew's head snapped up.

"Always look a man in the eyes! Never look down! No matter how humiliating your defeat."

Drew forced himself to look into the eyes of the man who had caught him playing knight. At first it took great effort, for the cleric's stare had the thrust of a broadsword, but the longer Drew looked, the easier it was for him to parry the cleric's gaze with his own. And, unless he was mistaken, there was a touch of humor in the corners of those steely eyes.

"Good," said the cleric. He tucked Drew's book under his arm and strode toward the door. "Follow me." He strode toward the hallway without looking back.

"What about my clothes?" Drew asked.

"You're wearing all the clothes you need for now," the cleric answered, without turning around.

Carrying the helmet under his arm, Drew followed—each clanking step announcing his presence—into the hallway and out to the courtyard.

The moment he stepped outside, Drew wished he could turn around and go back. The king's reception was over and it looked like half of England's nobility was milling about the courtyard. Heads turned toward him with the first clank of his armored foot on the cobblestone walk.

Their response was silence and Drew hoped they'd let him clank away into the night, but he wasn't so fortunate. It just took a while for his presence to sink in. After all, there hadn't been a knight at a royal reception for several hundred years.

"Well, bless my soul! It's Sir Lancelot!" someone shouted. Everyone roared with laughter.

Several men hurried toward him. Drew walked away as fast as the suit of armor would allow. A balding man with a large potbelly who had obviously indulged himself liberally with the king's wine pretended he was riding a horse. He challenged Drew to a joust.

"If you're looking for a virtuous maiden to rescue," shouted a man with a dark-haired lady draped on his arm, "you won't find one in this castle." His lady friend shrieked with laughter and punched her escort in the ribs.

The cleric seemed oblivious to the raucousness as he strode purposefully down the walkway past the keep and toward St. George's Chapel. Drew did his best to keep pace.

Seeing their sport getting away, two men grabbed Drew's arms and attempted to turn him back toward the courtyard.

"Leave the boy alone!" It was the cleric's high-pitched voice.

At first, the taunters were reluctant to release their source of entertainment until they recognized who had issued the command. When they saw the cleric holding the chapel door open for Drew, they released him immediately.

Drew clanked toward the open door as fast as he could.

"What's with the knight, your grace?" one of the men shouted.

The cleric answered him by shutting the door.

Chapter 2

THIS book gave you away." The cleric held up the book from Drew's cloth bundle as he would a piece of evidence in court.

Drew found himself standing in a small, sparsely decorated room behind St. George's Chapel. The furniture consisted of a small wooden desk and two upright chairs, one behind the desk, the other beside it. Miscellaneous papers and maps littered the top of the desk, some of them hanging over the edges, anchored to the desktop by a stack of books. The only wall ornamentation in the room, besides a couple of candleholders, was a crucifix above the desk. This wasn't the kind of office where someone would entertain guests, but more like a retreat in which to work uninterrupted.

The cleric pulled out the desk chair and lowered himself with dignified ease. He made no offer of a chair to Drew, which was just as well because Drew wasn't sure his sitting aim in armor was good enough to hit a chair. The cleric lay Drew's book on his ample midsection and folded his hands over it. For a while he said nothing. He just studied Drew. Slowly, a parental smirk spread across his lips—the kind seen by children after they have been caught in the act.

Patting the volume on his chest, the cleric said, "I knew where you were because of this book. The pile of clothes on the floor merely confirmed my suspicions." A quizzical look formed on his bemused face. "Why was the book bundled in cloth?"

Drew cleared his throat. "My father didn't want me to bring it to London."

There was an uneasy silence as the cleric waited for further explanation.

Drew fidgeted. The armor creaked. "My father thinks I spend too much time reading. So I hid the book in my clothes trunk."

"And it was your plan to read the book while wearing a suit of armor?"

"No." Drew blushed. "The reception was boring, so I sneaked out and got the book. I read for a while, then thought I'd explore the castle. This," he motioned to his armor, "was sort of spontaneous."

The cleric lifted the book and read the title aloud, "*The Days of the Knights* by Geoffrey Berber." He smiled a boyish grin. "I must have read this book fifty times when I was boy." He looked up, unsuccessful in his attempt to stifle a laugh. "Trying on a suit of armor is exactly the kind of thing I would have done as a boy, had I the chance."

Drew fidgeted as the cleric turned his attention back to the book, flipping through pages as if looking for something. Drew was perplexed. This wasn't what he'd expected. The clergyman had browbeat Elkins and intimidated the drunken noblemen with a single sentence. When Drew entered the room he'd prepared himself for an onslaught of righteous indignation. Yet, in front of him sat a giddy cleric wearing a silly grin.

Suddenly, the cleric snapped the book shut and said, "Who's your favorite knight?"

"Favorite knight?"

"Your favorite knight. Surely you have one."

"Well," Drew stammered as the armor squeaked, "I guess

if I had to pick a favorite, it would be Sir Gawain."

The cleric's brow furrowed. "Gawain? Gawain, not Lancelot? Lancelot was the greatest champion!"

Drew fidgeted again. Evidently he'd picked the wrong knight. But at the moment he was experiencing a greater discomfort than being wrong. He ached to sit down, to fold his arms, to do anything but just stand there and creak. Now he realized why knights were always pictured standing straight and tall—it wasn't because they were virtuous, but because they couldn't bend over.

"Lancelot was the champion," he said, shifting the helmet to the other arm. "He was best at jousting and fighting, but he was weak morally. He couldn't control his lust. And that weakness destroyed the Round Table and killed King Arthur."

"I see." The cleric stroked his pointed beard with a mixture of amusement and thoughtfulness. "Tell me, Andrew. Have you ever felt as strongly for a woman as Lancelot felt for Guinevere?"

"Of course!" Drew said.

The cleric's eyebrows shot up.

"Well, maybe not as strong. But there are more important things in this world than women!"

"Oh? An unusual statement coming from one who is . . . what? Seventeen? Eighteen?"

"Eighteen."

"I see. Then tell me, Andrew, from the wisdom of your years, what things are more important than women?"

"Justice, for one . . . and loyalty! That's where Lancelot failed! He betrayed his king and his fellow knights when he bedded the queen."

The cleric laughed, but not in disapproval. "Are you sure you're Lord Percy Morgan's son?"

Suddenly, a din of angry voices escalated from the hallway.

As the door burst open, Lord Morgan stormed in, followed by Lady Evelyn and Philip, Drew's mother and brother.

Even when storming a room, Drew's parents were every inch English nobility. Lord Morgan was a man who believed in putting his money on his back. His dark-green velvet doublet with puffed, slashed sleeves was stitched with gold thread and lined with gems. Over the doublet he wore a heavily furred sleeveless gown. A gold chain and medallion, with the image of a sneering collared reindeer, dangled around his neck. He wasn't a tall man, but what he lacked in height he made up for with noise. More than once Drew heard his father say, "A short man with a big voice is a giant."

If there was anyone in England who could match, and at times exceed, Lord Morgan's volume, it was Drew's mother. She was also her husband's equal when it came to fashion. Here was a woman who was eternally grateful she lived in an age when discretion and modesty were not in vogue. From head to toe she dressed the part of a woman flaunting her status. For the royal reception she wore a wig of golden hair, far superior to her own lackluster brown covering. The wig had been fashioned by Lady Morgan's hairdresser from the golden hair of a ragged beggar child she saw during a shopping trip to London. She lured the frightened girl into her carriage and offered her twopence for her hair. The passing of the coin and cutting of the hair occurred before the little waif had time for second thoughts.

Lady Morgan's golden wig was supported in the back by a rabato, a wired collar in the shape of wings and edged with lace. The front of the lady's white dress featured a triangular stomacher, studded with precious gems. It was a flat piece of material that looked like an inverted triangle with a point at each shoulder and one stretching just below her waist. Her skirt flared fashionably at the hips. Its length was just short enough to reveal her gem-ornamented stockings.

Lady Morgan's clothes were the envy of most of the court. However, she was not satisfied with most. She wouldn't be happy until the entire court envied her. This she accomplished with her pearl necklace.

Her jewelry for the reception had been the subject of intense planning and negotiation months prior to the event. She would not be satisfied unless she could create a jealous stir among the fashionable people of London that would last for weeks after the event. Her choice of jewelry had been specifically chosen to achieve this goal.

The pearl necklace she wore was the crowning treasure of Sir Francis Drake's famous voyage around the world. Drake acquired the necklace—along with so much gold, silver, and precious stones that the *Golden Hind* sailed home well below her watermark—in a series of raids on Spanish settlements along the California coast. Until now, the only woman in England ever to wear the necklace in public was Queen Elizabeth. Upon the Queen's death, the necklace was quietly returned to the Drake family, where it remained locked away until the Morgans purchased it.

This reception was the necklace's first public appearance in decades. And it graced Lady Morgan's delicate white neck, which at the moment was red and strained in anger.

Lord Percy: "We are the laughingstock of the kingdom! You have done some imbecilic things in the past, but never anything so . . ."

Lady Evelyn: "Months of planning, a small fortune, and for what? Is everyone talking about the Morgan jewels? No, they're talking about my idiot son walking around in a suit of . . ."

Lord Percy: "You couldn't have chosen a worse possible time! We waited for hours to talk to King Charles and no sooner were we introduced . . ."

Lady Evelyn: ". . . than this crude man barges into the hall and tells everyone that my son was caught sneaking around the castle wearing a . . ."

Lord Percy: "You are the most stubborn and obstinate boy I know! When we get home . . ."

"Lord Morgan!" the cleric shouted.

Lady Evelyn: "I have never been so embarrassed in my . . ."

Lord Morgan: "You will be whipped until your hide is . . ."

"Lord and Lady Morgan! Will you please!!"

The cleric's voice was shrill, but it had volume and an authority that cut through the wailing of the two martyrs.

Lord Morgan whirled around to see who dared interrupt him. When he saw the cleric who was now standing, Lord Morgan's face drained of color. His mouth fell open.

"Bishop Laud!" he stammered. "Your grace, forgive me, I didn't see you. The clod who informed us failed to mention it was you who was holding this worthless son of mine. Rest assured, the boy will be severely punished. His actions are idiotic, inexcusable. When I get him home he will be whipped with a . . ."

With raised hand, Bishop Laud cut off the nobleman. The room was mercifully silent. The bishop didn't speak right away. Drew couldn't tell if he was thinking or just enjoying the silence. As Drew shifted his weight from one foot to the other, the armor squeaked. His mother rolled her eyes and let out a disgusted sigh.

The Morgan family parted as Bishop Laud made his way toward Drew. The bishop looked him in the eyes. Drew caught himself just as he was about to lower his eyes. Then he remembered the bishop's words, *"Don't look down! No matter how humiliating your defeat, never be afraid to look a man in the eyes!"* Drew held a steady gaze as he looked into the eyes of Bishop Laud and the bishop smiled.

"No harm has been done. Don't punish the lad."

"If that is your wish," sputtered Lord Morgan. "But may

I say this is not the first time the boy has played the fool. If you ask me, the best way to deal with imbeciles is to . . ."

"Andrew and I have a lot in common," Bishop Laud interrupted. "A love of books (the bishop patted the volume in his hand). A love for Arthurian legend." Turning toward Lord Morgan, the bishop continued, "I like your son. He has character and, I believe, a great capacity for courage."

"We have tried to give him every opportunity, your grace," Lady Morgan said, "but the boy is lazy and undisciplined. Even though we sent him to Cambridge . . ."

The bishop turned. "You attended Cambridge?"

Drew nodded.

"I was chancellor at Cambridge. I'd like to reminisce with you about it some day."

"The point is," Lord Morgan said, his voice rising, "the boy does nothing but daydream."

"The point is," Bishop Laud countered with equal intensity, "I want him to come to London and live with me. I have work that suits his talents."

"You want to make my son a priest?" Lady Evelyn asked.

The bishop snorted. "No, madam, not a priest. I need courageous young men for special assignments. He will assist King Charles and me in rescuing England from her enemies. Drew, are you interested?"

"Yes, your grace. I'm interested," he said.

"Good!" boomed the bishop. To Lord Morgan he said, "Let me have your son for a couple of years. After that time, I will return him to you equipped to lead the Morgan family to unparalleled wealth and greatness."

Drew smiled. The bishop knew exactly how to get what he wanted from Lord Morgan. Drew's father agreed.

"Andrew," the bishop said, "get out of that armor. Then come back and see me before you return home for your things. There's something I want to give you."

Chapter 3

T HE day he rode from Windsor Castle to London was supposed to be the exciting first chapter in the adventures of Drew Morgan. Instead, it was a nightmare of nagging delays. It was as if the god of the underworld had commissioned a score of mischievous demons to dog his steps and pull and tug at him in every direction except the one in which he needed to go.

The morning began with promise. The journey from Windsor to London was a glorious ride. The wind slapped Drew's cheeks with a chilly hand. His regal black steed's strutting hoofs became a drum cadence announcing to the world that Drew Morgan was riding toward his destiny.

He had never traveled to London alone, but today marked a new era. Today his mission was twofold: he rode on family business, to pick up a set of chalices his father had commissioned from a London goldsmith; more important, he rode for England, his first mission on behalf of the Bishop of London.

His passport to royal adventure was a letter he carried close to his heart, signed by the Bishop of London himself, authorizing the loan of a book from the bishop's personal library. This was why Bishop Laud had wanted to see him again before he left Windsor.

When he handed the letter to Drew, the bishop instructed

the new assistant regarding his assignment. "Andrew," he said, "England's greatest enemy is no longer Spain, nor any other continental force. The greatest threat to England today is sedition from within. The minds of many Englishmen are filled with heresy, and their hearts harbor sedition. You cannot tell them by their dress, for some are rich, some are poor. Yet their hearts are evil. They freely walk the streets of every city and village parading innocent faces. It is our crusade to unmask these traitors and prosecute to the death those who would seek to destroy England. Ours is not an easy task, for we seek cowards who prey on weak minds, while hiding behind a cloak of anonymity."

The bishop showed Drew a pamphlet, the cover of which had a woodcut picture of a dog with Bishop Laud's face and wearing a bishop's miter. "This is a sample of their work," he said. Turning to an inside paragraph he read,

Laud, look to thyself, be assured thy life is sought. As thou art the fountain of all wickedness, repent thee of thy mountainous wickedness before thou be taken out of the world. And assure thyself neither God nor the world can endure such a vile counselor or whisperer to live.

The bishop folded the pamphlet. Patting it, he said, "The wretch who wrote this has been caught and punished. He was unmasked by the diligent work of a young man, much like yourself. Listen carefully to what I say. Always be alert to every bit of conversation, every scrap of evidence that might uncover the writers, printers, and publishers of seditious tracts like this one."

A pained expression crossed the bishop's face. He looked like a man suffering a recurring malady. "There is one writer in particular" he muttered. "I want him. Justin . . . not his real name. I'm sure of that. If you hear anything about Justin, the smallest scrap of news, I want to know about it immediately! Understand?" The muscles in the bishop's jaw tensed as he spoke; the flesh of his face was blood red. Drew was glad he wasn't Justin. He'd hate to be the object of the bishop's anger.

Drew nodded submissively.

"With God as my witness," the bishop swore, "I . . . will . . . have . . . him!"

The bishop's emotional storm passed quickly. Moments later he was cheerful again to the point of giddiness. "Give Timmins this letter," he said with boyish excitement. "It instructs him to give you one of my favorite books, better than Berber's *The Days of the Knights!* You'll love it, of that I'm sure." Placing his hands on Drew's shoulders he said, "Andrew, come to me in London as quickly as you can."

Drew's mission to London today was fortuitous. While there he could pick up four silver chalices his father had commissioned from a goldsmith on The Strand. This would not only save the Morgans from having to make the side trip to London, considering their son's exploits in a suit of armor the day before, but it would also limit their risk of further public ridicule.

Lord Morgan had intended to give Drew directions to the goldsmith's shop. However, Drew woke early and, anxious to begin his journey, he left before his father was awake. He wasn't aware he needed directions—he knew which goldsmith his father patronized.

It would take Drew the better part of the morning to reach London. He would pick up the bishop's book and his father's chalices and then meet the family at the King Alfred Inn at Basingstoke before dark. There, Lord Morgan would flaunt the finely crafted silver chalices before his old friend, the mayor of Basingstoke, and amuse himself with the mayor's futile attempts to suppress his envy.

That was the plan—before the score of mischievous demons were loosed against him.

To enter London Drew crossed Knight's Bridge, an event which he thought was no small coincidence as he began his first assignment for the bishop. He urged Pirate, his black steed, right at the triple fork which split north to Paddington, east to St. Giles, and south toward the Thames.

Pirate was feeling especially ornery that day, undoubtedly goaded by the demons. On a good day, he was quick to respond and seemed to crave adventure as much as Drew. On a bad day, and this was one of his worst, he was vicious.

Drew rode straight to London House, the city residence of the bishop. He rapped on the wooden door which a moment later swung wide to reveal a large round man wearing a large white cooking apron.

To say the man was round was an understatement. It was almost as if God pieced him together using balls of flesh. His round head sat on a round body. He had no visible neck. Two round breasts, as large as any woman's, poked out both sides of the apron, balancing precariously atop a protruding round belly.

"Ah! You're a young one," he said, his cheeks like red balls glued to the corners of his mouth which bounced back and forth when he talked. "And what might you be wanting?" He vigorously wiped his plump hands with a towel.

Out of politeness, Drew removed his cap. The gesture obviously delighted the man, for the red cheeks bounced to the far sides of his face, separated by a gap-toothed grin. "I'd be wanting . . . I mean, I'd like to speak to Mr. Timmins."

"Oh, now that's a pity," he said, digging the towel deeply into the crevices between his fingers. "You'll not find him here today. You'd best come back on the morrow."

"Tomorrow?" There was a touch of panic in his voice.

"There now," he said, taking Drew's predicament to heart. "If your business is urgent . . ."

Drew nodded that indeed it was.

". . . you might look for him at Whitehall."

Whitehall meant delay. Drew would have to go there, find Timmins, then come back here to get the book. It would take much too long.

"Maybe you can help me," Drew said.

The idea seemed to please the round cook.

"Could you get a book for me from the bishop's library? I have a letter from the bishop . . ."

The cook recoiled, his mouth as round as the rest of him. "Oh no! I couldn't possibly go into the bishop's study without his permission!"

"But I have a letter . . ."

The round cook's head bounced back and forth vigorously.

"Is there anyone else who could help me?"

"Only Mr. Timmins, I'm afraid."

The demons of delay were pulling him toward Whitehall whether he wanted to go there or not.

Two hours later Drew stood impatiently beside a sundial in the Privy Garden at Whitehall, the residence of King Charles I. The gardens were composed of sixteen blocks of assorted grass, flowers, and hedges laid out in a four by four square pattern. Drew knew there were sixteen blocks because he had counted them, several times. He had also watched the sun clock creep along its dial for more than an hour and a half while waiting for Timmins.

An expressionless palace guard had ushered him to this spot, telling him to stay put and not wander around. By the way the guard fondled the hilt of his saber, Drew thought it best to obey his instructions.

Finally, a short, balding man with a precise, businesslike stride approached him. A puff of snow-white hair rimmed the back of his head from ear to ear. His posture was rigid and his hands were clenched.

"Are you the young man with a message from Bishop Laud?"

"Are you Mr. Timmins?"

"Don't be impertinent, boy. Do you have a message?"

"I'm sorry if I seem impertinent, sir, but my letter is for a Mr. Timmins."

"I am Timmins!"

Without saying another word, Drew handed him the letter. Timmins opened the letter, glanced at it and swore. "A book?" He crumpled the letter and threw it into the hedge. Then he turned and stomped away.

At first, Drew didn't know what to do. Retrieving the letter, he straightened it as he ran after Timmins. Darting around the official, he planted himself in Timmins' path.

"I apologize if this is an inconvenience for you, Mr. Timmins, but coming to Whitehall to find you was an inconvenience for me. I'm leaving London within the hour. The bishop wants me to take this book with me. Are you going to follow his instructions or not?"

Timmins scowled at him with such anger that Drew would have felt more comfortable standing at the pointed end of the palace guard's saber.

"Be at London House in *precisely* an hour and a half." Timmins marched past Drew toward the palace.

An hour and a half? Drew could almost hear the demons howling with glee.

Morning passed into early afternoon and Drew was still in London. At least there was some consolation to his predicament. He could pick up his father's chalices in the interim. That would take about half an hour, giving him an hour of free time in the city he loved.

For Drew, London was everything home was not. The constant rumble of the carts and coaches was the heartbeat of a vibrant city; except for the frequent banshee cries of his mother, Morgan Hall was silent and dead. London was constantly changing, every day bringing a different challenge; at Morgan Hall the only challenge was to escape the constant bickering—his father screaming at his mother over money, his mother shouting at whoever was within sight, his brother whining and sniveling about.

As Drew and Pirate navigated the jumble of merchants, construction workers, and water carriers that crowded The Strand, he broke into a laugh. In a few days, this would be his new home. Men and women huddled on street corners, the sound of hammers beating in the background. Women with jugs gathered at the community water tankard which was running full tilt. Sweating porters labored down the street under the weight of their burdens. He loved it.

There were over fifty goldsmiths on The Strand. Drew rode straight to the shop where his father did business. However, when he inquired about his father's chalices, the owner of the shop, a man named Carados, said he had never received an order from Lord Percy Morgan for four silver chalices. Drew insisted the chalices had been ordered. The answer came to both of them at the same time. Lord Morgan had ordered silver chalices, but from another goldsmith. Carados was enraged.

"Twenty years I endure his insufferable bickering over prices! Twenty years I sell to him for less than anyone else. And what does he do? Stabs me in the back! I'll bet he went to Bors! That cutpurse! Ingrate! Out! Get out! And tell your Judas father I wash my hands of him!"

Fifty goldsmith shops on The Strand. Which one had his father's silver chalices? The demons roared.

Bors. Carados said it was probably Bors. Might as well start there. But where was Bors' shop?

A half hour had passed by the time he located the small goldsmith shop owned by Simon Bors. The scene inside was similar to the one in Carados' store. Lord Morgan had promised the job to Bors, but the order was never placed. Now Bors knew why and he was livid. Drew was thrown out of his second goldsmith shop in one day.

Now what? There were still forty-eight other goldsmith shops and he didn't have a clue where to begin.

"Psst! Over here!"

A scrawny man called to him from an alley. Drew recognized him as one of Simon Bors' shop assistants. He was motioning frantically to Drew. "For a pound, I'll tell ya who made your father's chalices." The man's eyes never rested, darting this way and that, startled at the slightest movement.

"A pound!" Drew looked at the man suspiciously.

"I'm the one that steered your father toward the better deal." He held out his hand for the money.

Drew didn't trust him, but what other choice did he have? He reached into his pocket and pulled out a pound. Clenching it in his fist, he said, "First, the name of the goldsmith."

"What do ya take me for? A common thief?"

"First the name."

"All right," the man hissed. "Gareth."

"And where would I find Gareth's shop?"

The man muttered a curse, "You are a babe in the woods, aren't ya?"

Drew started placing the coin back in his pocket.

Another curse from the shop assistant. "At the far end of The Strand, just across from the stone cistern."

Drew handed the man the coin.

"Tell your father next time to send someone who's been weaned," the man sneered.

The *far* end of The Strand. Where else would it be but at

the *far* end of The Strand! The traffic in the street increased. The demons were ganging up on him now, goading every person, animal, and cart to get in Drew's way. The closeness of all the people and animals created an unbearable stench. Nerves were raw. Tongues were sharp. It took him twice as long as it normally would, as he was jostled the length of The Strand. By now Pirate had had his fill of the city. He balked at Drew's handling and even tried to bite a pedestrian, luckily getting only the man's hat.

Finally, an exasperated Drew reached Gareth's shop. The goldsmith was eager to show his handiwork to Drew, but Drew was in too much of a hurry. He would never get back to London House on time. Pity. Gareth was one of the few friendly faces he had seen today.

Drew loaded the chalices, each one wrapped in velvet, in his satchel. He mounted Pirate, and set out to travel the length of The Strand one more time.

"I said *precisely* an hour and a half!" Timmins shouted, as the door to London House flew open. The round cook stood in the background wringing his plump hands. "Do you think I have nothing better to do than play governess for some inconsequential whelp?" Timmins threw an oversized volume at Drew and slammed the door.

The size of the book caused Drew to stagger. It was an enormous volume, much larger than he'd expected. He was beginning to wonder if he was going to have to carry it all the way to Morgan Hall on his lap. With a good deal of effort, he was able to wedge the book into his satchel. The chalices lay in the bottom, so a third of the book stuck out. The flap of the satchel wouldn't begin to stretch over the top of the book, but it didn't matter. The book was wedged so tightly in the satchel that nothing was going to fall out.

The sun was low in the sky before Drew was finally ready to embark on the last leg of his journey. However, the pesky demons weren't about to let him go without a parting shot. Just as Drew reached for Pirate's reigns, the horse bit his hand, crushing his finger and slashing a dark red gash across his palm.

Drew took the horse ferry across the Thames. The river slapped lazily against the wooden sides of the ferry. Unlike Drew, it was in no hurry. In response, Drew fidgeted impatiently; he had to make up for lost time. Already it was late afternoon and Basingstoke was still a half-day's ride away. He wouldn't arrive until well after dark and his father would be furious.

The ferry reached Lambeth landing and Drew urged Pirate into a gallop, hoping to outrun the demons that had dogged him all day. He was a good hour south of London when he saw her lying on the side of the road in tall grass next to a wooded area. A donkey grazed only a few feet away. As he got closer, Drew could hear a weak moaning. Her blonde hair was scattered in disarray around her head, her face was covered by her forearm.

Jumping from his horse, Drew rushed to her side. The woman was young and obviously poor; her clothes were tattered and her forearm soiled. The stains were old. They were not the result of her recent accident.

She started as Drew touched her arm.

"I won't hurt you," he said. He gently lifted her arm from her face. Drew guessed her to be about fourteen or fifteen years of age. She was remarkably pretty. Her eyelids fluttered open, revealing sparkling blue eyes. At the sight of him, she struggled to sit up. She faltered and Drew grabbed her shoulders.

"Thank you for stopping, sir," she said in an innocent, sweet voice.

Drew was captivated by her beauty; never had he seen such a fair maiden. Most of the young women he knew labored unsuccessfully for hours to reproduce this woman's natural features—her cheekbones were set high and colored with a slight blush, her eyes were framed with lashes like the rays of the sun, and her lips were so full and lovely that it was a sensuous pleasure just to watch them form words.

"Are . . . are you hurt?" Drew stammered.

"I don't know," the fair maiden answered, arching her back and swinging her head from side to side, apparently testing for pain. "It was so kind of you to stop and help me," she purred.

Drew lowered his eyes in modesty. "I couldn't just ride by and leave you lying here. It's something anyone would do."

"No," the maiden protested, "not just anyone . . ."

Drew looked back up.

The fair maiden's face was twisted, distorted by a wicked sneer. ". . . not just anyone," she snorted, "only a fool!"

Thud! A thick, jagged force slammed into the back of Drew's head. He slumped into the arms of his fair maiden. She pushed him off. The last thing he remembered was the tops of the trees against a late afternoon sky.

The shouts of angry voices stirred him awake. Where was he? Home? It wouldn't be the first time he was awakened by verbal warfare.

"Just kill him!" one of the voices shouted. It wasn't his mother's voice.

Drew's eyes snapped open but all he could see was grass. "Kill him!"

He remembered now. The girl . . . the pain. He was lying in grass face down.

"I'll hold him, you kill him!"

Drew tried to jump up. His attempt was checked by a stabbing pain in the back of his head.

"I'll hold him, you kill him!" the voice shouted again.

Drew recognized the voice. It was the woman he had stopped to help.

Fighting the pain, he struggled to his knees in the tall grass. The throbbing was so intense it blurred his sight and drugged his sense of balance. It took several efforts to rise up on his knees. He held his hands in front of him, hoping to ward off his attackers until his head cleared.

"Kill him! Kill him!" she screamed.

No blows came. No attack. Drew's outstretched arms felt nothing. As his head slowly began to clear Drew realized that the voices were distant. He turned toward their direction and blinked several times. Each blink brought a greater measure of sight.

In the middle of the road he saw his fair maiden and a short, dirty man. They were chasing Pirate in circles. The girl was holding the reins and the horse was rearing and kicking. The man cursed as he reached for the satchel. He would no sooner get a good grip on the book when Pirate would turn his head and bite the man. His bloody left arm gave testimony to several successful bites.

"Hold him still! Keep his head forward," the man shouted.

"I can't," the girl shouted back. "Just kill him!"

"Stop!" Drew shouted. Instantly he wished he hadn't. The pain in the back of his head exploded with the word. His eyes glazed over again, then slowly cleared.

The old man pulled a dagger from his belt. Pirate whinnied and tried to rear, but the girl pulled him back down. Drew started toward the thieves, holding the back of his head in an attempt to relieve the pain which stabbed at him with each step he took.

"Pa!" the girl screamed, motioning toward Drew with her head.

The old man swung around, his knife leveled at Drew. "Come here, boy," he hissed through huge gaps in his blackened teeth. "There be cups at the bottom of that knapsack and I'd be willin' to bet they're gold or silver. I want 'em and you're gonna get 'em for me."

"Cups?" Drew said with a puzzled expression.

"Don't you play me for a fool!" the old man yelled, running his hand through matted salt and pepper hair. "I felt 'em through the sack."

"Oh, the pewter cups," Drew said. "They're not gold, and certainly not worth your effort."

"And what would a lad dressed in such fine clothes be doin' carryin' around four pewter cups?"

"Who knows when you might run into three friends with a keg?" Drew said.

"Ahhhh!" the man cursed and jabbed at Drew with the knife. Drew had to jump back to keep from being slashed. The horse reared again and this time the girl almost lost him.

"I'll make ya a deal, boy," the old man sneered. "You get the cups from the bottom of that sack and I'll let you walk away from here. The cups for your life. Deal?"

Drew looked at the knife, the old man, the girl. He had never fought a man with a knife before, in fact he had never really fought anyone before other than his brother when the little weasel goaded him. He needed some kind of weapon, but what?

"I give you the cups and you'll let me and my horse be on our way?"

"Don't trust him, pa!" the girl shouted.

"I ain't trustin' no one!" the old man spat back at her. Then to Drew, "You get the cups out, then we'll talk." To the girl, "Prissy! You hold on tight to them reins, hear? Don't let him grab 'em!"

The man with the knife stepped away from the horse, but he stayed within striking distance. Drew approached Pirate, speaking to him in soothing tones. He patted the horse on the neck and looked at the girl. She was wild-eyed and tense as she held the reins tight.

It took Drew several minutes of working the book from side to side before it was free. When the book was two-thirds out of the satchel, Drew gave one last pull.

Just as the book popped out, the old man lunged at Drew, shoving him to the side. The weight of the book and the force of the blow sent Drew reeling. He stumbled but managed to maintain his balance.

Holding the knife between his teeth, the old man plunged both hands into the satchel. He pulled out two of the silver chalices, held them up, and grinned victoriously.

Drew saw his chance. With both hands, he swung the oversized book like a broadsword, and the volume smashed into the man's face, knocking him to the ground. The thief grabbed his face and screamed as the knife cut into him. The chalices were sent flying. Blood poured from the man's nose, a vicious cut laid open his left cheek, and his rotted back teeth could be seen through the open wound.

Drew stood dumbfounded, still holding the book. The man struggled to his knees holding his crooked, broken nose with one hand and his sliced face with the other. A swift movement caught Drew's eye. The girl had grabbed the dagger and was charging toward him, blade held high over her head. She lunged at him and he raised the book to protect himself. The knife ripped through the cover and into the heart of the book. It was buried so far into the book that the girl was unable to pull it out for a second attempt. Drew shoved the book forward, sending the girl stumbling backward against her father. Then, he gripped the dagger and yanked it out of the book.

The girl looked up at him in terror as her father whimpered at her feet. Drew stood over them both, the book in one hand and the dagger in the other.

"Take your father and get out of here," he said.

The girl stared at him, her expression alternating between terror and confusion.

"Go on, get out of here!" Drew shouted.

Slowly, the girl helped her father to his feet. She glanced behind her at Drew several times before they disappeared into the woods.

For a long time Drew stood staring after them. A trail of blood marked their departure. He couldn't stop his arms and legs from shaking. His stomach retched and his head pounded in agony. There was no telling how long he would have been there if he hadn't been moved to action by a new fear. *What if the girl returns with help?*

With trembling hands and wobbly legs he picked up the chalices, rewrapped them in their cloths, and returned them to the satchel. As quickly as he could, he wedged the wounded book back in its place, mounted Pirate, and headed for Basingstoke. It took almost an hour for his shaking limbs to steady as his mind replayed the scene over and over. He realized how lucky he'd been. He might have been killed while he lay unconscious on the ground. He might have been stabbed to death. The thieves might have been successful in stealing his father's precious chalices.

The more he thought about it, and the farther away he traveled from the scene of the failed robbery attempt, he began to feel quite proud of himself. He'd handled himself well. He acted out of compassion when he stopped to help the girl. He fought with courage when he could have run away. It was his first battle against evil and he'd emerged victorious.

The lateness of the hour and the trials of the day had drained him of energy; nevertheless, he rode straight and tall, like a knight returning home from battle.

Chapter 4

KING Alfred Inn was a medieval lodging house that catered to the rich and noble. For more than 150 years its wooden sign, hanging from a single beam jutting out above the doorway, welcomed kings and queens, dukes and duchesses, lords and ladies. Legend had it that the inn was Henry VIII's favorite rendezvous whenever he was courting, which was frequently. According to legend, he shared the hospitality of the inn with four of the six women who eventually became his wives. The inn's status grew from there and its registry became a who's who of English politicians and nobility, including those who simply wanted a place to rest after a full day's journey or a lavish getaway to meet their secret lovers.

The building stood boldly on the edge of the street. With only two steps, guests could exit their carriages and be inside the inn's large dining room where they would be waited on like royalty.

The inn's namesake was Alfred, king of Wessex, popularly known as Alfred the Great. Alfred's courage and compassion was part of English folklore and storytellers gained a ready audience whenever they told of how the West Saxon kings laid down their arms to superior Danish forces, that is, everyone except Alfred. The lone dissenter secretly raised an army and attacked the Danes seven weeks after Easter 878, in the Battle of Edington. Not only were the Danes defeated, but their King Guthrum was baptized in the Christian faith, with King Alfred as his sponsor.

Alfred the Great was an appropriate spiritual guardian for English travelers because he himself was a well-traveled man, including two visits to Rome, once in 853 and again in 855. His love for books dictated the decor of the inn that bore his name. Alfred believed that the best way to make England a leader of nations was to educate her young. He surrounded himself with books and even helped to translate a few essential volumes of his day into English. King Alfred Inn had a rather impressive collection of volumes, which Drew Morgan loved to browse whenever his family journeyed back and forth to London.

Lord Percy, Lady Evelyn, and Philip had arrived in Basingstoke in typical fashion. Several of their servants preceded them, delivering to the innkeeper a list of the things the Morgans would require during their stay. Special emphasis was placed on what they would eat and who should and should not be invited to join them.

At the first sight of the Morgan carriage, bell ringers heralded their approach. The mayor officially welcomed them when they reached the city limits, and a parade of officials and musicians ushered them to King Alfred Inn.

In return for this lavish reception, the Morgans were generous with their praise and their money. Lord Morgan ostentatiously presented a sizable monetary gift to the city on behalf of the poor and needy.

Everyone played their roles to perfection and thus the established order of society was preserved. If the city had not treated the Morgans in this fashion, the family would not have felt like nobility, and without nobility the commoners would question the financial stability of their country. If the Morgans had not showered the people with money in return, they would have betrayed the class of country gentlemen.

Worse yet, if their generosity had been questioned in any way, people might think that the Morgans were not as wealthy as they seemed—which, in fact, was actually the case. Lord and Lady Morgan lived well beyond their means and it was painful for Percy Morgan to release even a farthing. But, for appearance sake, he swallowed his stinginess and loosened his purse strings while at Basingstoke.

In this way, the Morgans appeared noble, the commoners were grateful, and English society was preserved.

A stableboy appeared from nowhere with a lantern bouncing at his side before Drew had time to dismount.

"Master Morgan?"

Drew uttered an affirmative grunt as he dismounted.

"We's been expectin' you for hours." The boy, about six or seven years old, was wide-eyed with concern. It was a look that recognized trouble and was glad he wasn't in the middle of it.

"Is my father angry?"

The stableboy nodded, his eyes growing even wider.

Drew reached under Pirate to unbuckle the strap holding the satchel. The horse offered no resistance. London's heavy street traffic, the battle with the thieves, and the long journey had taken away all his fight.

"We'll get that for you, sir. You'd best go in straightway."

Drew pulled at the satchel strap. "No, I'll get this . . ." The strap wouldn't budge. He yanked again, this time hard enough that a tired Pirate felt obliged to issue a warning grunt. Still the strap didn't move.

"Hold the light under here so I can see this buckle."

The boy lowered the lantern and Pirate's mud-crusted underbelly came into view.

"So that's why they didn't just remove the satchel!" Drew exclaimed. "The strap is wedged in the buckle!"

Drew stood up and began pulling at the bishop's book. "I'll take these things in myself," he told the stableboy. "Have your blacksmith look at that buckle. See if he can get it off."

"Yes, sir." the boy answered, as he watched Drew shove the huge book back and forth, working it out of the satchel.

With an angry father waiting for him inside, a buckle that didn't work, and a stuck book, it seemed to the stableboy that this particular traveler had an unusual number of things going wrong.

As Drew worked to free the book, he began formulating his explanation for his delayed arrival. His premise was simple: While the rest of the family enjoyed a leisurely trip from Windsor to the lavish accommodations of Basingstoke, he had fought a pitched battle with a score of delaying demons and had barely survived a near fatal battle with thieves. He would convince them that instead of being castigated, he should be congratulated for his perseverance and triumph. The bishop's book, the knot on the back of his head, and the thieves' dagger would document his story. The crowning piece of evidence would be the silver chalices themselves. Against tremendous odds he would safely deliver them into his grateful father's hands.

As Drew removed the first of the four chalices from the satchel, the cloth covering slipped. A beam from the boy's lantern hit the silver and bounced off, like a brilliant star. The beam of light gave Drew a wonderful idea. *This chalice is my Holy Grail! It is the symbol of my victory, a reminder of the day I overcame the persistent forces of evil! Like a knight presenting the Holy Grail to his king, so I will present these four grails to my father.*

Drew hurriedly arranged the chalices for presentation. He unwrapped each one. Using the coverings like tablecloths, he draped them over the bishop's book. Then, he arranged the four chalices on top of the covered book and placed the dagger in the center. He inspected his display admiringly; it represented battle and victory.

The stableboy did his best to act like Drew's actions were normal behavior for all the inn's guests. It was not his position to be amused by anything his superiors might do, no matter how odd. As Drew carefully balanced his regal presentation with both hands, the stableboy opened the inn door. Drew stood erect, yet humble, took a deep breath, and entered the inn ready to accept his family's praise.

"Where have you been?" Lord Percy Morgan thundered.

The voice came from the far side of the room. Although it looked as if things were breaking up, the mountains of bones and rinds, together with wine bottles scattered about the table and floor, suggested it had been quite a feast. Both parents were standing on the far side of the table; Philip was by himself at one end. There were still more than a dozen guests remaining in the room, but the mayor was not one of them.

Before Drew took a second step inside the door, his mother shrieked. She was pointing at the chalices. Lord and Lady Morgan rushed to Drew and snatched the chalices off the book. With their backs to the guests, they tried to hide the chalices beneath the folds of their clothes.

"Hey, Percy! Watcha hidin' those silver cups for?" yelled one of the guests. Drew had never seen the man before. He reclined in his chair, belly up and very drunk. "Bring 'em over here. Let's take a drink out of 'em."

Neither Lord nor Lady Morgan moved. "Give them to me," Lady Morgan whispered. "I'll take them up to our room."

Lord Morgan looked over his shoulder. The eyes of everyone in the room, dinner guests and servants alike, were on them. Suddenly, he cursed. With a wild swing he backhanded Drew across the face.

Drew never saw it coming. The blow knocked him against the doorpost, slamming his already injured head against the wood. There was a flash of light, then exploding pain as he slumped to the floor. He couldn't see anything, but he heard the book and dagger hit the floor next to him.

The blow was sufficient to cause Lord Percy to lose his grip on the two chalices he was attempting to hide. They clanged to the floor. Instantly, Lady Morgan dropped to her knees attempting to hide them under the folds of her skirt. This time Lord Morgan stopped her.

"Ladies and Gentlemen," he shouted, pausing long enough to bend over and pick up the two silver chalices that lay on the floor. "May I be the first—no, make that the second," he shot a sarcastic glance at Drew who was picking himself up from the floor, "to place on public display the newest addition to the Morgan family silver collection. Tonight's unscheduled exhibition is compliments of my idiot son, Andrew Morgan!"

Lord Morgan slammed all four of the chalices on the nearest table and led the room in mock applause for Drew. Through blurry eyes, everywhere Drew looked he saw people applauding and laughing at him, including some of the servants.

"Why did you hit me?" he shouted at his father.

"What's this?" Lord Percy cried, his tone heavy with ridicule. "The idiot has a voice! He's not dumb . . . just stupid!"

Laughter erupted throughout the hall.

"Why did you hit me?" Drew asked again.

"Shut up and go upstairs to our room!" Lady Morgan yelled. Her arms were folded over her midsection; she rocked back and forth like a little child with a bellyache.

"No!" Drew complained. "I want to know what I have done to deserve this kind of treatment!" Rarely did Drew go head to head with his parents; that was more Philip's style.

Maybe he was running on adrenaline from the successes he'd enjoyed earlier in the day, but he decided there was enough fight left in him for one more battle.

"The boy wants to know what he's done wrong," Lord Percy shouted in disbelief. "Is there *anyone* in this room besides this *dolt* who doesn't know that he's done wrong?"

A roar of hoots and guffaws went up. The remaining guests were clearly enjoying this spectacle that was proving to be more entertaining than the recorder and mandolin duet performed earlier in the evening.

"All right," Lord Percy said, placing his hands on his hips, warming up to the his son's public challenge. Lord Morgan proceeded as though he was bringing a petition of complaint to the Court of the Star Chamber. "Lord Chancellor," he bowed to his big-bellied drunken friend, "members of the Privy Council," he motioned to one side of the room, "and Chief Justices of England," he motioned to the other side of the room. "I intend to prove to you that this dunce," he pointed at Drew, "did commit the high crime of public stupidity."

Drew folded his arms in disgust.

"He claims ignorance, your honors," Lord Percy continued. "That I will readily grant him. He is ignorant. He is also stupid, brainless, and muddleheaded!"

The room echoed with laughter and shouts. "Guilty! Guilty! Guilty!" some of the guests shouted, banging their tankards on the tabletops.

"Get to the point," Drew shouted.

Lord Morgan raised his hands for silence. "Yes, the point. I will get to the point by asking the accused a question. Have you ever taken a trip with your family before?"

"Of course, I have!"

"Of course, he has!" Lord Morgan ridiculed. "And when you have taken trips with your family, who always unloaded the luggage from the carriage?"

"Philip and I," Drew answered slowly. He was beginning to see his father's point.

"This time I had to do it all myself while my dumb brother played knight in London!" Philip said. His speech was slurred; apparently he had been sipping the wine while his parents weren't watching. He wasn't about to miss out on the chance to ridicule his brother in public.

Lord Morgan raised his hand again. "One stupid son at a time, please!" Turning to Drew, "Can you tell us *why* I have you and your brother carry the luggage when there are so many ablebodied servants around to do it for us?"

Drew knew his father had him. It was common knowledge that some servants, while carrying luggage to the rooms, would shake the bags and listen for the jingle of money, or evaluate a bag's contents by its shape and weight. If they suspected money or valuables, they would pass this information to their cohorts who would waylay the travelers the next day several miles down the road. To counter such thievery, Lord Morgan always had his boys carry the luggage.

"I get the point," Drew said humbly. "I didn't think . . ."

"He didn't think!" Lord Morgan wasn't about to let up. "That's the first intelligent thing the boy has said in years!"

"I made a mistake. I'm sorry!" Drew shouted.

"Now he's sorry," Lord Morgan made a pouting face to the court. "Half the thieves in England are lining up between here and Winchester to see which of them gets to rob me first, and he's sorry!"

Drew turned to leave the room. Lord Morgan grabbed his arm and pulled him back. "We're not done yet," he said. "I want to know how you got the chalices in the first place, since I didn't tell you which goldsmith in London made them."

"I went to Carados' shop first."

"But he didn't have them, did he?"

"No."

"And what was his reaction when you asked for something he didn't make?"

"He was angry."

"Angry?"

"Well, very angry. He said he never wanted to do business with you again."

Lord Morgan stroked his chin thoughtfully. "I see," he said. "But how did you know who made the chalices?"

"Mr. Carados thought Simon Bors was given the job."

Lord Morgan winced. "Simon Bors! But he didn't have the chalices either, did he?"

"No," Drew said sheepishly. "One of Mr. Bors' assistants told me you commissioned Gareth to make the chalices."

"So now, Ladies and Gentlemen of the court," Lord Morgan shouted, "not only are half the thieves in England waiting to rob me, but half the goldsmiths on The Strand will never do business with me again! What have I done to deserve a son like this?"

Howling laughter.

Drew had had enough. It was a mistake bringing the chalices inside uncovered, and it was a mistake for him to leave Windsor without waiting for instructions, but he was determined these people know what he went through to see that the chalices arrived safely.

"Don't you want to know why I was so late?" Drew shouted at his father, "or why my clothes are torn and dirty? Or why I have a huge gash on the back of my head?"

"There's more! A tale of adventure!" Lord Morgan cried. He perched on the edge of a table and folded his arms. "Please, thrill us with your exploits."

"Well," Drew began, "just outside of London, I was attacked."

"Attacked? Why would anyone want to attack a poor fool riding out of London balancing four silver chalices on a book?"

A roar of laughter.

"People see that in London every day!" Lord Morgan added.

The big-bellied man laughed so hard he fell out of his chair.

"The chalices were in my satchel!" Drew had to shout just to be heard. "Two thieves attacked me. One hit me over the head. They tried to steal the chalices, but I fought them off."

The room grew quiet.

"I suppose the thieves were both seven feet tall," Lord Morgan said.

"No, they weren't seven feet tall." Drew began to admit to himself he was arguing a losing cause.

"Tell us more about these dangerous thieves," Lord Morgan prompted. "They were both grown men, weren't they?"

"One was a man."

"And what was the other one? A monkey?"

"One was an old man and the other was a girl."

"This is my son who would be a knight!" Lord Morgan shouted. "Single-handedly, he fought off the overwhelming forces of a little girl and an old man!"

"They had a knife!" Drew protested. He picked up the knife from the floor and held it up.

"And tell me," his father said, "how did you disarm this dastardly duo?"

Drew explained how he protected himself with the bishop's book. He held up the book and inserted the dagger to show everyone how far the dagger had penetrated the book.

Lord Morgan walked solemnly to his son and took the book from him. He examined them carefully.

"This is the bishop's book?" he asked.

Drew nodded.

Lord Morgan held the book over his head. "Ladies and Gentlemen of the court, the Bishop of London's book! My son has killed the Bishop of London's book!"

Everywhere Drew looked people were laughing at him. Some were holding their sides, while others wiped tears from their eyes. Their faces were red and strained. One man broke into a violent coughing fit.

"In one day my eldest son, the hope of the next generation, has tipped off the thieves of England against me; he has ruined me in London's business district; and I will undoubtedly be excommunicated because he killed Bishop Laud's book!"

Drew turned and stormed out of the inn. This time, no one stopped him.

The next morning, as the Morgan family prepared to leave Basingstoke, Lord Percy Morgan arranged for a public ceremony during which he gave the four silver chalices to his friend the mayor with instructions to sell them and use the money for the poor and needy of the city. Secretly, he'd arranged to have one of the mayor's servants return the chalices to him several miles down the road. Naturally, the arrangement cost him dearly, but under the circumstances it was the only way he could think of to keep from being robbed.

Drew had another fight with his father, this one private. He informed his father he had decided to return to London immediately, without going back to Morgan Hall. Lord Morgan refused, and in light of the previous day's events, he said he'd have to rethink whether or not Drew should return to London at all. Drew threatened to run away; Lord Percy threatened to disinherit him and give the rights of the first-born to Philip. If it was just money, Drew wouldn't have cared. But he couldn't walk away from Morgan Hall; there was too much history tied into the house and property. He couldn't let Morgan Hall fall into the hands of his weasel brother. Reluctantly, Drew agreed to return home.

From Basingstoke to Morgan Hall, Drew rode Pirate as an outrider, to keep a watchful eye for any sign of trouble. For Drew it was preferable to being inside the carriage with his parents and brother.

The rest of the ride home was agonizingly slow and boring. When a sudden storm turned the road slick, the pace slowed to walking speed. Twice the carriage mired in the mud. Both times Drew sullenly helped the servants push it out.

Finally, they approached the city of Winchester, only five miles from home. The Morgan party turned east on High Street and passed the Great Hall which housed King Arthur's Round Table. Normally, Drew would have arranged to stop before catching up with his family. Today he plodded by the Great Hall without even a glance its direction.

The Morgans passed through Kingsgate, one of the city's five original gates, built in the thirteenth century. As they crossed over the bridge and into the country, Morgan Hall loomed in the distance. A two-story country house, it was one of the finest in England, with only Theobalds and Longleat to rival its magnificence. But to Drew it was the most dreaded prison in England.

Chapter 5

THE teasing caress of her fingernail on the back of his hand sent a pleasurable jolt through Marshall Ramsden's body. His eyes closed and rolled upward as he fought the urge to respond to her playful touch.

"We don't have time," he whispered. "We have to get this printed before dawn."

"I know," she pouted, as she outlined the ink stains on his hand. "But I was hoping we'd get done early tonight so we could be together."

Marshall shoved the printing press bed along its runners, sliding it into position under the platen. Going to the side of the press he reached up with both hands and gripped the bar that would lower the platen and press the paper against the metal type. With a giggle, Mary ducked under the bar and between his arms so that they were face to face.

"You're crazy!" Marshall said with a smile.

"Crazy," she replied with a playful peck on his lips, "when it comes to you."

Marshall released the bar and pulled Mary Sedgewick to him. Any resistance he once had was gone as he passionately embraced his lover, who also happened to be his professor's daughter and his partner in crime.

Marshall Ramsden, a third-year theology student at Cambridge University, was the son of a noted London printer.

His father, a hardworking member of the printer's guild, had worked his way through the ranks to become one of the king's printers. In 1611, he was one of a select group of printers chosen by King James to print England's Authorized Version of the Bible which came about as the result of the Hampton Court Conference. For Marshall's father, that printing contract fulfilled a lifelong dream. He was a devout man who deeply loved the Bible. It brought him great satisfaction to think that generations of English families would be guided by copies of God's Word printed on his presses.

As an only child, Marshall was raised to continue his father's trade. But even when he was a young boy he showed more interest in reading what was printed than he did in printing it. And since much of his father's work was religious in nature, he was exposed early to spiritual writings.

For years Marshall harbored secret thoughts of pursuing a career in theology. He feared telling his father, thinking he wouldn't understand and might be hurt that his son would desire another profession. Finally, one spring Sunday as the family rode home from St. Paul's Church, God presented Marshall with the opportunity he needed.

As the carriage crossed the London Bridge, he and his father had been discussing the Scripture reading from the service. It was from the first chapter of Jeremiah's prophecy. God was speaking to the prophet. He said: "Before I formed thee in the belly I knew thee; and before thou camest forth out of the womb I sanctified thee, and I ordained thee a prophet unto the nations." Marshall's father said he was captivated by God's foreknowledge of the prophet. Marshall said he was especially drawn to a verse that appeared later in the chapter, "Behold, I have put My words in thy mouth."

It was then that he told his father he felt God had set him aside to study and teach theology, that God was putting His words in Marshall's mouth, not ink under his fingernails.

Marshall couldn't have been more surprised at his father's reaction.

"I have spent all my life printing what other men have written," his father said, "hoping that in some small way I could have a part in proclaiming God's Word to England." He gripped his son's shoulders. "And now you're telling me that God is calling you to spread His message through your words and pen!" His father paused to gain control of his emotions. "I'm overwhelmed with happiness!" he cried. "My only prayer is that I will live long enough to print your words on my press."

For whatever reason, God chose not to honor the printer's request. The senior Ramsden died during Marshall's second year at Cambridge, but not before he passed on his love for the Bible to his son.

It was this love that motivated Marshall to print Justin's illegal pamphlets on the Cambridge University printing press. Through his theology professor, William Sedgewick, he was exposed to the teachings of the Puritan preachers. And it was through his theology professor's daughter that he was exposed to the thrills of romance and the dangers of illegal printing.

The English Puritans believed strongly that the Bible was God's blueprint for life. There was an escalating concern among them that high church officials, principally Bishop Laud, were steering the English people back to Roman Catholicism. The bishop worked his agenda with a heavy hand. His first task, after being promoted to the bishopric of England, was to present King Charles with a list of the names of English clergymen. Beside each name he had printed an "O" or a "P". Those clergymen who were Orthodox would be promoted as opportunities arose. Those who were Puritans would be passed over for promotion, frustrated, and harried out of the ministry with every available force.

Among the dissenters there were basically two responses to Laud's persecution. Some felt that the situation was hopeless. They fled the country — first to Holland and then to the New World. Because they chose to separate themselves from the Church of England, they were called Separatists.

The second group comprised those who would not easily abandon their church. They set out on a course to purify the church from this papist influence and so were known as Puritans.

The Puritans were determined and persistent. They firmly believed that God would have them rescue the Church of England. The thought of fleeing as the Separatists had would show a lack of faith. If it took several generations, they were determined to reclaim their churches. Their goal was to base their lives, their churches, and their country on the Bible, not on ritual or tradition.

The Puritans' weapons were preaching and pamphlets, both of which Bishop Laud targeted. To control the preaching, the bishop instituted a series of reforms that restricted church services to the order prescribed by the Book of Common Prayer. Since preaching is a public form of communication, it was easy to monitor. However, stopping the pamphlets was another matter.

By law, publishing in England was limited to a few London printers and the two university presses, Oxford and Cambridge. All printers had to obtain a license for each publication that was printed on their presses.

These laws drove the Puritan pamphlet industry underground. Penalties for defying the laws were harsh. If a Puritan writer was captured, he was tried in the Star Chamber. Punishment often included the severing of one or both ears and branding on the cheeks with the letters "S" and "L" — for seditious libeler. The Puritans, however, reassigned the letters to different words: *Stigmata Laudis* — the marks of Laud.

These were the penalties Marshall Ramsden and Mary Sedgewick faced if they were caught. Although they had never met Justin, a pseudonym chosen in honor of an early Christian martyr, they believed in his message. Unlike other pamphleteers, Justin's style was not antagonistic, nor did he attack Laud personally. His arguments were biblical, reasonable, and powerful. Justin's commonsense approach stirred the passions of believers like Marshall and Mary to the extent that they would risk a public trial and branding to see that his words were spread throughout England.

Mary was one of the first to join the Cambridge resistance. It was she who introduced Marshall, a more than welcome addition since he knew how to use the printing presses. It was Mary's task to see that the printed pamphlets were delivered to distribution points near the campus city. And what began as a common passion for the writings of Justin had developed into a more personal passion between Marshall Ramsden and Mary Sedgewick.

Whenever a man and a woman are locked in the kind of embrace that held Marshall and Mary during those pre-dawn hours in the print shop, the universe is reduced to a simple equation: one man + one woman = the entire universe. Kings, countries, schools, politics — all cease to exist. Families, relatives, and friends all vanish as if they were never born. Even time takes a holiday. For the two lovers, nothing else mattered except the singular universe they shared.

The door of the shop slammed open, then slammed shut a fraction of a second later. The sound so startled Mary that she banged the back of her head on the press bar. Leaning against the safe side of the door was a student named Essex Marvell, one of the strangest but most loyal friends Marshall ever had. "Just call me 'S'," he said the first day they met. "Everyone does."

"S" was out of breath, his clothes were wet with perspiration, and he had a look of alarm in his eyes, the kind that kicks a person's adrenal glands into emergency production.

"They're coming!" he shouted.

He didn't have to explain who "they" were because it really didn't matter. Anyone caught with Justin's pamphlets might as well hand over both ears and turn his cheek for branding.

Marshall took charge.

"Mary, you can't be seen. We'll take care of the plates and the pamphlets."

Mary hesitated for but a moment, looking at him with frightened eyes, wishing there was time to tell him of her love. Marshall smiled at her. He understood.

"S," Marshall pointed to the stacks of pamphlets drying on a shelf, "put those in the bag. I'll get the plate off the press."

"Should I bar the door?" "S" asked frantically.

"No," Marshall shouted back. "Just work on those stacks."

"S" ran to the stacks of pamphlets and furiously began stuffing them into a large canvas sack which was used to sneak the illegal pamphlets off the university campus. Marshall grabbed the bar on the old press and pulled it toward him until it stopped. Removing the bar from its hole at the top of the worm screw and placing it in another hole, he pulled again. The new presses lifted the platen from the paper with a single stroke of the bar. But universities seldom have new equipment. Unless Marshall could move faster, that simple fact of university economics would result in his capture and imprisonment.

There wouldn't be time to take the printing plate apart and redistribute the type to the typecase. Marshall would have to get the plate off the press and hide it. He glanced up. No sign of Mary. "S" was shoving pamphlets into the bag as fast as he could.

Marshall worked the worm screw and prayed it would be fast enough. Two more turns should do it. Midstroke, the screw jammed. He heard movement outside the shop. He reached for the ligatures on the edges of the plate and unscrewed them.

The door slammed open for the second time that morning just as Essex was throwing the canvas bag into a lower cabinet. This time, however, the door didn't close, it hung open like a gaping mouth. Out of the mouth jumped two soldiers followed by a finely dressed nobleman. The soldiers leveled their weapons, one on each student.

Marshall recognized the nobleman as George Macaulay, the official who licensed all presses and publications in Cambridge. Marshall had obtained printing licenses from him before. The nobleman was abnormally tall and thin to the point of sickly. His mouth formed a perpetual frown, a completely inverted U, which made him look like a puppet.

"Good morning, gentlemen," the puppet mouth greeted them. His deliberately long strut portrayed a confidence that this morning's events would earn him well-deserved praise.

"Top of the morning to you, sir!" Marshall replied brightly.

Macaulay stopped and glared. He didn't appreciate criminals with a sense of humor. Essex didn't have Marshall's nerves. The younger student leaned against the cabinet door, the one in which he'd just deposited the bag of pamphlets. His legs were crossed at the ankles as were his arms across his chest. The boy's fingers fidgeted nervously in his armpits.

"It's a mite early to be working on anything legal," Macaulay said, as he walked toward Marshall and the press. "You do have a license for this print job, don't you?"

"Well, to be honest, sir, no I don't. Frankly, I didn't bother because I knew you wouldn't grant it."

Macaulay was angered that his prey wasn't afraid of him. "Let's take a look at that plate," he growled.

"I'd like to oblige," Marshall said with a grimace, "but it's stuck in the press. I can't budge it."

Macaulay motioned to the soldier covering Marshall and said, "Help him get the plate out."

The soldier set his weapon against the side of the press.

"You grab that side and I'll grab this one," Marshall instructed. "It's really stuck tight but I think one good pull should get it. Ready? On the count of three. One. Two. Three!"

The two men yanked with all their might. The plate came flying out of the press. Loose type flew everywhere. The scarecrow nobleman had to cover his face with his hands as the lead alphabet showered down upon him. Some of the letters found their mark on his skin and clothes, printing imperfect d's and k's and w's.

"Well! I guess it wasn't stuck after all!" Marshall grinned.

The guard who had been Marshall's unwitting accomplice was not amused. Still holding the empty platen in his hands, he swung it at the laughing printer, hitting him with the flat surface and sending him sprawling on the floor. He stood over the fallen printer with his foot on Marshall's chest.

"We'll see who is laughing when you come to trial in the Star Chamber," Macaulay shouted, dabbing at the spatters of ink on his clothes with a handkerchief. "Search that cabinet!" he shouted to the second guard standing next to Essex. "Your friend wasn't quite fast enough," Macaulay said with a snort.

The guard shoved the lightweight Essex aside. Then, he had to get down on all fours to reach the canvas bag in the back of the cabinet.

Essex stood nearby, waiting for the guard to climb back out. When the emerging guard reached the moment of imbalance between bending and standing, Essex grabbed the bag, pushed the guard to the ground, and bolted toward the back door. Marshall tripped the guard standing over him as he attempted to intercept the fleeing Essex.

The back door flew open and Essex was gone. In two blinks the first-year student came flying back into the room. A huge oafish guard appeared in the doorway.

"Do you think I'd be stupid enough to leave the back door unguarded?" Macaulay jeered.

"If you're asking, yes, I think you would be stupid enough," Marshall replied. The guard he'd tripped up silenced Marshall with a kick to the ribs.

To the oversized guard in the doorway Macaulay shouted, "Take out one of the pamphlets and read it aloud. Let's see if it's as humorous as the funny printer on the floor."

"I don't read so good, Master Macaulay," the guard protested.

"All the better," Macaulay replied. "You'll be reading these boys' prison sentences. I'm sure the funny printer will be happy to help you with any hard words."

The guard shrugged. He wasn't sure, but he took Macaulay's response to mean he should read a pamphlet anyway. He lowered his huge paw into the sack and pulled one out. With clumsy fingers he worked the pages open and stared at the words. A grin spread across his face. Looking up he said, "Hey, this is good!"

"Read it aloud!" Macaulay shouted.

The guard began reading:

DELILAH AND THE DEAN'S DOWNFALL

Having heard that Dean Winters was crude,
She decided to see for herself.
When he entered the class she was . . .

"Ahhhh!" Macaulay screamed, grabbing the pamphlet from

the guard. He flipped through the pages randomly reading it for himself.

Still on the floor Marshall smiled. "It's not as good as Shakespeare, but I kinda like it."

"Me too," said the guard.

"Dunce!" Macaulay shouted, turning to the guard closest to the cabinet. "You grabbed the wrong bag!"

"There was only one bag in there!" the man protested.

"Look again!"

Macaulay stood over him, hands on hips, supervising the search of the cabinet. The guard got down on all fours and crawled halfway into the cabinet. With his rear end protruding, he shouted, "Just like I said," his voice echoing from inside, "there's nothing else in here!"

Marshall stood up under the careful watch of his guard. "Look, I don't know what you expected to find here. But guys around here go wild for this Delilah series. They can't get enough of her. They're willing to pay half a crown easily!"

"Enough!" Macaulay shouted. "Search the rest of the shop!" The guards opened every drawer and cabinet. Every printed piece of paper was scanned. They found half-finished textbooks, play scripts, and bills of advertisement, but no Puritan propaganda pamphlets.

"Get them out of here!" Macaulay huffed, after the last drawer had been searched.

Marshall and Essex were marched out of the shop. Macaulay was the last one out. He took another look around, cursed, and closed the door. He held the bag containing the lewd literature; at least he wasn't coming away empty-handed.

The first rays of morning pierced the shop windows, highlighting the ceiling rafters. The scene below looked like the eerie aftermath of student vandalism. Printer's type and leading littered the floor. The flatbed press platen was half up and half down on the worm screw. The press itself was dirtied with ink. Drawers and cabinet doors hung half open. Random shapes and sizes of papers were scattered everywhere. All was still.

Then, as the sunshine reached the top of the wall and began its daily descent from ceiling to floor, a small creak disturbed the silence. It was the sound of wood against wood, the kind of noise the top of a wooden barrel makes when it's pried open. From inside the cabinet that had earlier displayed the back half of a British guard, a tiny, feminine hand reached out and shoved the cabinet door open wider. Out crawled Mary Sedgewick from her cramped hiding place behind the interior wall of the cabinet. Behind her, she dragged a canvas bag, identical to the one Macaulay took from the shop. This bag, however, contained the Puritan pamphlets written by the infamous Justin and printed by her beloved Marshall.

Mary wasted no time. She made her exit through the back door. She threw an oversized cloak over her shoulders to protect herself from the morning chill and also to conceal the bag she carried in her arms. Her gait was brisk, like that of any young woman out for a morning walk.

She made here way to Bridge Street and turned north. A few minutes later she crossed the Cambridge River which gave the university town its name. Proceeding past Magdalene College between St. Peter's and St. Giles, and past an old medieval castle, she headed for the countryside. She turned down the road leading to the Platt farm.

As she walked, she congratulated herself for holding up so well. It was a short-lived confidence. A moment later, trembling hands and unsteady legs betrayed her.

"Mr. Platt!" she cried, barely able to control herself.

A kindly, elderly man emerged from the barn, dressed for another day of battle with the soil, animals, and elements. When he heard Mary's voice and saw her disheveled appearance, he held out his arms and let her run into them. Between sobs she told him of the events in the print shop.

"They arrested Marshall for the obscene pamphlets?" Platt asked.

She nodded.

"Good," he said. "Damage was minimal. We may have lost a printer, but not the press."

"But Marshall and Essex will be dismissed from the university!" she wailed.

"Yes," he agreed, "but they will escape the Star Chamber."

Mary wiped her nose. "I'm just glad Marshall's father isn't alive to see this. He'd be so disappointed that Marshall won't graduate from Cambridge."

"Don't sell our brother short, missy. From what Marshall has told me about his father, he was a man of God. He'd be proud his son has the courage to stand up for his faith."

"It just makes me angry," Mary said, straightening up. "Why does there have to be any punishment at all? Why couldn't we put some harmless pamphlets or blank pieces of paper in the sack when we make the switch?"

Farmer Platt inhaled deeply. He had attended the meetings of the Puritan resistance committee when the plan was discussed. Several ideas were presented, including the ones just mentioned by Mary, but the plan that had been worked to perfection in the print shop this morning was the one that was adopted.

"You have to understand human nature, missy," the farmer explained. "Macaulay knew something illegal was being print-ed. And he wouldn't rest until he found it, even if that meant tearing apart the walls of the shop. So, we give him some-thing illegal to find. Granted, it's not what he was looking for, but it is a crime. His sense of duty is fulfilled and he gives up after a cursory search."

Mary laid her head against Platt's chest. The reasoning was

sound, but it didn't stop her heart from aching. "Are these pamphlets really worth that kind of danger?" she asked.

Platt responded by reaching into the canvas bag and pulling one out. He began to read:

There comes a time in every man's life when he must make a decision. I'm not talking about the kind of decision that determines the outcome of his day, or his year, or even his life. I'm talking about the kind of decision that goes far beyond his personal interests, far beyond his own life—a decision that will set in motion the destiny of the world for generations to come.

The time has come for us to make such a decision.

The choice that confronts us is not complicated. Simply put, it is this: Will we observe the laws of God or will we conform to the desires of men? Shall we obey the Bible, or shall we obey the dictates of a London bishop?

The question before us is simple; so must our answer be simple. Borrowing Peter's words our response should be: "We ought rather to obey God than men" (Acts chapter V, verse 29).

As Christians of conscience, how can we decide otherwise without denying our faith?

The Bible alone is God's perfect statement of how we are to live. The Lord God, determining to set before our eyes a perfect plan, is both able to do it and hath done it.

It is natural that God should be so explicit in the instructions regarding His people, since it is the virtue of a good law to leave as little undetermined as possible.

The explicitness of God's moral and judicial law is

a clear indication of God's mind. And His law is permanent. It cannot be repealed by any earthly king, any earthly council, or any earthly bishop.

Either the Bible is God's perfect Word, or it is not. Either we will choose to obey Him, or we will not. The choice before us is a simple one. Making our decision is not difficult; living according to our decision will require great courage and faith.

These are perilous times. Who knows the full measure of the price we will yet pay? However, the choices we make, we make not only for ourselves, but for our children and our children's children. Whatever the price, it will be worth it.

This is not the time for the weak of heart. Nor is it the time to turn the other cheek, for we have not been insulted. We have been deceived. It is time for godly men and women of England to choose their future.

I, for one, choose God. I would rather fail attempting to obey God, than to succeed in any attempt to please men.

Platt rested the pamphlet on his lap. "Marshall will be proud that he had a part in getting this message out," he said.

Mary wiped her eyes and nodded.

"You'd better get home, missy," Platt said. "I'll take the pamphlets from here."

Later that day, Justin's pamphlets left the Platt farm hidden in the false bottoms of milk containers on a dairyman's cart. The dairyman passed them to other contacts who took them east to Newmarket and Thetford and into the city of Norwich where one of the pamphlets was delivered to Reverend Thomas Calmers, the parish priest of Spixworth.

Reverend Calmers shut the door to his study as he read

Justin's challenge. On the desk before him lay a circular from Bishop Laud addressed to the churches of Norwich. In the circular, the bishop instructed the priests always to wear the proper surplice attire when preaching. Instructions were also given regarding the placement of the altar at the east end of the church. A rail was to be built around the altar, setting it apart from the congregation. Failure to follow the circular's instructions would bring immediate disciplinary action, including, but not limited to, the suspension of the pastor's living.

Tears stained Justin's pamphlet as Reverend Calmers finished reading it. In all his thirty-two years of ministry, he never thought it would come to this. Yet he could not ignore the two opposing forces inside him. Like an unhappy couple, his faith and his church were claiming irreconcilable differences. Once inseparable, they now hated each other. How could he choose between them?

For most of the afternoon, Calmers wept and prayed over the pamphlet and circular as they lay side by side before him on the desk. As the sun set and the room darkened, Reverend Calmers rose slowly, as if he were lifting a great weight. Picking up the two printed items on his desk, he placed the pamphlet in his pocket and the bishop's circular in the fire.

A country gentlemen from Corby delivered Justin's latest pamphlet to points north—Peterborough, Leicester, and Nottingham. In Derby, just west of Nottingham, a father of nine read the pamphlet to his family at the supper table. He prayed that God would keep his children strong in the faith. Then he offered a prayer of thanks for Justin's parents and the influence they undoubtedly had on the writer's spiritual upbringing.

To the south the pamphlets made their way to London and Canterbury. From there, they were carried to the southwest—Bristol, Exeter, and Plymouth. In Edenford, a little village situated on the River Exe, Ambrose Dudley, the town's scrivener, studied the pamphlet word for word. He circled several phrases in the pamphlet that were distinctive of the author's style, folded the pamphlet and placed it in the back of his Bible.

It would be difficult for an Englishman to travel to any part of England and not find someone reading Justin's pamphlets—sailors at Portsmouth, candlemakers at Swindon, lawyers at Ipswich, and a schoolmaster at Coventry.

It was one of Laud's boys in Northampton who first laid his hands on Justin's latest pamphlet. As instructed, he delivered it immediately to Bishop Laud at London House.

It took no small amount of courage to hand over the pamphlet. He had heard stories from the other boys about Laud's violent reactions to seditious literature. But what he had heard had not prepared him for what he saw that day.

The bishop received the pamphlet and rewarded the boy with a shilling, commending him for his diligent work. Then he dismissed the boy so he could read the pamphlet in private. Feeling somewhat cheated that he didn't get to see the bishop throw a tantrum, the boy sneaked back down the hallway and cracked the door just wide enough to watch. The bishop was slumped in a chair before a fireplace, reading intently. There was no yelling; he didn't throw things; he didn't stomp about. Nothing. Just the rhythmic rising of his chest as he read.

Disappointed, the boy was about to leave when the bishop tore half a page from the pamphlet and placed it in his mouth. Slowly, with forced determination, he chewed the paper and swallowed. He tore another piece off and chewed and swallowed it. Then another and another. As the bishop chewed page after page his face grew redder and redder, and beads of sweat formed on his forehead and ran down the sides of his face.

The only sound to be heard was the tearing of the pages and the eerie noise of a man forcing himself to swallow. Minutes later, he was finished. The pamphlet was gone. The bishop stared at the fire, his face still red and drenched with sweat. Then, a low rumbling came from his chest and formed into words, "I will meet them as a bear that is bereaved of her whelps, and I will rend the caul of their heart, and there will I devour them like a lion: the wild beast will tear them, Hosea chapter 13, verse 8."

Chapter 6

MORGAN Hall, the lavish country estate of the Morgan family, was disputed territory between two generations of Morgans. Built during the glory days of Queen Elizabeth and financed with pirated gold from Spanish ships — a practice encouraged by the queen, Morgan Hall was originally designed to reflect the personality of its seafaring owner. However, in recent years the stately mansion was systematically being refurbished to suit the tastes of a new generation of Morgans who were more concerned with wealth and status than with the wishes of the original builder.

Admiral Amos Bronson Morgan, one of England's most revered naval heroes, built Morgan Hall in 1590. The unschooled son of a Plymouth shipbuilder, Amos was an articulate man, his education coming from extensive reading. He was an expert on modern ship design and Greek classical literature.

Amos Morgan's vast knowledge could be attributed to his father; some his father taught him directly and some Amos learned because his father forbade him to learn it.

A self-made businessman, Edward Morgan thought book learning a waste of time. He refused to let Amos attend public school and took it upon himself to give his son a practical education. The boy learned math by adding price columns of supply lists and workers' pay slips; he graduated to higher math by calculating ships' buoyancy distributions. Lessons in logic involved solving management resource problems on the docking berth. Amos' reading primer was a stack of production orders, timber schedules, and delivery invoices. By the time he was fifteen, Amos knew every aspect of his father's shipbuilding business.

In spite of his father's restricted syllabus, Amos developed a penchant for reading; by the time he was a teenager he craved books like most boys his age craved the opposite sex. He dreamed of matriculating at Oxford University with its magnificent libraries and robed professors, but Edward Morgan wouldn't hear of it. The boy had all the learning he needed to run the family business. Subject closed.

Edward Morgan had violated a principle of parenting—forbid a boy to do something, even if it's studying, and that's exactly what he will want to do. Such was the case with Amos Morgan.

Amos used almost all the money he earned to purchase books from the local bookseller in Plymouth. At night or whenever he could steal a few minutes away from the docks, he pored over his forbidden purchases. He quickly developed a fascination with Greek literature. Homer was his favorite, especially the voyages of Ulysses. Amos read the *Odyssey* so many times he could close his eyes and recite lengthy portions of it word for word. It was Homer who convinced the boy his destiny was in sailing ships, not in building them.

Amos Morgan's first taste of nautical adventure came aboard the *Minion*. John Hawkins, the *Minion's* skipper, was the son of an English family who made their fortune trading African slaves.

One spring afternoon, while the senior Morgan negotiated a contract to build four new ships for the senior Hawkins, Amos negotiated his future with the younger Hawkins. Impressed with the boy's determination, John Hawkins signed

Amos on as a member of his crew. When Edward Morgan learned of the deal between the younger men, he was so furious he nearly scuttled the shipbuilding contract. But Amos was of age and there was nothing his father could do short of physical violence to prevent him from going. Amos Morgan paid a high price for his change of career: his father never spoke to him again.

Although John Hawkins was twenty-six years his senior, he and Amos became close friends. Their friendship was based on shared danger, like the time they put in for repairs at San Juan de Ulua.

There were ten English ships in all. For months they had been on a slaving expedition in the Caribbean, exchanging Africans for West Indian sugar, gold, and hides in defiance of Spanish commercial regulations. The Spanish thought they owned the New World and made regulations accordingly. The English had little regard for Spanish claims or regulations. If there was anything an English seaman liked as much as raiding Spanish territories, it was breaking Spanish regulations.

The day after John Hawkins' ships dropped anchor at San Juan de Ulua, Spanish ships appeared. The Spanish captain relayed a note to Hawkins that his ships needed supplies; would Hawkins be so kind as to make room for them in the harbor? Since the Spanish fleet was already blocking the entrance to the harbor, Hawkins didn't see that he had much choice. He maneuvered his ships close together and the Spanish proceeded to squeeze into the harbor next to them. No sooner had they dropped anchor than armed Spanish sailors began pouring over the sides of their ships. The English were overwhelmed.

It was Amos Morgan's first battle; it was also the first day he ever killed a man; by sunset he was quite experienced at it.

The day did not go well for the English sailors. Only two

ships escaped, the *Minion* and Drake's *Judith*.

For months afterward, the incident at San Juan de Ulua worked in Amos' belly like a bad potato. He lost several friends that day. He also developed a hearty hatred for Spanish arrogance and was constantly formulating ideas and schemes for revenge. However, there was little he could do about it—until John Hawkins was appointed treasurer of the English navy. When the new treasurer called upon his ship-building knowledge to settle the score with the Spanish, Amos responded eagerly.

John Hawkins and Amos Morgan developed a new class of English ships. The design was risky. To begin with, the ships were smaller than the Spanish galleons. All the guns were moved broadside and toward the center line, thus improving stability. Then the ships' sides were sloped inward from the lowest gun deck up to the weather deck. The result was that these ships were lower, faster, and more seaworthy than any others sailing the ocean.

Reducing the size of the ship meant reducing the size of her guns as well. Hawkins and Morgan equipped the ships with a long-range culverin type of gun, with shot ranging from 9 to 32-pounders. The guns were much smaller than the Spanish 50-pounders but had greater range and accuracy.

The new design called for new strategy. The standard naval warfare tactic was to run at the enemy, fire the guns, ram the ship, and loose a boarding party. These new English ships, however, were designed for off-fighting. They would be no match for the Spanish if they used traditional tactics. For a new battle plan, Hawkins called upon Sir Francis Drake who devised a strategy for the English fleet. When the strategy was complete, everything was in place. All that was needed was an opportunity to put their new ideas to the test. The opportunity came in July 1588.

The great Spanish fleet was first sighted off Cornwall heading toward England. Philip II of Spain, with the blessing of the Pope, had sent his seemingly invincible armada to conquer England and return the country to the benevolent fold of Roman Catholicism. Neither Philip nor the Pope cared that England didn't want to be returned to the fold; they had decided it was God's will and set out to accomplish it.

The alarm sounded. Amos Morgan, now captain of his own ship, the *Dutton*, responded with the rest of the captains. Charles Howard, commander of the English fleet, summoned the ships to assemble at Portsmouth. It was nearly a fatal mistake. The converging Spanish ships almost succeeded in trapping the English fleet in the harbor. With the ships bottled up in the harbor, the English would be forced to fight a close battle, one they would most certainly lose. It was the new ship design that saved the day.

The lighter, faster English fleet bolted from the harbor and tacked westward across the bows of the Spanish ships which were not fast enough to cut them off. Upon reaching open sea, the English now had the wind advantage and could implement Sir Francis Drake's new strategy.

In three encounters, the smaller, faster English ships danced out of reach of the heavy Spanish guns. The long-range culverin guns peppered the tightly bunched Spanish ships with shot. The smaller guns weren't large enough to destroy the Spanish ships outright, but like bees they swarmed and stung the ships repeatedly. Powerless to hinder the assault, the Spanish ships retreated to the Calais harbor.

For days the Spanish sat there, hoping to lure the English into the harbor where they could fight a traditional battle. The battle was a stalemate, at least until Sir Francis Drake came up with another plan.

Just after midnight, six English ships were set on fire and sailed into the harbor of Calais. The Spanish captains were forced to cut loose their anchors and flee the harbor, sailing

right into the guns of the waiting English ships. The Spanish
Armada was routed; they never again regained their fighting
formation.

Even the winds turned against the Spanish fleet. "The
winds of God," Drake called them, as if God Himself were
fighting for the English cause. The Spanish fleet was scattered
and largely wrecked. Of their 130 ships that sailed for England, only 76 ever made it back to Spain. For the English it
was a total victory. They suffered fewer than 100 casualties,
and not a single ship was sunk by the once-invincible Spanish
Armada.

The Spanish threat thwarted, people and queen were eager
to show their gratitude to the daring Englishmen who had
saved them. John Hawkins, Francis Drake, and Amos Morgan became national heroes. Among other rewards, Amos
was promoted to admiral. He soon became a regular at court
functions, and was showered with adulation and wealth—
more wealth than he could possibly spend in a lifetime, especially considering the fact that he led an austere life centered
around his ship and a growing library of books.

It was Queen Elizabeth herself who suggested an invest-
ment for his growing estate. Buy some land and build a
house, she advised. When he expressed little desire to own a
house he would seldom occupy, the queen predicted that
things would change as he got older, that one day he would
welcome a place where he could sit comfortably in front of
the fire and read his books. More out of politeness than
desire to own a home, Amos Morgan began looking at houses
and land. The more he looked, the more interested he
became.

It was the idea of a personal library that most captivated
him, a desire for a repository for his growing number of
volumes and a place to which he could escape when he was
not sailing. So Amos Morgan purchased a large tract of roll-

ing acreage just east of Winchester, not far from Portsmouth where his ship was docked.

Maybe it was his shipbuilding skills rising to the surface or maybe the wisdom of the queen's words were taking hold, but for the first time in his life Amos Morgan was consumed with a personal building project. He involved himself in every aspect of the house, from design to interior detail. When Morgan Hall was finished, Amos Morgan's creation proudly took its place alongside England's finest country homes.

There was Longleat, a glorious Italian Renaissance home constructed in 1580, known for its magnificent tapestries, paintings, porcelain, and furniture, and, of course, its great hall with massive wooden beams and giant Irish elk antlers mounted on the walls.

And there was Theobalds with its woodland motif, King James' favorite retreat. It had indoor trees, bushes, and branches so natural looking that when the doors were left open birds flew in and roosted in them. Theobalds also had garish touches of the spectacular, notably the room displaying the stars of the universe on its ceiling, complete with a clock-work mechanism that moved the sun and planets in keeping with the seasons.

Morgan Hall was a handsome addition to the stately manors. Like the others, it reflected its builder's interests. The mansion was a mixture of Amos Morgan's three great loves: classical Greece, the ocean, and the printed word.

A visitor to Morgan Hall would ascend eight marble steps formed in a half circle, to reach the twelve-foot arched doorway, passing between six majestic Corinthian columns.

Inside, he would find himself in a domed entryway with three identical open-arched doorways leading to different parts of the house. Between the arches stood twin pillars, these too of marble and of ancient origin, having been discovered and excavated from the bed of the Tiber River in Rome.

Glancing up, the visitor would look past the railings of the second floor to the dome overhead where there was a painting of God in His heavens, surrounded by the seemingly mandatory cherubs and half-clothed women so prominent in classical art.

Passing through the northern archway, the visitor would find himself in the drawing room. Continuing farther, he would be in a cedar dining hall.

The eastern archway led to two sets of stairs, one against the wall on the right and one against the left wall, each with a corner landing. The left stairway was for women, the right stairway for men; the difference between the two was the panels of the railings. The men's panel was an elaborate cut-wood design. The women's panel had the same design, but only in relief, protecting the ladies' ankles from the crude stares of men. The admiral was more of a gentleman than most of those who sailed under his command.

The south portal in the entryway was the one used most often by guests. It led to the great hall where parties, balls, and banquets were held. The hall was long and expansive with a wooden floor so shiny that details of the wall hangings could be clearly seen in its reflection. The walls were adorned with huge panoramas—tapestries as well as paintings—of ships at sea. The ceiling had several circular bas-relief designs which featured oval paintings of blue sky and friendly clouds in their centers. Standing in the room one always had the feeling of fair weather and good sailing.

In the middle of the eastern wall of this great hall, two heavy oak doors led to the admiral's favorite room, his personal library. It was here that he kept his most treasured possessions—his books, mementos from the queen, and a variety of weapons, including his first cutlass, the one that saved his life so many times in the bay of San Juan de Ulua. His book collection included Cicero, Livy, Suetonius, and

Diodorus Siculus. He also owned Gerard's *Herbal*, Elyot's *The Governour*, and the poems of Sidney.

Three of the four walls of the library were lined with bookshelves from floor to ceiling. The eastern wall was a series of double glass doors leading to a covered walkway and then out to the gardens. Except in inclement weather, these doors were always open, flooding the room with light and fresh air. When the weather was bad, the admiral could still enjoy the outdoor light as it streamed through the glass panes. Morgan Hall was one of the first houses in England to use glass for windows let alone for doors. The glass had been imported from the Continent at great expense. The thick square panes were set in lead casings and the glass itself was not very clear; one could see only vague shapes moving on the other side of the doors when they were closed, but they were clear enough to let the light in and that's what the admiral wanted.

In the private living quarters upstairs, the rooms were in the center of the house, without outside windows or doorways. A hallway along the perimeter of the house and glass doors led to small balconies at regular intervals around the circumference. Often, the admiral walked the perimeter of the house, spyglass in hand, surveying his property, much the same way he walked the decks of his ship at night before turning in.

Morgan Hall was the admiral's retreat, and the site of the occasional party required of a man in his position. To everyone's surprise, especially the admiral's, Morgan Hall also became a newlyweds' love nest.

The admiral wasn't looking for a wife. He had always thought it unfair for a woman to be married to a sailor, since her husband would be gone for months or possibly years at a time. His philosophy regarding the fairer sex was rational, considerate, and typical for a confirmed bachelor. Its fatal flaw was that it neglected to factor love into the equation.

Georgiana Reynolds was serendipity. Or, as the admiral would tell it, she was a sailor's dream—a tropical paradise that unexpectedly crested the horizon of his life.

Their meeting was not by accident. A powerful force, Queen Elizabeth, brought them together. The queen had always liked the admiral; he was modest, kind, and not self-seeking, thus a rarity in the English court. It was her royal opinion that such a man needed a good wife, so she took it upon herself to find him one. When she settled on Georgiana Reynolds, the queen all but decreed they get married, an action that was unnecessary since the two were smitten with each other from the moment they met.

Georgiana was as fair as a sunny day. The young, modest daughter of an English nobleman, she became the light and life of Amos Morgan's existence. Two months after they met, Amos and Georgiana were married. Life at Morgan Hall had never been so sweet. The couple shared a love of books and the outdoors. Morgan Hall was always open to the wind and sun, and each evening the giddy couple strolled arm in arm around the grounds.

Amos Morgan's new bride expanded her lover's horizons by introducing him to the wonders of their native isle. Amos discovered that traveling in a coach with Georgiana was better than the best day at sea. Knowing his love of history, Georgiana charted a tour that took in several major historical sights. In the north they saw Housestead's Roman Fort along Hadrian's Wall and remnants of the Fosse Way in the south. They visited Stonehenge, Scarfell Pike, and Land's End. For five months the couple toured in wedded bliss. Then, quite suddenly, their tour came to an abrupt halt. Georgiana took to her bed. She was with child.

The admiral had never really thought about being a father. The more he thought about it now, the less he liked the idea. A baby would be an intrusion, an unwanted rival for

Georgiana's attention and affection. He knew he was being selfish, but he didn't care. His beloved wife had become the center of his existence. It wouldn't be the same with a baby in the house.

Georgiana, on the other hand, couldn't have been happier. She was excited to bear the admiral's child and took the pain of pregnancy in stride. She knew of the admiral's reservations about the child, but had convinced herself that once the child was born, he would change his mind.

Some women are not equipped to bear children, and Georgiana was one of these. Her pregnancy was difficult from the start. As the months passed, her sunny countenance faded. At the time of birth, Georgiana was weak and sickly.

For over eighteen hours Georgiana labored to deliver her baby. She writhed and screamed and clutched the hand of her midwife and gritted her teeth in agony. The baby wouldn't come. Twice her wet bedding had to be replaced with fresh sheets. She was exhausted. As one attendant described it, "She was more worn out than a bar of soap after a hard day's wash." Even so, Georgiana refused to give up. Nothing was going to stop her from delivering her child.

The attending midwife described the birth as an exchange of life. Throughout the ordeal it was clear that there would be only one survivor—either mother or child. When the moment of birth came, to hear the midwife tell the story, it was as if Georgiana willed her life into the body of her infant son, for the moment the baby was born, Georgiana died.

If Amos Morgan had known no greater joy than when he met Georgiana, he knew no greater sorrow than when she died. His life was shipwrecked.

To take his mind off his sorrow, he retreated into the bosom of his first love—the sea. He hired nannies and tutors to raise his son in his absence. From the time Percy was two months old until he came of age, he and his father were together for little more than occasional holidays and a few special days each year. As a result, the two were not close. This was never more evident than when Percy chose a bride and brought her home to Morgan Hall.

Percy Morgan married Evelyn North—one of *the* Norths. He didn't marry her because he loved her. In fact, there was no romance between them at all; their marriage was a meticulously negotiated alliance designed to benefit both sides. But it was a marriage the romantic admiral never understood, let alone approved. Both the groom and bride were ambitious opportunists and each had something the other wanted. Although the Norths were quite wealthy, their empire was endangered by an insufficient cash flow. That's where the Morgans came in. The admiral was flush with cash. On the other hand, the Norths had what Percy coveted most—a higher level of nobility. Queen Elizabeth was dead and the king on the throne knew not Amos Morgan. It's true, the admiral was still respected by the court, but at a polite distance; he could move among them, but he wasn't one of them. In the marriage negotiations, Percy Morgan bargained with his father's cash for the Norths' nobility.

From the moment Evelyn Morgan became the lady of the house, she set out to change things. The admiral, feeling his age and no longer able to sail, spent his days in his library retreat. He had no great love for his new daughter-in-law, but tried his best to tolerate her. When she spoke of making changes in Morgan Hall, he politely but dogmatically refused every proposal. And that, in the admiral's opinion, was the end of it. However, he underestimated his daughter-in-law's determination and guile.

When it came to getting her way, Evelyn was a bloodhound; she never let up until she had what she wanted, and when it came to her new house, she wasn't about to back down to some washed-up sailor. On every opportunity that presented itself, and in many she created, Lady Morgan voiced her displeasure over room colors, paintings, and furniture. Whenever guests came to Morgan Hall, she would rail about the complaint *du jour*. She nagged her husband every night in bed until Percy started sleeping in another room. During the day she indoctrinated the servants about everything that was wrong with Morgan Hall. In short, whoever had ears to hear heard how much Evelyn Morgan despised the house Amos Morgan built.

Her favorite target was the dark wood paneling of the drawing room. "It makes me *absolutely* depressed!" she would rail. Evelyn's opinions were always stated in the absolute; there were no gray areas in her tastes. "It's *absolutely* as dark as a dungeon in here. I swear I can't live another day with this room like this!" When guests arrived she would always show them the drawing room first, to set the tone and subject for the evening. "Isn't this *absolutely* ghastly?" she would ask. "Don't you think this room would look more attractive in light oak or ash?" When her guests politely agreed, she would make it a point to bring it to the admiral's attention in their presence. "Now see, dear," she would say, touching his arm in the same way an adult would touch a child, "Margaret agrees with me. All that dark wood in the drawing room is *absolutely* impossible. Something *has* to be *done* about it."

Like the steady drip, drip, drip of water against rock, Evelyn Morgan began to wear away the admiral's resolve.

It was late spring of 1625 when Lady Evelyn Morgan won the battle of the drawing room and had it repaneled with oak. For the admiral it was a tactical blunder. He thought that by allowing her a victory, he could have some peace; but just the opposite was true. The bloodhound was on the scent and forged ahead with greater intensity. Her next target was the sea paintings in the great hall.

"All these pictures of heaving waves and silly boats make me *absolutely* nauseous," she would say, holding a dainty white hand across her midriff. "Why, I turn green every time I look at them. Don't they affect you that way too? Something *must* be done about them."

She replaced the seascapes with paintings typical of the period—plump, pink naked women lounging on sofas or being abducted by satyrs while horrified cherubs hovered overhead. "It looks like a brothel," the admiral spat disgustedly.

Picture by picture, panel by panel, room by room, Lady Evelyn Morgan stole Morgan Hall from Amos until all he had left was his library. It was there he took his stand.

Drew was fourteen at the time. He remembered his grandfather arming himself with his cutlass, the one that had tasted the blood of Spaniards at San Juan de Ulua, and threatening Lady Morgan with bodily harm should she ever attempt to enter his library without his permission. Flush with victory, Lady Morgan's response one evening was to barge into the room uninvited and unannounced. Amos went wild. There were several moments when Drew thought for sure his mother was going to be run through as the admiral's blade slashed within inches of her. That night the admiral drove Lady Morgan out of the library just as he had driven his enemies off the deck of his ship. She never ventured into the room again in his lifetime.

For the rest of his life the admiral spent his days in seclusion. His health was too frail to fight the sea or to sustain an extended battle with his daughter-in-law. He withdrew to his world of books.

Drew often spent whole days in the library with his grandfather, sometimes to escape his mother's moods, sometimes to hear his grandfather's sea stories. A special kinship developed between grandfather and grandson. They provided each other a balance in life. With his sea tales Admiral Morgan brought adventure to Drew's otherwise drab life; and Drew brought hope to the admiral that with the next generation Morgan Hall would be back in the possession of someone who shared his values and priorities. Their special relationship made life bearable.

Drew was still brooding when the family entourage arrived home from their Windsor Castle excursion. Philip was the first out of the carriage with Lady Morgan close behind. Lord Morgan, anxious to check on his expensive ponds of tropical fish, went directly to the garden without going into the house.

Drew eased himself down from Pirate, who had plodded all the way from Basingstoke, matching his rider's depressed state of mind. He loaded himself down with his bags from the carriage, the bishop's wounded book, the thieves' dagger, and, of course, Geoffrey Berber's *The Days of the Knights*. Even from out here he could hear his mother and brother yelling inside, something about windows and servants and a drunk, or was that a trunk? *How could I ever think of leaving my happy home?* Drew mumbled.

The massive oak door hit something and stopped midway when he pushed it with his hip. He poked his head through the opening and saw an old sea chest blocking the door. *What's that doing there?* Drew pushed harder. The chest moved with surprising ease. *Must be empty*, he thought as he squeezed by it.

To his right in the great hall his mother was screaming and banging on the closed double doors that led to the admiral's library. "You've been swinging that sword again, haven't you, you old dog!" She pounded the doors with her fists. "It's freezing in here, thanks to you!"

"Leave Grandpa alone!" Drew shouted at her. "It's his house!"

"Don't talk to me like that!" Lady Morgan turned on him, her face flushed with anger. "You're in more trouble than he is," she screamed. "Go to your room!" Turning back to the door, she shouted, "And if you think you can barricade the door with your stupid sea chest, you're sadly mistaken! It was a feeble attempt, old man!"

Lady Morgan paused, expecting a response. There was none. The admiral had never been shy about cursing back at Lady Morgan before. Drew moved toward the doors, listening for any sound from behind them. Still nothing.

"Maybe he's sick," Drew said.

"Maybe he's dead," Lady Morgan replied. Then, liking the sound of her words, a grin lit up her face then quickly faded. "Not possible. I'm not that lucky."

"Grandpa?" Drew shouted.

No answer.

He tried the doors. They were locked.

"*Grandpa!*" Drew glanced at his mother with mounting horror. Her expression sickened him. The grin was back, accented by the heavy paint on her face. It was a grin of triumph.

Dropping his armload of things on the floor, Drew yanked at the doors with both hands. They wouldn't open.

Running out of the hall, he circled around toward the library's glass doors through the domed entryway, between the twin stairways, and out the back door. He could see his father on his hands and knees bending over his fish pond, his face inches from the water. Drew sprinted toward the library doors. They were open—every one of them. Drew's momentum carried him past the doors; he smashed against a doorjamb trying to make the turn into the library.

"Grandpa!" he yelled.

Drew scanned the room. Over the back of his grandfather's favorite chair, situated in front of the fireplace, Drew could see the old man's head. Single strands of gray hair arched up from a smooth surface, much like grass poking through cracks in granite rock. And just like a rock, his grandfather was motionless. The only movement Drew could see was the dance of the flames in the fireplace.

Drew approached the unmoving form of his grandfather. "Grandpa?"

No answer.

He hesitated. If his grandfather was dead, he didn't want to know it. But what if he needed help? Slowly, Drew peeked around the edge of the chair. Admiral Morgan's eyes were closed. A big grin covered the rest of his face.

"Have a good trip, boy?" Admiral Morgan asked.

The news that the admiral was still alive ruined the rest of Lady Morgan's day. Drew remained in the library with his grandfather, the only place where he felt safe from his mother's needling gibes.

"Disgusting!"

Propping himself up with his cutlass, the admiral stood by an open glass door watching his son, Lord Morgan, peer into the fish ponds. Drew slouched idly in a chair with one leg draped over the side, flipping through the pages of a book.

"Is he kissing those fish?"

Drew glanced up. "He talks to them."

The admiral shook his head. "He's kissing them!"

With a lazy moan Drew got up and wandered over by his grandfather. Lord Morgan was still on his hands and knees, his face less than an inch from the water. His lips were moving. On the other side of the surface there was a wavy splash of bright orange color.

"He's kissing them," Drew agreed.

The gardens were Lord Percy Morgan's addition to Morgan Hall. He had personally directed a staff of gardeners in transforming a lazy meadow into a maze of hedges, walkways, and waterfalls.

Lord Morgan divided his magnificent garden into what he called "lands." There was a land of fruit where oranges, apples, and a half-dozen different kinds of berries grew. There was a wooded land which featured a miniature forest patterned after the fabled Sherwood Forest. A valley of grass featuring a covered table with benches was called the land of the spring meadow. All of this was impressive even by nobility's standards, but Lord Morgan's most ambitious and impressive project was his land of tropical fish.

Throughout this land was a series of cascading saltwater ponds. It took Lord Morgan and his gardeners over three years to devise a system that would sustain saltwater tropical fish. The system had to be replenished twice a month with fresh saltwater carted by wagon from the sea. To populate the water, Lord Morgan had standing orders with several ships' captains for tropical fish from the Caribbean. This was profitable for the owners of the ships: it gave them return cargo after unloading their cargo of African slaves in the West Indies. The fish-loving lord of Morgan Hall was known to spend as much for a rare fish as the merchant could get for a sturdy young male slave.

"That's the difference between us," Admiral Morgan said to Drew, his cutlass poking the air toward his son beside the fish ponds. "In my day Englishmen battled Spanish aggression. Today's Englishman battles fish fungus."

With a loud snort, the admiral hobbled back to his chair in front of the fire, using his cutlass as a cane. Drew watched him with concern. *Am I overreacting to the recent scare, or is Grandpa moving more slowly than usual?* Upon reaching the chair the admiral navigated his backside toward the seat, much like a ship approaching a dock. His bottom hovered for a moment over its target. Then, with a "humph" he plopped into his chair. Seventy-one years old and ancient by the world's standards he sat with his eyes closed, catching his breath.

"You see before you the ruins of time," he said with tired, raspy voice. "My boy, my day is fast coming to a close. And I'm glad it is. I don't want to live any longer in this miserable age."

Drew said nothing. It wasn't the first time the admiral had spoken like this. The fact that he was talking about death didn't disturb Drew; sometimes he was most alive when he was talking about it. That's why Drew remained silent, hoping his grandfather would leap into a tale of the past and take him along.

The admiral continued, "Drake is dead. Hawkins is dead. The days of English glory are dead and buried." He sighed a deep long sigh. "Dead is best. It's a curse to live too long. At least Drake and Hawkins aren't forced to watch their beloved England rot before their very eyes."

Well, Drew thought, *it's a start. At least he's talking about John Hawkins and Sir Francis Drake. Maybe he just needs a little help.*

"Grandpa, why didn't some people like Sir Francis Drake?"

The admiral opened one eye and peered through it suspiciously. He recognized Drew's attempt for what it was. Nonetheless, he smirked, closed his eye, and laid his head back against the chair.

Success! This was his grandfather's standard storytelling posture. Drew waited while the admiral conjured up images of the past; he would have given anything to be able to see the things his grandfather could see on the other side of those wrinkled eyelids.

"Most men hated Drake," the admiral said. "Parvenu they called him." He pronounced the word with an exaggerated French accent.

"Parvenu?"

"Upstart. Bounder. Drake was never known for his social graces. Always had that west country accent." The admiral smiled. "If he hadn't been kin to Hawkins, the great Drake would have lived and died a penniless dirt farmer." Amos let out a laugh which sent him into a coughing spasm, then wiped his mouth with a handkerchief before continuing. "But didn't he have the gall! That parvenu got us out of more scrapes because he would do things that no sane man would think of doing."

Another coughing spasm, this one more violent. When it passed, the admiral slumped back into his chair, weak and sweaty.

"But now Drake's dead," he murmured breathlessly. "Hawkins too." A pause. "So why am I still here?"

"Maybe," Drew said hesitantly, "because I need you."

Amos smiled at that. He reached over and patted his grandson's hand. "We've been good for each other, haven't we?" he said. "But your time has come. It's time for you to go and live your own adventures."

Drew was reminded of his recent encounter with thieves outside London. "I almost forgot! I did have an adventure!" Drew leaped up and retrieved the bishop's book and the dagger from the other side of the double doors. Displaying them with pride, he narrated the adventure to his grandfather who listened intently. The admiral held the knife close to his failing eyes and meticulously examined the book, asking questions and congratulating Drew on his ingenuity of using the book as a weapon. Drew also related Bishop Laud's invitation for him to come to London.

"The Bishop of London?" The admiral winced. "Never had much use for those religious types myself. What exactly would you be doing for him?"

"The bishop says I'll be protecting England against internal enemies. I'll report to him and he reports directly to King Charles."

"Internal enemies, huh?" The admiral leafed through the pages of the wounded book, looking to see how deep the dagger had pierced. "Good book," he announced. "I like Layfield. Gives you plenty of facts, but doesn't let 'em get in the way of the story."

He handed the book back to Drew and then continued. "Internal enemies . . . they're the hardest to spot. It was easier in my day. You knew who your enemies were. They were the ugly ones swarming over the side of your ship, cursing in Spanish, and trying to run you through with a sword."

"Are you saying I shouldn't go to London?" Drew asked.

The admiral pondered for a moment, started to speak, then was racked with another coughing fit. When the coughing finally subsided, he was left gasping for air. Finally, he said, "No, I didn't say that. In fact, I think you should go. Tonight."

"Tonight?"

"Why not?"

"I can't go now. If I go now Father will give Morgan Hall to Philip. I don't want to lose Morgan Hall, especially to Philip. I want to save it for you, Grandpa, restore the sea paintings, make it like you once had it."

The admiral leaned back in his chair and fought for a breath of air. "No one knows better than I how hard it is to leave Morgan Hall," he wheezed. "But there's more to life than Morgan Hall. And sometimes when you allow yourself to wander from the things you love, you find something you love even more. Like my Georgiana." At the mention of his wife, the admiral's eyes turned moist. "You know, we had a system, Georgiana and I, whenever we'd leave Morgan Hall. I'd set out the trunk. She'd pack. Then we'd go on a holiday. Whenever I was with her I forgot all about ships and adventures. I even forgot about Morgan Hall." As he turned to Drew, a single tear worked its way down a wrinkled ravine on his cheek. "Nothing in this world means more to me than Morgan Hall. Except you. Drew, don't stay here for me. Go. Tonight. Discover your own adventures. Build your own Morgan Hall. Go out there and find your Georgiana."

"No, Grandpa. I can always go later..."

The old man raised his hand to stop Drew from saying anymore. "Every captain worth his salt would willingly give his life to save his ship. But there are times when the ship can't be saved and it takes a wise captain to recognize that time and to give the command, 'Abandon ship.' My son, Drew, the battle is lost. Abandon ship."

Drew was torn. He wanted to go to London, but he didn't want to leave his grandfather. And the thought of Philip inheriting Morgan Hall was unbearable.

"I want you to have this." Admiral Morgan held out his sheathed cutlass.

"Grandpa! Your cutlass? I can't take that!"

"Nonsense! You'll need it if you're going to protect England from her internal enemies. I'd like to give you my books." His eyes gazed lovingly over the rows of volumes. "But there are too many of them. This you can carry with you. And it will always remind you of me."

Reverently, Drew accepted his grandfather's cutlass. "I'll try to make you proud of me," he said. Then he added, "But I still haven't said I'm going yet."

That night Drew was awakened by coughing noises in the hallway outside his room. It was the admiral. Drew listened as the sound made its way slowly past his door. He started to get up, then stopped. Maybe Grandpa was resuming his nightly inspection ritual. If so, he wouldn't want to be disturbed. Drew listened as the twin sounds of shuffling feet and coughing made their way to the end of the hallway, turned the corner, and proceeded along the far side of the house. As the sound grew distant, Drew could no longer hear the shuffling sound, but the cough was still clear. His grandfather apparently had rounded the far corner and was on his way back, because the cough was getting louder.

Then there were voices. Curses, actually. Both Lord and Lady Morgan were yelling at once. Lord Morgan called the admiral stupid for wandering around at night, and Lady Morgan screamed at him for opening all the doors and windows along his route. The shouting continued as they took the old man back to his room. Drew heard a door slam; then nothing.

The next morning, Drew rose late. He wandered downstairs to the kitchen to find a servant to get him something to eat. No one was there. He wandered down the hall past the servant's quarters. They were vacant. The dining room, the drawing room, still no one. It wasn't until he was through the entryway and into the great hall that he saw something that alarmed him. The double doors leading into the library were standing wide open. Grandpa rarely kept those doors open. As Drew approached the doorway he saw that the library was darker than normal, because the garden doors were closed. He walked closer and saw the first sign of life that morning. Alicia, the maid, was dusting the bookshelves. All the other servants were scurrying about, moving things and cleaning. Standing in the center of the room was his mother, hands on hips, directing the servant traffic.

"What are you doing in Grandpa's library?" he shouted. "He told you never to come in here!"

"It's my library now," she said coolly.

"It'll never be your library! Not while Grandpa's still . . ." Drew couldn't finish the sentence. The smile on his mother's face was the same painted smile she wore yesterday when she thought the admiral had died.

"He can't be dead!" Drew shouted. "I heard him in the hallway last night!"

"You heard an old man dying." she said curtly, then ordered two of the male servants to remove Grandpa's chair from in front of the fireplace and put it in storage.

Drew couldn't witness any more desecration of his grandfather's library. He wheeled around and ran from the room. Up the stairs he flew to his grandfather's room. The admiral lay uncovered on his bed when Drew entered his room. He was in his night clothes, cold and still on top of the bedclothes. No one was attending him, no one mourning him. His son was probably in the garden feeding his fish. Who knew where Philip was? And his daughter-in-law was busily removing the last vestiges of the admiral from Morgan Hall.

Drew found a blanket and covered his grandfather. Drew had never felt much need for religion, but now he wished he knew a prayer to say. He struggled to formulate some appropriate words in his mind, but his thoughts were far from anything resembling a prayer. They were thoughts of mounting fury. Drew Morgan looked at his grandfather's covered form one last time and knew what he had to do.

Driven by his rage, he ran to his own room, grabbed the admiral's cutlass, and headed downstairs to the library. He burst into the room like a one-man army attacking a stronghold.

"Out! Everyone get out!" he shouted slashing the cutlass at frightened servants who dropped books and whatever else they were carrying and ran in horror.

"Drew Morgan! Just what do you think you're doing?" his mother screamed.

Drew whirled to face her. Years of hatred welled up inside him. Later when he would think back on this incident, Drew would testify that he had murder in his heart and that the only thing that kept him from killing his mother was the restraining hand of God.

"You!" he leveled the tip of the blade at his mother. "Get out of this room! This isn't your room. This will never be your room! Get out!"

"How dare you!" she screamed. She not only stood her ground, but took a defiant step toward Drew.

Drew countered with a swipe of the sword, clearing the top of the table with one stroke. A vase, a couple of books, and an empty cup flew halfway across the room. "If you're not out of here by the time I count to five," he threatened, "you'll join Grandpa on the count of six! One!"

"Drew, don't be stupid." She didn't retreat, but she didn't advance either.

"Two!"

All the servants fled the room.

"Three!"

Drew took a step toward his mother. She began inching her way toward the double doors leading to the hall.

"Four!"

Just inside the doorway, she planted her feet and took a last stand.

"Five!"

Drew charged at her, sword raised. Lady Morgan fled, but not before vowing to return with Drew's father.

Drew slammed the double doors behind her and locked them. Then he locked doors leading to the garden and stationed himself in the middle of the room, prepared for the siege he knew would come.

A barrage of threats and curses from behind the doors followed. For hours Lord and Lady Morgan screamed and shouted at the doors of the library. Philip let loose an occasional taunt, but he tired quickly and the battle came down to

Drew and his parents. Late into the night they grew hoarse and finally retreated.

There, in the silence of the library, Drew mourned the death of his grandfather. He ran a reverent hand across books on the shelves as he whispered the titles; for some of them he remembered his grandfather's assessment of the authors' abilities or lack of them. He sat in a chair and recalled stories he had heard in this room, expecting to look up and see the storyteller—head back, eyes closed, in his usual storytelling position; then, at times, he sat on the floor in the middle of the library, his arms wrapped around his knees, and just wept.

Shortly before morning, as the dark on the other side of the glass doors grew lighter, Drew evaluated his position. He had no food, no supplies of any kind. How long could he hold out? Then what? Reclaiming the library seemed the right thing to do, but holding on to it was a completely different matter. Now that rational thought regained a foothold in his thinking, holing up in a library seemed rather ridiculous, unwise . . . *"It takes a wise captain to recognize the time to give the command, 'Abandon ship.'" Isn't that what Grandpa said? The battle is lost. Abandon ship. Abandon ship.*

As the first rays of the day slipped over the eastern horizon, Drew went up to his room and gathered his things, including the bishop's book and the dagger. With his grandfather's cutlass leading the way, he crept downstairs and out the servant's door toward the stable. He quickly saddled Pirate, careful not to awaken the stablehands, and rode away from Morgan Hall.

Looking back one last time he saw the sea chest sitting on the front porch next to one of the huge Corinthian columns. In all the commotion of the day, the servants hadn't found time to put it away. Just then his grandfather's words came to him:

"We had a system, Georgiana and I, whenever we'd leave

Morgan Hall. I'd set out the trunk. She'd pack. Then we'd go on a holiday. Whenever I was with her I forgot all about ships and adventures. I even forgot about Morgan Hall."

The admiral had left Morgan Hall for the last time. He was with Georgiana again. Undoubtedly enjoying a holiday.

Chapter 7

"E VER killed anything?"
"What do you mean?"

"Bugs. Flies. You ever kill 'em?"

"Sure. Why?"

"Anything larger?"

Drew didn't like the direction this conversation with Eliot was taking. "Let's talk about something else," he said.

Eliot Venner made a snorting sound. "No. Not till you answer my question. You ever kill anything bigger than a bug?"

Drew looked at his Sunday companion as they walked down a dirt road leading away from London. He had known Eliot only a few months, but he knew enough about the strange redheaded boy to realize that this conversation was nothing unusual for him. "There was a snake once, in my father's garden," Drew said warily. "My brother and I cut it in half with a shovel."

"Did it feel good?" Eliot's eyes lit up as he asked the question.

"What do you mean, 'Did it feel good'?"

"Did you feel good after you killed it?"

"You're sick, Venner."

"I know." Eliot smiled as he said it. "When I squish a bug, I get a tingly feeling all over me." There was a moment of silence when Drew didn't respond. Then Eliot asked, "Ever wonder what it would feel like to kill a man?"

"Shut up, Eliot."

Eliot shrugged. He was a wild-looking boy who had led a wild life. His savage appearance came from two pronounced features: a pair of frightful eyes and a head of strikingly red hair. The pupils of his eyes were engulfed by an abnormally large sea of white, making him look like he was in a constant state of shock. More than once Drew had seen Eliot use his queer eyes to his advantage by combining them with a truly wicked grin. The effect was eerie and intimidating. Once you were able to get past those eyes, you saw his unruly red hair. Beyond unkempt, his hair looked like it had exploded from his head.

Shorter than Drew, Eliot was actually a few years older. His face was heavily pockmarked and he walked with slight limp, both maladies resulting from a hard upbringing on the streets of London. Eliot Venner was tough and intimidating, but Drew liked him. There was a remnant of a little boy in Eliot and he was fun to be with, except when he started acting weird like he was now.

"How much farther?" Drew asked.

The two boys trudged north along the dusty road. It was a sunny afternoon and road traffic was busier than usual for a Sunday, all heading the same direction. Drew hoped the amount of traffic wouldn't cause too much attention. The last thing he wanted was to be arrested attending an illegal event on the day before his first assignment.

"Another mile," Eliot said. "It'll be worth it. Trust me."

"I don't know. Bearbaiting doesn't sound like entertainment to me."

"You'll love it!" Eliot squealed. "I was right about Rosemary, wasn't I?"

For three months Eliot Venner had served as Drew's tutor

in everything from the basics of spying to an introductory course on London's late-night entertainment. When it came to ferreting out Puritans, Eliot was Bishop Laud's most successful operative, though his motives were hardly spiritual. But for a boy who was weaned on the streets of London, it was the perfect job. He could lie, steal, sneak around, and get paid for it.

The bishop had paired the young men together because he wanted Drew to learn from his best operative. But he was disappointed when Drew willingly joined Eliot's late-night escapades. The bishop knew all about Eliot's carousing; he didn't approve, but he allowed it. He knew how difficult it was for Eliot to act like a Christian for weeks or months at a time in order to gain the confidence of his prey. After all, the young man needed a release for his youthful lusts. Between assignments was the best time for him to do it. Bishop Laud didn't expect moral behavior from Eliot, nor did he cultivate it; it would only interfere with the young man's work.

As for Drew, the bishop had more noble plans. But knowing the intensity of young male desires, he decided it would be a mistake to forbid Drew to accompany Eliot. So, for the moment, Bishop Laud looked the other way. The time was coming when Drew's training would end and the two young men would part company.

Meanwhile, Eliot Venner acquainted Drew with the diversions of local taverns. Drew preferred solitude to social gatherings and had never developed a taste for wine or beer. Even while a student at Cambridge, he preferred staying in his room and reading to going on drinking binges with his classmates. But Eliot taught him to drink and Drew became his willing student. It wasn't unusual for teacher and pupil to wake up in a heap on the cold stones of a London street lying in their own mess.

Getting drunk wasn't the only social disgrace Eliot taught

Drew. He also initiated his pupil into the ways of working women. At a tavern on Mile End Road, Eliot introduced Drew to Rosemary. He said it was Drew's reward for successfully completing his first week of lessons. When Eliot presented the girl, Drew had already crossed the threshold from sober to drunk; he thought Eliot was setting him up for a date and politely declined. Appalled at Drew's slowness, the entire tavern burst into ribald laughter. Everywhere he looked black gap-toothed mouths howled in derision as Rosemary slinked seductively toward him. Drew's face flushed hot. He pushed past the jeering trollop. He had to get away, to get out of there.

The next morning he awoke sick—physically from the drink, but also sick at heart over his encounter with raw lust. He had always fantasized his first time would be a romantic interlude with his version of Guinevere, a fair-skinned beauty for whom he would willingly sacrifice his life. He doubted anyone in the tavern last night shared his romantic fantasy. Had Eliot really expected him to sleep with a tavern wench who smelled of sweat and stale beer and who was willing to accommodate him with the passionless effort of a common worker earning a wage?

Drew ferociously washed himself and vowed never to carouse with Eliot again. But a few weeks later, when the disgusting memory dimmed, Drew celebrated another training milestone with his tutor at a different tavern.

Now as Eliot and Drew approached Fleet Ditch, the proposed site of the Sunday bearbaiting event, they saw hundreds of spectators, a pagan congregation of London commoners. As the time for the event drew near, there were the usual sounds of anxious anticipation—raucous laughter, boisterous wagering, and crude jokes. The illegality of the event only sharpened the crowd's excitement. As Eliot led Drew through the crowd, it was evident that he felt at home; Drew, on the other hand, had never been around so many unwashed people in his life.

The center of attention was a caged brown bear that looked sickly and was obviously frightened by the noise. One eye was clouded and half closed, its left side and shoulder bore massive scars where the bear's fur had never grown back. A murmur passed through the crowd that the animal was too old and broken down, that the promoter of the event was cheating them. When word reached the promoters, one of them grabbed a long pole and viciously jabbed at the bear through the bars. It responded with a roar that made even the seasoned spectators jump back. A ripple of laughter followed as those closest to the cage ribbed each other about being scared. Thus, the critics were satisfied and the promoter was pleased with himself.

"Told you this would be good," Eliot poked Drew with his elbow.

Drew didn't respond.

The entertainment began after the spectators were ushered into a natural amphitheater along the side of a large ditch which had been cleared of all shrubbery. A large wooden pole stood in the center.

Suddenly, a wretched donkey bolted in from the right side of the ravine, chased by four dogs. A terrified screaming monkey was its jockey. The crowd roared with laughter as the curious sight streaked in front of them, Eliot the loudest of all. His laughter was as odd as the rest of him, an explosive series of high-pitched bursts. Drew thought he sounded like an agitated hyena. Workers at the far end of the ravine scared the donkey into reversing his course and making another pass in front of the crowd, monkey still screaming and hounds nipping at his legs.

It took several burly men to remove the bear from his cage and chain him to the pole. As they finished, one of them lit some firecrackers and tossed them at his feet. As they exploded, the old bear howled and danced in terror, much to the delight of the crowd. Fresh dogs were loosed and three of them charged at the bear.

The spectators grew increasingly animated, shouting obscenities at the bear, urging the dogs on as they dodged the bear's ferocious swats. Drew glanced over at Eliot and saw barbaric anticipation in his eyes as he repeatedly bit his lower lip. A trickle of blood crept down his chin. Drew scanned the crowd. He was surrounded by Eliots—wild-eyed, frenzied beasts hungry for violence, crying for blood, anxious for death. It made him sick.

The bear was holding his ground against the dogs.

"They send out the old dogs first," Eliot shouted to Drew, wiping the blood off his chin with the back of his hand. "They don't want the bear to die too quick."

The dogs barked and lunged at the bear, occasionally catching a bit of fur. More frightened than hurt, the bear held them off with wild swipes of his enormous paws. For the most part the dogs stayed out of the bear's reach. One grew a little too careless and one ferocious swipe sent him sprawling across the dirt. The dog let out a yelp, a few convulsive spasms, and then he was still. His entire side had been ripped open by the bear's claw.

The crowd screamed curses at the bear and demanded for more dogs. Three more were released—mastiffs specially trained to attack and kill bears and bulls at such events. They charged the bear as if possessed; their eyes fixed with rage, they snapped and tore at things indiscriminately—the bear, the older dogs, even each other.

The old brown bear began to tire. There were just too many adversaries. Just as he would swat one dog away, three would tear at his legs. Sensing his fatigue, the dogs began jumping at his head and shoulders, trying to drag him to the ground. The bear flung one of the mastiffs clear out of the arena. The crazed dog hit the ground and rolled several times, but was quickly back on his feet and into the fray, oblivious to his wounds.

All around Drew spectators began chanting for the bear's death. Their faces were scarlet, their necks strained, veins bulging, and their eyes were blood red and frenzied. These were ordinary people who worked at a variety of trades in London every day. But on this bright afternoon they were death's fanatics. The only thing that would satisfy them was the demise of a bear.

Suddenly, the bear threw off two of the mastiffs that had fastened themselves to his upper torso. Slowly, majestically, he rose to his full height. It was as if he was oblivious to his surroundings. Tall and strong again, he surveyed the sky above the ridge of the amphitheater and let out a long roar. It wasn't a cry of pain, it was a proud roar, strong, clear, the kind of noble cry he might have made as young cub alone in a field on a spring day.

The dogs weren't impressed. They tore at him unmercifully. The crowd came to its feet when the dogs managed to pull the bear to the ground. Their mouths red with the bear's blood, the dogs attacked with even greater frenzy. The people clapped and jumped and cheered.

"Didn't I tell you it would be great?" Eliot was ecstatic as he and Drew walked back toward the city.

Drew couldn't find it in himself to respond.

"Wasn't the best I've seen," Eliot said, mentally comparing it to previous events, "but it was good. Sometimes the bulls fight better than the bears. Why, last summer I saw this one bull stick a dog and throw him all the way . . ."

Drew quickened his pace and walked ahead.

Eliot stopped and stared after him. "Guess bearbaitin' ain't for everyone." Catching up with Drew he said, "But I was right about Rosemary, wasn't I?"

Monday morning dawned bright and Drew was up early with an emotional hangover. On the one hand, he was excited because he would receive his first assignment from the bishop today; on the other, he had dreamed of bearbaiting all night and was still haunted by the bear's death. In his dream the bear always looked directly at him, as if Drew could do something to prevent its death. Drew was disgusted with himself for not being able to shed the uneasy feeling, but he couldn't get the bear's face out of his mind.

Bishop Laud was already in the garden, on his knees wielding a trowel, fashioning wells around the base of his roses.

"Andrew!" the bishop greeted him enthusiastically. "Lovely morning, isn't it?"

Drew's response was politely unenthusiastic.

The bishop sized up his condition. "Been out with Eliot again, have we?"

Drew nodded.

"Hangover?"

Drew shook his head.

"None of my business, huh?" The cleric rose, brushing the dirt from his knees. He was obviously disappointed. "Well, we won't get into that now You know how I feel. On another subject, I received a letter from your father."

This got Drew's attention. He had not had any direct communication with his family since he ran away.

"He was responding to my letter. The one I sent when we returned Pirate."

When Drew left Morgan Hall after his grandfather's death, he rode straight to London House. When he arrived, he explained to Bishop Laud the circumstances that prompted his return to London. Upon the bishop's advice, Pirate was returned to Lord Morgan the next day. That way Drew could not be accused of horse theft. Otherwise, the bishop was delighted to receive Drew into his house, even under less than ideal circumstances. He had listened in rapt attention as Drew described how the bishop's book had saved his life. Bishop Laud showed no anger that his book had been damaged. In fact, he was thrilled that the book was the instrument of Drew's salvation.

In the days that followed, the bishop kept Drew constantly by his side. He even had a bed for him moved into his bedchamber. Drew felt strange with all the attention the bishop was giving him. Yet, never in his life had he been given the attention and care the bishop showed him, and he liked it.

Late at night in the darkness of the bedchamber they would talk of the days of King Arthur and of the crusades and of life at Cambridge. To Drew's delight, the bishop would reveal dirty little secrets about some of the prim and stodgy professors at Cambridge who had intimidated him.

When Drew began carousing with Eliot, he was given his own bedroom. But the other bed was not removed from Laud's bedchamber and Drew still slept there whenever the bishop and he got carried away discussing the days of chivalry.

For the most part, Drew had never been happier. The thought of his grandfather's death and losing Morgan Hall to Philip was still painful, but he was very content with his new life and home. The large round cook who had greeted him during his initial visit to London House still giggled and bubbled every time he saw him. Drew thought him strange but came to love the meals he fixed. And Timmins was his usual stoic self, not speaking to Drew unless necessary, which suited Drew fine. In short, London House had become his home and Drew hadn't thought of his family or Morgan Hall until the bishop mentioned the letter from his father.

"Don't you want to know what he says?" the bishop asked.

"Not especially."

"Well, he doesn't say much," the bishop continued, ignoring Drew's remark. "Your grandfather's funeral was well attended."

"I'll bet it was a real celebration for my mother."

"And he thanks us for returning the horse."

"Us?"

"Well, me actually."

"He didn't say anything to me directly at all, did he?"

The bishop hesitated.

"I thought so," Drew said. "It doesn't matter. I have a new life now and I'm anxious to start on my first assignment."

The bishop stared at Drew. He looked as if he was about to say something pastoral but then changed his mind. "You're right," he said. "Let's get started. I have something for you in my study."

Bishop Laud's private study was impressive, much like Admiral Morgan's library at Morgan Hall except that the titles were more theological.

Bishop Laud handed him a Bible. "I want you to have this," he said. "It's a gift."

Drew leafed through the pages of the Bible.

"Have you ever read the Bible before?"

"No. This is the first time I've even held one."

If the bishop was surprised he didn't show it. "Well, it wouldn't hurt you to read this one, but that's not why I'm giving it to you. Look at the front matter."

Drew turned to the title page.

"This is the version King James printed, oh let's see . . ." the bishop paused while he calculated in his head, ". . . almost twenty years ago. I want you to have this specific Bible for two reasons: First, it will drive the Puritans crazy They'll think you are a heretic for using it and will try to convert you to reading the Geneva Bible. They are an unreasoning, stubborn people when it comes to this new translation. If you pretend to be won over by their arguments, you will gain their sympathy. Use that to your advantage. But the second, and more important reason I'm giving you this Bible is that you will use it to communicate with me secretly."

Drew looked up, confused.

The bishop explained. "I've developed a simple code for you to use whenever you send a message. The code is based on this version of the Bible. I'll be able to use the same version to decode your messages. To anyone else, the message will look like nonsense."

The bishop proceeded to teach Drew the encryption method he had devised. His method was based on assigning numbers to the various parts of the Bible. First, the books of the Bible were numbered, Genesis being number one and Revelation number sixty-six. The chapters and verses were already numbered and, if necessary, the words in each verse could be numbered. Based on this system, any message could be relayed by stringing words from the Bible together as if they had been cut out and pasted to a separate sheet of paper.

"Ideally, you will use entire verses or phrases from the Bible," the bishop continued. "For example, say you uncover someone we're looking for. Your message might look like this .." The bishop handed Drew a scrap of paper. A series of numbers was written on it: (43/1/45/8-11).

"Now remember," the bishop prompted, "book, chapter, verse, words."

Drew opened his Bible to the table of contents and counted down to the forty-third book. "The Gospel according to John," he said aloud.

"Correct."

Drew turned to the page number indicated in the table of

contents. "First chapter, verse 45," he said aloud again. He counted past the first seven words. "The message reads, *'We have found him.'* "

"Excellent!" the bishop exclaimed. "The better you know the Bible, the easier it will be for you to form messages. Here, try this one. It's a message from me to you." The bishop handed him another scrap of paper. Printed on it was this encrypted message: (6/1/17/20-23) (40/5/14/13) (5/1/7/5-6).

Drew wrinkled his brow and set to work. The sixth book of the Bible was Joshua, chapter 1, verse 17, words 20-23 read, *"God be with thee."* He jotted these down on the piece of paper. Then, from the Gospel of Matthew came a single word, *"on."* He added the word to the previous phrase. Next came two words from Deuteronomy, *"your journey."*

"Read it aloud," the bishop instructed.

"God be with thee on your journey." Without looking up he said, "This is great! But why didn't Eliot teach me this?"

"Eliot doesn't know about it," the bishop said, putting his hand on Drew's shoulder. "This is a personal code. You and I are the only ones who know about it."

Drew tensed. The bishop felt his reaction and changed the subject. "Your first assignment is in Norwich. See what you can find out about a man named Peter Laslett. He's the curate of Norwich and I suspect him of being a Puritan sympathizer."

The curate of Norwich was a humorless man of fifty who took his faith seriously; in fact, Peter Laslett took everything seriously. He was convinced that too much fun was not a good thing and seemed determined to provide a counterbalance in his church services. The hymns plodded along at a miserable pace, their tempo slow enough to reduce the heartbeat of everyone singing them. But the hymns galloped along compared to Laslett's sermons.

When the curate of Norwich preached, he paused at the

end of every phrase. His eyes rolled back as if he were searching a dark closet in the back of his head for his next words.
After enduring one of Laslett's services, Drew was confident
that if he was successful in removing this man from the pulpit, all of Norwich would rise up and call him blessed.

Following the first service he attended, Drew approached
the curate requesting assistance. For his first assignment,
Drew chose one of Eliot's most successful schemes. He arrived in Norwich dirty, ragged, and hungry. In preparation
for his arrival, Drew had worn the same clothes for a week
and hadn't eaten for two days. *"Nothing gets 'em more than
hearing your belly growl,"* Eliot had said. *"It's something you
can't fake."*

Drew told the curate his mother and father had died when
he was young, and the only life he knew was begging on the
streets of London. But times being the way they were, beggars couldn't live on handouts anymore and were forced to
steal in order to eat. Some hardened criminals caught him
working their territory and beat him up, forcing him to steal
for them. Tired of all the thieving and lies, he ran away from
London. All he wanted now was to find a place where he
could earn a decent, honest living.

Laslett bought it.

"The more miserable you are when you come to them, the
more they like it," Eliot had instructed Drew. "That way it
makes a better story come testimony time."

A widower, Laslett invited Drew to stay with him. However, in Norwich Drew didn't use his real name. Laslett knew
him as Gilbert Fuller. When the church ladies heard there was
a second eligible bachelor living with the curate, they had no
end of dinner invitations from lonely women and mothers
with daughters of marrying age. One such invitation came
from an elderly spinster named Mistress Adams.

Drew made a few slips at Mistress Adams' house during

dinner one Sunday afternoon. Her brother Orville, a London undertaker, was visiting her and he grew suspicious when Drew couldn't recollect the names of some of London's back streets. Drew claimed brain deprivation from a prolonged lack of food; or possibly his forgetfulness was due to the life-threatening mystery malady he barely survived the previous winter. Everyone seemed satisfied with his explanation and Drew forgot all about it. As the days continued, Drew began to feel a strain from remembering the lies he was weaving.

A few weeks later when Drew rose and dressed for church, the curate was absent from the house. It seemed odd to Drew, but he figured something important had arisen. He was sure he would learn the reason for the curate's absence at church. The moment he walked through the doorway, Drew saw that several violations which he had noted for his report to Bishop Laud had been corrected. The most noticeable was the sanctuary altar. It had been moved to the far east end of the church and there was a crude, hastily built railing around it. Then, when the service began Peter Laslett appeared wearing a minister's surplice. It was the first time he had worn one since Drew arrived. Drew was surprised, but not alarmed.

As was the custom in Norwich, the hymns droned on as they did every Sunday. Drew settled in for another ministerial marathon as the Reverend Peter Laslett began reading his text from Jeremiah 9. As he read, he shot quick glances at Drew when he paused at the end of sentences.

"Let every one take heed of his neighbor," the curate read, "and trust you not in any brother, for every brother will use deceit, and every friend will deal deceitfully."

Laslett wiped his brow, then continued.

"And everyone will deceive his friend, and will not speak the truth: for they have taught their tongues to speak lies, and take great pains to do wickedly. Thine habitation is in the midst of deceivers; because of their deceit they refuse to know Me, says the Lord. Therefore thus saith the Lord of hosts: Behold, I will melt them, and try them, for what else should I do for the daughter of My people? Their tongue is as an arrow shot out, and speaketh deceit: one speaketh peaceably to his neighbor with his mouth, but in his heart he lieth in wait for him."

The curate looked up. It was several moments before he spoke, but when he did, his tone was measured and deliberate. "Brothers and sisters, you have heard the Scriptures speak of the slandering neighbor. I believe we have such a neighbor among us today. A neighbor of deceit. One who lies in wait, hoping to trap us." Laslett spoke in his usual turtle pace, but he had the attention of everyone in the congregation.

"This false neighbor is one who sought our help, and we took him in. He shared the hospitality of our homes and ate from our tables, but he is not one of us."

Peter Laslett looked straight at Drew, his courage building as he spoke. "Claiming to be the product of London streets, he knows not the street names. Claiming to have received no education, he uses the vocabulary of a person who is well read. Claiming he has no family but street dwellers, he shows remarkable table manners. Brothers and sisters in Christ, I fear we have in our midst a neighbor who is in league with the devil, that master deceiver."

The preacher closed his eyes and bowed his head. Everyone in the sanctuary held his breath, waiting for what would come next. There had never been this much suspense in one of Peter Laslett's services in his thirty years of ministry.

"Master Gilbert Fuller, if that is your real name, would you please stand and give us your testimony to the glory of God!"

All eyes turned to Drew. Some had an astonished look in them, others the look of the attack dogs at the bearbaiting. Drew jumped from his seat and made his escape through a side window. He held on tightly to the Bible the bishop gave him and didn't stop running until he was a couple miles out of town.

Eliot had prepared him for this possibility. His instructions were to take a slow circuitous route back to London. For the bishop's safety, it was imperative that no one follow him back to London House.

Drew traveled north to Sheringham along the North Sea coast. There, he penned a coded message to the bishop.

Bishop Laud was about to sit down to dinner when he received Drew's message. To the protestations of his round cook, he excused himself and went to his study. He reached for his Bible, the twin of the one he had given to Drew. The message was brief, consisting of a single entry of seven words: (23/6/5/4-10). Translated, it read: *"Woe is me! For I am undone."*

In Drew's second assignment he fared better. The bishop sent him to Bedford in the fertile valley of the River Great Ouse, just north of London and west of Cambridge. Determined to learn from his mistakes, Drew used a story that was easier to remember and more in keeping with his background. Upon arriving in the town he attended church services and afterward arranged to speak with the pastor. Robert Sewell's services were a pleasant surprise after Peter Laslett's church. Drew was especially impressed with his speaking ability. He probably had taken some courses at Cambridge or Oxford.

Immediately upon entering the sanctuary Drew knew he had a possible conquest. The altar was not set against the eastern wall and the minister was not wearing a surplice. These things were violations, to be sure, but what really caught Drew's attention was the lack of priority given to the Prayer Book. All ministers were under strict orders to adhere to the Book of Common Prayer for their services. They were discouraged from preaching their own sermons. The bishop was adamant about this. Preaching lent itself to personal opinion, which would not be tolerated. The bishop had determined that every church in England should worship in like manner; it was this commonality in the worship service that made them the Church of England. The bishop also discouraged prayers not in the Prayer Book. If a person was allowed to pray anything he wanted, who knows what he might say? Better that he use the approved prayers of the church.

There was no doubt in Drew's mind that Robert Sewell, the pastor at Bedford, was a Puritan. He prayed his own thoughts and preached his own messages. Drew listened, took notes, and took aim.

There was only one problem. Her name was Abigail and she was the minister's daughter. In the three months Drew was at Bedford, he and Abigail grew very close. She was sweet, shy, and had the deepest dimples Drew had ever seen. The two of them would spend evenings strolling through a large grassy area behind the parsonage, just talking—nothing important, as they shared their hopes and dreams, their likes and dislikes. It was the first time Drew had ever felt comfortable with a girl.

It was a good thing he didn't stay in Bedford any longer than he did, because he began to develop real feelings for Abigail. And feelings can be deadly for a spy.

Bedford was Drew's first victory. When confronted with his crime, Sewell freely and unashamedly admitted his guilt. As a result he was censured for his actions and forced to relinquish his living as the parish minister. Everything had gone right for Drew; he got the information without being discovered and transmitted it to Bishop Laud via code. It was the first time Drew signed his note. While flipping through the first part of the New Testament during a sermon, he made a surprising discovery. In his coded message, after informing the bishop of his success, Drew signed the note: (41/3/18/2). The 2 translated: *"Andrew."*

All in all Bedford was a gem of a victory, but admittedly a gem with a minor flaw—Drew's feelings for Abigail. The outcome would have bothered Drew more except that he didn't see Abigail once the charges were brought against her father. Whether it was coincidence or by her father's design, Drew never knew, but it was easier on him not having to face her.

If Drew's second assignment was a success, his third one was a coup. This time he was in the eastern city of Colchester. His assignment was another minister, the Reverend Preston Oliver. And although Oliver was found guilty of Puritan sedition, Drew uncovered a greater prize.

Drew's story for Colchester was that he had been thrown out of Cambridge University for his Puritan leanings. Reverend Oliver was not only sympathetic to Drew's plight, but introduced him to a young lady who had a gentleman friend with a similar story. The lady's name was Mary Sedgewick; her friend, Marshall Ramsden, had also been expelled from Cambridge. The official story was that he was caught printing pornographic literature. However, Oliver let it be known that there was more to the story, that Marshall was a godly young man with the highest ideals, and that his expulsion from the university was because of his unpopular theology.

Drew liked Mary the moment he met her. She was open and cheerful, friendly almost to a fault. When she heard Drew's story, she grabbed him by the hand and literally pulled him through the streets of Colchester to a blacksmith's shop where Marshall had found work as an apprentice.

At first Drew felt threatened by Marshall's good looks and easy manner and, even though he had just met her, jealous of the way Mary looked at him. But those feelings quickly passed and soon the three of them became inseparable. They laughed late into the night telling Cambridge stories; they shared meals on Sunday afternoons; they discussed their favorite books.

It wasn't long before Mary invited Drew to accompany her on one of the pamphlet distribution runs. Just for company, she said; if they should happen upon dangerous men intent on doing them harm, Drew could protect her. Marshall showed no signs of jealousy. He trusted Mary and gave every indication he trusted Drew.

Before long, Drew was working with Marshall at a secret press, printing the pamphlets of the notorious Justin. The two men enjoyed each other's company. Drew was shown the escape routes and the hidden-door ploy. Mary would often bring them a late dinner. At times their laughter and horseplay got so loud it was a wonder they were able to maintain their secrecy.

To that point in his life, the hardest thing Drew ever did was to hand over Marshall Ramsden and Mary Sedgewick to Bishop Laud. He had never had a closer relationship with anyone else, and it was hard for him to think of Marshall and Mary as a threat to England. There was no doubt they were lawbreakers, but Drew liked them. He delayed his report to the bishop for two weeks while he agonized over the decision.

Marshall and Drew were in the middle of a print run when the shop was raided. As before, there was advanced warning and Mary was hidden, the press type was scattered, and the print bags were switched. However, this time there was no Essex Marvel to assist with the switch. Instead, there was Drew Morgan, Bishop Laud's undercover operative.

Marshall Ramsden and Mary Sedgewick were arrested, tried, and convicted based on Drew's evidence.

The Ramsden/Sedgewick case was the first of Drew's assignments to be tried in the infamous Star Chamber, so named because the ceiling was studded with stars. Drew watched in anguish as his deposition was read, followed by the presentation of physical evidence. There was no jury. At the conclusion of the presentations the members of the court pronounced their sentences one by one, beginning with the least of them; their consensus was announced by the lord chancellor. To the charge of seditious libel against king and crown — guilty.

As sentence was pronounced and then carried out, neither Marshall nor Mary showed any remorse. They were whipped and their cheeks were branded with S.S. — "Sower of Sedition." Since Marshall's crime was greater, his left ear was also cut off.

Chapter 8

WHAT'S troubling you?"

"Huh?" Drew looked up from his book. He was sprawled over the arms of a chair in Bishop Laud's library. The bishop, seated behind a desk overflowing with papers, laid his pen aside and studied the boy.

"You've been staring at that same page for a long time."

Drew cleared his throat and sat up. "My mind was wandering."

The bishop didn't return to his work, apparently waiting for a more specific response.

"I was thinking about my last assignment."

"A first-class job, Andrew," the bishop exclaimed. "I couldn't be more pleased. In fact, I was thinking..." He rose, stretched, and came to the front of the desk. Resting his bulk on the edge, and scrunching several pieces of paper in the process, he continued, "I'm going west on a trip. A hunting trip actually, although I *despise* the sport. But the king has requested I accompany him and I've declined too many similar invitations already. I'd like you to go with me. It'll be a good break for you, just what you need. And your company would make the trip more pleasant for me." He paused. A sly grin appeared on his face as he said, "Besides, you'll meet an old friend there."

"Oh?"

"Elkins."

Drew furrowed his brow. He didn't recognize the name. "You know—you met him at Windsor Castle." The bishop's grin grew enormous. "At the time I believe you were wearing a suit of armor."

Lord Chesterfield's manor was a spacious mansion designed and built by a young, promising architect named Inigo Jones. Traditional in design, the exterior of the manor was formal and symmetrical; from an eagle's viewpoint it would look like a giant capital E. Inside were splashes of the architect's promising genius, with vaulted ceilings and serene pastoral paintings.

The mansion lay on the edge of a gently sloping grassy expanse that led down to the edge of the forest where the royal hunt would be held. Drew leaned against the building with arms folded and surveyed the gathering of hunters through squinted eyes. The sun had barely peeked over the horizon, backlighting the costumed figures as they buzzed about. There was a chill in the air; puffs of breath hung in front of people's faces as they talked. The grass was heavy with dew revealing a myriad of trails as the hunters crisscrossed back and forth across the lawn.

Drew was in no hurry to join them. He was content to lean against the mansion and feel the sun's warmth. Closing his eyes, he retreated to the privacy of his thoughts. He hadn't wanted to come to Devonshire, but Bishop Laud insisted, saying it would do him good. The four-day journey to the southwest of England proved both interesting and boring. Nothing exciting happened along the way and the trip was long, but he had never journeyed to this part of the country, and the anticipation of new discoveries around every bend in the road was a mild form of entertainment. The bishop was also right about the healing benefits of a holiday. The farther

Drew traveled from London, the less he was haunted by the disfigured faces of Mary Sedgewick and Marshall Ramsden. This morning there was only sun, grass, trees, and the promise of an uncomplicated day.

"Well, if it isn't Sir Drew!"

Drew smelled him before he saw him. Elkins. The groundskeeper's breath was the rancid odor of stale beer, and he looked like he was wearing the dirt and sweat of a week's work. Grinning yellow teeth lingered inches away from Drew's face.

Drew closed his eyes without responding. In truth, he couldn't think of anything to say. How does one defend one's right to be caught wearing a suit of armor? He just wished the smell would go away and take Elkins with it.

"Now laddie, is that any way to treat a friend who is the bearer of urgent news?"

"News?" Drew open his eyes.

"Why news from Lady Guinevere, o' course," Elkins guffawed. "She's in her chamber waitin' for ye, if ye know what I mean."

"You're disgusting. Leave me alone." Drew closed his eyes again.

"What kinda knight are ye? Every knight I know is always ready for action."

Exasperated, Drew took a deep breath which he regretted immediately The warm pungent odor of the unwashed groundskeeper nearly choked him. "Excuse me," Drew said, pushing his way past Elkins. "I think the bishop needs me."

"I'll join ye," Elkins said, falling in step with him. "The bishop and me's got a meetin'."

Drew surveyed the sloping lawn for the familiar round figure of Bishop Laud. Everywhere he looked lords and ladies were dressed in their finest hunting attire. The scene before him was more like a costume party with a hunting theme than an actual hunt. Men with plumes in their hats flirted with ladies in full dresses wearing a touch of jewelry and an abundance of frills. The guests gathered around low tables set underneath the outstretched limbs of majestic trees. A crystal stream ran along the base of the slope, jumping and splashing over smooth rocks.

The tables were laden with cold veal, cold capon, beef and goose, pigeon pies, and cold mutton. And, even though it was early morning, there were wagons and carts filled with barrels of wine, not rotten drams but noble wine rich enough to make men's hearts swell.

Everywhere he looked, Drew saw people making extraordinary effort to balance their gaiety and nobility; too much of the one and they could be accused of acting like commoners; too much of the other and they would miss all the fun.

A waving motion caught his eye. It was Bishop Laud gesturing for Drew to join him. At first, he had to shield his eyes against the sun to verify that it was indeed Bishop Laud. There were two others standing with the bishop. He couldn't quite make out who they were. In fact, he wouldn't have recognized the bishop except that he had seen the same pudgy arm movements hundreds of times before. The bishop didn't get out often, so he exercised daily by holding books in both hands and elevating them over his head. The movement that caught Drew's eye was the exercise minus the books.

It wasn't until Drew was a few steps from the threesome that he recognized one other member of the party — Charles, King of England.

"Your majesty," the bishop said, "allow me to introduce Andrew Morgan."

Drew bowed from the waist. "Your majesty."

"So this is the young man you have been telling me about," the king said, appraising Drew with an amused eye. "The bishop's quite taken with you, young man," he continued, "and he's not easily impressed."

"Thank you, your highness." Drew bowed again.

The thirty-year-old king was surprisingly personable, a trait not inherited from his stiff and humorless father, James. Before now, Drew had seen the king only from a distance. Up close, the monarch's most striking features were his calm, almost lazy eyes framed by a full head of long, dark hair. His ready smile was punctuated with a mustache and pointed beard which had become the fashion of English noblemen. Long, thin fingers cradled an ornamented goblet.

A quick glance behind the king revealed that everyone around them—lords, ladies, magistrates, court officials—were spectators of this royal conversation. They still carried on their own conversations, to be sure, but always kept a ready eye and ear in the direction of the king.

"And this," the bishop gestured to the third man of the party, "is Lord Chesterfield, our gracious host."

Chesterfield nodded toward Drew. His countenance was as cold and stiff as the ruffs he was wearing. Drew had never seen so many ruffs and lace on a man. From his mother's lifelong passion for delicate lace, Drew had become quite familiar with it. Lord Chesterfield's lace was the finest he had ever seen.

Drew returned Lord Chesterfield's nod.

"I'm really quite surprised you came," the king said to Bishop Laud.

"You invited me, your majesty."

"I know, I know," the king waved off the obvious remark with his goblet, spilling wine everywhere. "But I was sure you would dig up some emergency that would keep you in London. You always do."

The bishop's face turned red. "My only wish is to serve you," he replied weakly.

"Oh, don't be so blasted sensitive, my dear bishop," the king said with an exasperated tone. "I didn't mean anything by it." Turning to Lord Chesterfield the king added in a stage whisper, "The bishop isn't much of an outdoorsman. However, I'm sure he would be a more willing participant if you had stocked your park with Puritans instead of deer."

Lord Chesterfield laughed obligingly at the royal humor, a laugh that was cut short when a boy about eight years old with messy black hair darted between the king and himself. Chesterfield made a kicking motion at the boy but missed. Then he gestured to Elkins who had halted a discreet distance from them.

Elkins muttered a low curse and chased after the boy.

"Excuse my son, your highness," was all Chesterfield said, but he was obviously infuriated.

Drew unsuccessfully tried to suppress a smirk. He recognized the parental fury in Lord Chesterfield's face. It wasn't long ago that he was the little boy running around at regal functions. Today he stood with the King of England, Bishop Laud (without doubt the second most powerful man in the country), and a prominent nobleman. In a few short months he had risen to prominence. But he was most proud of the fact that he was recognized for his actions on behalf of England, not for how much wealth he had. His grandfather, Admiral Amos Bronson Morgan, had consorted with the Queen of England. Today, Admiral Morgan's grandson carried on that noble tradition. This was a day Drew would never forget.

At Lord Chesterfield's signal the trumpets announced the beginning of the hunt. The grassy expanse became a seething staging ground for horses, hounds, and hunters. Well-bred mounts mirrored their masters' nobility as they allowed preening touches from stablehands. Dogs barked and strained at their leashes as masters rubbed vinegar on the hounds' nostrils to increase their scent. With great pomp Lord Chesterfield paraded his magnificent greyhounds. He had a full kennel of bloodhounds, but since this would be a sight hunt, he chose the greyhounds. Besides, the speed of his dogs would shame the slower bloodhounds of his guests. The hunters inspected their bottles to insure they carried enough wine with them, checked their weapons, and gave one last kiss or witty remark to their ladies before embarking on the hunt.

To say the event was a hunt gives too much credit. Although many of the assembled were expert hunters and falconers, this particular event was a social event, and so the killing was staged. Once the trumpets sounded the hunters would storm the woods which had been stocked with over 400 deer, chasing and shooting anything resembling an animal. They would do this until another trumpet call would gather them to a staging area where a paling had been erected. The servants would flush the deer from the woods into a funnel of pales. The frightened animals would be packed together by the narrowing fence and the nobles would kill them. This was a gracious host's way of seeing to it that every guest went home with a kill.

"Drew, I want you to come with me." The bishop pulled at Drew's arm. The cleric was carrying a crossbow and some arrows. Drew smiled wryly. There was something about a churchman with hunting weapons that struck him as odd.

"Do you know anything about these things?" the bishop asked.

"The crossbow?"

The bishop was examining the weapon as if he didn't know which end to point away from himself. In answer to the bishop's question, Drew took the weapon and loaded it. Trumpets sounded. The bloodhounds were cast off and Lord

Chesterfield let slip his greyhounds. There was a thunder of hooves as the party descended into the forest. Drew carefully handed the loaded bow back to the bishop.

"Have you ever shot a crossbow?" Drew asked.

"When I was younger . . . much younger." The thought of younger days brought on by the feel of the crossbow seemed to fill the bishop with a youthful vigor. He took a deep breath and said, "You know, I feel good being out here. I just may get one of those deer today. Wouldn't that be something if I could get one in the wild? I could mount his head in my library, in that space over the small desk next to the fireplace. That would be a good spot for it, don't you think?"

Since coming to live at London House Drew had seen Bishop Laud in a variety of moods, from depression brought on by intense anxiety to his present state of giddiness. Drew liked the bishop this way best.

"Let's go get my deer!" The bishop started jauntily down the hillside toward the forest. "Where's Elkins? He's supposed to join us."

"I'm sure we can get your deer without his help, your grace," Drew offered.

The bishop swung around with a surprised look on his face. "'Your grace?' Why so formal, Andrew?" An eyebrow raised as he caught on. "Ah, it's Elkins, isn't it? You don't want him coming with us." The bishop put his arm around Drew and spoke softly. "I share your feelings. He's a dirty, disgusting creature, but he serves our purpose for the time."

Scanning the area the bishop spotted his Devonshire informant near the edge of the forest. The groundskeeper had apparently caught up with Lord Chesterfield's son and now the person chasing had become the person chased. The boy was buzzing around the groundskeeper like a pesky bee, jumping at him, grabbing first an arm then a leg. Elkins was trying to shoo him away.

"Elkins! Come here, I need you!" the bishop yelled.

The groundskeeper turned and nodded, lectured the boy with a stern finger, then proceeded toward the bishop. The boy was unimpressed. He attached himself to Elkins' leg like a leech.

"Son, go away!" The bishop made a shooing motion with his hand. "Go on, we have business. Go on, I say."

The boy released the groundskeeper. He stood, hands on hips, and sized up the bishop, as if debating whether this was a voice to be obeyed. The boy chose not to challenge the bishop, or maybe he just thought of something better to do, for he ran toward the woods and disappeared.

With his hunting party assembled, the bishop and the others entered Lord Chesterfield's wooded park, going in the opposite direction from all the other hunters. This was for two reasons: first, the bishop had business to discuss with Elkins and didn't want to be overheard; second, Elkins claimed to know a place where the deer fed. This fueled the bishop's desire of getting a deer in the wild.

Drew lagged behind slightly. He was doubtful they would see a deer, let alone come close enough to shoot one. Elkins' smell would frighten them all away.

As they stalked through the woods, the groundskeeper gave his Devonshire report to Bishop Laud in a loud whisper. There was a strong Puritan element in Devon, Elkins told him. Feelings and commitments ran deep, but so far there had been no outward actions he was aware of that could be prosecuted. He reported that although Lord Chesterfield was not sympathetic to the Puritan cause, he didn't want to persecute them because they were industrious workers and good tenants. Their products, especially their bone lace, were of the highest quality and brought a handsome profit. Chesterfield didn't want to do anything that might endanger this revenue.

Just that morning, Elkins continued, the local curate of

Edenford, a man by the name of Christopher Matthews, delivered the yearly wool production report to Lord Chesterfield. Upon hearing the name of the curate, the bishop held up his hand for Elkins to stop. The bishop searched his memory for a moment, then bid the groundskeeper continue. Elkins said he overheard his master talking to the curate. He quoted Lord Chesterfield as saying, "As long as you do your work and pay your rent and keep your beliefs to yourselves, you will be left alone."

This last statement brought a loud "Humph!" from the bishop, loud enough to frighten a rabbit from under a bush. The animal darted in front of them, ran down the path a short way, then slipped into heavy brush.

"Oh, no!" Elkins cried. His eyes were wide and his mouth had a strange twist to it.

Drew couldn't believe the man's fear. *What kind of groundskeeper is this to be frightened by a hare?*

"The hare! It's an evil omen!" Elkins cried.

"Nonsense!" said the bishop, continuing forward.

"If by chance by the way," Elkins was quoting from some unknown source, "you should find a hare, partridge, or any beast that is fearful, living upon feeds or pasturage, it is an evil sign or presage that you shall have but evil pastime that day!"

"I say it again, superstitious nonsense!"

The bishop, with Drew right behind him, pressed on down the narrow path. The shaken groundskeeper reluctantly followed from a distance.

Their business concluded, Bishop Laud returned to his earlier giddy nature as he stalked through the forest with his crossbow, calling out to the deer in a singsong whisper.

It was a curious sight in Lord Chesterfield's forest that morning: three would-be hunters crouched in a line as they sneaked up on the feeding grounds, an oversized bishop leading the way and carrying the only weapon, followed by a skinny would-be adventurer, with a filthy commoner trailing behind. It would be a miracle indeed if this unlikely hunting party even saw a deer.

"I never knew hunting was so exhilarating," the bishop whispered back to them.

The groundskeeper held a dirt-crusted finger to his lips, signaling quiet. Then, with the same finger, he jabbed the air, pointing just beyond a thick row of bushes. The deer's feeding place. As quietly as his inexperienced bulk would allow, the bishop pushed past the bushes with the crossbow at the ready.

His disappointment was unmistakable.

When Drew made his way into the small clearing, he saw a tiny brook but no deer. As if to vindicate himself, Elkins pointed out every evidence of their prey. He showed them the trees upon which the deer frayed their antlers; from the height of the marks on the trees he judged their height and said the marks indicated the deer's antlers had a crowned top. Judging from one set of tracks he guessed one of the deer to be an adult buck; the heel marking was large and widely cleft.

But the bishop wasn't interested; he was too disappointed at not finding something to shoot.

Suddenly, there was a rustle in the bushes to their right. The three hunters froze. Another rustle.

Drew's heart was pounding as he watched the wide-eyed bishop raise the crossbow at the thick row of bushes. The bushes moved again, as if an animal was eating berries from them. The bishop took aim. It was definitely a larger animal, not a rabbit. The bishop steadied himself.

Elkins whispered to him, "Hold your breath before you shoot."

The cleric drew a deep breath and held it. The bushes rustled again. Drew smiled; Bishop Laud would be telling people about this kill for years to come.

There was a click and whoosh as the bishop fired. The arrow slipped through the air and penetrated the bush with a thud. A second heavier thud indicated the bishop had hit his target. There was the sound of feet pawing helplessly at the ground, then silence.

"You got it!" Drew shouted.

"Excellent shot, your grace!" Elkins echoed.

The short, chubby bishop straightened himself to full height. In his mind Drew could already see the proud cleric relishing in the event before King Charles and their host. To have excelled in this manly sport would increase the bishop's stature among all the men in the king's court.

The bishop handed the crossbow to Drew and triumphantly proceeded behind the bushes which concealed his prey. He spread the bushes apart and then froze.

Something was wrong. Dreadfully wrong. The bishop's shoulder's slumped and he made a whimpering sound.

"Bishop?"

No response. The bishop stood there, dead still.

The bushes were so thick, Drew had to steady himself on the bishop and lean around him to see what the cleric was staring at. Fear gripped his throat when he saw it.

Lord Chesterfield's son!

The bishop's arrow had pierced the boy's left cheek and was protruding out the back of his head. His left hand still gripped the arrow's shaft. He was trying to pull it out when he died.

"My God, forgive me!" Bishop Laud sank to his knees and wept.

Chapter 9

THE note appeared on Drew's bed pillow three nights after he returned to London from Devonshire. There was a single encrypted notation on it: (18/3/3-8).

Even before he translated it, the message made Drew uneasy. The handwriting was jagged and uncertain, uncharacteristic for the bishop who normally penned large, sweeping numbers and letters. But that wasn't all that bothered Drew about the note. Never before had the bishop sent him a coded note while they were both at London House. There was no need. What prompted a secret note now? Why couldn't the bishop tell him face to face?

Ever since the hunting accident Bishop Laud, the rock of England's Church, had been unstable. During the four-day return trip to London he was silent and sullen. He ate nothing. Drew never saw him sleep. For the entire journey the bishop propped himself up in the corner of the carriage and stared out the window. He looked like a rag doll as the rocking motion of the carriage jostled him back and forth. When they arrived at London House, the bishop marched up the steps to his room like a condemned prisoner going to his execution. A locked door shut him away from the rest of the world.

Several attempts were made to get the bishop to open his door. He didn't respond to the round cook's sugary pleading

Nor did he respond to Timmins who tried first the quiet tones of diplomacy, then the loud demands of authority. Drew added his voice of concern, all to no avail. For two days London had no bishop. It was as if he were dead. Then the note appeared on Drew's pillow.

As far as Drew knew, this was the bishop's first communication with anyone since the accident. He opened his Bible and found the passage. It was from the book of Job. Drew scribbled the translation on the paper below the code:

"Let the day perish wherein I was born, and the night in which it was said, 'There is a man-child conceived.' Let that day be darkness; let not God regard it from above, neither let the light shine upon it. Let darkness and the shadow of death stain it; let a cloud dwell upon it; let the blackness of the day terrify it."

He read the message over and over, not knowing what to do.

The next morning there was no change. Drew sat in the bishop's library after breakfast with the note in his hand. He ached to talk to someone about it, someone who would know what to do.

"Ain't ya got nothing better to do than sit around suckin' your thumb?"

Drew looked up. Eliot was standing in the door way. With jaunty cheerfulness Drew's wild-haired friend flopped into the chair opposite him.

"How was the hunt in Devonshire? Get a kill?"

"Not exactly."

"Not exactly? What does that mean? Either you killed a deer or you didn't."

"I didn't kill a deer."

"Not surprised. I'll bet you didn't even try, did you?"

Drew shook his head.

"No, I didn't think so. You're not the killing type." Eliot vigorously scratched the top of his head which only messed up his hair even more. "Where's the bishop?"

"In his room. I don't think he'll be available today."

"He sick?"

"Not exactly. Just unavailable."

"Unavailable? What's that supposed to mean? I have a meeting with him this morning—just got back from Scarborough." Eliot swung at the air, "Forget I said that, nobody's supposed to know. But then I guess the bishop wouldn't mind you knowing." Looking around to see if they were alone, Eliot Venner's discomforting eyes opened wide with fiendish delight, "There's a preacher up there who's gonna be sportin' a new set of letters on his cheeks. Laud's gonna love it—he's been after this guy for years!"

Drew stared hard at his pockmarked friend. He desperately needed to talk to someone about the bishop. Could he talk to Eliot? He was hardly the sympathetic type, but then his devotion to the bishop was beyond question. And the bishop's condition affected him too. Still Drew hesitated and he didn't know why. That disturbed him.

Drew had stared at Eliot so long it made Eliot uncomfortable. "Why are you looking at me that way?"

Drew searched for a way to begin. "The bishop really trusts us, doesn't he?"

Picking up on the somber tone of Drew's voice, Eliot leaned forward. "Yeah, what of it?"

Drew paused. Something inside him was telling him this was wrong.

"Come on, give!" Eliot shouted. "Something's going on with the bishop, isn't there?" Eliot leaped to his feet with a sudden realization. "He's not hurt, is he?"

"I don't know," Drew said.

"Again with 'I don't know'!" Eliot was getting angry. "Tell

me what's going on!" he shouted.

Drew told Eliot all about the accidental killing and the cover-up that followed. As the bishop wept over the still form of Lord Chesterfield's son, he had refused to be comforted. Nor could Drew pull him away from the boy. The arrow protruding from the boy's skull seemed to disturb him especially. A couple of times the bishop reached for it, then recoiled. So Drew grabbed the arrow by its shaft and extracted it from the boy's head. The task was harder and more messy than he'd thought it would be. He started to toss the arrow to one side when the bishop grabbed it. At first Drew feared the bishop might harm himself with the arrow, but it seemed to calm him down. He clutched the instrument of the boy's death to his chest and rocked back and forth.

Elkins was in no better shape than Bishop Laud. He stood there immobile with his mouth gaping open, staring at the dead boy.

A trumpet sounded, the signal for everyone to gather at the paling.

Drew tried again to get the bishop on his feet. He offered to explain to Lord Chesterfield. At the mention of their host's name, the bishop grew frantic. He grabbed Drew by the arm, squeezing it hard. Terror was in his eyes.

"No, no, he must not know!" the bishop cried. "No one must ever know!"

"But it was an accident!"

"No!" The bishop's face was red and wet. He fell to his knees. With one hand still clutching the arrow, he began scooping handfuls of dirt onto the dead boy with the other.

It was then that Drew took charge. After several attempts, he managed to coax Elkins into helping him. Together, they pulled the bishop away from the body and leaned him against a tree a short distance away.

There was a large bush beside the stream between two giant

oak trees. The limbs on the bush could be moved aside easily. Drew decided that was the best place to bury the boy; the freshly dug earth would be hidden underneath the limbs of the bush.

After scratching out a shallow grave using tree limbs for a shovel, Drew carried the boy and placed him in the hole along with the crossbow. He filled the grave and then asked the bishop if he wanted to say a prayer. The bishop turned away and said nothing.

Drew described to Eliot how he guided the bishop back to the Chesterfield manor just as the king was breaking up his deer to the cheers of the assembled party. The stag was lying on its back as the king approached it with a knife, the chief huntsman holding down the deer's head with his knee. The bishop whimpered and hid his face against Drew's chest as the king cut a slit along the brisket. The deer's flesh was thick, an excellent cut of meat.

Drew concluded his account, "We left just as they were forming a search party for Lord Chesterfield's son and arrived home three days ago. As far as I know, he hasn't spoken to anyone." Drew fingered the bishop's note in his hand. Should he show it to Eliot?

"Do you hear any sounds coming from his room?"

Drew shook his head no.

"Maybe he's killed himself!" Eliot started toward the stairs.

"Eliot, wait! There is this," Drew held up the bishop's note and handed it to Eliot.

Eliot began reading. "This ain't the bishop's handwriting," he said.

"No, it's mine."

"I thought you said it was from the bishop."

"It is. I can't tell you any more than that."

"What are these numbers on top?"

"Can't tell you."

Eliot looked up, exasperated.

"I can't tell any more than that I know it's a message from the bishop." Drew waited for Eliot to finish reading the note, then said, "What do you think? Do you think it's a suicide note?"

Eliot shook his head. "I don't know," he said. "Sounds too pretty for a suicide note. Why would he write a pretty suicide note? Where did you find it?"

"In my room. He must have left it while I was sleeping."

Eliot slumped into his chair again. "If this is a suicide note, why would he give it to you? Why not just let people find it when they find the body?"

That made sense to Drew.

Eliot crumpled the piece of paper and tossed it on the floor. He jumped up again.

"Where are you going?"

Eliot didn't answer. He bounded up the stairs taking two and three steps at a time. A moment later Drew could hear Eliot pounding on the bishop's bedroom door and yelling. This went on for several minutes. Then Eliot returned.

"Any luck?" Drew asked.

Eliot shook his head and resumed his place opposite Drew. He placed his head in his hands and rubbed his wild eyes. "He's alive. At least I know that much."

"How? Did he speak to you?"

"No, but I heard a scraping noise—a chair being moved or something like that."

For several minutes the boys sat in silence.

"Did I ever tell you how me and the bishop met?" Eliot hunched forward, resting his chin in his hands. "He caught me lifting Timmins' purse."

"No!" Drew laughed.

"God's truth!" Eliot laughed with him. "I must have been seven, maybe eight at the time."

"What happened?"

"Instead of turning me in, he took me home with him. Never explained why. But if he hadn't I sure woulda died. That was a plague year. Church bells played for the dead every day. Whole families were swept away; in my alley, thirty kids died. I was sick at the time and the bishop brought me here. He was the first person who was ever kind to me for no reason."

Drew smiled. "I know what you mean."

"Where did you first meet him?" Eliot asked.

Drew laughed and shook his head.

Eliot leaned forward eagerly. "This must be good. Come on, out with it. Where did you meet him?"

"At Windsor Castle."

Eliot shook his hand like he was playing a stringed instrument. "Well, lah dee dah! And?"

"It was during a reception for the king."

"AND?"

"He caught me hiding in a suit of armor."

Eliot howled. He laughed so hard he fell out of his chair and rolled on the floor. His hyena-sounding laugh brought the round cook flying into the room. When he saw who it was, he left, wiping his hands with a towel and shaking his head.

For most of the afternoon the boys shared Bishop Laud stories. Eliot told how the bishop bought him the first set of clothes he ever wore that hadn't been handed down or stolen. Drew told how the bishop had filled the gap in his life left by the death of his grandfather. There were solemn stories and hilarious ones. A passerby would have thought it was a wake for the bishop.

The shadows in the room were growing long when Eliot asked, "Can Elkins be trusted?"

"What do you mean?"

"Will he keep his mouth shut about the accident?"

Drew hadn't thought about it. "I guess so."

Silence.

Eliot stood. "If the bishop asks for me, tell him I'll be gone for a while."

"Just 'gone'? Nothing else? What about your report on Scarborough?"

"I can tell him when I get back."

Alone again, Drew sat at the bishop's desk and opened the cleric's King James Bible. Still unfamiliar with the contents, it took him the better part of the evening to find the right words to put into a note. It would have been easier to compose one using his own words, but since Bishop Laud saw fit to write him a coded note, he felt the return message should be in like form.

With a confident hand he wrote: (23/41/10/1-11) (20/17/17) (20/18/24/10-20) (41/3/18/2). Translated, it read: *"Fear thou not; for I am with thee: be not dismayed. A friend loveth at all times, and a brother is born for adversity. And there is a friend that sticketh closer than a brother. Andrew."*

He carried the note with him through supper, reading it several times. It wasn't until he retired to his bedroom that night that he went by the bishop's closed bedroom door and slipped the note under it.

The late summer morning light woke Drew as it spilled through the window onto his face. Birds were singing and he could smell the flowers from the bishop's garden. Drew rose from bed and stretched. As he did he saw a piece of paper on the floor. He recognized the bishop's perfectly formed numerals: (9/2/1/6-8) (22/5/4/1-2) (20/6/27/12-13) (66/22/5/29-32).

Without dressing, Drew grabbed his Bible and a pen. Pages flew back and forth as he decoded the note. As the message emerged he thought how much easier it was to translate a message than to write one. Setting his pen down, he read the translation: *"My heart rejoiceth, my beloved. Your friend for ever and ever."*

It was then he heard the bishop's humming and the clip, clip, clip of his shears in the garden. Drew smiled. *The bishop's back!*

"Christopher Matthews is a serpent."

The Bishop of London gestured toward Drew with his knife as he spoke between bites of mutton. "He's a dangerous man. If he and others like him are not stopped, the whole fabric of the church will be rent to pieces. He must be silenced."

Drew pushed his plate away and concentrated as his mentor instructed him on his upcoming mission. It wasn't unusual for the bishop to continue eating for fifteen to twenty minutes longer than everyone else at the table. Tonight it was just the two of them.

"I don't understand what makes him so dangerous," Drew said. "He's just the curate of a small village."

The bishop gulped hurriedly to respond. "That's *exactly* why he's dangerous," he said, poking his knife emphatically at Drew. "An Oxford dean wouldn't dare spout Puritan propaganda, because he knows we'd have him locked up before nightfall. It's the backwoods preachers in the small towns who do the damage. They deceive their unlearned church members." The knife waved back and forth furiously. "No, *deceive* isn't strong enough. They *bewitch* their people. For when the heretic is exposed, it's not uncommon for the very people who were bewitched to rise up and defend the heretic!"

"I still don't understand why small villages are a threat. What difference does it make if there are small pockets of dissenters on the fringes of the country? If you control the major learning centers, you control the country, right?"

The bishop beamed. "You're unlike any of my other boys," he said. "You ask intelligent questions. It's refreshing." He chewed a bite of potato while formulating his explanation. "It's a matter of unity, Drew. 'There is one body, and one Spirit, even as ye are called in one hope of your calling; One Lord, one faith, one baptism, One God and Father of all, who is above all, and through all, and in you all.' Ephesians chapter 4. The dissenters undermine the unity of our faith. It is for the sake of unity that we insist on conformity for all churches. Any member of the church should be able to walk into any church in England and be familiar with the worship service—that's why we have the Book of Common Prayer. That same member should know the minister is approved by the church and agrees with what the church stands for—the ministerial surplice is the symbol of an approved minister. And that same member would rightfully expect that the things of God are kept holy—that's why the altar is placed uniformly and set apart with a railing so that people don't profane it by using it as a common table to transact their business, or to lay their goods on it, or to write frivolous notes on it."

Bishop Laud helped himself to the last of the potatoes as he continued.

"The Puritans are determined to undermine the unity of the faith. They insist on preaching their own messages. Many of these men are illiterate, empty-headed fools, yet they claim to speak for God! Even in their public prayers, when they divert from the printed prayers, they spout their ignorance in the pretense of leading their people to the throne of God! For the good of the faith, for the unity of the church, these harmful simpletons must be silenced! And I will overcome every obstacle at any cost until England is rid of every last one of these heretics!" He paused, looked at Drew and chuckled. "Sermon's over."

Drew smiled back. It was good to see the bishop full of life again. "When do I leave?" he asked.

The question seemed to knock the wind out of the bishop. He stopped mid-bite and lay his knife down and shoved his plate away. Drew had never seen the bishop leave any food on his plate before.

"In the morning," was all he said. There were tears in the bishop's eyes.

Drew gulped hard and looked down.

"I had planned on sending Eliot on this mission," the bishop said. "But the Lord alone knows where he is."

"He'll come back. I'm sure of it," Drew offered.

"Oh, yes, I'm sure of it too. I trust Eliot. It's just that . . . well, I've been trying to convince myself that you're not ready for this mission. Just so I can keep you near me. But I've only been fooling myself. You are ready. You're just as qualified as Eliot for this mission, maybe even more so, because you're smarter. The truth is, this assignment may take several months and I don't want to let you go."

Drew blushed and fiddled with his dessert spoon. "You think it will take that long?"

"Edenford is a tightly knit village. You will not gain their confidence easily. It'll take time, but," Bishop Laud slapped the table with a pudgy hand, "I can't let personal motives interfere with God's work. May God speed your way to Edenford, Andrew, and may He bring you back to me soon."

The road west held haunting memories for Drew. Just a few weeks ago he had accompanied a stricken Bishop Laud along the road as they returned to London. He tried not to think about it, but occasionally a landmark would prompt a memory which prompted a sick feeling he would rather forget.

He decided the best way to fight the unwanted feelings was to keep his mind occupied with the mission. He reviewed his preparations and his plan. He would travel by horseback to Bridgewater. There, he would leave his horse and walk the rest of the way to Edenford, a little more than thirty miles through Wellington, Halberton, and Tiverton. He chose the long walk on purpose; upon arriving at Edenford he wanted to have a well-traveled, near-indigent look. He carried stale bread with him from London which would be moldy by the time he arrived at the village, a little trick the bishop suggested. The cleric said he got the idea from the Bible. Drew wondered if there were other espionage tricks in the Bible he could pick up. He determined to read the book more. Besides a few clothes, the only items he carried with him were the Bible, needed for coding and decoding messages, and his grandfather's cutlass to protect himself from highway thieves.

Drew entered Devonshire on his fourth day of travel. The road passed through a high ridge of hills displaying a vast panorama of enclosures and lesser hills, each with a steep ascent. At Tiverton he joined the River Exe, a clean, clear river whose source was in Exmoor and which emptied into the English Channel just below the city of Exeter, Devonshire's county seat. The river was Drew's traveling companion for the remainder of the journey, as the road to Edenford paralleled its course up and down a hilly tract. A stratum of slate nestled in the red soil of the hills on either side of the Exe, and an agreeable mixture of wood and fields made it a very pleasant land. As the road passed over the river on a stone bridge of three arches, Drew found himself in Edenford.

"Stop right there, young fella!"

Drew had barely cleared the town end of the bridge when he was challenged by a potbellied old man with wild white hair carrying a flintlock. Out of respect for the gun, Drew stopped.

"State your business," the old man wheezed. He spoke in a slow, lazy drawl. His eyes squinted and his lips pursed in an attempt to look mean.

"I don't have any business, directly," Drew said. "I'm just a traveler."

"Where do you call home?" The gun bobbed as the old man asked his questions.

"Well, you might say I'm between homes right now."

"You mean you got two homes?" The gun lowered and the fierce look faded as the watchman seemed to ponder the incredulous idea of someone owning two homes.

"No, I mean I don't have a home right now."

The sneer returned. The old man griped his firearm tightly and raised the sight to his eye. "Put your hands up!" he shouted. "You're under arrest!"

"Now wait a minute!"

But the watchman didn't wait a minute. "And drop that sword to the ground!" His left eye closed while the right one eyed Drew through the gun's sights.

Drew slowly lowered his grandfather's cutlass to the ground and held his hands high. "On whose authority am I being arrested?"

"On my authority, you blasted parvenu! I'm the watchman of this town."

Parvenu? Where did I hear that word before? That's right! That's what some people called Sir Francis Drake. Upstart. He hailed from this backward part of England, didn't he?

Maybe it was because everything is exaggerated when you're looking down the wrong end of a rifle barrel, but Drew didn't like the way this watchman's hands were trembling, especially the finger curved around the trigger. In a calm, overly polite tone of voice he asked, "And what, sir, may I ask, are the charges against me?"

"It's my duty to take up all rogues, vagabonds, and beggars."

"And which one am I?"

The trembling watchman didn't seem to have a ready answer for him. "Not quite sure," he said finally, "but you must be one of 'em. We'll let the scrivener decide which." Since the man was obviously weak-headed and strong-willed, Drew decided he welcomed the opportunity to put his fate in the hands of the unmet official.

The scrivener of Edenford was a scarecrow of a man named Ambrose Dudley who resided in a whitewashed brick house not far from the bridge. As he sat behind his desk, pen in hand, peering over the top rim of his glasses, he reminded Drew of a schoolmaster.

"What do you have, Cyrus?" the scrivener said, as Drew was directed to stand before the desk.

"I think he's a rogue, Ambrose," the watchman said in his slow drawl.

"A rogue, huh?" The scrivener began writing in a book.

"I'm not a rogue!" Drew protested.

The scrivener exhaled loudly, stopped writing, and looked up, displeased at having had his writing interrupted.

"At least, I don't think I am," Drew continued. "What's the legal definition?"

Ambrose let out a snort and turned to the front of his book. Upon finding what he was looking for, he read aloud in a flat tone, "A rogue is one who for some notorious offense was burnt on the shoulder." He turned back to his previous page and continued writing.

"Wait!" Drew cried. "That proves I'm not a rogue!"

The scrivener looked up disgustedly. "Does it?"

"Sure it does! Examine me if you want, you won't find a brand on my shoulder!"

The scrivener looked at the watchman who just shrugged.

"Beggar, then," the scrivener said, and returned to his writing.

"No! Wait! I'm not a beggar either!"

"Young man! If you don't stop interrupting me, I'll have you arrested for interfering with a public official in the performance of his duty."

"Sir, I don't mean to be impertinent, but can you produce anyone who will say that I begged from him or asked any kind of relief?"

The scrivener looked at the watchman who shrugged his shoulders again. With deliberate movements the scarecrow laid down his pen, removed his glasses, and clasped his hands on top of the ledger. "Then maybe you can help us clear up this matter," he said.

"In truth, sir, I am an honest man," Drew said earnestly. "I'll be happy to assist you in any manner you desire."

The scrivener nodded. "Then tell me, Master . . ."

"Morgan. Drew Morgan." Drew had decided ahead of time to use his real name during this mission for a couple of reasons. First, since this mission would be a lengthy one, the simpler his story, the better. Second, this far west, it was safe for him to be himself. The chances of any in Edenford having heard of his family, let alone having any dealings with them, was remote indeed.

"Master Morgan. Where do you live?"

"Well, my home is east of Winchester."

"You own or lease your home in Winchester?"

"Well, no, not exactly. It's not my home, it's my parents' home."

"I see," said the scrivener. "You live with them?"

"No," Drew replied. "Not anymore."

"I see. Are you traveling to a new home?"

"Just traveling, no place in particular. I thought I might go to Plymouth and enlist on a merchant ship, unless something else came up along the way."

"How long have you been a sailor?"

"Well, I'm not exactly a sailor, either. I mean, I think I'd like to be, but I haven't ever actually been on the sea."

The scrivener looked at the watchman. "Vagabond," they said simultaneously. The scrivener donned his glasses and resumed writing.

"No, wait!"

But before Drew could protest any further, the scrivener of Edenford turned to the front of his volume and quoted, "A vagabond: One who has no dwelling house nor certain place of abode."

Drew stood silent. He didn't know how to respond. He fit the description.

The scrivener continued writing as he said, "You'll be held while we send for the high constable, at which time you will have an opportunity to defend yourself against these charges."

"How long will that take?" Drew asked.

"A week, maybe more."

"You're going to put me in jail for a week?"

"We don't have a jail," the watchman said. "You'll walk the streets with me during the day. Our night watchman will guard you at night."

Drew envisioned himself being paraded around town with this potbellied watchman for a week. Everyone would see him. Their first impression of him would be that he was a criminal. How could he earn their trust after that? Had he compromised his mission already? How could he go back to London so soon? Eliot would ride him mercilessly. And the bishop would certainly be disappointed. He could hear the bishop's parting words, *"You're just as qualified as Eliot for this mission, maybe even more so, because you're smarter."* He had to do something to salvage the mission.

"Surely there is someone here in Edenford to whom I might plead my case," Drew cried.

"He don't talk like no vagabond," the watchman said.

"The law does not take a person's vocabulary into account," the scrivener shot back.

"But sir, my honor as a gentleman is at stake. Surely I have a right to defend my good name before it is irreparably damaged!"

Pondering Drew's question aloud, he said, "The law's pretty clear about these things. But there is a meeting at the town house tonight. We could seek their advice on what to do with you until the high constable arrives."

The Edenford town house was nothing more than a large, dirty barn adjacent to Market Street; it was lined with stalls, and soiled straw served as carpeting. The leaders of the town gathered shortly after sundown and were more than a little agitated over Drew's presence. As they wandered in many of them looked somewhat sourly on him; others asked suspicious questions about his recent whereabouts to which he tried to give courteous replies. There was a lot of finger pointing his direction, which made Drew wonder if his appeal to this gathering was a wise decision after all.

Drew was the first item on their agenda. They didn't argue his guilt or innocence; the fact that he fit the description of a vagabond was good enough for them. Their discussion was about what to do with him until the high constable arrived. One man, who Drew later learned was the innkeeper, suggested the town put him up at the inn. Others objected that this would bring needless charge to the town. Finally, it was agreed that unless someone offered to shelter him, he would walk the streets with the watchmen.

"The boy is welcome to stay with me."

All eyes turned toward the speaker. He was a kindly looking man of medium height with dark hair and eyes. A giant of
a man seated beside the speaker said, "That's taking Christian
charity too far. What about your daughters? What if he's the
one?"

The speaker looked kindly at Drew and patted his giant
friend on his hairy arm. "My offer stands," he said, loud
enough for everyone to hear.

Since no one had a better idea, it was agreed that Drew
would stay with the unnamed man.

The scrivener then raised the question as to whether Drew
should remain for the remainder of the meeting or be removed. The intensity of the discussion surprised Drew. He
couldn't imagine what a small village would have to discuss
that would cause such anxiety among its people. It was finally
decided that Drew would not be permitted to stay and that
Cyrus Furman, the watchman, should wait with him outside
the meeting place. This seemed agreeable to everyone except
Cyrus.

The watchman led Drew outside. As he did, a man beside
the doorway grabbed Drew by the arm and issued a threat
through dirty, clenched teeth. "If you so much as touch them
girls, I'll have your hide, boy!"

Cyrus Furman fulfilled the letter of his duty, but not the
spirit. He took Drew just outside the town house, then stood
near the door so he could hear what was going on inside. The
loud, anxious voices of those inside carried well outside into
the cool evening air and Drew had no trouble hearing the
discussion.

The town crisis had to do with a murder. A body had been
found a short distance up river from the north bridge. It was
a recent killing, and a brutal one. There were several stab
wounds to the chest and back, and the man's eyes and been
gouged out.

"Has the body been identified?" Drew recognized the voice as belonging to the scrivener, Ambrose Dudley.

"It has," an unknown voice replied. "It's the body of Lord Chesterfield's groundskeeper, Shubal Elkins."

Chapter 10

EDENFORD was a village with a secret. Most everyone in the village knew there was a secret, but not everyone knew what it was. There were some who thought they knew the secret, but they didn't; and those who knew were content to let those who didn't know continue in their ignorance.

Situated on a sloping range between a river and a mountain, Edenford was known throughout England for its wool serges and on the Continent for its delicate lace. The city was founded upon wool by the Chesterfields.

William Chesterfield, Lord Chesterfield's great-grandfather, was Edenford's founder and first known resident. In truth, a long forgotten Saxon king was there before him, as evidenced by his castle on the hillside. But no one could remember the king's name, when he lived or died, or anything about him. So, for all practical purposes, William Chesterfield was considered the town's founder.

The first structure on the Edenford plain was nothing more than a hut erected by its enterprising founder. Having inherited a flock of sheep, Chesterfield set out to make himself a fortune, which he did quite handily. Succeeding generations of Chesterfields built upon their ancestor's foundation until a traveler would have to journey almost five miles north to the outskirts of Tiverton before reaching the far side of the Chesterfield property.

William Chesterfield established the wool business in Edenford by increasing the size of his flocks and building houses for workers; his son expanded the family industry by erecting looms and huge dyeing vats and bringing in more workers; his son, Lord Chesterfield's father, built Chesterfield Manor, expanded the family trade, and brought in even more workers; Lord Chesterfield collected rent, saved the best lace for himself, and lived lavishly off the fruit of his ancestors' labor.

For almost 100 years Edenford and quality wool products had been synonymous, but not until the Matthews family arrived did the village earn its reputation for lacework.

The wife of Edenford's curate, Jane Matthews, worked a loom. She was a skilled worker, her hands were fast, her fingers nimble. However, she was bored with the repetition of her job and dreamed of doing something more challenging, more artistic—like making lace.

When her mother died, Jane Matthews inherited her mother's meager possessions. Among them was some delicate bone lace from Antwerp. Jane had always admired the intricate patterns. To her they conjured up impressions of summer daydreams and wistful fantasies. More than anything she wanted to create some white lace fantasies of her own.

For years she scrutinized her mother's Antwerp lace, following each delicate strand to its end. Then, while she was pregnant with her first child, she began her efforts. By the time her second surviving child was born two years later, she began showing her work to some of the townspeople who were favorably impressed. When her girls reached their twelfth and tenth birthdays respectively, word had reached Lord Chesterfield of her product and he called her to Chesterfield Manor to examine her work. He was impressed, not only with the quality of the lace but with the opportunity to make even more money. Jane Matthews was taken off the looms and set to work exclusively on lace.

Demand for her lace far exceeded her ability to produce it, so Lord Chesterfield ordered her to teach her craft to others. Although many of her students were competent, none could match the elegant work of Jane's lace, that is, until her two daughters took an interest. At the time of Jane's death, her oldest daughter's lace rivaled that of her mother.

Jane Matthews died of consumption during the winter of 1627. It was a deadly winter for all Edenford. Fourteen people died, nine of them children. Publicly, Lord Chesterfield expressed the proper amount of grief over Edenford's loss, especially the loss of Jane Matthews. Secretly, however, he was quite pleased with himself. Because he had insisted on Jane teaching others her craft, his lace industry would be unaffected by her death; her daughters would simply take her place.

Jane Matthews had been dead for nearly three years when her husband, Christopher, invited Bishop Laud's spy to stay with him and his family.

"Ugly business."

Drew's host led him past the village church situated on the edge of a grassy, tree-lined common.

"It's hard for me to understand what would motivate one man to kill another," he said, "and harder still to understand mutilating the body."

It was the same road that brought Drew into Edenford. It had a three-arch stone bridge at each end, both of them crossing the River Exe. To a traveler this north-south highway was a mere detour on the road between Tiverton and Exeter. That is, unless Cyrus Furman stopped him.

"I saw Cyrus standing near the door," Drew's host continued. "Can't blame him. This killing is making everyone nervous. Anyway, I assume you heard everything, even though you were voted out."

Drew looked at his host. There was no outward guile in the man. He was slightly undersized, but stocky and solid. Deep wrinkles around his eyes and bushy black eyebrows gave his face a look of constant concern.

"It was hard for me not to hear what was being said," Drew said.

The host laughed. It was a hearty laugh, nothing bashful about it. "There are a lot of things that can be said about the townspeople of Edenford," he said, "but being timid or quiet is not one of them!"

"Forgive me, sir," Drew stopped in the middle of the street as his companion turned a corner leading uphill away from the town common, "but I don't know who you are or where you're taking me."

His host turned toward him with a sheepish grin. "No, it is you who must forgive me," he blushed. "I'm afraid my manners have been distracted with all this turmoil." He extended his hand. "I'm the curate of Edenford. My name is Matthews, Christopher Matthews."

A slightly wicked grin crossed Drew's face as he gripped the man's hand.

The moon lighted their way as Christopher Matthews led his guest up a sloping road away from the village green. They turned left onto High Street, an upper road that ran parallel to the main thoroughfare. This road was not nearly as wide nor as well pitched as Market Street. It was a cobblestone lane lined with a series of small residences wedged against one another. The houses huddled together, as if bracing themselves against a common enemy. Supper smells of boiled fish and roasted beef filled the lane; the din of clearly audible voices and the dancing light of candles peeking through cracks in the shutters added a family element to the street. This was a close community in every sense of the word.

Matthews didn't slow down until they were one house shy of the end of the street. Had they continued walking, they would have walked into a cornfield. The curate reached for the door latch of a thin dwelling of two stories. The lower half rested on a granite stone foundation. Two shuttered windows to the left of a narrow wooden door filled the width of the house. Wooden beams jutted out overhead, supporting the second story and providing a covering over the doorway. Above the beams four smaller windows framed by white paneling looked out over the cramped street. A person could easily lean out the upper window and join hands with someone in the window of the house opposite. The entire edifice leaned noticeably to the left, a fact that would have concerned Drew, except that there were more than a dozen houses on that side to hold it up.

"This will be your jail cell for the night," Matthews said with a wry chuckle. Then when Drew didn't smile back, he said, "Forgive me, friend. It was a poor attempt at humor. Both Cyrus and Ambrose mean well. They are just doing their jobs, protecting the town. If I were you, I wouldn't worry about the charges. When the constable gets here on Market Day, we'll get everything resolved. You don't strike me as the dangerous sort. If I thought you were, I never would have volunteered to bring you home with me."

I'm more dangerous to you than you think, Drew said to himself. He was trying hard to dislike the curate, but finding it increasingly difficult to do.

Matthews swung open the door. At first glance, the girl setting the dinner table on the far side of the room made no strong impression on Drew. The sound of the door caused her to look up, throwing back her dark brown hair, revealing sparkling brown eyes and a relaxed, warm smile. It soon became evident that the sparkle and smile were reserved for her father. When she saw Drew her eyes clouded with suspicion and a tight nervous line replaced her smile.

"Good news, girls!" Matthews announced cheerily. "We have a handsome houseguest!"

The unsmiling girl at the table folded her arms. With knives in one hand and spoons in the other, she looked like an armed griffin on a knight's coat of armor.

A happier reception came from the stairway to the left. "Poppa!"

A slender form flew down the steps and jumped into Matthews' ready embrace. From her build it was clear she was no child, but still she was small enough to get lost in her father's arms. Bright blue eyes peeked around her father's shoulder for a look at the stranger. Her long straight hair, fair complexion, and pixie smile staggered Drew. There was something about her that touched him as no other woman had, a stirring inside of him so powerful it was almost frightening. For the first time in his life Drew Morgan understood how Lancelot must have felt the first time he laid eyes on Guinevere.

"Master Morgan, allow me to introduce my two greatest earthly treasures. This is my elder daughter, Nell," he gestured toward the unsmiling girl at the table.

Drew bowed slightly. Nell returned a nod and a curt, "Master Morgan."

"And this bundle of giggles," he squeezed the younger girl, "is Jenny. We just celebrated her sixteenth birthday."

"Master Morgan," she said coyly.

Drew mustered up a chivalrous tone in his voice. "Always pleased to meet a fair maiden," he said.

An exasperated sigh came from the far end of the room. "May I speak with you, father? In the kitchen?" Not waiting for a response, Nell deposited the utensils in a heap on the table and stalked through the doorway.

If Matthews was embarrassed about being summoned to

the kitchen, he didn't show it. "You can put your things over there," he pointed next to the fireplace. "If you'll excuse me."

Jenny trailed after her father, her long brown hair bouncing side to side. There was a quick, smiling glance backward before she disappeared into the kitchen.

Drew found himself standing alone in the curate's humble home. Humble was an understatement. Before him was a long narrow room which featured a common eight-foot fireplace on his right and a narrow staircase leading upstairs on his left. The fireplace, which was presently boiling supper, was the main source of light for the room after the sun went down. There were two candles on the dinner table and a soft light coming from an unknown source at the top of the stairs. The entire room was half the size of Drew's bedroom at Morgan Hall.

The furniture consisted of six chairs and two tables. Four straight-back wooden chairs were arranged around the larger table which had been left unset for dinner; a fifth chair was pushed into a smaller table under the twin windows overlooking the street, to Drew's immediate left. Stacks of lacework, lead weights, scissors, and balls of wool yarn cluttered the tabletop. A high-backed rocker sat motionless in front of the fireplace on a large woven rug, the only covering for the wooden floorboards.

Drew unslung his bag from over his shoulder and placed it quietly beside the fireplace. He was reminded of his confiscated cutlass and made a mental note to ask the curate about it.

A variety of whispers drifted through the open kitchen doorway, but Drew couldn't make out what was being said. He thought about edging his way toward the kitchen, then decided against it. *"The secret to learning people's secrets is to act uninterested,"* Eliot had instructed him. *"Don't be in a hurry to get information. Be patient, be friendly, and look for ways to earn their trust. That's the best way to get the goods on them.*"

Besides, the risk wasn't worth it. There was little doubt he was the subject of conversation in the next room. No matter which way the verdict went, he was determined to make every effort to stay at least for dinner.

"*The first meal with your prey is the most important—and the most dangerous,*" he remembered Eliot saying. The word *prey* never set well with Drew; for him, it brought his work down to the level of animals. Drew preferred to think of himself as an undercover operative infiltrating a traitor's camp.

Just then Jenny emerged from the kitchen carrying pewter plates. She didn't look at Drew directly, but the impish smile on her lips acknowledged his presence. Slender hands placed the pewter plates for each setting—one, two, three, four of them! A quick glance at Drew brought a flush to her cheeks. When she saw he was watching her, she made a hasty retreat to the kitchen.

"*I love it when my prey offers me dinner like sheep inviting a wolf to join them for a bite.*" Drew remembered Eliot's high-pitched chortle as he said this. "*And, let me tell you, religious people love to eat. And when they eat, they talk. Put a plate of food in front of a Puritan and he'll tell you the secrets of his life! As they eat I imagine what their cheeks will look like when they're branded!*"

"And what do you hope to find?"

Christopher Matthews placed another bite of mutton in his mouth and chewed thoughtfully as he looked at Drew for a response. A sparse meal of cold mutton, boiled corn, and wheat bread lay between the curate, his daughters, and their guest. Drew had just finished telling them the story he had fabricated for this assignment. Much of it was true, but embellishments had to be added in order to gain their sympathy.

For example, he told them he was the son of a wealthy English country gentleman and that he was raised in an abusive home. That was true. But he added that his father was a drunkard and subject to fits of violence, when, in fact, Lord Morgan shied away from alcohol. Two glasses of wine were enough to make him pass out. Drew also lied about his grandfather, saying that he was a deeply religious man. The curate was pleased to hear that a public hero the likes of Admiral Amos Morgan had a deep reverence for God. Finally, Drew lied about the fight that led him to flee from Morgan Hall. He claimed his father drove him out of the house at sword point when Drew started to take an active interest in religious matters. He concluded that he had wandered from town to town for nearly a year when he was arrested by Edenford's watchman.

"What do I hope to find?" Drew echoed his host's question. "I don't understand."

"In Plymouth. Why do you want to be a merchant sailor in Plymouth?"

Drew shrugged his shoulders and rearranged the corn on his plate. *"Act like you're confused and hurting,"* Eliot had tutored. *"They love that. In their minds it marks you as a prime target for salvation."*

The curate smiled. "Well, I know one thing for sure. God brought you here for a reason."

Matthews sat at the head of the table, to Drew's right. The girls sat opposite Drew, listening as the men dominated the conversation. Nell sat straight and formal in reserved detachment. Jenny stared at Drew outright, at least until he glanced at her, at which time she would lower her eyes.

"No matter how things work out for me," Drew said, "I want you to know I'm grateful for your gracious hospitality." He couldn't resist stealing a glance at Nell as he said it. Her expression remained unchanged.

" 'Be not forgetful to entertain strangers: for thereby some have entertained angels unawares,' " the curate quoted from the Bible.

Nell was incredulous. "Father! Certainly you're not suggesting Master Morgan is an angel!"

Matthews laughed his booming laugh. With a twinkle in his eye he teased, "One never knows!"

"I could believe it," Jenny said softly, then wished she hadn't. When everyone looked at her, she flushed and ran to the kitchen, empty plate in hand.

"Master Morgan," Nell pushed her plate away and rested her folded arms on the table in front of her. "You say your grandfather was a religious man. In what ways?"

"Drew. Please call me Drew."

Nell nodded and waited for a reply to her question.

"Well, for one thing he went to church a lot," Drew offered.

Nell nodded her ascent but waited for more.

"And, um, he was always praying."

"Praying?"

"Sure! Grandpa prayed for everything—the queen, Morgan Hall, his ships, the defeat of Spain . . ."

Nell smiled. Something he said amused her and it made him feel uncomfortable.

"And Grandpa read the Bible a lot too. He was always reading the Bible." Knowing how strongly the Puritans felt about the Bible, Drew felt he was on solid ground with this piece of information. "Grandpa was big on the Bible. In fact, he gave me a Bible just before he died. I carry it with me wherever I go. That was one of the things that upset my father the most—when I started reading the Bible. But I told him that the Bible was God's Word and no one could keep me from reading it. That's when he drove me out of the house."

Apparently the Bible gambit worked. Nell had sobered and was no longer amused with him. "You have the Bible with you now?"

Drew nodded and motioned to his bag by the fireplace.

"What version is it?"

The Bishop had said he could use his Bible version to his advantage. Now was his chance. "Version?" Drew pretended not to have the slightest idea what she was talking about. "It's an English version, of course," he said.

The smugness reappeared on Nell's lips. The look really intimidated him.

"There is more than one English version," the curate offered. His tone was warm and fatherly. It was quite evident he didn't share his daughter's condescending smugness. "May I see your Bible?" he asked.

Drew retrieved his Bible and handed it to the curate. Matthews opened the cover and read the title page. He looked up at Nell and said, "King James."

"It figures," Nell replied sarcastically. "I'd better help Jenny with the dishes." She rose, grabbed a few dishes from the table and disappeared into the kitchen.

"Is there something wrong with my Bible?" Drew pretended to be perplexed.

"You are our guest," the curate replied, handing the Bible back to Drew. "I'm sorry if we have offended you."

"No, please, I want to learn. It's evident you don't like my Bible and I don't know why. How is it different from your Bible?"

Matthews examined Drew's face to see if he was sincere or merely being polite. "Let's sit in front of the fire," he said.

While Drew pulled his chair over to the fireplace, Matthews went upstairs and returned carrying another Bible. He eased himself into the high-backed rocker. "This is my Bible." He handed it to Drew. "It was my father's Bible. He was a cobbler in Exeter. Like your grandfather, a very devout man."

Drew flipped the pages. "What makes this Bible different from mine?"

"This is called the Geneva Bible. It was translated in a time of great persecution, during the reign of Mary Tudor. In those days many godly men fled to the Continent, Geneva specifically. This version of the Bible was published by those exiled men with one thing in mind—to meet the spiritual needs of men and women who refused to be intimidated by an earthly crown."

"And mine is not a Geneva Bible?"

Matthews opened Drew's Bible and turned to the title page. He pointed to the words. Drew read aloud,

THE HOLY BIBLE
Conteyning the Old Testament, and the New:
Newly Translated out of the Originall Tongues:
and with the former Translations
diligently compared and revised,
by his Majesties speciall Commandement.

Appointed to be read in Churches.

IMPRINTED at London by Robert Barker,
Printer to the Kings most Excellent Majestie
Anno Dom. 1611
Cum Privilegio.

"Your Bible is the result of the Hampton Court Conference," Matthews added. "Have you heard of it?"

"I've heard the name."

"In 1603 when Queen Elizabeth died and James of Scotland was crowned king, he was presented a petition of Puritan grievances. It was called the Millenary Petition, because it had

1,000 signatures. My father was one of the signers. I was just thirteen at the time. I remember the excitement of the people as they passed in and out of my father's shop. 'Now we will have a king who agrees with our doctrine,' they said. It was widely believed that the new king would help us shed the last traces of Catholicism and establish a completely Bible-based church. It seemed as if God had answered our prayers."

The last of the dishes rattled behind Drew as Jenny removed them from the table. Nell slipped behind the two men, hurrying up the stairs.

"By order of the new king the Hampton Court Conference was held the next year. With much anticipation, we sent our best Puritan leaders. The conference was a disaster for us. When our representatives brought up the issue of reviving the preaching ministry in the church, the king flared up. He said that if ministers were allowed to deviate from the Book of Common Prayer, then every Jack and Tom, Will and Dick would be given opportunity to censure the king and his council at their pleasure. Turning to the Church of England bishops, he said that if the Puritans ever assumed their authority, the king would lose his supremacy. He told our representatives that he would make us conform, or harry us out of the land—or worse."

Matthews reached over and patted Drew's Bible. "This translation came as a result of that conference." The curate straightened in his chair and, taking the Bible from Drew, turned a few pages. "The king even had them print warnings against us in the preface," he said, as he scanned the print. Finding the section he was looking for he continued, "The translators expected to be 'maligned by self-conceited Brethren, who run their own ways, and give liking to nothing but what is framed by themselves, and hammered on their own anvil.' We are the 'self-conceited Brethren' to whom they refer. And here, 'Lastly, we have on the one side avoided the scrupulosity of the Puritans, who leave the old ecclesiastical words, and betake them to other, as when they put "washing" for "baptism," and "congregation" instead of "Church." But we desire that the Scripture may speak like itself, as in the language of Canaan, that it may be understood even of the very vulgar.' "

Matthews closed the book. "They were right in thinking we would not openly embrace their new translation when we already had a translation which came, not as a result of a conference of hate, but from godly men whose only wish was to serve God in peace."

"Poppa! You're boring Master Morgan!" Jenny stood in the doorway of the kitchen wiping her hands with a towel.

"No!" Drew objected. "I've learned a great deal."

"Are you and Nell finished with the dishes?" Matthews asked.

"Yes, Poppa."

"Then it's time you get to your journals."

"Nell's already upstairs," Jenny offered.

Matthews nodded in understanding. "Then you had best join her. Say good-night to our guest."

Jenny smiled shyly. "Good-night, Master Morgan."

"Drew, please call me Drew."

"Good-night, Drew." She giggled and ran upstairs.

"Can I get you anything before we retire?" Matthews asked.

"If you don't mind, I have one more question. Are you saying that my version of the Bible is not a good one?"

Matthews shrugged his shoulders. "I really can't say. I've never read it. In fact, yours is the first one I've actually held. Everything I've told you I've learned from others." He leaned forward with clasped hands, resting his forearms on his knees. "I can't bring myself to read the translation that bears the name of a man for whom I have no respect."

Drew had to stifle his reaction. Matthew's open antagonism against King Charles' father was foolhardy. Talking like this about a king of England, even a dead one, could get a man in serious trouble if the wrong person heard it. And for Christopher Matthews, Drew was definitely the wrong person. Drew attempted to get more. "What do you mean?" he said.

Matthews hesitated. Had he sensed Drew's surprise?

"King James may have been a learned man in matters of state and religion, but he was immoral, and for that he will be judged."

"Immoral?"

"Surely you've heard of his indiscretions. It's common knowledge that pimps and procuresses lived by the vices of his court, ranging from court laundresses ready to earn sixpence in a dark corner to highly paid courtesans. I've heard the king himself preferred men to women in this regard. And when it came to his family, his actions were abominable. When Prince Henry suffered fits of fever and diarrhea, the king abandoned him and fled to Theobalds, leaving the young prince to die alone. I cannot read a Bible that bears the name of such a man."

In truth, this was not news to Drew. In fact, Matthews' description of the court of King James was mild compared to the stories Drew overheard from his father. Even so, Drew spotted a flaw in the curate's logic and decided to press his advantage.

"It seems to me," he said, "that you're responding to this Bible as if King James himself wrote it. He commissioned it, true, but still it's a translation of God's Word, isn't it?"

A surprised look spread across the curate's face followed by a slow smile. He added to Drew's observation, "And hasn't God always used imperfect men to transmit His perfect Word? An interesting thought, Master Morgan."

Drew lay in front of the dying fire. With only two bedrooms upstairs, he was bedded down on the rug in front of the fireplace. For a long while a light shown from the upstairs landing as someone worked into the night. Drew could hear an occasional shuffle of pages and the movement of a chair. Then the light went out. Just before retiring, Drew searched his Bible for his first message to Bishop Laud from Edenford. He scratched it on a piece of paper and hid it in his coat pocket. It read: (9/24/4/20-40) (41/3/18/2). *"I will deliver thine enemy into thine hand, that thou mayest do to him as it shall seem good unto thee. Andrew."*

Drew turned over and slept contentedly.

Chapter 11

THREE days separated Drew from his trial. Plenty of time to gather sufficient evidence and flee Edenford before being brought up on charges before the high constable.

In their first encounter Christopher Matthews had revealed a fatal weakness—he had an openness about him that would get him arrested. The curate promised to be a veritable fountain of self-incriminating evidence. Still, Drew cautioned himself to be patient. This case was special to the bishop. Even so, given three more days before the trial, Drew felt confident he would have enough evidence to hang the man before Market Day.

Small villages like Edenford didn't settle legal matters on their own. They depended on local watchmen like Cyrus Furman, and civil servants like Ambrose Dudley, to detain lawbreakers until a duly authorized official could hear the complaint and render a decision. For most villages this was done once a month by the high constable, or constable of a hundred, as he was sometimes called. The acting constable dispersed legal judgments on behalf of the justice of the peace for a designated territory. He was usually a gentleman, but yeomen could be appointed as petty constables if there were no qualified or interested gentlemen in the district. However, Edenford had a high constable, a gentleman from Exeter by the name of David Hoffman.

A sober-faced fellow, Hoffman was nearly as wide as he was tall. From the age of eleven, the only growing he had done was in circumference. A short man, he spared no expense on food and spent very little on clothes. Consequently, he looked like an overstuffed sack of grain. His arms and legs extended well past the ends of his frayed and threadbare coat sleeves and pantlegs, and his shirt bulged open between every button and ribbon of his doublet.

An only child and never married, David Hoffman's great love in life was food. The Matthews family had witnessed the high constable's obsession with eating eleven years previous, on the day Christopher was appointed curate of Edenford. The Matthews had invited Hoffman to enjoy the hospitality of their home as they celebrated the appointment. Nell was just seven years old at the time. What she saw that day had a traumatic effect on her.

From the moment the high constable entered the house until the moment he waddled out, he did little but eat and drink. To the amazement of all, the man was an ambidextrous eater; both hands moved in concert, lifting food to his face. Nell remembered how for lack of air he periodically would be forced to pause; his head would fall backward and he would gasp like a fish. The longer he ate, the redder his face turned until sweat poured down his temples and dripped from the end of his cleanly shaved chin, staining the top shelf of his enormous belly.

For weeks afterwards Nell had nightmares. She dreamed that the high constable had burst all over their living room rug.

The high constable's gross eating habits aside, when it came to dispensing justice Edenford could have had worse. David Hoffman knew the major laws and most of the minor ones, and justice was usually served. This was due to the fact that he loved his work. True, the office could be burdensome at

times: the constable had to arrest rioters, felons, or vagabonds, and supervise inns. He was also called upon to present
those he arrested in court, and at harvest time he might be
called upon to find laborers.

Still, Hoffman labored to maintain a good record in all
these matters for several reasons. First, he enjoyed the respect
that came with the office; also, it provided him frequent opportunities to be someone's dinner guest, and thus pay hom-
age to his first love—food.

In the late summer of 1629, as the obese constable prepared to journey north on his regular rounds, his thoughts
were troubled. Reports from London indicated there was nas-
ty business brewing in the village of Edenford. Hoffman
hoped it was a mild tempest that would blow over quickly.
He didn't want anything adversely affecting his reappoint-
ment six months hence.

Drew had never known a family like the Matthews. He had
lived with other Puritan families in the course of his espionage work and had observed many more. None of them were
like this family. There was something different about them,
especially the curate.

For a while Drew couldn't put the difference into words.
Then, an analogy came to him that turned his impressions
into images. Most people, he observed, practice their religion
much like a schoolboy reciting his lesson or an apprentice
attempting to imitate the work of a master craftsman. They
try to become something they're not. Christopher Matthews,
however, didn't *practice* his faith. He and his faith were inseparable. To think of him practicing his faith would be like
thinking of a bird practicing flying. Birds fly because they're
birds. Christopher Matthews lived his faith just as effortless-
ly, just as freely, because it was part of who he was.

Every morning at the breakfast table Christopher Matthews would say, "Well now, what can we do for God this day?" The thing that astonished Drew most was not the fact that the curate asked the same question every day, but the fact that he meant it. When he walked out the door of his house, he looked for something to do for God, as if that was a natural thing for a man to do.

The curate followed a daily routine. He would no more think of diverting from his routine than a goose would consider forgoing his winter migration. Matthews rose between 3 and 4 in the morning to spend an hour or two in prayer. Then he would gather his family for morning prayers and the singing of psalms. He would read a chapter from the Bible to them and then pray again, bringing to God his daughters' prayer requests. In the evening, the Bible was read again, this time accompanied by instruction. Finally, each member of the household would retire to meditate on the day's Bible passage, examine their lives in light of it, and record their thoughts in a daily journal.

If it weren't for the presence of ladies, Drew would have felt he was living in a monastery.

For two days Drew accompanied Christopher Matthews in his daily activities. During this time he came to realize that the man was the closest thing to a mayor the village of Edenford had. Most of the land was still owned by the Chesterfields, a vestige of medieval times when the lord of the manor lived in a castle on a hill and was surrounded by serfs. The old political system had passed away, but economics still held much of its structure in place. Such was the case here. The family Chesterfield and the town Edenford were joined together in an economic marriage.

In this union, the family provided the land and the political and economic influence of the Chesterfield name; the village manufactured the goods that produced the revenue. Normally, the two sides got along agreeably. It wasn't a perfect marriage, but it was livable.

Christopher Matthews was the link between the two partners. When he and his young bride first moved to Edenford, he came as a simple cobbler, having learned the trade from his father. He had no ministerial or political ambitions. The village needed a cobbler and he desired a little village in which he could raise a family and quietly live out his days.

At that time the village was serviced by the parish priest of Tiverton who held livings in several towns. This was not uncommon. A minister often combined the livings of several smaller towns if a single parish could not support him. Rarely could he do justice to all the villages he serviced; but, for towns like Edenford, it was better than having no minister at all.

It was a dispute between the Chesterfields and the priest that changed the pastoral leadership at Edenford. The priest had performed a wedding ceremony for Lord Chesterfield's daughter against her father's wishes. He did it because the groom's father, Lord Weatherly, paid the priest's living for Taunton. The marriage didn't last long and neither did the priest's living from Edenford.

To prevent this kind of thing from ever happening again, Lord Chesterfield decided he needed his own minister, one who answered to him alone. While shopping for one, he decided he didn't want a professional. Professionals tended to take their religion too seriously and often meddled in things that were none of their business. He wanted a man of the earth, not of the cloth. He saw several benefits in this: for one, the living would be cheaper since the layman would also have a trade; another benefit was that a lay minister would be kept busy with his trade and wouldn't have time to sit around evaluating the spiritual condition of the Chesterfields. Basically he was looking for someone who would keep the people happy with the required Sunday services, be available to him for religious matters when called upon, and stay out of his way the rest of the time.

He found just the right man in his own village. Christopher Matthews was the most religious layman in Edenford, and so the cobbler was offered the position. At first Matthews declined, feeling ill-equipped to be a spiritual leader; it was his wife, Jane, who persuaded him to accept. She reasoned this was a God-sent opportunity to establish a biblical foundation in the village. Yielding to his wife's faith in him, the cobbler became the curate.

Within months the number of village crimes decreased and the work productivity increased. When Lord Chesterfield inquired about the change, he discovered it was the result of Christopher Matthews' quiet leadership and strength of character. The curate had visited each house in the village, convincing the residents to try godly living. He challenged them to test God's ways for themselves for six months. If they weren't better off after that time, they could do whatever they wished and he would leave them alone. Within two months it was a new village and Christopher Matthews was their Moses, their prophet and leader.

At first, Lord Chesterfield felt threatened by Matthews' sudden increase in power over his village. The dilemma was that he liked the increased productivity and decrease in problems. His dilemma was solved by a stroke of genius. Instead of reining in the curate, he decided to give him additional authority and power and—this was the key—the curate would be responsible directly to him for all matters pertaining to the business of Edenford.

Matthews' initial response was to decline. He did not seek additional power; his only wish was to be the people's spiritual leader. Again, it was his wife who convinced him otherwise. She saw the position as a two-way street. Not only would he represent the Chesterfields to the people, but he could represent the people to Lord Chesterfield and possibly improve the living conditions of the villagers.

Under Matthews' leadership, the Edenford wool industry prospered as never before—from raising the sheep, to shearing, to spinning, weaving, dressing and scouring, fulling and drying, and dyeing of the serges. The greatest addition to the Edenford merchandise, however, was the intricate bone lace crafted by the Matthews women.

The shadows of Edenford were beginning to lengthen as Drew and Christopher Matthews and David Cooper strolled toward the village green. All morning long Drew had followed the curate from business to business, astounded at their reception. As a boy he had witnessed his father's transactions and had concluded that business was a matter of shouts, threats, and confrontations. Not so in Edenford. The owners of these establishments greeted Matthews with genuine warmth. Business was transacted with friendly tones and handshakes. By midday Drew wondered aloud if Matthews had any enemies.

"That's an odd question," the curate responded. He glanced at Cooper who scowled at the question. "Why would you want to know if I have enemies?"

It was an unfortunate slip, one that cast suspicion on Drew. "Forgive me if I offended you," he stammered. "It's just that where I come from, business is a hostile transaction. Everyone here is so friendly."

"It's because we're more than just neighbors. We're family."

Family . . . Not like my family! They were never this kind to each other.

Every place they visited, the curate treated each person he was talking to as the most important citizen of Edenford. And Drew saw that his fear of being branded as a criminal by the townspeople was totally unfounded. In fact, he had to remind himself he was under this man's legal custody. Everywhere they went, Matthews introduced him as if he were a visiting London dignitary.

Drew had met Mrs. Weathersfield, a widow who said she prayed every day that Matthews' daughters would find suitable husbands. It was no secret she also prayed for a husband of her own, preferably the curate himself. Matthews gave her some shillings for food. Later, when Nell learned that the money was not from the church, but from Matthews' own pocket, she was upset. It wasn't the first time her father had given away too much of their money so that they didn't have enough to buy food. This, in addition to his bringing Drew Morgan home with him—another person to feed.

Drew had also met David Cooper, the village cobbler and boyhood friend of Matthews from Exeter. The two buddies had their fathers' profession in common when they were growing up. Cooper was the one who sat next to Matthews in the meeting hall the day Drew was arrested. He was a large, hairy man with an equally large smile. His heavy black head of hair, beard, and thick arms reminded Drew more of a blacksmith than a cobbler. He had come to Edenford upon Matthews' invitation when Matthews became Lord Chesterfield's representative and the village was left without a cobbler.

At the cobbler's shop Matthews pretended to be a shoe inspector and ribbed Cooper about sloppy workmanship, which was difficult to do since the shoes were masterful products. Then the two friends decided to play hooky from work for the remainder of the day. They took Drew with them.

The three of them spent a lazy afternoon at the bowling green. The two friends were evenly matched, and were better players than Drew, who had handled a bowling ball only once in his life. Bowling was considered a commoner's sport, beneath the dignity of noblemen.

After the first two games, the curate winning both, Drew was content to lie on the grass and watch. He was amused at their competitiveness. After Matthews' third straight win, the cobbler's temper flared and he dented the grass with a few bowling balls. The curate quipped that the force of the balls was undoubtedly creating earthquakes in hell, which made the cobbler chuckle. His anger passed as quickly as it had appeared.

"Is this the way you guard a prisoner?"

The angry voice came from behind Drew. It was Ambrose Dudley. His face was flushed as his yellow teeth spit out the words. Old Cyrus Furman, carrying the town's aged musket, lolled behind him.

"Master Morgan isn't going anywhere, are you, Drew?" Matthews emphasized Drew's name and title, in contrast to Dudley's use of the term "prisoner."

Drew, still lying on the grass, smiled and shook his head no.

"This is irresponsible. Completely irresponsible!" the scrivener shouted. "For all we know, this boy may be Shubal Elkins' killer!"

Again the curate addressed Drew. "You're not a murderer, are you?"

"Nope." Drew picked a blade of grass as he said it.

The curate was in a playful mood. Ambrose Dudley was not. His clenched jaw worked back and forth as he looked from man to man.

"Now, Ambrose," Matthews walked toward him, "the boy's not going anywhere. He'll be here on Market Day."

Dudley refused to be consoled. "If he isn't here, it'll be on your head! Come, Cyrus." The angry scrivener turned and stalked away. His elderly companion shrugged his shoulders and lolled after him.

Matthews looked at Cooper. "Think we should have invited them to bowl a game with us?"

The three walked across the road that separated the village green from the river and descended the slope to the water's edge. As they lay on their backs, hands folded behind their heads, Cooper spoke of a special shipment of shoes going to London on Market Day. The curate asked Drew if he had ever been to London. Drew casually mentioned his family's recent trip to Windsor Castle, leaving out the part about the armor and Bishop Laud.

"Have you been to St. Michael's Church?"

"I've been in it once," Drew replied. "Not for services, though."

"Last time I was in London I went there," the curate said. "I'm not sure I could worship God there."

"Why not?" The question came from Cooper.

"A couple of things bothered me. First, the sanctuary is so magnificent. To me it's distracting. I'd probably find myself looking at it instead of thinking about God. Then, outside the building, the poor, homeless, and the hungry gather on the steps. They live there. Twice a day, a groundskeeper tries to chase them away. In some ways I can see his point. They do leave a mess, urinating on the pillars and discarding their trash all over the steps. The thing that bothers me most is that those people think that by being close to a church building they are close to God."

The talk went from church buildings to the controversy in the church between the bishops and the Puritans to the persecution of the Puritans since William Laud was appointed Bishop of London. The shift in topics made Drew uneasy, but there was no indication that the conversation was an attempt to elicit his views on the matter.

"When I think of Laud, I think of a story I heard recently," Matthews said as he sat up.

"Everything reminds you of a story," Cooper jibed.

"True. But I think Laud's actions will come back to haunt him."

"So, what's the story?"

Matthews rose to his feet with a groan. "There's no time for stories now. We need to get home."

"Oh no you don't!" Cooper cried. He pulled Matthews to the ground and pinned him. "Not until I hear your story!"

Drew watched this horseplay with unconcealed amusement. He'd never seen grown men acting like this. The men he knew would never joke with each other. It lowered too many barriers. Someone might see it as a weakness and exploit it.

"All right! I'll tell the story. Just get off of me, you big ox!" Matthews cried. "I can't breathe!"

Cooper eased up but was prepared to pounce again if Matthews made any attempt to get away. However, Matthews made no false moves and, after brushing himself off, he began his story:

"There once was a man, a poor man, who got it into his head to become a highway thief. He explained to his wife that it would be a much easier and more profitable way of making a living than working day in and day out. And so the next morning he went, club in hand, and walked down the London Road, somewhere between Newark and Grantham. There, a gentleman on horseback overtook him. The poor man waited for the gentleman to get close and when he did, the thief caught hold of the horse's bridle.

" 'Stand and deliver!' he shouted with club raised.

"The gentleman on horseback began to laugh! 'Would that a thief should rob a thief?' he cried. 'I am one of your trade, you poor wretch! But surely you are either a fool or one who has recently started this trade, for you are doing it all wrong!'

" 'I have never done this trade in my life before.'

" 'I thought as much,' said the gentleman. 'Therefore, take

my advice and mind what I say to you. When you have a mind to rob a man, never take hold of his bridle and bid him stand; the first thing you should do is knock him down. And if he talk to you, hit him another stroke and say, "You rogue! Cease your babbling!" Then, you have him at your will.'

"Thus they walked for about a mile, the gentleman teaching the poor man his art. As they were going through a certain town, they came to a bad lane. The poor man said to his teacher, 'Sir, I am better acquainted with this country than perhaps you are. This lane is very bad and anyone traveling it is in danger of being robbed. But if you go through this gate and along the field side, you will miss the bad part of the road.'

"So the gentleman took his advice and followed the poor man through the gate. Coming to the other side, the poor man knocked the gentleman over the head with a blow that brought him to the ground.

"The gentleman cried out, 'Sir! Is this your gratitude for the good advice I gave you?'

" 'You rogue!' shouted the poor man. 'Cease your babbling!' And he gave him another knock. And so, having him wholly at his mercy, he took almost fifty pounds from him and the man's horse. Then the poor man rode home to his wife as fast as he could go.

"When he arrived home, he said, 'Good wife, I find this a very hard trade that I have been about and I am resolved to have nothing more to do with it, but to be content with what I got. I have a good horse here and fifty pounds in my pocket from a gentleman. And I have considered that since he too is a thief I cannot be prosecuted for it; therefore I will live at ease.' "

David Cooper rubbed his whiskers and chuckled. "I like it," he said.

Drew added his favorable consent.

"A question though," said Cooper. "How does Laud remind you of this story?"

Christopher Matthews stood to his feet and stretched. "It's getting late," he said. "I'll tell you on the way back."

The others joined him. By now long shadows stretched their direction.

"The way I see it," he explained, "England is the poor man in the story—hungry, desperate, and looking for a way to survive. Along comes Bishop Laud, the gentleman of the story. He tells them that he too is concerned about England's plight and that Puritans are to blame for their wretched condition. So he teaches them to hate and to kill Puritans. What he doesn't realize is that someday the hate he taught them will be turned against him. I believe that when all is said and done, England will survive. Laud will not."

The trio walked across the village green in silence.

The curate broke the silence when he said, "I pray that God will open his eyes before it's too late."

On the third day of Drew's captivity, the day before Market Day, Matthews left Drew at home with Nell and Jenny. Important, confidential business, he said following morning devotions, as the two of them walked to the village well for water. He gave Drew a choice: he could stay at the house with the girls or Matthews could arrange for him to walk the streets with the watchman.

Drew visualized his choices: spend the day with two attractive ladies or shuffle through the streets of Edenford with a slow-witted old man. It didn't take him long to decide. An afternoon of flirting with Jenny excited him. What surprised him was his eagerness to spend the day with Nell as well. Her intellect and self-assurance intimidated him, yet he felt an attraction to her he couldn't explain.

As the two men pulled water from the well, David Cooper

rushed toward them and pulled Matthews aside. A few moments of furious whispering passed between them. Drew continued drawing water and tried to act like he wasn't listening. In truth, he was straining to hear what they were saying. He didn't catch much, just a few words—"shipment" and "delivery" and "distressed."

"I'm afraid I'm going to have to leave you here," the curate said, returning to Drew. "Tell Nell and Jenny I might not be home until late tonight. They'll understand." Then, with a sheepish grin he added, "Happens all the time in my line of work."

Drew watched the two friends hurry up the street toward Cooper's cobbler shop. They hadn't gotten far when they ran into Ambrose Dudley. A heated discussion ensued as several times the angry scrivener pointed a bony finger at Drew. A moment later Matthews and Cooper continued on their way. Dudley was left standing with his hands on his hips, glaring at Drew.

Pretending not to notice him, Drew lifted the water buckets by their rope handles. Instead of walking toward High Street and the Matthews' house, he went down the hill to Market Street, the street that led to the south bridge and out of town. Just as he rounded the corner of the row of houses, he glanced out of the corner of his eye. Dudley was in quick pursuit. Drew quickened his pace as he followed the road along the back side of the houses on High Street. By the time he reached the end of the row, he had a good lead on the scrawny scrivener. He darted to his right up the road between the cornfield and the houses and then right again on High Street. Without knocking he burst into the Matthews household, startling Jenny and Nell who were doing their lacework at the table before the open window.

"Shhhh!" He hurriedly set the buckets down and pulled up a chair so that he was facing the open window.

"Master Morgan! What on earth . . ."

"Shhhh!" Drew insisted, pointing toward the open window.

The girls shared puzzled expressions but stared out the window nonetheless. For several long moments nothing happened. In fact, Drew was beginning to wonder if anything was going to happen. Maybe Dudley gave up on him.

Just then a long nose slowly appeared at the edge of the open window followed by the remainder of the scrivener's drawn face. He was met by three people staring at him.

"Good morning, Master Dudley," Jenny said brightly.

Drew waved.

The scrivener, surprised and embarrassed, said nothing. With a loud snort, he straightened himself and strutted down the street.

The three enjoyed a good laugh, Jenny with her girlish giggle and Nell with a light but full laugh. Again Drew was surprised at his feelings. The sight of Nell laughing captivated him. Her brown eyes twinkled and her white even teeth highlighted a perfect smile. He loved seeing her like this and was pleased with himself that he was part of something that made her laugh.

"What was that all about?" Nell asked.

Drew picked up the buckets full of water to take them to the kitchen. "I guess he was afraid I'd run away. Your father left me at the well. He went with Master Cooper and said he wouldn't be home until late tonight."

The statement sobered Nell instantly, her face registering genuine concern. It caught Drew's attention because Nell was far past the age when a girl would show disappointment when her father didn't make it home for dinner. There was more to the curate's absence than Drew was led to believe.

Nell resumed her work with a stoic expression. "Thank you for relaying the message," was all she said.

"And thank you for not running away!" Jenny beamed. This brought a scowl from Nell.

For most of the morning Drew watched the girls make lace. Mostly he watched the girls. Nell worked studiously, her dark brown hair curled around the edges of her face as she leaned slightly forward. The broad bridge of her nose separated those intriguing brown eyes of hers, highlighted by thick, full eyebrows; her lips were full. A hint of laughter seemed to reside in the corners of her eyes and mouth. Drew hadn't noticed it before.

Jenny was slightly smaller than her sister. Her skin was fair, a perfect match for the straight brown hair that fell down to her waist. Drew loved to watch her throw it over her shoulders whenever it fell forward and got in her way.

The girls were dressed similarly. Muslin blouses were covered by cloth bodices and skirts of muted colors. The most striking similarity between the sisters was their long graceful fingers that could tug and pull when needed, or deftly wind delicate threads with artistic confidence.

Drew had never seen such intricate work in progress. But then, being the product of a wealthy family, he had never seen much of any kind of work in progress.

"It's called *punto a groppo*," Nell said.

"Bone lace," Jenny translated.

First, a geometric pattern was drawn on a piece of parchment and holes were pricked in it to indicate where pins were to be placed. The pins would hold the threads in place while the lace was being made. The parchment was then placed on a pillow and threads attached to the pins. The other ends of the thread were wound around bobbins. Originally bones were used, which gave the lace its name. Finally, the threads were looped, interlaced, braided and twisted around the pins, forming rows of deep, acute-angled points joined by narrow bands. The finished product was a delicate, open-cut design that was the envy of all fashion-conscious people.

However impressive and intriguing the bone lace was to Drew, it was not nearly as captivating as the delicate hands making it. Nell's slender fingers danced with a skilled confidence around the pins. Her hands moved in coordinated rhythm to a silent tempo, like a gentleman and his lady dancing on a ballroom floor, each so familiar with the other that every move is anticipated and perfectly matched.

"Master Drew, it isn't polite to stare." Nell had a slightly amused look on her face.

"Forgive me," Drew stammered. "I was just fascinated with your work."

"Haven't you ever seen a person work before?"

Her dry reproach was not lost on Drew.

"Nell! Master Drew is our guest," Jenny came to his defense. "You shouldn't speak to him like that!"

"Maybe not," Nell replied with an unrepentant tone. "I suppose I'm just not used to having a healthy man sit around the house and do nothing all day long."

"Nell!" Turning to Drew she said, "I enjoy your company, Master Drew, even if my sister doesn't."

Drew sat back in his chair, arms folded. "I'll gladly do whatever I can—as long as it's legal."

His joke died for lack of response.

"There is something you could do to help us pass the time, if your offer is sincere, Master Drew."

"Tell me what it is and I'll gladly do it."

"Do you have a good reading voice, Master Drew?" Nell asked.

Drew shrugged. "I suppose so."

"It would help us pass the time if you would read to us while we work."

"I could do that," Drew said. "What would you like to hear?"

"The Bible would be my choice," Nell said.

Drew spied an opportunity to give Nell a dose of her own sarcastic medicine. "Excellent choice!" Drew exclaimed. "And I'm sure you won't mind if I read from my Bible, the one translated by order of King James."

Jenny gasped. "Oh, I don't think Poppa would like that," she said.

If Nell was as shocked as her sister, she didn't show it. She looped and twisted a thread. "I'd like that very much," she said evenly.

"Nell!" Jenny dropped her work in her lap and stared in disbelief at her sister.

"But if you don't mind," Nell continued, "since you chose the Bible version, I feel it's only fair that I choose the passage you read."

Drew retrieved his Bible from his bag beside the fireplace. "Fair enough," he said.

Nell didn't announce her choice until Drew returned to his seat. Jenny just sat there, immobilized by her sister's willingness to allow the rogue translation to be read aloud in their home.

"What would you have me read?" Drew asked, falling into his chair.

"Song of Solomon, chapter 4."

Drew went right to work to find the book in the Bible by turning to the table of contents. Beginning with Genesis he scanned the contents with his index finger. "Let's see . . . Song of Solomon . . . Song of Solomon . . ." He failed to notice the crimson coloring rising in Jenny's cheeks.

Nell watched him with amusement. "Read the Bible often, Master Morgan?"

"All the time," Drew said, without looking up.

"It's near the middle of the . . ."

"Found it!" Drew flipped the pages to the appropriate page

number. Then he said aloud, "Chapter 4 . . . verse 1. Here it is!" He straightened himself in the chair and began to read, "Behold, thou art fair, my love. . . ." He stopped, an embarrassed look crossed his face. Jenny began giggling uncontrollably. Nell maintained a straight face.

"Please continue," she said. "You're doing a fine job."

Drew realized he'd been tricked, but he wasn't about to back down now. This was a battle of wits and he intended to outlast Nell Matthews. With a loud voice he continued reading, "Thou hast doves' eyes . . ."

"Master Morgan?"

Drew looked up, perturbed at being interrupted.

"Would you mind beginning again . . . from the start? And please forgive my little sister's giggling."

Jenny sobered slightly.

Drew cleared his voice and began again, this time even louder. "Behold, thou art fair, my love; behold, thou art fair; thou hast doves' eyes within thy locks: thy hair is as a flock of goats, that appear from Mount Gilead. Thy teeth are like a flock of sheep that are even shorn, which came up from the washing; whereof every one bear twins, and none is barren among them. Thy lips . . ."

Drew was beginning to weaken. Jenny was giggling uncontrollably; even Nell was having difficulty maintaining her composure.

". . . are like a thread of scarlet, and thy speech is comely; thy temples are like a piece of a pomegranate within thy locks. Thy neck is like the tower of David builded for an armoury, whereon there hang a thousand bucklers, all shields of mighty men. Thy two . . ."

This time Drew turned red. He had translated a few coded words from this book of the Bible, but he had never read it. And he had certainly never heard the priest at his church in Winchester read this passage in a church service. "Don't stop now," Nell laughed, "you're doing so well."

Drew gritted his teeth. "Thy two breasts are like two young roes that are twins, which feed among the lilies."

Just then two women walked by the open window, their eyes wide with shock. Jenny hid her face in a pillow, her shoulders shaking uncontrollably as she tried to muffle her laughter. Nell could hold it no longer. Tears ran down her cheeks as she tried to suppress her laughs.

Drew closed the book. "Well, that's enough Bible reading for today," he said. "I think I'll take a walk." As the door shut behind him, he could hear howls of feminine laughter coming from inside.

Chapter 12

MARKET Day was dark and cold. Heavy gray clouds lumbered overhead, threatening rain but never living up to their bluster. On any other day, the mood of the residents would match the grayness of the day, but not today. This was Market Day, and the hardworking people of Edenford weren't going to let a few dark clouds deprive them of a diversion from their daily drudgery. Besides, this particular Market Day had excitement on its agenda; this was the day of Drew Morgan's trial.

The trial was scheduled for mid-morning. This was because High Constable Hoffman was not an early riser. Then, of course, he would have breakfast, which would sometimes last until lunch. The townspeople took the high constable's schedule in stride. They were in no hurry; if the accused hadn't run off by now, it was safe to assume he'd still be around whenever Constable Hoffman finished eating.

In the meantime the people of Edenford made every effort to enjoy themselves. The womenfolk strolled from booth to booth in groups of three or four, whispering and laughing as they bought vegetables, fruit, and cheese. The menfolk usually gathered on the church steps or in front of David Cooper's cobbler shop. Their conversation ranged from the wool trade to politics and religion (for in these times you could not talk of the one without talking about the other), to weekly bowling scores, or to just plain gossip. The young men usually ended up on the grassy area next to the church where they would wrestle or race or kick a ball around.

Of course, it wouldn't be Market Day without the aromas. The musty, heavy smell of a wool town gave way to the sweet odors of fresh bread and rolls, flowers, cheeses, and the earthy smell of freshly picked vegetables.

Drew accompanied the Matthews family down the hill to Market Street. All of them, including the curate, were carrying some kind of bundle or basket. The girls had packed food, their Bibles, and odds and ends that would be needed during the course of the day. A stiff blast of air sent Drew's felt hat flying down the road toward the south bridge. The Matthews waited for him while he chased it. He was halfway to the bridge before he caught up with it.

Maybe I should just keep going, he thought. In spite of Chrisopher Matthews' assurances that everything would be all right, the thought of a trial unnerved him. Maybe the hat was an omen warning him to escape while he still could. After all, he wasn't even supposed to be here. He thought he'd be gone by now. But the last few days had turned up nothing new. Then there was the matter of the town's secret. How could he leave knowing there was a secret and not knowing what it was? Drew pulled his hat down tightly around his head and walked into the wind, toward the waiting Matthews and his trial.

Just beyond the Matthews, shouts and grunts could be heard coming from the village green. Nell and Jenny had already turned that direction to see what the commotion was all about. Two men stripped to the waist were locked in a wrestling match. One of the men was a hairy red giant; the other was of medium height with a dark complexion. Jenny leaned toward Nell and whispered something. Nell shoved her away.

The redheaded giant was toying with his smaller, weaker foe. The dark-haired man, whom Drew had never seen before, was scowling and intense. No matter what he tried, he wasn't able to gain a hold on his opponent who was larger, stronger, and quicker. The harder the dark man tried, the more frustrated he became. Lowering his head, he charged. Drew thought he looked like a bowling ball rolling toward a taller pin. An instant before impact, the giant stepped aside, grabbed the passing man's torso, and sent him flying. The dark man, arms and legs flailing, landed with a thump at the feet of some spectators.

Acknowledging the cheers, the red giant raised his hands in victory. Then he caught sight of Nell and his sweaty grin grew even larger. He seemed especially pleased that she had witnessed his victory.

However, the dark-haired wrestler wasn't ready to concede defeat: the red giant's arrogance enraged him. Struggling to his feet, fists clenched, he attacked the giant from behind, landing a solid blow to his kidneys.

The pain of the blow registered on the giant's face. With surprising quickness he whirled around, slammed the dark man to the ground, and proceeded to pummel him.

It took four strong men to pull the giant from atop his bloodied opponent. One of the men was Christopher Matthews. Coming face to face with the curate brought a look of shame and embarrassment to the red giant's face, as he wiped a bloodied nose with the back of his hand. He glanced at Nell who wore a look of disgust. She shook her head, turned her back, and walked toward the market booths.

"Nell, wait!" The red giant called after her.

No response. Nell continued walking away.

"Nell," he whined, "he hit me first!"

Drew leaned toward Jenny. "Is there something going on between Nell and him?"

Jenny smiled, enjoying her closeness to Drew. She leaned toward him to get even closer. "He'd like to think there is," she whispered, "but he's wasting his time."

"Why doesn't Nell tell him she's not interested?"

"It's not that easy for her. Our family has been friends with the Coopers since before we were born. They're like family."

"Coopers? He's a Cooper?"

Jenny nodded and stole a glance at Drew's lips. "His father is David Cooper, the cobbler."

Now that he knew the family connection, Drew could see some resemblance—the massive arms and chest, a thick forehead jutting out over deep-inset eyes. He was bigger than his father and just as hairy. It was the red coloring that was so different.

"Nell and James were born within two months of each other," Jenny continued, "and our families have just assumed that they would get married someday. Especially James."

"Does your father expect Nell to marry James?"

"I've never heard him say it directly, but he and Master Cooper are best friends. He'd be pleased if they did."

Convinced that Nell wasn't going to speak to him, the red giant shuffled back to his friends, his shoulders slumped. Glancing up, he saw Drew standing close to Jenny. His eyes focused hard on Drew as he raised himself to full height.

It seemed inevitable. Drew knew that unless he could complete his business in Edenford quickly, their paths would cross. He didn't like the prospect.

The high constable was awake and well fed by 10:30, with enough time to hold a court session before lunch. On clear days the hearings were usually held on the village green beside the church; on the day of Drew Morgan's trial, however, the blustery weather forced the gathering inside the church. Drew entered the building alongside Christopher Matthews. The wooden pews were already packed with spectators. Nell and Jenny managed to find seats halfway to the front as Drew and the curate walked up the center aisle. James Cooper and a few other young men sat directly behind them. Nell's head was bowed as they passed. Was she praying or simply trying to ignore the red giant seated behind her? Jenny smiled reassuringly as she wiggled her slender fingers in a little wave.

The shutters were closed against the wind, making the inside of the church dark and gloomy. An occasional shrill whistle howled as the wind tried to force its way in through the cracks in the shutters.

Although every seat was taken, people continued to pour in. They stood against the walls, lining the edges of the building two and three deep. To Drew everyone seemed in a surly mood, as if they were looking for a fight.

As Drew and Matthews sat on the front pew, reserved for defendants and witnesses, Drew couldn't help but smile when he saw the communion table in violation of Bishop Laud's directive: it wasn't against the eastern wall, nor was it railed off. In fact, the bishop would be incensed—the obese high constable was hunched behind the table, using it for court proceedings.

Two other cases were addressed before the charges against Drew were read—a money dispute between two men who were building a cottage together, and a property loss settlement involving the death of a pig. Apparently a drunken man had stabbed his neighbor's pig when he mistook it for a demon.

After the high constable fixed the amount between the two building partners and ordered the pig killer to pay restitution, he called Drew to stand before the assembly. Ambrose Dudley, in his capacity as town scrivener, read the charge against Drew. From the platform Drew could clearly see Nell and

Jenny. Nell's face remained expressionless; her hands worried a few strands of fringe on her shawl; Jenny was biting her lower lip.

Dudley's high voice cut through the crowd's restless murmur, "Master Drew Morgan is hereby charged with being a vagabond."

Then the scrivener was asked to present his case. "Performing his rightful duty, Cyrus Furman, town watchman, detained Master Morgan three days past. Master Morgan was traveling from the north on Bridge Road entering Edenford. He was armed with this."

Using both hands Dudley raised Drew's grandfather's cutlass over his head so that everyone could see it. The level of murmuring rose.

"Suspecting Master Morgan of being a vagabond, or worse, Cyrus brought the boy to me, whereupon I questioned him extensively. My examination revealed he had no permanent place of residence from which he was coming, and no permanent place of residence to which he was going—hence, a vagabond."

The high constable leaned over his book and wrote something while everyone waited. The scratchings of his pen and the whistling of the wind through the shutters were the only sounds. Lifting his head, he said, "Anything else?"

The scrawny scrivener straightened his doublet while he cleared his throat. When he spoke next the tone of his voice was lower and deeper, to lend an added note of authority. He said, "There is. I suspect Master Drew Morgan of murdering Shubal Elkins!"

As if by cue, the room exploded with noise. Several men jumped to their feet and leaned forward over the backs of the pews, shouting and shaking fists at Drew. Like a flowing tide, they began moving toward him, a cursing, shoving, jostling wall of angry faces. Head and shoulders above them was

James Cooper. The red giant wore a twisted grin as he pushed his way forward.

To old Cyrus Furman's credit, the town watchman positioned himself between his prisoner and the furious tide. He had nothing with which to protect his prisoner except his bare hands, since firearms were not allowed in the church. The high constable was on his feet, frantically hammering the communion table and shouting for order. Christopher Matthews leaped to the town watchman's side and loudly called for calm, but the noise of the angry sea of townspeople drowned him out.

The curate shoved Drew against the wall and shielded him with his body. The angry tide continued advancing. Not until it was within a foot of the curate did it stop. No one was willing to lay hands on the curate. They shouted and cajoled, but the curate of Edenford refused to move.

Matthews took advantage of the impasse. "This man did not murder Shubal Elkins!" he shouted.

"The scrivener says he did!" A man with a large forehead and a splotchy black beard became the self-appointed voice for the mob. The tide of men surged as they shouted their agreement. Christopher Matthews was beginning to understand. The scrivener had orchestrated this vigilante effort.

"On what evidence?" Matthews shouted back.

"He did it with his sword!" the black beard said.

"Is that what the scrivener told you? That the murder was committed with the sword?"

He was answered with affirmative nods and shouts.

"That's interesting, since Ambrose Dudley didn't examine the body. I did. So did Cyrus and David Cooper." He scanned the crowd for the town watchman and found him off to the side, restrained by two men. "Cyrus, could the wounds on Shubal Elkins' body have been made with a sword?"

"Not likely," Cyrus replied. "The cuts were too small

More like the work of a small knife."

"Cooper?" the curate shouted across the sea of accusers to the cobbler who was standing at the back of the church.

"Had to be a knife," Cooper shouted back. "There's no way it could have been done with a sword."

"Morgan could have done it with a knife!" The voice was Ambrose Dudley's. He was standing safely away from the action on the far side of the church behind the communion table and the high constable.

At this point the high constable intervened. "Did you find a knife on the boy?"

"He could have thrown it in some bushes or the river, or buried it." The scrivener's voice was high pitched and uncertain.

"You found no knife on the boy when he was arrested?" the high constable repeated.

"No, we did not." the scrivener said grudgingly.

The high constable followed up with another question. "Do you have any other evidence that would link this boy to the murder?"

"He was in the area at the time of the murder!" Dudley replied. "The body was found late last Sunday. Drew Morgan came from the direction of the murder on Monday. Your lordship, I still believe Morgan did it. I have a feeling about Master Morgan. I can always tell when people are hiding something, and he's hiding something!"

The oversized constable produced a lace handkerchief and wiped large beads of perspiration from his brow and the side of his face. "Master Dudley, as you are well aware, impressions are not admissible evidence. Nor is a man guilty simply because he was in the vicinity of a crime. Unless you have something more substantial, I will not accept the charge of murder against Master Morgan."

"There is still the matter of his being a vagabond!" said

Dudley. "Of that there is no doubt!"

"That is a matter we will decide." The high constable spoke firmly with a touch of exasperation. "But as for you, town scrivener, let it be known that your actions in this matter have been reprehensible! You have let personal opinion outweigh fact. You stirred up this town needlessly with your wild accusations. At the conclusion of this trial, I will meet with town officials and we will determine suitable punishment."

An unplanned recess followed as everyone returned to their seats. Drew thanked his protectors before returning to his place on the platform. The sea of faces before him was decidedly mixed; some, like Jenny and Nell, were pale from fright, others eyed him suspiciously, while still others looked genuinely disappointed that they weren't going to hang him.

When all was quiet, the high constable addressed Drew. "How do you respond to the charge that you are a vagabond?"

"I am a traveler. Nothing more," Drew replied. "I am no threat to this town."

"His response doesn't answer the question!" Dudley shouted.

A perturbed, angry look crossed the high constable's face. "If you don't mind, Mr. Dudley, I know my job, if you'll let me do it."

Dudley folded his arms and scowled.

"He is right, Master Morgan," the high constable continued, "your response does not answer the question. Do you have a permanent place of residence?"

There was a long pause as Drew tried his best to come up with something that would acquit him of this nagging petty charge.

"Is the question too hard for you, Master Morgan?"

Christopher Matthews stood. "Master Morgan has a permanent residence in my home, should he choose to dwell there."

Jenny silently clapped her hands together, cheering her father. Nell's mouth dropped open for an instant; then she snapped it shut with tightly pursed lips.

"A noble gesture, curate," Hoffman replied, "but hardly relevant. Your gesture comes after the crime has been committed. Let me rephrase my question. Master Morgan, four days ago when you were detained by Edenford's watchman, did you have a permanent place of residence?"

"No, sir," Drew replied. "But I still contend I was no threat to the town. I was passing through on my way to Plymouth."

"Plymouth? For what purpose?"

"To enlist as a crew member aboard a trading ship."

"I see." The high constable played with the folds of flesh under his chin. "Was a ship's captain expecting you?"

"No, sir."

"Have you ever been a crew member of a ship before?"

Drew thought about lying that he had, but remembered the problems he encountered during his first assignment at Norwich where too many lies proved to be his undoing. Better to keep his story simple and look for another way out of this. "No, sir," he said.

"Do you have any evidence that could convince us that your story about Plymouth is true?"

"No, sir."

A rumble of voices reverberated through the church as the high constable scribbled something in his book. When he was finished he addressed Dudley. "I am fully aware how trite this next question is in light of the recent outburst, but to satisfy procedure, I must ask it. Was Master Morgan carrying any weapons when he was detained?"

"He was," Dudley said quickly, obviously pleased. The

scrivener laid the cutlass on the communion table in front of the high constable. The constable pulled the cutlass from its sheath and held it up, examining the blade.

"Does this cutlass belong to you?" he asked Drew.

"Yes, sir, it does."

"Why were you carrying it?"

"For protection, sir."

"Protection? Protection from what or whom?"

"Highway robbers. The roads of England are hardly safe for travelers."

The high constable agreed with a grunt as he continued to examine the sword. "I was in Collumpton a few weeks ago," he said in a tone that sounded like he was thinking out loud. "Seems there was a highwayman who was working the stretch of road between Collumpton and Bradninch. You wouldn't happen to be that highwayman, would you?"

"No, sir!"

"This is a navy cutlass unless I'm mistaken," the high constable noted. "Yet, you say you have never been to sea."

"It was my grandfather's." Drew debated whether or not to use his grandfather's name, then decided it might impress the constable. "My grandfather was Admiral Amos Morgan."

Another murmur throughout the church, this one louder and sustained by whispers.

The high constable turned from the sword and examined Drew. "Impressive!" he said. "Is Admiral Morgan still alive?"

"No, sir. He died earlier this year."

"Hmm," was all the high constable said.

There was a moment of silence.

The high constable placed the cutlass on the table. "It's just as well. I'm sure such a noble man would be ashamed to know his grandson has become a common vagabond. Do you have anything else to say in your defense?"

Drew's mind raced. There was no sense of panic; it was just

that he was perplexed. Try as he might, he couldn't think of a way to extricate himself without endangering his mission in Edenford. Could his efforts be salvaged if he was found guilty? What was the penalty for being a vagabond anyway? He didn't know.

"May I say something?"

All eyes swung from Drew to the speaker rising from the front pew. It was Christopher Matthews.

The high constable acknowledged the curate with a nod.

"If I may, I would like to speak on behalf of the accused."

Another nod from the constable.

"According to the definition read by our scrivener, there seems to be little doubt that Drew Morgan is a vagabond."

"Father!" Jenny couldn't constrain herself. Even stoic Nell had a shocked look on her face.

Matthews continued. "He may be a vagabond, but he's not an evil person and he's certainly not a threat to our town. Although I have known him for only three days, I have spent more time with him than anyone else in this room."

"Hardly relevant testimony!" Ambrose Dudley said, jumping to his feet. He addressed the constable. "Christopher Matthews was entrusted by the good people of Edenford to guard the prisoner until this hearing. A job, I fear, he has performed miserably. On one occasion I caught them bowling together! The curate was entrusted with guarding him, not entertaining him!" Laughter rippled through the room.

"On another occasion the curate left the prisoner completely unguarded in the street! The boy could have run away!"

"Which proves my point exactly!" Matthews countered. "Drew has had every chance to run away and he didn't!"

"He didn't run away because he knew I was following him!" the scrivener shouted.

"A single occasion," Matthews replied. "I still contend that if Drew Morgan intended to run away, he could have done so. If he intended to do us harm, he could have done so. He has done neither. If he is truly a criminal, he wouldn't be here today." Matthews sat down.

The high constable sighed. This was taking longer than he had hoped and he was getting hungry. He looked at the scrivener who would undoubtedly want to respond.

"The fact remains," Dudley said, "Drew Morgan had no permanent place of residence on the day he was arrested. By English law he is a vagabond and ought to be sentenced as such." Dudley sat down in apparent triumph.

With great reluctance the high constable asked, "Does anyone else have something to say?"

Drew scanned the room. Nell and Jenny were huddled together. Their heads were bowed. Behind them redheaded James Cooper had lost interest in the trial. He was staring blankly at the ceiling. David Cooper stood in the back against the wall, his huge hairy arms folded across his chest.

"If I may speak again," Christopher Matthews stood, this time with his father's Bible in hand.

Ambrose Dudley rolled his eyes upward.

Just then the back door of the church swung open, letting in a gust of cold air. Complaints from those standing in the back were short-lived when the latecomer was recognized. The constable sat up straight in his chair. When Drew saw who it was, his face drained of color. It was a good thing everyone was looking toward the back door because it took him a moment to compose himself.

Lord Chesterfield closed the door behind him. Totally self-absorbed, he acted like he had stepped into an empty room. Removing his outer cloak he took great care in arranging his clothing, smoothing wrinkles, straightening the lace on his shirt and sleeves. Like most noblemen, he was used to being stared at and waited on; in fact, he expected it, even enjoyed it. After making himself presentable, he looked at the high constable. "Continue with whatever you were doing," he said, with a casual sweep of his hand.

"It is an honor that you should join us," the high constable said. "I would be further honored if you would join me on the platform."

After another series of hand waves, as if brushing aside the constable's offer, he said, "Continue your business. When you're finished, I have something to tell the townspeople."

Four men seated on the back pew offered the lord their seats. He took all four places, spreading out his cloak. For Lord Chesterfield's sake, the high constable reviewed the charges, pointing toward the defendant. Drew Morgan watched intently for Lord Chesterfield's reaction. There was a flash of recognition, then a slight frown. A moment later Lord Chesterfield's expression became that of a bored nobleman who was forced to endure the trivial squabbling of commoners.

The high constable told Christopher Matthews to continue. Had the high constable known what the curate was about to say, he would have declared Drew guilty and been done with it.

Matthews cleared his throat. "As I was saying, according to English law there is little doubt that Master Morgan is guilty of being a vagabond. However, there is a higher issue at stake."

Ambrose Dudley grunted his disagreement.

"Hear me out, good scrivener. For we know you to be a good Christian man." Ambrose Dudley visibly started when the curate addressed him directly. "Master Dudley, how long have you lived as a resident of Edenford?"

Dudley went rigid. "Three years," he replied curtly. "For one year and two months as town scrivener."

"Three years and two months we have known this man,"

Matthews said. "With minor exception, he has fulfilled his duty with distinction. He attends church services faithfully. Even considering his actions regarding Drew Morgan we can only conclude that he is doing what he thinks is best for Edenford."

Puzzled faces appeared all around, especially on the face of the high constable. There was no question among the people regarding the character of Ambrose Dudley. What they didn't understand was why the curate would be saying these things now.

In answer to their puzzled expressions, the curate said, "I say this to make it clear that the issue at hand is not the performance of the scrivener's duty, for as always he has done his job with our best interests in mind according to English law. However, I contend that the real matter at hand is not whether Drew Morgan is a vagabond by English law, but whether the English law regarding vagabonds violates God's law!"

Ignoring the anticipated verbal reaction from the crowd and before the high constable could stop him, Matthews pressed on.

"According to English law, it is unlawful to travel the roads of England as a wanderer, not having a clear destination or a permanent place of residence. If Abraham, God's chosen father of the nation Israel, was alive today and subject to English law, he would be standing next to Master Morgan right now!" Opening his Bible the curate read, " 'By faith Abraham, when he was called, obeyed God, to go out into a place, which he should afterwards receive for an inheritance, and he went out, not knowing whither he went.' In fact, according to English law, the entire nation of Israel would have to be arrested!" Again the curate read, " 'And the LORD made them wander in the wilderness forty years.' Both Abraham and the entire nation of Israel would be guilty of breaking

English law. It makes me wonder, whom else would we have to arrest?"

The curate posed the question rhetorically, however a soft voice answered him from the pews. "We would have to arrest Jesus! Our Lord Himself admitted He was a vagabond." It was Nell. Quoting from memory, she continued, "Jesus said unto him, 'The foxes have holes, and the birds of the heaven have nests, but the Son of man hath not whereon to rest His head,' the Gospel according to Matthew, chapter 8, verse 20."

Another voice, this one husky and masculine from the back. "All of us should be arrested," David Cooper said. "Doesn't the book of Hebrews say we are all strangers and pilgrims on the earth?"

The high constable slapped the communion table with his hand several times. "The curate is the only one recognized to speak," he said. Then addressing the curate, "I will grant you that there have been other wanderers. However, they lived in a different time and a different place. This is England, in the year of our Lord 1629. And it is against the law to be a vagabond."

Matthews nodded. "My point is this: As Christians, what should we do when God's law and England's law do not agree? Which law should we obey?"

The constable was unnerved. This was clearly a question he did not wish to rule on. He glanced back at Lord Chesterfield for help. Chesterfield stared back at him, his face expressionless.

For several moments the high constable sat motionless, his head propped up by his arm resting on the communion table. "You still have yet to demonstrate that God's law says anything regarding vagabonds that is contrary to the laws of England," he finally replied. "The references you cite merely point out that the laws of biblical days are different from the laws today. You have not convinced me that God has given any specific instructions regarding vagabonds." The constable sat back in his chair, pleased with himself.

His victory was short-lived. The curate opened his Bible to a place marked with a piece of paper. It was then that Drew realized this was anything but an impromptu defense. The curate had carefully orchestrated the proceedings to this point. "From God's law as found in the book of Leviticus, chapter nineteen, verse 34, 'But the stranger that dwelleth with you, shall be as one of yourselves, and thou shalt love him as thyself: for ye were strangers in the land of Egypt: I am the Lord your God.' This is God's law regarding a sojourner, a traveler like Abraham or like Drew Morgan."

The high constable scratched the top of his head. He looked at Drew as if trying to understand why all this fuss was being made over him.

Looking to the back of the room, the high constable said, "Lord Chesterfield, this is your town. I defer to you. The boy seems harmless. What would you have me do with him?"

Lord Chesterfield sniffed, obviously unconcerned about the matters at hand. "I care not what you do with the boy," he said.

Upon hearing that Lord Chesterfield didn't care how he ruled, the high constable said, "In the case of Drew Morgan, it is my ruling that we should welcome him into Edenford as a stranger according to the dictates of God's Holy Word."

The brief celebration that followed was meager. Celebrating was confined to the Matthews family and a smile from David Cooper. Many of the people were disappointed, for the ruling meant there would be no punishment to add to the Market Day excitement.

In the years to come, Drew's trial would be overshadowed by the more memorable event of the day, Lord Chesterfield's announcement.

Following the trial, Lord Chesterfield went to the front of the church. There was a general buzzing among the townspeople.

On behalf of the town, the curate offered condolences regarding Chesterfield's missing son.

Lord Chesterfield acknowledged the comment with a casual nod, and cleared his throat. Then he informed the people of Edenford of two items of news that affected them directly. First, by order of King Charles, a tax to support the English navy was to be increased from 50 pounds to 75 pounds. This increase would compensate for the 25-pound decrease in ship money required of neighboring Tiverton.

Second, the people were informed that John de la Barre, a prominent Exeter clothier who had purchased the largest share of Edenford's serges, had been granted a protection by the king. In other words, not only would the town not receive the 850 pounds the clothier owed them, but they could not take legal action against him.

The double blow to the town's economy was catastrophic. It destroyed more than a year's worth of work and the people were powerless to do anything about it.

Edenford wasn't the first town to be affected this way. The king's action in these matters was not arbitrary. His rulings against Edenford followed a clear pattern. As in so many other villages, the king had ruled against them because they were Puritans.

Chapter 13

THE prey had defended the predator. This irony of his trial was not lost on Drew. Had Christopher Matthews remained silent and let the obese constable and the scarecrow scrivener do their jobs, he could have saved himself from the long arm of Laud. But then, the curate didn't know he was defending his enemy.

A quiet week had passed since the trial. Drew was lying on his bedding in front of the fire in the curate's sitting room. As he reviewed the events in Edenford, he came to one conclusion: Christopher Matthews was making his job easy.

He took mental inventory of the evidence he had against the curate: The man had libeled King James, accusing King Charles' father of immorality; and the church communion table was not properly placed, nor was it railed off. This was an irrefutable charge. The whole town witnessed its abuse by the high constable during the trial. Even if none of the townspeople would bare witness against their curate, there was always Lord Chesterfield. He saw it too.

The thought of the lace-covered lord made Drew wonder if Lord Chesterfield recognized him at the trial. For an instant it seemed as if he did. Now Drew wasn't so sure. That led to another thought, a disturbing one. Would Lord Chesterfield testify against the man who was instrumental in his highly profitable wool business?

A noise at the head of the stairs diverted Drew's attention. It was the sound of a heavy book closing followed by the scraping of a chair pushed across the wooden floor. Drew guessed it had been over an hour since Nell, Jenny, and the curate had said their good-nights. However, there was still a light coming from the curate's study. He was probably working on Sunday's sermon. Drew let out a sigh. He wished the curate would go to bed. He didn't feel safe decoding a message from Bishop Laud until everyone was asleep.

He'd received the message early today, delivered to him by—who else?—Christopher Matthews. The curate said the courier had been told Drew might be found in either Tiverton, Exeter, or Plymouth. The curate saw it as God's providence that the courier happened to inquire about Drew while passing through Edenford. Of course, Drew knew divine providence had nothing to do with it. The courier had been told exactly where Drew could be found.

Drew looked upstairs again. The light was still burning. Was the curate going to stay up all night? Drew unfolded the paper bearing the bishop's message. He reasoned the chances of his being interrupted at this late hour were few and decided to risk it.

The familiar round numbers on the page made Drew homesick for London—the library at London House, the round cook's meals, the late night talks with the bishop about knights and adventures. All these things stood in sharp contrast to his present shabby surroundings.

Opening his Bible, he stretched out on his belly in front of the fire and decoded the message. It read: (50/1/3) (53/2/3/1-8) (20/11/5/11-18) (53/2/5) (60/4/17/1-9) (50/4/1/4-21). *"I thank my God upon every remembrance of you. Let no man deceive you by any means. The wicked shall fall by his own wickedness. Remember ye not, that, when I was yet with you, I told you these things? For the time is come that judgment must begin. Dearly beloved and longed for, my joy and crown, so stand fast in the Lord, my dearly beloved."*

Drew frowned. The message disturbed him. Sitting up he read it again. Why was the bishop concerned about the mission so soon? The message was couched in friendly talk, but still there was clearly a measure of doubt in the bishop's mind. *"Let no man deceive you."* What made the bishop think someone was deceiving him? *"Remember ye not, that, when I was yet with you, I told you these things?"* Drew strained his memory to identify the conversation to which the bishop was referring. Was he referring to their discussion following Marshall Ramsden's trial? That could be it. Maybe the bishop was concerned that he might get emotionally attached to Christopher Matthews. Or was someone feeding the bishop erroneous information?

Then there was the sentence about time: *"For the time is come that judgment must begin."* Was Laud saying his time in Edenford was short? If so, how short? And why?

Even though the message concluded with a sentimental ending which he had come to expect, it disturbed him that Laud had doubts about his ability to complete this mission.

As the last of the flames in the hearth died leaving only glowing embers, Drew placed the coded message in the front of his Bible, lay on his back, and stared at the darkened beams running from wall to wall across the ceiling. He thought fondly of the bishop, the man who called him away from the misery of Morgan Hall, one of two men responsible for his deliverance—his grandfather being the other. The one called him away, the other sent him away. *"Abandon ship! Abandon ship!"* He smiled as he remembered his grandfather's words. Now that he had been away for several months, he couldn't understand his attraction to Morgan Hall. Let Philip have it. In time, he'd build something grander, something that was his and his alone, something no one could take from him.

Of course, at that time the greatest attraction of Morgan Hall was the admiral. Drew wondered if he would have stayed had his grandfather not died.

"Never had much use for those religious types." Wasn't that what the admiral had said about the bishop? Drew chuckled softly. He wondered if his grandfather and the bishop would have been friends had they met.

They're so much alike, Drew thought, *both passionate idealists, wanting glory for England at any cost. The bishop fought for England's glory through the church, the admiral on the sea.*

Another similarity between them was that they were both alone. Neither had close friends. Well, the admiral had John Hawkins and of course Georgiana, but that was before Drew's time; and the bishop had Timmins, hardly a friend though, more like a trusted advisor. To his knowledge Drew was closer to both men than anyone else. He was good for them. And they were good for him.

From humble beginnings both the admiral and the bishop had risen to the pinnacle of their professions. The admiral was a shipbuilder's son and Laud came from a family of clothiers. This is what Drew admired most about them: they were strong men who would not be denied their dreams; passionate men who knew what they believed and who were willing to fight for it, no matter what the cost.

Just then an uneasy realization lodged in Drew's mind, a cold-water realization, the kind that douses the fire of grandiose thoughts. Then, before he had time to digest the first realization, it spawned a second one, equally disturbing. Drew's eyes darted back and forth as he wrestled with the twin disturbances.

The first disturbing realization was that he, unlike the admiral and the bishop, had no strong beliefs to fight for. Who ever heard of a knight without a cause? The bishop fought to preserve the Church of England, a cause for which he would

willingly die. The admiral fought to protect England from
Spanish aggression, a noble cause for which he nearly died.
What am I fighting for? England? The king? And who am I
fighting against? Who are my enemies? Grandfather hated the
Spanish, Laud the Puritans. Whom do I hate?

He thought of Marshall Ramsden and Mary Sedgewick and
felt no hatred for them. *What about Christopher Matthews?*
Jenny? Nell? Are they my enemies? Drew found it difficult
to imagine them being a threat to England's crown, nor could
he muster any hatred for them. The things they stood for
were crazy and their actions were illegal, but the Puritans
weren't the seditious plotters of rebellion he expected
them to be. His lack of passion against his enemy disturbed
him.

The second disturbing realization, born out of the first, had
to do with the fact that he was all alone. Not only did he not
have a cause, but neither did he have a friend, someone his
age he felt close to.

In his stronger moments Drew told himself he didn't need
anyone else. But there was something inside him that longed
to be close to others, a wife certainly, but also male friends.
He had none.

He envied Christopher Matthews, a man surrounded by
love. He loved his daughters and they loved him. He had
close friends, David Cooper for one, but the whole town
seemed to love him. It seemed that even God loved him!
Drew had never seen a man so openly love God and live in
the certainty that God loved him.

Who loves me? The closest persons in my life are the bishop
and Eliot. Who else? Nobody. Whom do I love?

His lack of an answer made him feel even more alone and
empty. Like two specters, these twin disturbances haunted
Drew most of the night. He had no cause and he knew not
love.

Drew stirred fitfully as sleep finally overtook him. His last thoughts were of Nell Matthews.

The old wooden chair creaked as Nell leaned back and shoved her journal to the back of her father's desk. She angrily rubbed her tired eyes, then folded her arms across her chest. The journal, a quill, and an inkwell were bunched in front of her, together with her Bible and a few sheets of blank paper. The journal lay before her, ready to receive her daily spiritual reflections. The page was blank and that infuriated her. It wasn't for lack of thoughts, since her mind was cluttered with them. It's just that they weren't spiritual thoughts. They were thoughts of Drew Morgan.

"Well now, what can we do for God this day?"

Christopher Matthews' hands were folded on top of his Bible following the morning prayers and daily Bible reading. He looked from person to person seated around the table, expecting an answer.

Drew was still pondering the Bible reading. In the passage Jesus had healed a man born blind. The healing attracted great opposition, for reasons Drew didn't understand. He wanted to ask the curate to explain, but Nell would probably look at him like he was a dunce, so he didn't ask. The thing that he liked about the story was the way Jesus stood up to His enemies. Something Jesus said so impressed Drew he asked the curate to repeat it so that he could write it down, no matter what Nell thought of him. "I must do the work of Him who sent Me, while it is day. For the night comes when no man can work." Jesus was a Man with a mission. Like his grandfather and the bishop, Jesus had a mission to fulfill and no one could stop Him.

There it was again — mission. It seemed like everyone had a mission. Everyone except himself.

Then, almost miraculously, the clouds in his mind parted and he saw his mission. He saw it clearly. *What have I always wanted all my life? Adventure and glory. The life of a knight! I want stories to be told about me, young boys to want to be like me, my name to be mentioned alongside Arthur, Lancelot, Gawain.*

My mission is myself! I will build myself a reputation of fame and wealth and glory. How can I fulfill this mission? By earning the gratitude of king and court. The king is the dispenser of glory and fame and wealth. And if the king wants Puritans in exchange for these things, I will give him Puritans.

Drew felt a heady rush of excitement. He was a man with a mission. And nothing was going to stop him. "I must do the work of Him who sent Me." Drew liked the words. He also asked the curate for the reference. It would be a good line to use in his next message to the bishop.

Nell was the first to answer her father's question. "Jenny and I have Lord Chesterfield's lace to complete. It will take us most of the day to finish. And, if I know Lord Chesterfield, he'll send a servant down two or three times today to see if it's ready. I pray the Lord will grant us an double measure of patience, a measure for us and a measure for Lord Chesterfield."

Matthews looked at his younger daughter. Keeping her eyes fixed on the table in front of her, she said, "Nell already said what we'll be doing today. And now that the trial's over, I just hope we can convince Master Morgan to stay in Edenford." She blushed and lowered her head still further.

"I could always stay and read the Bible to you and Nell while you work," Drew offered.

Now both girls blushed. Jenny started giggling. Nell joined her. The perplexed curate looked from them to Drew and back to them. "Am I missing something?" he asked.

Giggles turned to guffaws.

Grinning, Matthews said to Drew, "I suppose you're responsible for this."

Laughing with the girls, Drew shrugged his shoulders, feigning innocence.

Still grinning, Matthews rose and signaled Drew to accompany him. He led Drew out the door. "Drew," he said, "I want you to know you're welcome to stay with us as long as you like. It's the least we can do, considering how the town has treated you."

"Thank you," Drew responded. "But I've presumed on your hospitality too much already."

"Have you given any thought to what you're going to do now?"

Recently, Drew said to himself. To Matthews he said, "I'm not sure. I should probably continue on to Plymouth. I don't know. I'm just not sure I want to be a sailor anymore."

"I wouldn't blame you for wanting to get out of Edenford as soon as possible. We didn't exactly give you a grand reception."

Drew chuckled. "This may sound crazy," he said, "but it wasn't that bad. I've grown to like this town. With a few exceptions the people are friendly. Everyone seems happy. It's like a big family. I only hope that someday I can be part of a town like this one."

"Why a town *like* this one? Why not become part of Edenford's family?"

Drew intentionally hesitated before answering. "I'd like that . . . it's just that I don't know anything about making wool. And I don't have a place to live."

"If you're worried about a place to live, you're welcome to stay with us."

There it was, just what Drew was fishing for. And it came so easily.

"I don't know," he said. "It would be a hardship for you.

Besides, I don't have a job."

"I've been thinking about that too. I'd like to make a proposal," Matthews said.

They reached the end of High Street and turned toward the south bridge. Neither man looked at the other when they spoke; they focused on the ground before them as they ambled down the road.

"Drew, in the short time I've known you, I've come to admire you. I was watching you carefully during the trial. You held your composure in a tense situation. That's a rare gift. I remember thinking to myself, 'God has great plans for this young man.' And now I'm more convinced of that than ever." The curate paused a moment, letting that thought sink in. Then he said, "I want to help you find God's will for your life."

This is too easy, Drew thought.

"I want to make you my apprentice."

"As curate?" Drew stopped and stared at Matthews in disbelief.

The curate laughed. "In a sense, yes. The position would include teaching you about spiritual things. Whether or not you became curate would be up to God. I was thinking more in terms of Edenford's woolen industry."

Drew resumed walking. The idea left him cold. "I'm flattered," he said.

It was Matthews' turn to stop. He faced Drew squarely. "For me, it would be an answer to prayer. Let me explain. In the Bible, the Apostle Paul had a son in the Lord—an adopted spiritual son whose name was Timothy. For years, I've been praying that God would send me a spiritual son." The curate paused, his eyes lowered. With broken voice he said, "Drew, I believe you're God's answer to my prayer."

Drew didn't have to fake a reaction. The curate's emotions moved him. He didn't know what to say.

"All I ask is that you pray about it. We don't have much to offer you except the space in front of the fireplace, but it's yours for as long as you want it, or until you can afford a place of your own. If you would feel more comfortable elsewhere, we could probably work a deal with Charles Manly, our innkeeper."

Aside from the unexpected display of emotion, Drew couldn't have asked for more. Christopher Matthews continued to make his job easy; he was inviting Drew into the town's confidence, and once he had their confidence he would learn their secret. With hushed voice, Drew said, "I'll think about it."

Of course, there was nothing to think about. Like fishing, he threw out a baited line and the fish jumped at it. Now all he had to do was haul in the catch without losing him.

For weeks Lord Chesterfield's devastating news hung like a dark cloud over the people of Edenford. The gloomy economic forecast colored every aspect of town life a depressing shade of gray.

Sunday dawned clear and bright. It was the kind of day that made atheists wish they believed in God, just so they could have someone to thank. The wild flowers alongside the river waved their faces heavenward to the glory of God. The crisp air, warm sunlight, and blue sky formed a trio of praise while the fields and trees and waters danced beneath them.

All this was lost on the people of Edenford. The king's ship tax and his favored protection of clothier de la Barre covered their eyes like a pair of sooty lenses.

David Cooper didn't see the sparkling blue canopy overhead as he stepped outside the cobbler shop on the way to church. The stack of unpaid receipts on his bench loomed high in his mind. He would greet the people whose names appeared on those receipts and see that they were wearing shoes he made, shoes for which they had not paid. And how could they pay? The king had robbed them of their livelihood. He understood their situation, but did they understand his? He had a choice. He could buy leather to make more shoes or he could buy food for his family. He couldn't do both.

Cyrus Furman, town watchman, shuffled his normal shuffle on the way to church, his ailing wife clinging to his side with thin pale arms. The past winter had been a sickly one for his Rose, almost a deadly one. Twice she had stopped breathing, only to be spared. But not before the disease had taken its toll. It had consumed her strength and a large portion of flesh, leaving nothing more than a frail frame. Since her illness it took the Furmans twice as long to walk the short distance to church. Rose had to stop and rest every ten steps. Patiently Cyrus held his wife's hand against his arm while she caught her breath.

He was blind to the wild daisies waving to him from the side of the road. He wondered what would happen to Rose. As town watchman his income depended on the sale of serges. How could the town pay him, now that de la Barre's debt was forgiven? How would he care for Rose?

Charles Manly and Ambrose Dudley, both bachelors, walked together to church like always. The warmth of the sun's rays were ignored. The only heat they were aware of was the heat in their conversation.

"We should refuse to pay the ship tax!" Manly grumbled.

"Barnstaple tried that," Dudley replied.

"What happened?"

"The dissenters were whipped and pilloried."

Manly mulled the thought in his mind.

"The thing that angers me," Dudley said, "is that the ship tax isn't needed."

"How do you know that?"

"The last time I was in London, I ran into the Earl of Northumberland. He told me that last winter he patrolled the coast in miserable weather. Not only did he not encounter hostile forces, but he encountered almost no foreign ships at all! He said he finally returned to port in disgust. There is no emergency. No danger."

"So why the tax?"

"The king wants more money, plain and simple. So he creates an imaginary crisis and levies a new tax."

The bachelors were usually the first worshipers to reach the church building on Sundays, besides the curate and his daughters. This Sunday was no exception. The two men thought it odd that the front doors were closed when they arrived. Had the curate overslept? To deepen their minor mystery, when they pulled on the latch, they found the doors locked.

"Master Manly, Master Dudley, over here!"

The men turned in the direction of the soft voice. It was Jenny Matthews. "We're having church over here today." She led them under some trees on the south side of the church building. The village green stretched before them. There they found the curate, Nell, and Drew Morgan.

"God be with you, gentlemen," the curate greeted.

The bachelors frowned as they shook his hand, obviously not pleased with the new arrangement.

The curate explained, "It would be a crime against God to meet inside on a wonderful day."

Their expressions showed their displeasure. Nor were they alone in their opinion.

The children loved it. They chased each other and rolled in the grass. The adults huddled in small groups and Drew thought they sounded like beehives. One huddle appointed a churchwarden to voice their disapproval to the curate. Christopher Matthews listened politely, then proceeded to convene the service.

"Where are we going to sit?" someone yelled.

Matthews spread his arms wide, indicating the grass.

More grumbling, this time louder with comments bordering on insurrection.

The curate was ready for them. "The Feeding of the Five Thousand," he shouted. "I quote, 'And Jesus commanded the multitude to sit down on the grass,' Matthew 14:19." He stood firm with authority in his eyes. "If our Lord did not think the grass an undignified place to sit, neither should we."

Drew learned something about Puritans that day. They'll do anything if the Bible approves it. To his surprise, everyone—the bachelors, the churchwardens, the Coopers, even old Cyrus and Rose Furman—found a place to sit on the grass.

The church service began. Although the setting was unusual, the service was exactly the one being performed at St. Michael's Church in London and at all other state churches in England. In distraught Edenford, the service served its purpose. The familiar phrases spoken by the curate, the responses by the congregation at appropriate times, the traditional hymns, all these things brought a sense of order and peace to their troubled lives, like a ship's anchor during a summer squall.

This part of the service would have pleased the Bishop of London. Phrase by phrase, word by word, it followed the sanctioned order of service. It was what followed that would have unnerved him—the preaching, especially the unrestricted preaching of an unlearned, unlicensed preacher.

The old homilies of 1563 were written for ill-educated preachers and were to be read aloud to the congregations. But the Puritans would have nothing to do with them. They preferred prophesying, a message from the Bible interpreted and applied by their preacher. They wanted to know what the Bible said about life, about marriage, about children and work, about ship taxes and capricious monarchs. They desired more than the anchor of tradition, they wanted a fresh breeze from the Captain of their ship.

Prophesyings became so popular that many Puritans required two sermons on Sunday. Bishop Laud forbade a second service, ordering catechism to be held on Sunday afternoons instead. So hungry were the people for preaching that many Puritans would walk to a neighboring town for a second sermon if their church had only one.

The curate of Edenford preached twice on Sundays with catechism between services. The families planned accordingly. They brought baskets of food and ate on the village green in between events.

With the spirit and urgency of an Old Testament prophet, Matthews prophesied to the townspeople of Edenford regarding the recent devastating news.

" 'What are we going to do?' That's the question I've heard most often since Market Day. 'What are we going to do?' I've been asked the same question by women at the well, by workers at the dyeing vats, by shopkeepers, by husbands and wives in their homes, by my daughters at my own dinner table. 'What are we going to do?' "

Matthews paused. The unanswered question hung over the people like an executioner's blade.

"We're asking the wrong question," he continued. " 'What are we going to do?' is the question of a hopeless and helpless people. It's the question of a people looking to themselves for answers. And the people who look only to themselves for answers to life's problems are drawing from a shallow well.

"What question should we be asking? I'll tell you. We should be asking ourselves, 'What would God have us do?'

"Are we so filled with pride to think that something strange and unusual is happening to us? That we are the only people who have faced a crisis like this? That God is so shortsighted He has failed to supply us with sufficient guidance with His Word?"

The curate opened his Bible. "An incident similar to ours occurred in the days when God's Son walked the earth. In those days the Roman emperor levied taxes. The Jewish people didn't like the emperor's tax any more than we like the king's tax. Some advocated not paying the tax, but Jesus had a word for them."

The curate read from his Bible, " 'And they sent unto Him their disciples with the Herodians, saying, "Master, we know that Thou art true, and teachest the way of God truely, neither carest for any man: for Thou considerest not the person of men. Tell us, therefore, how thinkest Thou? Is it lawful to give tribute unto Caesar, or not?" But Jesus perceived their wickedness, and said, "Why tempt ye Me, ye hypocrites? Show Me the tribute money." And they brought Him a penny. And He said unto them, "Whose is this image and superscription?" They said unto Him, "Caesar's." Then said He unto them, "Give therefore to Caesar the things that are Caesar's, and give unto God those which are God's." ' "

The curate pulled a coin from his pocket. In silence he deliberately examined both sides. Drew was too far away to identify the coin. It might have been a shilling, possibly a half-crown.

"This is an English coin. It bears the image of an English monarch. And we are subjects of the English crown. Were Jesus standing here today and were we to hand Him this coin and ask Him our question, 'What would God have us do?' He would undoubtedly say, 'Render therefore unto your king the things which are the king's, and unto God the things that are God's.' "

The curate replaced the coin in his pocket.

"What would God have us do? Pay the king's ship tax!"

There was no vocal dissent. This was not a town meeting; it

was a church service and the town's prophet was prophesying. However, some of the men shifted uneasily.

"Now I know what most of you are thinking," the curate said, anticipating their reaction. "You're saying to yourselves, 'But *how* are we going to pay the ship tax?'"

Several men in the congregation nodded.

The curate opened his well-worn Bible to a second place. Before reading from it, he set the scene. "I imagine it was a day very much like today when Jesus spoke these words. The sun was shining. The sky was clear. And Jesus' followers were sitting on a hillside waiting for a word from God. They were poor people, working people. They were not learned people, for if Jesus had wanted to address the learned, He would have spoken to the Sanhedrin. They were not rich and noble, for if Jesus had wanted to address the rich and noble, He would have gone to the palace. Instead, He was on a hillside addressing men and women who had little money and no security. This is what He told them, 'Therefore I say unto you, be not careful for your life, what ye shall eat, or what ye shall drink: nor yet for your body, what ye shall put on. Is not the life more worth then meat? and the body than raiment? Behold the fowls of the heaven: for they sow not, neither reap, nor carry into the barns: yet your Heavenly Father feedeth them. Are ye not much better than they? Which of you by taking care, is able to add one cubit unto his stature? And why care ye for raiment? Learn how the lilies of the field do grow: they labor not, neither spin: Yet I say unto you, that even Solomon in all his glory was not arrayed like one of these. Wherefore if God so clothe the grass of the field which is today, and tomorrow is cast into the oven, shall He not do much more unto you, O ye of little faith? Therefore take no thought saying, What shall we eat? or what shall we drink? or wherewith shall we be clothed? (For after all these things seek the Gentiles) for your Heavenly Father knoweth that ye have need of all these things. But seek ye first the kingdom of God, and His righteousness, and all these things shall be ministered unto you.' "

Slowly, reverently, the curate closed his Bible. He looked into the faces of his congregation. Rose Furman lay back against her husband's chest, her eyes closed and her wrinkled face lifted toward the sun.

In soft tones the curate repeated a portion of the Scripture passage. " 'Therefore take no thought . . . for your Heavenly Father knoweth that ye have need of all these things.' What would God have us do? He would have us pay the king's ship tax. How are we going to pay it? God knows our needs. He will provide a way. In the meantime, we must live by faith in God's Word. Faith does not wear a long face. Faith does not fret. Faith will not waste a beautiful day like today with concern for tomorrow. 'This is the day which the LORD hath made: let us rejoice and be glad in it!' "

Edenford's response to the curate's sermon amazed Drew. Although the circumstances were unchanged, everything was different. People were chatting and laughing, children were playing. By their mood, you would have thought the king had rescinded his tax and John de la Barre had agreed to pay the money he owed them.

Families gathered together all across the village green; some sat in the shade of the trees lining the road, others enjoyed the sun. Nell and Jenny had prepared a lunch of bread, cheese, and fruit. As Drew ate with the Matthews, a stream of people came by to talk to the curate. David Cooper was one of the first.

"Thanks for reminding me that God's in control," he said, giving his friend a bear hug. James was with him and knelt beside Nell, saying something so low Drew couldn't hear it. Nell's response was a cool shrug of her shoulders.

No sooner had the Coopers left than Cyrus and Rose Furman stopped by. The curate inquired into Rose's health and assured the elderly couple that something would be worked out regarding the watchman's pay.

The Furmans were followed by the bachelors, Manly and Dudley, and the Pierce family. And so it went until the whole village had stopped by. The conversation was almost identical with each group.

"It's like this all the time," Jenny whispered, as Drew watched the curate fail in his fourth attempt to take a bite of bread. "The typical life of a curate's family," Nell added.

Sunday afternoon was reserved for catechism. The curate taught the children, assisted by his daughters who took turns every other Sunday. That Sunday it was Jenny's turn. Much to his delight, Drew was left alone with Nell.

Together, they packed the remains of lunch in the basket. Afterward, Nell leaned against a tree, arranging her dress neatly across her outstretched legs which were crossed at the ankles. While surveying the residents of Edenford at play on the green, she rubbed her hands. Starting at the base of each finger she worked her way toward the tip. It looked like she was forcing the knots out of the ends of her fingertips. That done, she leaned her head against the trunk, folded her arms and closed her eyes.

Drew was reclining on his side, his head propped against his hand. He watched some men bowling on the far side of the green. Trying not to be obvious, he stole occasional glances at Nell. When she closed her eyes, he was more obvious about it. Smooth skin stretched over her cheekbones, then down a shallow hollow toward her chin. Her nose had a gentle slope to it, coming to a slight peak before curving under to join her full upper lip.

"Are you staring at me?" she demanded, her eyes still closed.

"Don't flatter yourself!"

"Well, if you are, it wouldn't be the first time."

Drew looked away. In the middle of the green a group of young men had gathered in a circle. James Cooper stood in the middle, arms locked in a wrestling hold with another boy. The shouts of the bystanders caused Nell to open her eyes. Her eyes flashed when she recognized James. She leaned her head back against the tree and let out a disgusted groan.

"What's the matter?"

"That!" She pointed at the wrestlers.

"I don't understand."

Her voice heavy with sarcasm, she replied, "I'm not surprised. But James Cooper will certainly get it if his father finds out he's been wrestling on Sunday again."

Playing his part as an ignorant pagan, Drew said, "He's not supposed to wrestle on Sundays?"

"Of course not!"

Drew knew full well that the wrestling match, and other Sunday recreational activities were protected by decree of King James, much to the chagrin of the Puritans.

For a dozen years Sunday afternoon recreation had been a controversial issue in England. It began in 1616 when a delegation of servants and laborers waited in Lancashire for King James to return from Scotland. When he arrived they complained that church leaders prevented them from all recreations on Sunday afternoons. The upshot of the incident was King James's *Book of Sports* which authorized people to enjoy themselves on Sunday afternoons with various sports. The king's decree angered the Puritans and they were not shy in expressing their opposition. Their arguments fell on deaf ears.

To emphasize his authority over the Puritans, King James ordered that his *Book of Sports* be read from the pulpit in all churches. Most ministers grudgingly complied. Some exercised creative interpretations of the decree which were designed to fulfill the letter of the law, yet still give commentary on the act. For example, one church had the churchwarden read the *Book of Sports* while the minister sat in the front pew with his hands over his ears. Another minister read the *Book of Sports* and followed it with a reading of the Ten Commandments. He then urged his congregation to choose which they would follow. There were a few cases where daring clergymen refused to obey the king's command. If discovered, these were punished.

"You really think it's wrong for them to wrestle on Sunday?"

"This is the Lord's Day," came the curt reply. "And more importantly for James Cooper, his father believes it's wrong."

"Are you going to tell Master Cooper?"

An anguished look crossed Nell's face as she looked at the young men now rolling on the ground. "If I'm not here to see it, there will be nothing to tell," she said, getting up. She brushed the grass from her dress and stepped into the road. Turning to Drew who was still reclining on the ground, she said, "You're not going to let a helpless maiden wander off by herself, are you?"

It's a good thing Drew was already on the ground; for if he hadn't been, Nell's invitation would have felled him. Jumping to his feet, he joined her.

"Where are we going?"

She held out her arm for him to take. "I'm not going to tell you. You'll just have to trust me."

Nell Matthews led Drew Morgan up Chesterfield Road toward Chesterfield Manor. The dirt road rose before them at an increasingly steep angle. They passed the ends of two rows of houses, packed together like the ones on High Street where the Matthews lived. Edenford's looms were housed in a large building behind the second row of houses. "That's where my mother worked before she began making lace," Nell said. Behind the looms was a field and the base of the mountain.

Drew took little note of buildings and scenery. His awareness focused on his closeness to Nell. To feel her arm entwined in his, to brush against her side, to be inches away from her face—these sensations intoxicated him. As she pointed out other industry-related sights, he looked at her cheeks which were flushed from the walk, the rebellious wisps of hair that blew across her forehead, and the flecks of gray in her brown eyes.

"Let's rest here a moment." They had reached the tree line on the mountain. Nell stopped, pulled her arm from Drew's, and turned back toward the village. Reluctantly, Drew followed her lead. With their arms no longer linked, she stepped a discreet distance away from him.

From this elevation, they could see all of Edenford, the rooftops of the houses, the church building, and the village green where the wrestling match was still going on. Dominating the scene was the River Exe with Bridge Street crossing it twice over identical three-arched stone bridges.

A sparkling light caught Drew's eyes in the far distance to his left. "What's that over there?"

Nell followed Drew's gaze. "Oh, that's Williams Lake. And the forest on the far side is Lord Chesterfield's forest. He stocks it with all sorts of game and invites his rich friends to play hunting with him."

Where Bishop Laud killed Lord Chesterfield's son, Drew thought. *And where Shubal Elkins' body was found.*

"It's an interesting lake," Nell continued. "It never freezes over, even in the winter. Probably fed by thermal underground springs. I'll take you there this winter, let you see for yourself. That is, if you're still around."

If you're still around. It was meant to be a casual remark, but to Drew it had the weight of prophecy. If all went as planned, he would not be around. But then neither would Christopher Matthews. The thought provoked unwanted feelings; he was determined to fulfill his mission, and he forced himself not to think of what that would do to Nell.

"Come on." Nell grabbed his hand. "This is what I wanted to show you." She pulled him off the road and up a grassy slope.

As they crested a ridge, ancient castle walls overlooking the valley rose up before him. The crumbling walls were partially hidden by trees on three sides, as if the forest were reaching out to reclaim the land taken from it by the builder of the castle.

Nell walked to the center of what had once been a large room. Patches of weeds carpeted the floor under her feet. "Do you like it?"

"This is great!" Drew's gaze followed the tops of the broken walls as they stretched farther into the forest. None of the stone walls was over three feet high, but the layout of the castle was still plainly evident—doorways, halls, rooms, storage areas. It was magnificent.

"Just think, someone used to live here," Nell said. "She stood right where I'm standing and probably worried about her children playing in the river, wondered if her husband would come back from a war, or whether they would have enough food for the winter."

"Who used to live here?" Drew asked.

"Nobody in town knows," she replied. "All anyone knows is that it was a Saxon king."

"Sad, isn't it?"

"What?"

"That a person or maybe an entire family lived and died and nobody even remembers them. I mean, these people had hopes, dreams, ambitions; and nobody remembers anything about them. They might as well never have been born."

The two were silent, lost in thought about the unknown family.

Nell and Drew followed each other from room to room exploring the ancient stones, taking turns describing how they thought the completed structure once looked, guessing the identity of the various rooms, and imagining what it must have been like to live in the castle.

After a while Nell sat on a wall beside a low tree limb. Drew perched on a large rectangular stone opposite her. The large stone seemed out of place. It was the same type of stone as the walls, but was too large to be one of the wall stones. Neither did it look like it belonged anywhere else. It was a mystery, just like the mystery of the castle's occupants and the secret of the little village situated below it.

"My father is quite taken with you." Nell's statement brought them back to present time.

"What makes you think that?"

"I can tell." Nell pulled the tree's low branch toward her and played with the leaves as she talked, wiping them clean and layering them like a fan. "Poppa likes everyone, but he's very selective about the people he respects. He respects you. If he didn't, he never would have left you alone with Jenny and me the other day."

"I'm glad he did."

"I just don't know what he sees in you," Nell sniffed.

Drew frowned. "Why do you say that?"

Nell let go of the leaves and the branch sprang back into place. She placed her hands on the edge of the wall and leaned forward. "You have no trade, no future, and no personal faith. In fact, I'm not even sure you believe in God."

"I believe in God!" Drew protested.

"Oh? What do you believe? Tell me about your God."

"Well," Drew searched his mind, he had never before been

called on to put his spiritual beliefs into words. He was confident he had some, or at least he thought he was confident, but putting them into words was a different matter.

"I'm waiting." There was a smugness in Nell's voice that infuriated Drew.

"Well, for one thing, He's up there!" Drew pointed upward.

Nell looked up. "In the trees?"

She was toying with him. "Of course not! He's in heaven!"

"I see," said Nell. "And what does He do in heaven all day long?"

Drew had never thought about it before. The only images that came to mind were those of Greek mythology where the gods were promiscuous and spiteful, amusing themselves by complicating people's lives. "He answers prayers and does other God things!" Drew stammered.

"God things?" Nell stifled a chuckle.

"Sure, God things. How do I know what God things are? I've never been to heaven!" Drew hopped off his stone perch and walked away from the amused curate's daughter. He walked only a short distance. "Did you bring me up here to make fun of me?"

Nell stopped giggling. She reached for the tree limb again. "No. I'm sorry." She began picking at the leaves. "That was mean of me. I just find it odd that someone who carries a Bible with him on his travels knows so little about it."

"Maybe I want to learn more about it."

Now it was Nell's turn to be embarrassed. She stared at the leaves as she picked them from the limb one at a time. "If you truly want to learn the Bible, my father's the one who can teach you," she said.

"I know." Drew welcomed the change of subject, anything that shifted attention away from himself. He walked casually to where Nell was sitting and sat on the stone wall next to her, but not too close. "He really surprised me this morning. He's a much better preacher than I thought he would be."

"Most people are surprised." Nell smiled with unconcealed pride.

"Has your father had any university training?"

Nell shook her head. "No, everything he's learned, he learned from his father in a cobbler's shop."

"But he knows the Bible so well! And he presents it so well in his preaching." A thought occurred to Drew. Here was a chance to fish for some information about the curate. "I'll bet he's a good writer as well," he said.

Nell laughed. "No," she said. "No, my father communicates well verbally. God has blessed him with an incredible speaking ability. But when it comes to writing, he gets all knotted up. I think it's because he takes it too seriously and tries too hard."

Drew's hook came back empty. Since the curate was good with words, Drew thought he might possibly be one of the infamous Puritan pamphleteers, maybe even Justin himself. Nell's comment destroyed that theory. Unless, of course, she recognized the question as a trap and was protecting her father.

The conversation lagged. Neither seemed in any hurry to leave, but they didn't know what to talk about next. Nell was the first to break the silence.

"Drew, what do you want out of life?"

This woman isn't one for casual conversation, Drew thought. *First, she's asking me about God, and now she wants to know the meaning of my existence. This is not your typical courting conversation.* He had already been cut once today by Nell's barbed wit, so he was cautious. "I really don't know," he said.

"Well, what kind of things do you dream about?"

He looked hard at her. There was no hint of playfulness on her face. Her eyes were soft and inviting. "I'm not sure I want to tell you," he said.

Nell's eyes and mouth expressed disappointment. She hopped down from the wall. "Maybe we should go back now," she said.

"Nell!" Drew pleaded. "It's just that the things I dream about can't possibly come true."

"Why not?"

Drew hesitated. He wanted to be open with her, but he knew that if he was, he would be making himself vulnerable. *What if she laughs?* "They can't come true because . . ." he stopped. He looked at her again. She was intent and serious. "They can't come true because they're past. I dream about the past."

Nell smiled. It wasn't the smile of a predator about to pounce; her smile was warm and understanding, the kind that says, "Thank you for sharing your feelings with me." It filled Drew with an unusual warmth. "Any particular time period?" she asked.

He was in it this far, he might as well go all the way. "This one," he said pointing to the fallen stone walls. "The age of Camelot and King Arthur. The age of chivalry and might for right. I think I like it because everything was simpler. You knew who was good and who was evil. Men fought to make the world a better place, not just so their house could be bigger than someone else's or so their clothes better or so their wives could wear more expensive jewelry."

"You're an idealist!" Nell cried, showing genuine surprise. "It's not a very easy thing to be in today's world."

"Not very realistic, that's for sure."

Nell was looking at him with an expression he had never seen before. It was a look of admiration.

"Well," Drew said, "now it's your turn. What do you dream about?"

Nell turned to leave. "It really is time we started back."

Drew blocked her way. "Oh, no you don't. It's only fair. What do you dream about?"

She tried stepping around him. Drew grabbed her by the shoulders. Fury flashed in her eyes like the drawing of a sword. Had he made a fatal mistake? Apparently hers was a reflex action, because an instant later the fury faded. She searched his eyes with hers. Now it was her turn to decide if she wanted to make herself vulnerable. She smiled and turned away, choosing not to look at him as she spoke.

"We have something in common," she said softly. "I'm an idealist too. We're different in that you dream of the past, while I dream of the future. I dream of a place where people can speak without fear of being killed for expressing themselves. I dream of a country where honesty is the national heritage, where people spend more time amassing friends than they do amassing wealth." She glanced over her shoulder to gauge his reaction before continuing. Picking a leaf from the same branch she picked earlier, she folded it with tiny folds. Her voice was softer as she continued. "I dream of a community where God is King and where all the townspeople are committed to loving and serving God and one another. There is no need for a watchman, no jail, no court. They're not needed because everyone is just as much concerned about others as they are about themselves. And everyone lives in freedom . . . freedom from hate, freedom from fear, freedom to love and be loved." Nell dropped her folded leaf to the ground. "Pretty idealistic, huh?"

Drew matched her soft tone. "When you find your community, let me know. I'd like to live there too."

As Drew Morgan and Nell Matthews left the castle remnants, late afternoon shadows stretched down the hillside toward the village, like giant arms pointing them toward home and reality. They walked side by side in silence. At times their arms or hands would brush against each other. Drew wanted to take her hand, but he didn't.

"Thank you for bringing me here," he said.

Nell's reply was a smile. To Drew that was better than words. He never knew he could get such good feelings by making someone smile.

As they descended to the town, Drew caught a glimpse of Christopher Matthews emerging from the front doors of the church. Reality. Why must everything be so complicated? To achieve the honor and glory he craved, Drew had to reveal the curate's illegal practices. However, he hadn't counted on falling in love with the curate's daughter.

Chapter 14

MONDAY morning would tell if the aura of good feeling generated by the curate on Sunday had any lasting value.

For the Matthews household the morning began like all others. Christopher Matthews was up first, praying and studying his Bible. Then, he slipped outside and prayed some more as he walked through the cornfield at the end of High Street.

Nell and Jenny awoke next. They tiptoed around the sleeping Drew on the floor of the sitting room. He awakened to the sounds of the girls in the kitchen, rose and hurriedly dressed. The inconvenient part of staying with the Matthews family was his lack of privacy. He was tucking his shirttail in when Jenny emerged from the kitchen door with a bowl of apples in her hands.

"Oh!" That was all she said as she quickly ducked back into the kitchen.

"It's all right. I'm dressed," Drew called after her.

For whatever reason, she didn't return.

As Drew rolled up his bed of blankets, the front door creaked open and the head of the household entered.

"Master Morgan!" beamed the curate. "It's a fine morning God has given us." For most people saying good morning was a ritual. It could be said without effort or thought and had absolutely nothing to do with the person's opinion of the day. Not so for the curate of Edenford. When Christopher Matthews said, "It's a fine morning," he meant it. The tone of his voice, the sparkle in his eyes, and his cheerful smile combined in a convincing display of sincerity.

"You've been much in my prayers, young man." The curate thumped Drew on the back. Before Drew could respond something behind him caught the curate's eye. "Now there's a vision of loveliness!" he beamed.

Jenny had emerged from the kitchen, carrying the same bowl of apples she had earlier. "Poppa!" She flushed with embarrassment.

Going to her, the curate gave his youngest daughter a one-armed hug. "And where's my other beauty?" he asked.

Nell came from the kitchen. Maybe it was the interior light, or the lack of trees or ancient stone walls, but the magical radiance that surrounded her on the hillside was gone. *Maybe I'm expecting too much,* Drew reasoned. *After all, she's fixing breakfast, not making a ballroom entrance.*

The curate hugged his elder daughter with his remaining arm. "Well, Master Morgan, how long are you going to keep us in suspense? Will you stay with us, or will you be leaving?"

Drew surveyed the faces of the family before him. Oddly enough, of the three, the curate's face was most hopeful. There was a touch of pleading in Jenny's eyes. Nell wasn't even looking at him. She was looking at her father.

"Well . . . if you'll have me . . . I'd like to stay."

"God be praised!" the curate shouted, hugging his daughters even tighter. Then he bounded toward Drew to congratulate him.

Drew extended his hand. The curate shoved it aside and embraced him, adding a few breath-stealing slaps on the back. Whirling around toward the girls he said, "Isn't that wonderful news?"

"Yes, Poppa! Wonderful news!" Jenny's eyes twinkled as she spoke.

"Just wonderful," Nell said, as she placed the utensils on the table. Her response stymied Drew. The words were there but the emotion was flat.

"I have a confession to make," the curate said. All eyes turned to him. "I already knew you would stay."

Drew was skeptical.

"I knew because God told me," the curate said. It was a simple straightforward statement. He said it in the same way someone would announce news from a neighbor. "It was just this morning. I was walking in the cornfields and God told me you were staying." The curate grabbed Drew by the shoulders and looked him square in the face. "My boy, God has something important for you to do in Edenford."

Drew tried to decide if he believed the curate or not. Ministers were always saying things like that. They were forever saying it was God's will that an offering be taken, or it was God's will that their living be increased, or some such nonsense. It was usually an attempt to invoke God's authority to get their own way. But from what Drew had seen, Christopher Matthews was different from the other clerics he had known. This man was without guile. He was sincere and direct in everything he said and did. If Christopher Matthews said God had spoken to him, there was little reason to doubt him.

The week couldn't have gone better for Drew. Everything went according to plan; no, everything went better than planned. It was incredible. By the end of the week, not only had he gained the confidence of the people, but he was the town hero.

Monday was a day of politics. Drew shadowed Christopher Matthews from shop to shop and house to house as the curate lobbied the townspeople to adopt an economic plan. By mid-afternoon there was a town meeting to consider the plan. The meeting was held at the town house, the site of Drew's introduction to the menfolk of Edenford. At Nell's suggestion the women gathered at the church. While the men deliberated, the women prayed.

During the meeting the curate harvested the seeds he had sown all morning. The result was that Edenford had a working plan to cope with their economic crisis.

Simply put, Edenford temporarily became a closed economic system. A common granary and food dispensary was established to distribute fairly the town's food supply without cost to the townspeople. In exchange, farmers received equitable compensation in services and goods from the other merchants. In all other matters, the town switched from a monetary system to a barter system. David Cooper was appointed arbiter to settle any disputes. Finally, a town bank was established, funded by the people's money. The bank would purchase goods not produced by the town. Also it would pay the ship tax money in a lump sum, saving the high constable the trouble of having to go house to house to collect it. The bank would be the true test of the town's solidarity. It was one thing for a people to agree to united action, and quite another for them to hand over their money to a community chest. But that's just what they did.

The sense of cooperation and willingness among the townspeople was impressive. The credit belonged to the curate. During the proceedings Drew remembered thinking this kind of cooperation could never be found in Winchester or London. He remembered his father's partners moving through financial waters like grinning sharks, circling and circling until they found a weakness in someone's position. Sometimes all that was needed was the scent of fear in one of their own. They attacked en masse and wouldn't let up until their victim was bereft of all he possessed, stripped, and tossed aside like a carcass.

The town meeting wasn't entirely peaceful. There was a moment of violence when Edward Hopkins expressed his opposition to the ship tax. Hopkins was the angry dark-haired man who had punched James Cooper in the kidneys during their wrestling match. He claimed to have heard reports that the cities of Witheridge, Halberton, and Crediton had been treated similarly by the king and were equally incensed. There was talk of resistance, armed resistance if necessary. Individually, Hopkins said, they were no match for the king's forces. But if all the towns in Devonshire banded together, they could raise a militia and force the king to rescind his blasted tax.

A good number of the Edenford men, including James Cooper, supported the idea of armed action and several volunteered for the militia. Then someone suggested they kidnap the high constable when he came to collect the tax and hold him hostage. The mounting anger eased when a wag pointed out that kidnapping the obese official would be self-defeating. He said the ship tax would cost them much less than feeding the captive constable.

However the laughter was brief and the support for armed resistance escalated. David Cooper stood and spoke against the use of force. That's when Drew saw the sharks begin to circle. Mistaking his call to reason for fear, they attacked. It began with name-calling and insinuations about the cobbler's courage. Hopkins accused Cooper of being a royalist, the king's boy sent to suckle his crying subjects. James Cooper sprang from his seat. Before anyone could stop him, he was on top of the dark-haired Hopkins. Like a spark to powder, the attack ignited a brawl. A farmer grabbed David Cooper by the shirt and cocked his fist. The cobbler was too quick for him. With a head-butt to the farmer's face, the cobbler knocked him to the ground and then fell on top of him. They rolled around the floor like a bowling ball, knocking several other fighting men to the ground.

Blam!

The sound of a musket reverberated against the barn's splintered walls. Everyone froze, but no one released his grip. The smell of gunpowder wafted through the room as heads swiveled frantically in search of the gunman. A swirling puff of smoke rose to the ceiling directly over Edenford's curate.

It was the only time Drew saw Christopher Matthews holding a weapon. It looked out of place in his hands, just as peculiar as Bishop Laud looked holding a crossbow. The weapon was a pistol, held high over the curate's head, pointed at the ceiling. Drew had no idea where the weapon came from or whose it was.

Shaking the pistol, the curate said, "Will this solve our problems? Do you really believe that we can make this a better world by killing those who disagree with us?"

He had their attention, but no one backed down. They were frozen in action, like subjects in an oil painting, angry men clutching each other's clothes, muscles straining, faces red and wet. The focal point of the scene was Christopher Matthews who stood tall over them with arms stretched overhead, his right hand still holding the smoking pistol.

Slowly the painting dissolved. Men released their grip without apologies. But not until everyone resumed their places did the curate lower his arms and drop the weapon. It hit the wooden floorboards with a hollow thud. "We have weapons more powerful than guns. We have God's weapons, prayer and faith!"

"Prayer ain't gonna stop the king from taxin' us!" Hopkins yelled.

"Who do you think is stronger, the King of England or God?" Matthews shouted back. "With God's weapons Moses defeated the powerful Pharaoh of Egypt! With God's weapons Joshua felled the walls of Jericho and entered the Promised Land! With God's weapons the sun stood still, fire fell from heaven, and men were raised from their graves! What does the King of England have that can compare to weapons like these?"

No one answered him.

Matthews continued, " 'Not by might, nor by power, but by My spirit, saith the Lord of hosts!' I, for one, choose to fight with the weapons of God. Who will join me?"

The curate walked to the center of the building and dropped to his knees in prayer. Without a word, one by one, the assembled men of Edenford knelt around their curate. First David Cooper and old Cyrus Furman, followed by the bachelors Manly and Dudley, then James Cooper. Even Edward Hopkins joined them. The entire male population of Edenford followed Christopher Matthews in humbling themselves before God.

Drew alone remained standing. He was off by himself, leaning against the outer wall of the structure. He considered joining them, but decided against it. It was too early.

He stared in awe at the curate. *Who is this man?* Never before had he seen anyone have this kind of power over other men. *How does he do it? Is it the words he uses?* At one point it was clear he was quoting Scripture. *Do the Bible words act like an incantation? Do they have some kind of magical power?*

It was while the men were praying that Drew realized the difference between Bishop Laud and Christopher Matthews. The similarities between them had always been obvious: They both worshiped the same God. They both read the Bible. They both believed strongly they were doing God's will, although their beliefs pitted them against each other. This town-meeting scene made their differences equally as obvious: The bishop wielded political power like a sword to defend God, his church position, and himself. The curate, on the other hand, believed that God could defend Himself. Instead of trying to protect God, the curate found protection in God.

When the last amen sounded, one final action was taken. Thursday was set aside as a day of prayer and fasting for all ablebodied men and women. This too was the curate's idea. "On Thursdays our meat and bread will consist of prayer and supplications to God. We will find our strength in Him," he said. Then, with a grin, he added, "We shouldn't overdo it, though. We wouldn't want to grow spiritually fat!"

Tuesday was a setback for the town.

It began well enough. The new community order was implemented as David Cooper arbitrated between the merchants and the farmers for a fair exchange of goods and services. Ambrose Dudley was elected the town's banker. A council of five men was chosen to determine what needed to be purchased and how much money was to be spent.

Spirits were high in the face of worsening conditions. Most families would be able to eat meat only once a week, maybe twice; some not at all. Many of them would have to exist on watery vegetable soups and bread sliced so thin it looked like parchment. Mothers braced themselves for the changes that would occur among the children. Their cheeks would grow hollow, their eyes would yellow, and their skin would take on a grayish cast. Drew remembered the look. He had seen it on the faces of the street children in the alleys of London. It had never bothered him before because he only saw them briefly as he passed by on his horse or in the family carriage. Now he would be living among them. He had to remind himself it was temporary. Before long he would be back at London House, sitting at the round cook's table.

Because of the scarcity of wood, houses would have to go

unrepaired and roof leaks unpatched. A delegation led by Christopher Matthews journeyed the short distance to Lord Chesterfield's manor to request the use of some of the trees in his forest for the more urgent repairs. Chesterfield received them kindly, but refused their request. If he allowed them to take his trees, he explained, his game animals would be deprived of places to live.

Drew felt the first pangs of real hunger on Tuesday. Not the it-must-be-time-to-eat-again hunger, but the kind of hunger that weakens a person, feeding on his disposition as well as his body. Drew encouraged himself by making it a test of his manhood. *The Round Table knights knew hardship and hunger,* he reasoned. *If they could endure hardship, so can I. Besides, being one of the hungry in a town full of hungry people works well into my plan.*

Tuesday's great setback came when it was discovered that Rose Furman had died. Drew was accompanying the curate on his visitation rounds when they entered the Furman home and found old Cyrus sitting in a rocking chair, rocking back and forth, holding an emaciated Rose in his arms.

Drew had heard somewhere that old people sometimes acted infantile. He thought Cyrus was merely obliging his senile wife by rocking her to sleep. Then, as he got closer, he noticed her one eye was half open and her limbs were stiff. She had been dead for some time.

"I should have told someone," Cyrus cried. "But I knew if I did, you'd take her away from me." He brushed thin gray hairs from her eyes, wrapping them behind an ear. "Forty-three years. We've been together forty-three years. When I let her go, it's over. I just wanted it to last a little longer."

Christopher Matthews placed a hand on Cyrus' shoulder. "You hold her as long as you want."

It didn't matter now. The spell was broken. Drew and Matthews had intruded on the final intimate moment between a man and his wife. It was over. Gone forever.

The news of Rose Furman's death weighed heavily on the village. It wasn't death itself that depressed them; to the people of Edenford death was an unwelcome but frequent guest. It was the death of Rose. Maybe it was because the Furmans were unable to have children; all they ever had was each other. True, they were an oddly amusing couple. Rose was strong-minded and determined while Cyrus was easygoing, slow-witted, and clumsy. She would yell and complain, he would grin and shrug, but they loved each other. For forty-three years they loved each other, and it was difficult for the townspeople to imagine one without the other.

If it hadn't been for the distraction of the miracle on Wednesday, the townspeople would have nursed the loss of Rose Furman for months.

Wednesday was the second full day of Drew's tutelage at the hand of Edenford's curate. As he did the previous day, Christopher Matthews woke Drew at 4 o'clock for Bible study and prayer. Since Drew's arrival in Edenford, the curate had learned two important things about him. First, Drew wasn't a Christian; and second, he loved adventure, especially in his reading material. Using the latter to address the former, the curate chose the life of Paul as the subject of their Bible studies. On the first day of study the curate had Drew read from Acts 27, the account of Paul's shipwreck in the Mediterranean Sea. Drew was fascinated with the nautical detail of the story, like passing to the lee of Cyprus and Crete due to unfavorable winds; the ill-fated gamble to reach Phoenix, a harbor that faced both southwest and northwest, in which the ship could winter; and binding the hull of the ship with ropes during a storm to hold it together. He was also intrigued by the adventurous spirit of Paul. This apostle wasn't like the churchmen of England who hid from the world behind church walls, wearing robes and attending councils and complaining that Englishmen were no longer interested in religion. Not the Apostle Paul. The idea of an adventurous preacher struck Drew as odd but intriguing.

Wednesday morning's Bible reading came from Paul's defense of his ministry in 2 Corinthians 11:22-33. "Are they Hebrews? so am I. Are they Israelites? so am I. Are they the seed of Abraham? so am I. Are they ministers of Christ? (I speak as a fool) I am more; in labours more abundant, in stripes above measure, in prisons more frequent, in deaths oft. Of the Jews five times received I forty stripes save one. Thrice was I beaten with rods, once was I stoned, thrice I suffered shipwreck, a night and a day I have been in the deep; In journeyings often, in perils of waters, in perils of robbers, in perils by mine own countrymen, in perils by the heathen, in perils in the city, in perils in the wilderness, in perils in the sea, in perils among false brethren; In weariness and painfulness, in watchings often, in hunger and thirst, in fastings often, in cold and nakedness. Beside those things that are without, that which cometh upon me daily, the care of all the churches. Who is weak, and I am not weak? Who is offended, and I burn not? If I must needs glory, I will glory of the things which concern mine infirmities. The God and Father of our Lord Jesus Christ, which is blessed for evermore, knoweth that I lie not. In Damascus the governor under Aretas the king kept the city of the Damascenes with a garrison, desirous to apprehend me: And through a window in a basket was I let down by the wall, and escaped his hands."

The curate and his student discussed the Bible reading as they walked the road beside the cornfield. It was getting late in the year and the stalks were brown and sagging. There was a chill in the morning air, enough to turn their speaking into wisps of fog.

"It's hard for me to believe he endured all those things.

What kept him going? What was he looking for?" Drew asked.

"Paul kept going not because he was *looking* for something, but because he had *found* something."

"I don't understand."

"I know. You don't understand because you're still looking for what Paul found."

"What did he find?"

The curate smiled. "Something worth living for; something worth dying for."

"His faith in Jesus, right?"

The curate stopped and studied his student. Drew's remark was an academic one, not a life-changing one. He resumed walking. "Paul's faith in Jesus Christ changed him so dramatically that he spent the rest of his life traveling throughout the known world, enduring whatever trials and hardships came, to tell others about his discovery."

"It still doesn't make sense to me. People didn't want to listen to him. They hated his message. What did he gain?"

"Until you experience what Paul experienced, it won't make sense to you. Believe me, there is sufficient motivation. Someday, Drew, you'll understand him."

After breakfast and family devotions with Nell and Jenny, Drew assisted the curate in gathering information for his monthly report to Lord Chesterfield. To complete the report they had to inspect each phase of the wool industry in Edenford, from the tending of the sheep to the stored serges.

The shepherds gave him a total head count, the number of sheep lost to predators (with explanation, since it was the shepherd's duty to protect the sheep), and the number of new births. Those suspected of having a disease were inspected. Everything was recorded by Drew precisely according to Christopher Matthews' directions.

The spinning wheels were housed in family residences.

Each house was visited and a record made of the production total for each worker. The looms were next. They were all under one roof. Again, production was checked as well as the status of the equipment. A list of needed repairs was appended to the report.

The two men had to cross the village to get from the looms to the fulling mill beside the river near the village's south bridge. Drew had never realized the amount of work that went into making simple wool cloth. For the Morgans it had always been a matter of sending a servant to town to get the needed material. The servants then sewed their own clothes. Of course, the Morgan family's clothing was purchased and fitted in London at the finer tailor shops.

It was at the fulling mill that Drew saw the danger of cloth-making. There, the material was thickened and scoured by soaking and pounding it. After the serges were soaked, they were drawn out and pounded with notched timbers that looked like giant teeth. The mill drew the serges with such violence that if a person were standing too close, the giant teeth could grab a bit of his clothing and pull him to his death in a moment. At first it seemed that the process would injure the serges, but the finished product proved otherwise.

The scoured serges were then taken outside and placed on racks lining the banks of the river. Each piece was about twenty-six yards long. The long strips of white cloth waved gently in the breeze as they dried. From here most of the serges were taken to be hot-pressed, folded, then cold-pressed and stored for shipment to Exeter. Other strips were sent to the dyeing vats before being pressed.

The vats for dyeing were located on the west side of the village in a large wooden structure next to the grazing fields that rose gently toward the mountains. Racks of dyed serges stretched across the fields making the countryside look like a giant patchwork quilt of blue, green, yellow, black, and red.

Actually there were only four vats of colored dye, one for each primary color and one for black. The green cloth was made by dipping the serges twice, first in yellow, then in blue. The blue, yellow, and black vats were housed in one large room. The vat holding the scarlet dye had a room all to itself, since it was the most changeable dye and needed stricter control.

To dye the cloth, the serges were stretched across the vats between two horizontal poles which were rolled by two men, one at each pole. The serge was lowered into the vat by unrolling it from one pole and pulled out of the vat by rolling it onto the other pole. When the end of the serge was reached at one pole, the process was reversed. In this way the cloth was dipped back and forth until it was the desired color. A furnace of coal under the dye vats kept the liquid hot, almost to the boiling point.

As Drew and Christopher Matthews entered the room of three vats, Drew immediately recognized one of the workers at the blue vat by his red hair. It was the fiery James Cooper standing on a platform and turning one of the dipping poles. Seated at his feet was a little boy. Drew assumed it was James' brother, since he had seen the small boy with the Cooper family Sunday afternoon on the village green. As for the other worker, Drew couldn't recall ever meeting him.

"Good afternoon, James, William," the curate said. Then with note of surprise upon seeing the little boy sitting on the platform at his brother's feet, "And little Thomas!"

"Hi, Master Matthews!" Thomas waved enthusiastically.

"Curate," the redheaded man acknowledged dutifully. He didn't look down at them. His eyes were fixed on the man across from him on the far side of the vat. It was a look of animosity, which didn't surprise Drew. Every time he had seen James Cooper, the redheaded giant was at odds with someone.

"Good morning, curate," William said as he steadily un-rolled the serge from his pole. The serge had to be kept moving to keep it from being unevenly dyed.

"What's Thomas doing here?" asked the curate.

James pulled in the serge as he answered. "Mom's fixin' up Mrs. Furman for her burial. Dad's arbitratin' between the farmers and tailors. So I got stuck with him." The dark blue cloth rolled out of the vat with gentle ease. Splashes of blue dye on the wooden platform indicated the process did not always go this smoothly.

"Do you think it's wise for him to be up there on the platform with you?"

"It's the only way I can keep an eye on him."

The curate looked around. "I suppose so. Just be careful. How many serges have you dyed today?"

James almost spat out the answer. "Two." William kept his head lowered and continued to unroll the cloth from his pole into the vat.

"Is that all?"

"That's all," James answered through clenched teeth.

The curate bent over and looked under the vat. "Here's your problem. Fire's almost out. The embers are barely alive." He straightened up. "Why is the fire almost out?"

Both workers began yelling at once, each accusing the other for being responsible for the dying fire.

The curate held up his hand for them both to stop. "I don't care whose fault it is. Work it out peaceably"—he em-phasized the word *peaceably*—"between the two of you, but finish that serge and relight that fire. Understood?"

"Yes, sir," William said. James nodded his head, still glaring at his coworker.

Matthews looked at the dyers a moment and decided the matter was settled. He indicated to Drew where to record the work output for the blue vat and turned toward the yellow vat to check the progress there.

Drew recorded the number. When he looked up the dyers of blue cloth had reached the end of the serge.

"One more time," William said.

James shook his head no. "It's finished."

"One more time!"

"No!"

William began rolling up the serge on his pole for one more pass, but James held his pole firmly in place. As the slack in the serge was taken up, the blue cloth rose out of the dye. To force the issue, William gave his pole a jerk. Blue dye splattered on the sides of the vat; some fell to the floor.

This gave James an idea. He released his grip and the cloth inched downward. He wanted William to think he was conceding to one more pass. Just as the cloth dipped below the surface, the redheaded giant yanked back on his pole. His plan was to snap the cloth taut and spray William with blue dye, but the plan backfired. The cloth snapped taut, sending the dye flying. Liquid blue sprayed all over James and his little brother.

William laughed to the point of hysterics at his coworker's failed attempt. Drew joined him. James and Thomas looked like they had been attacked by a band of renegade blueberries.

Thomas was crying, partly from the surprise, but also from the heat of the dye. He was trying to wipe it off his arms which only succeeded in smearing the dye all over him.

William laughing at him and his little brother bawling made James furious. He grabbed the blue serge with his hands and yanked it with all his might. William's pole spun wildly, knocking him off balance. He fell onto the platform and almost into the vat. Now there was fury on both sides of the vat. William struggled to his feet and grabbed his end of the serge. A tug-of-war ensued over the vat of hot blue dye.

William was no match for the redhaired giant and Drew

feared he would be pulled into the vat. Confident in his superior strength, James pulled William until his midsection was against the pole, then he pulled a little more until William would have to let go or fall in. Then James would let up. Once William regained his footing, the giant would pull him against the pole again. William knew he was overmatched, but he wouldn't let go.

"James! William! Stop this right now!" It was the curate. The incident at the blue vat had everyone's attention now. "Both of you, let go!" he yelled.

"He started it!" James yelled back. He looked down at the curate as if to plead his case.

William saw this temporary distraction as his opportunity. He tugged sharply. It was enough to cause the red giant to lose his balance. But only for a moment. His attention drawn back to the tug-of-war, he strengthened his grip and reset his feet.

Suddenly, his right foot slipped on the wet platform and his legs flew from under him. Releasing the serge, he tried to catch himself on the pole, but his arms slapped against the wad of blue serge wrapped around his pole. As he tried to grab it, his right hand fell on slippery, wet cloth and came up empty. His left hand slipped off the cloth too and slid down to the wooden pole where he managed to gain a hold. With only one hand secure, the momentum of his falling weight swung him sideways, knocking little Thomas into the vat of hot blue dye.

The little boy didn't have time to scream. In an instant he disappeared beneath the surface.

"Thomas!"

James released his grip on the pole and landed on the wooden platform with a thud. Scrambling over onto his belly, he reached into the vat after his brother.

"AAHHHHHHH!" he screamed, pulling his hand from

the hot liquid. It was blue up to his wrist.

The instant Drew saw little Thomas plunge into the vat, he dropped his papers and sprinted up the steps to the platform. When James reached into the vat, he had held onto the giant's shirt to keep him from falling in too.

James' eyes were frantic as he nursed his hand.

"You've got to pull him out!" Drew yelled at him.

"It's too hot!"

"If you don't, he'll die!"

James whimpered. "I can't. He's already dead."

Drew searched the surface. There was no sign of Thomas. "Get out of the way!" he yelled.

"What are you going to do?"

"Just get out of the way!" Drew yelled again, trying to pull the giant aside. He wouldn't budge.

"James!" It was the curate. "Move aside!"

It took a second for the voice of authority to reach its mark. When it did, James moved to the side of the platform.

Drew fell to his stomach and plunged his arm into the dye up to his shoulder. Every nerve in his arm exploded with pain, crying to him to pull it back out. His teeth were clenched, he grimaced with agony but kept his arm in the vat, searching for little Thomas. Each swish brought greater heat and greater pain; his fingers numbed; even if he found the boy he didn't know if he would be able to get a grip on him. There! For an instant he thought he felt something. Drew closed his grip and pulled.

Nothing.

By now the curate was standing on William's platform. All the other workers in the building encircled the vat. They stood at a cautious distance from the hot sides.

"Look there!" the curate pointed to the middle of the vat. The back of a small hand had floated to the surface in the middle of the vat. It was too far away.

"Is there a long pole or something?" Drew yelled.

"Over here!" a worker pointed toward the corner of the building.

Just then the small hand sank below the surface.

Drew cursed. Pointing to William he yelled, "Stretch the serge tight!" William gripped his pole. The curate moved into position to help him. Turning to James, "Pull the serge tight and hold it taut!"

James just sat there, his forehead propped up by the back of his blue-stained hand.

Drew knocked his arm away. "James, help me save your brother!"

The giant looked at him dumbly. There was a large blue stain in the middle of his forehead. "He's dead! I killed my little brother!" James sobbed.

"He's not dead!" Drew grabbed the giant's shirt and tried to pull him up.

The giant was too heavy.

"He's not dead!" Drew yelled again. "Help me save your brother!"

"Not dead?"

"Not if you help me!"

Drew's assurance nudged the giant into action.

"Pull the serge tight! As tight as you can get it!" Drew yelled.

James pulled slowly at first, then with more determination. The serge cloth rose out of the vat and stretched tight.

Drew ducked under the pole and balanced on the edge of the platform. He inched his toes over the edge the same way he would if he were diving into a lake. He would have only one chance. He couldn't afford to slip.

He leaped onto the serge. The sudden weight brought grunts from William and the curate as they tried to hold it tight. The serge was slippery and wobbled from side to side.

Wrapping his arms and legs around it, Drew fought to keep from rolling over. The heat from the vat below rose all around him. He felt like a pig on a open spit.

"All right. Now lower me to the surface!" Drew yelled.

As the serge dipped slowly, Drew scanned the surface for Thomas in the area where he was last seen.

"Stop!" he yelled. "That's close enough!" Drew was just inches away from the hot blue liquid. To balance himself, Drew spread his legs wide and pivoted to his right, keeping his hips in the center of the serge. There was a moment of imbalance. Drew steadied himself, but not before his left foot dipped into the hot liquid. He grimaced, laying his head against the wet serge.

"Drew, let us pull you in," the curate said softly. "It's probably too late anyway. We don't want to lose you too."

Drew shook his head. "Just hold the serge steady."

The curate nodded. "Lord, help him!" he prayed.

For the second time, Drew plunged his arm into the liquid. Burning pain engulfed it. Tears streamed from his eyes as he fought to ignore the pain and concentrate on reaching little Thomas.

There! His hand brushed something. Just beyond reach. He stretched farther and bumped it, pushing it further away.

"No!" he screamed. The pain was more than he could take. A darkness began to close around him. He pushed it away. *If you lose consciousness, you die*, he told himself.

He had to stretch farther, but there was only one way for him to do that. He didn't want to. He didn't know if he could. *The boy is dead. Save yourself.*

He took a deep breath and plunged his head, shoulder, and upper torso into the hot liquid. The pain was incredible. Hot dye filled his ears and seeped through his eyelids, stinging his eyes. He could hear muffled cries from the bystanders on the other side of the surface.

The dark that surrounded him was more than just the absence of light; it was a hot, burning liquid darkness. It was not alone. Another darkness accompanied it, the darkness of unconsciousness. He'd fought it once, but it was back, stronger than before. A third darkness joined them, the darkness of death. It was curious sensation. It was cold. In the midst of burning liquid, the hands of death were still cold.

His hand brushed against something. An arm. Then a body. Drew pushed past the pain and reached through the darkness; he grabbed the boy's shirt. With all his might Drew Morgan pulled himself and little Thomas Cooper to the surface.

The last thing he remembered was what seemed like a hundred hands pulling him out of the vat.

Chapter 15

A rustling sound was the first thing Drew remembered, following the vat incident. The sound reminded him of his boyhood when he would lie in bed at night pretending to be asleep. Julia, his nursemaid, would quietly move about the room so as not to wake him. With his eyes closed Drew would track her movements and actions by the sounds she made. He could tell where she was by the rustling of her skirt. The creak of the rocking chair meant she was either reading or knitting—reading if he heard pages turn, knitting if she sighed. Julia always sighed when she knitted, once every few minutes. The best sound of all was a rustling away from him followed by the click of the door latch. It meant he had fooled her. He could stop pretending and get out of bed, as long as he was quiet about it.

But this wasn't Morgan Hall and the rustling sound wasn't coming from Julia. It was accompanied by a soft humming. Julia never hummed.

Drew tried to open his eyes. His effort set off a series of painful jabs in both eyes, which brought a wince, which hurt his cheeks and lips, which caused him to lift his right hand to his face, which sent a stabbing pain up his arm. With a moan he ceased all movement and fell limp. His eyes and cheeks and arm throbbed in unison, and still his eyes were closed! The rustle of skirts moved toward him and then quickly away, followed by footsteps descending stairs with a hushed voice trailing after.

"Poppa! Poppa! He's awake!"

To a chorus of "Amens," Drew heard thumping sounds coming up the stairs—a pair of heavy thuds followed by the pitter-patter of lighter feet.

"Drew! Thank God!" The voice belonged to Christopher Matthews.

"How are you feeling?" The second voice was Jenny.

Drew formed a slow grin. It was painful, but he found it easier than trying to open his eyes. It took him a while to respond. Matthews and Jenny waited patiently. "Well . . ." He found it difficult to speak. He was incredibly thirsty; his mouth was devoid of moisture making his tongue and lips and gums sticky. ". . . as you might expect, I'm feeling a little blue."

There was an uncertain pause, then a huge guffaw. It was a good sound, one that Drew would always associate with the curate of Edenford. Jenny laughed and sniffled at the same time.

"Half the village is downstairs praying for you," Jenny said. "They've been praying through the night."

"Through the night? What time is it?"

"Almost 10 o'clock in the morning," Jenny answered. "Thursday morning. When the townspeople heard what you did, everyone stopped working so they could pray for you and Thomas."

"Some have been here all night," Matthews added. "Others are at the Coopers' house."

The mention of the Coopers begged another question, one Drew wasn't sure he wanted to ask. He didn't know if he was ready to hear the answer.

"Is Thomas all right?" Drew needed to know, one way or the other.

"He hasn't awakened yet." The curate delivered the news somberly. "He's alive, but he's badly burned."

"Is he going to die?"

"God alone knows the answer to that question."

Flashes of remembered pain darted through Drew's mind as bits and pieces of the incident came back to him.

Unexpectedly, the bed tilted to the right. Someone was leaning on it.

"Can you open your eyes?" Matthews' voice came from directly overhead.

"I tried once," Drew responded. "It hurt. A lot."

"We've sent for a doctor. He lives in Exeter and probably won't be here until tomorrow. If it hurts too much, don't try to open them. Best wait for the doctor to get here."

The sound of the curate's voice traveled from side to side over him. He was probably examining one eye, then the other.

"I'd like to try again. At least one more time." He assumed the curate consented, the weight lifted from the side of the bed and Drew was level again.

It was such a simple thing really, opening one's eyes. Drew had done it every day of his life without giving it a thought. Not so on this day. With great effort he forced his eyelids to raise. His effort was rewarded with pain. There was the pain of the burn, the pain of light as it poked through the tiny opening, and the pain of raw flesh against raw flesh where the folds of his eyelids overlapped. It took him more than a minute, but he successfully opened both eyes halfway. Tears stung the corners of his eyes and the overflow burned saltwater trails down the sides of his face.

His first sight was Jenny. Her hands were folded and pressed to her lips; the corner of a handkerchief dangled from between her palms. Next he saw the curate. His right hand was on his hip, the back of his left hand wiped away tears.

"I hope I don't look as bad as the two of you," Drew said.

There was no answer. Instead the curate turned silently and went downstairs to inform the townspeople of Drew's progress. Drew wanted to ask why Nell wasn't with Jenny and the curate, but he didn't. For one thing, he didn't want anyone to know he was particularly interested in her whereabouts; for another, he was being fawned over by a beautiful lady. It didn't seem appropriate to ask about her sister.

"You really are a sight," Jenny said, half-laughing, half-crying.

"Am I really all blue?"

Jenny nodded and giggled. "Wait right here!" she ran out of the room.

Wait right here? Where does she think I'm going?

A moment later she was back with a hand mirror and held it in front of his face. At the first sight of himself he laughed, then wished he hadn't. The pain was intense.

Jenny pulled the mirror away. "I'm sorry!" she cried.

"No, don't be. It's not your fault." Drew paused to take a few deep breaths. "I'd like to see the rest of me."

"Are you sure?"

Drew nodded slightly. He directed the mirror's positioning. "Hold the mirror up higher. Now angle it down, no, too much. Up a little more, there." Drew could see his arm. It was puffed and blistered. Funny blue sausages were attached to the end of a bloated hand. His fingers. They too were puffed, red with blisters, and, of course, blue.

"Do you want to see your foot too?"

That's right. With all the other areas of pain, he'd forgotten about his left foot. He took a quick mental inventory. The skin felt tight and it hurt when he flexed it, but otherwise it wasn't too bad. "I suppose it's blue too?"

Jenny nodded and gently sat on the edge of the bed. Instinctively Drew shuddered; she was awfully close to his burned arm. Internal warning signals sounded, urging him to pull his arm to safety or ask her move away from it. But there was a soft, hazy look in Jenny's eyes. It was more than a look of compassion; her eyes were filled with tenderness and romance. Drew ignored his warning signals. *What's a little pain compared to the chance to be this close to someone so beautiful?*

She slowly, gently lifted a few strands of hair that had fallen to his forehead and brushed them back. "You're remarkable," she said in a half-whisper. "You're a gentleman. You're handsome. And you're brave."

She leaned over him further so that her face was directly above his. Her long brown hair fell to both sides of Drew's face. Now it was just the two of them; Jenny's canopy of hair shut out the rest of the world. For Drew the sensation was torture—her hair tickled and stung his burned cheeks as the beauty of her twinkling blue eyes, petite nose, and soft lips lingered over him. As she lowered herself, the pain was shoved aside by the smoothness of her skin and the moist warmth of her breath. Tenderly she closed her eyes and brushed her lips against his. There was no pressure—she didn't want to hurt him. Somehow that made the kiss even better.

Jenny's long hair swept across his face as she rose. At the door she turned toward him with an impish grin and was gone.

Drew learned that he was in the Matthews' house, upstairs in the curate's bed. He assumed as much since Jenny roamed freely about and knew exactly where to find a hand mirror.

The curate's bedroom was dark and spartan. Since it was in the middle of the house, sandwiched between the girls' bedroom and the study, it had no windows. The only natural light came through the doorway. Rough beams peaked above him and the walls were bare. There was a washbasin on a small stand in the far corner and a small chest of drawers against the wall next to the door. It was a room for sleeping and dressing, nothing more.

After securing Drew's consent, Christopher Matthews began ushering grateful townspeople to his bedside. First came David and Shannon Cooper. The large, hairy cobbler and his petite wife showered him with tearful thanks. They were accompanied by their middle child, Margaret. Drew guessed her to be about ten years old. She stood silently behind her parents, uncertain about the blue stranger in the bed and the intense emotion of the situation. The fiery-headed James wasn't with them.

Old Cyrus Furman shuffled up the stairs to visit him. Because of the events surrounding the vat incident, Rose's funeral had been postponed until Friday. Everyone in Edenford was praying that the funeral service wouldn't be a double one.

"I guess we was wrong about you," Cyrus drawled. He leaned over and patted Drew on the chest. "God bless you, son."

Ambrose Dudley was a surprise. In contrast to the other visitors, the scrivener stood ramrod straight beside the bed, hands clasped in front of him. He held a letter which he worried with his fingers as he spoke. The sharp lines of his thin face and hard eyes provided Drew little comfort. "I suppose we are indebted to you," he said matter-of-factly.

Drew nodded curtly.

"This came for you," he said, tossing the letter on Drew's stomach. "It was delivered by an unwashed, undisciplined young man with wild hair. A friend of yours, I'm sure."

As the scrivener left Drew grabbed the letter with his good hand and slipped it under the bedclothes. He couldn't take the chance of someone offering to read it to him.

How ironic. If Ambrose Dudley only knew he was delivering a message from Bishop Laud!

The messenger was undoubtedly Eliot and that disturbed Drew. The fact that the bishop had Eliot deliver the message increased its urgency significantly. He'd decode the message as soon as he was sure he'd be left alone. And, he would need to have someone bring him his Bible.

Drew received the rest of the townspeople as graciously as he could, considering that they all said the same thing, "What you did was wonderful. We didn't know you had it in you. Thank you. God bless you."

Finally, the last person left the room. Still, there was no Nell.

"I'm sure you're tired," the curate said. He stood at the door, his hand on the outside latch. "I'll close the door so you can get some sleep."

"Wait! Before you leave, could I have my Bible?"

The curate's face brightened at the request. He retrieved Drew's Bible. "Would you like me to read to you?" he offered.

"Um, no thanks. I think I'd like to be alone."

The curate nodded. He set the washbasin on the floor and pulled the stand next to the bed. Lighting a candle, he said, "This way you can blow out the candle when you're ready to sleep."

"Thanks. Um, where's Nell? I haven't seen her."

The curate playfully knocked himself on the head. "I should have told you earlier. She's at the Coopers'. James blames himself for the accident. As you've probably noticed, he's an emotional person. Well, he started saying crazy things about hurting himself, wouldn't listen to anybody. You don't know this, but he and Nell have been close ever since they were kids. She's always been able to handle him. So she's with him now, trying to keep him from doing something stupid."

Drew held in his thoughts and simply nodded acknowledgment.

"Oh," the curate stopped at the door, "just a suggestion. You might read Galatians 6:7-9. I know you're in a lot of pain right now; I just want you to know that what you have done will not go unrewarded. God will see to that. If you need anything, just call." The curate closed the door and Drew was alone.

The thought of Nell consoling James Cooper grated on him. He cursed quietly as he flung open his Bible. Retrieving the letter from under the covers, he worked at opening it with his good hand, hoping it was a short message. He didn't feel like decoding it now, but he wouldn't be able to rest until he knew what was so important that the bishop had Eliot deliver the message.

The paper tore in two as he fumbled to open it. He cursed again. The news about Nell's whereabouts disturbed him more than he cared to admit. He shook open one half of the letter. It wasn't code! It was handwritten. He dropped the paper on his chest, reached for the second half, and shook it open. Matching the two pieces of paper together, he held them up to the candlelight. The message was written in a nearly illegible scrawl. *"Urgnt! Met me rivrs ege nr brig. Sat. 10p. Eliot."*

Drew lay still in bed, scowling behind half-opened eyelids. *Maybe it is nothing. It says urgent, but Eliot set the meeting two days away. And why does Eliot need to talk to me personally? Has something happened to the bishop? Is my mission in Edenford in danger?*

Drew folded the pieces of the note and looked for a place to hide them. If found, this note would be more dangerous than the others. Drew wedged it between the pages of his Bible.

Just as he was about to extinguish the candle, he remembered the Scripture passage the curate suggested he read. What was it again? That's right, Galatians 6:7-9. Looking in the index, he found the page number for Galatians. By the light of the flickering candle he read, "Be not deceived; God is not mocked: for whatsoever a man soweth, that shall he also reap. For he that soweth to his flesh shall of the flesh reap corruption; but he that soweth to the Spirit shall of the Spirit reap life everlasting. And let us not be weary in well doing: for in due season we shall reap, if we faint not."

Drew awoke shortly before dinner. He could smell bread baking and—was it beans? He couldn't quite tell. The aroma of food goaded his stomach to complain loudly.

"Good, you're awake!" Jenny shoved the door open with her side. She carried a tray of food. Scooting the candlestick aside with the edge of the tray, she set the food on the stand beside the bed.

The Bible is gone! Drew distinctly remembered placing it on the stand beside the candle before falling asleep. He tried looking over the edge of the bed to see if it was on the floor.

"What are you looking for?" Jenny asked.

"Did you remove my Bible from the stand?" he asked.

"No."

"Is it on the floor?"

Jenny looked around the legs of the wooden stand. "No, I don't see it."

Drew tried to suppress the anxiety welling up inside him. "That's funny," he said. "I placed it on the stand just before going to sleep."

Jenny was unconcerned. "Maybe Poppa borrowed it." She scooted the stand closer to the bed. "I brought you supper," she said cheerily.

"Maybe Poppa borrowed it" . . . *What if he finds Eliot's note?*

"Open up!"

Jenny aimed a spoonful of corn at his mouth.

"I'm capable of feeding myself." His irritation over the

missing Bible fouled Jenny's playful mood.

The spoon retracted and a kernel fell to the bed. A pouting lower lip appeared. "I thought you'd enjoy this."

Her pout worked.

I can't do anything about the note right now, Drew reasoned. *If Matthews reads the note, I'll just have to make up a story.* "You're right," he said to Jenny. "I would enjoy it."

A coy expression replaced her pout as she extended the spoon. Drew leaned forward. The combination of his hunger and his server made this the best meal he'd eaten in months.

The meal was a typical one for Edenford, considering their economic woes—corn, beans, and coarse bread. Since water was free, it was the standard drink, and Drew was drinking a lot of it lately.

The best part of the dinner was the after-dinner kiss under the flowing canopy of Jenny's hair. This time, her lips pressed firmly against his and remained longer. A small sigh escaped her as their lips parted.

Nell didn't come to see him until late that night. Standing in the doorway she looked haggard and worn. She wore a sweet smile and there was kindness in her eyes, but her conversation seemed formal and guarded. They talked of the accident. Little Thomas was still not awake; James was doing better, no longer feeling self-destructive.

It pained Drew when she spoke of James. He tried to ignore it, but couldn't. He reasoned he had no right to feel jealous, especially considering what had happened between him and Jenny today. Still, the thought of Nell comforting that redheaded ox soured his mood. Did she hold his hands? Hug him? Just what did she do to console the oaf?

Knowing Nell would disapprove of his jealousy, he tried to keep his feelings hidden. "I'm glad James is doing better," he said in measured tones.

If Nell detected bitterness, she didn't show it. With eyes half-closed, she wiped her forehead with the back of her hand. "If you don't mind," she said wearily, "I'll excuse myself. There are still some things I have to do before retiring. I wish I could stay longer. But I'm afraid I wouldn't be very good company. Perhaps tomorrow."

"I understand," Drew said flatly.

"Would you like me to close the door?"

"If it wouldn't be too much trouble."

Nell closed the door halfway, then poked her head back in the room. "By the way," she said, "you look adorable all blue." She smiled prettily and closed the door.

Drew lay awake for several hours reviewing the events of his abbreviated day—the gratitude of the townspeople, the obvious pride Christopher Matthews was taking in him, his mixed conversation with Nell, and, of course, Jenny's kisses. Then there was the problem of the Bible. Who had it? And more importantly, had they found Eliot's note?

His conglomeration of thoughts turned fuzzy and blended together as he drifted asleep. The last thing he remembered was the sound of a chair scraping the floor. It came from the curate's office. He must be working late again tonight.

By Saturday Drew felt well enough to try to get out of bed. When he first awoke, a movement in the doorway caught his eye. Jenny smiled sweetly at him.

"How are you feeling?"

Drew didn't answer right away. He hadn't quite completed the transit from the realm of dreams to conscious reality. He struggled because the two realms don't share a common language. One is based on a series of irrational images; the other on a rational sequence of word-symbols. Drew struggled, much like a foreigner who was attempting to decipher the English language.

Jenny giggled as Drew wrestled with question. "Is the question too hard for you?"

"I'm doing pretty well, I think." The language of the conscious realm was coming back to him.

"Would you like something to eat?"

Another question! Drew thought hard. "Yes, I think so."

Jenny was in the room now. "Your eyes are open all the way."

She was right. Drew rubbed them with his left hand. "Ow!" He'd forgotten that he couldn't do the little things, like rubbing one's eyes in the morning, without giving them a thought.

"Are you all right?" Jenny was beside the bed now, looking directly over him, her long brown hair falling toward him.

"I just have to be careful what I do." Drew looked up at her. *What a lovely vision to wake up to,* he thought.

"I'll go get your breakfast." She turned and left.

Drew was disappointed. He was expecting another kiss.

"Well, are you going to sleep all day?" A smile accompanied the question. Nell stood in the doorway, her arms folded.

"Actually, I thought I'd join you ladies downstairs today."

"Are you going to read the Bible for us?"

"Only if I can choose the passage."

Nell chuckled. Her smile widened, accompanied by laughing eyes. Seeing her like this brought a warm wave of good feeling over Drew. *What is it about this woman that attracts me so? Except for that one Sunday afternoon, she has kept herself distant. She is not as pretty as her sister, so why am I attracted to her? Why does it make me feel so good to see her smile?*

Jenny brought the breakfast tray in and set it on the little wooden stand, just like before.

"Come on, Jen, let's get to work," Nell turned to leave.

"I thought I'd stay with Drew while he ate his breakfast."

"He's a grown man. He can eat his breakfast all by himself. Let's go, we've lost a couple of days this week."

Jenny's lower lip appeared. Her expression appealed for Drew's intercession.

Drew smiled apologetically. "Thanks for the offer." A genuine frown formed on Jenny's face.

Drew almost fainted trying to go downstairs. He should have been forewarned by the extensive effort it took to dress himself. He wore a single shoe—his swollen and bandaged left foot wouldn't fit into one. Overall he felt pretty good. His right arm and face throbbed from his exertion, as did the foot, but other than that he felt strong and he was anxious to get out of bed and move around. Besides, he had to regain his mobility if he was going to make the rendezvous with Eliot.

It was fortunate for him that a railing was on the side of the stairs as he descended. A little more than halfway down, a white fog rushed to his head bringing with it a cold sweat. He fell on the railing and tried to clear his head. The white fog grew more dense and began to darken.

The next thing he knew, Nell and Jenny were holding him up, one on each side. They helped him down the stairs and into a chair. A few minutes later his head began to clear. Jenny gently mopped the moisture from the sides of his face and his upper lip.

"Why didn't you call us?" Nell scolded.

Drew shrugged. "I thought I could make it by myself."

Nell shook her head and returned to her working place by the window which opened onto High Street.

When his strength returned, Drew offered to read from the Bible, using it as a chance to inquire about his missing Bible. Jenny said she still hadn't seen it. Nell said she thought it was in the curate's study upstairs, and so Jenny went to look for it. A few moments later she returned, carrying the Bible.

Under pretense of finding a passage to read, Drew looked for Eliot's note. It was still there. In the same place, he thought, but he wasn't sure. Even so, there was no way of knowing if the curate had read the note and placed it back in the Bible. Then another thought occurred to him. What if Nell was the one who was using the Bible? She knew where to find it. Had she read it? If so, how could he explain Eliot's note?

The Scripture passage Drew read was selected by joint effort. True to her word, Nell left the decision to Drew. He wanted to read more about the adventurous Apostle Paul—*about* him, not *by* him, he emphasized—but he had no idea where to look. "Why not start at the beginning of his adventure?" Nell suggested. She guided him to the book of Acts, chapter 9. He scanned the chapter silently for embarrassing references before beginning to read.

"What's the matter? Don't you trust me?" Nell teased.

As Nell and Jenny pinned, looped, twisted, and tied their lace, Drew read most of chapter 9 (under Nell's direction he skipped the last eleven verses as well as chapters 10, 11, and 12 since they were about Peter) and chapters 13 and 14.

A wild thought troubled Drew as he read about Paul and Barnabas at Iconium, where there was a plot to stone them. Fortunately, the plot was uncovered and the apostles fled. Drew wondered what the townspeople of Edenford would do to him if they knew the reason for his presence among them.

Following lunch and a nap, Drew felt good enough to leave the house. Nell insisted someone accompany him. So Christopher Matthews asked if he felt up to a little walk. When Drew said he was, the curate handed him a walking cane, a gift from old Cyrus Furman.

It felt good to get outside. The slight breeze was stimulating, cold on his face and foot, and, although bright, Drew welcomed the sun like a long-lost friend. Walking the streets of Edenford, he felt like a returning battle hero. Everyone they passed said a kind word and thanked Drew again for saving the Cooper boy. With each encounter Christopher Matthews beamed like a proud father.

The curate led Drew to the Cooper residence, located above David Cooper's cobbler shop. The upper room was extremely warm with no windows or source of circulation. Lying prostrate on the bed was a swollen and blistered Thomas. His mother was beside him, dabbing his limbs with a wet cloth. The boy's eyes were closed. Drew was beginning to wonder if coming here was a good idea. Seeing the boy like this caused him to feel faint.

"Is he going to be all right?" Drew asked.

"He's in God's hands," the cobbler said.

"What did the doctor say?"

The curate answered this time. "He didn't come." No further explanation was offered, and from the resentful looks on the faces of the curate and the boy's parents, Drew didn't ask for one.

"He's just now beginning to respond to us," the cobbler said.

Drew walked to the side of the bed. Thomas' features were engulfed in swollen skin.

"Thomas," he said. "This is Drew."

No response.

"I hope you get better. I'd hate to be the only blue person in the village."

It took a moment, but then the corners of the boy's mouth turned upward and a tear trickled down the side of his face.

As they descended the stairs the Cooper family heaped "Thank yous" and "God bless yous" upon Drew. There were so many of them he ran out of ways to respond, so he just smiled a lot and nodded. There was a tense moment as Drew reached the foot of the stairs. James was seated on a stool hammering a heel to the bottom of a shoe. He hadn't been back to the vats since the accident, choosing instead to work with his father. The hand that gripped the hammer looked like it was wearing a blue glove; and there was a prominent blue stain on his forehead. At the sight of Drew, James dropped his hammer and stalked out the back door. The smiles that had been everywhere moments before vanished, as the two visitors took their leave.

"It's not you," the curate said. "He's angry with himself for causing the accident, and even more so for failing to rescue his brother. Like the stains on his hand and forehead, you remind him of his failure. It's difficult for him. Every time he sees his reflection, he sees the mark of Cain."

"The mark of Cain?"

"In the book of Genesis. Cain killed his brother Abel, so God put a mark on Cain as a warning to others. Cain's punishment was having to live with the guilt of his actions. That's how James feels."

As they turned on to High Street Drew said, "I've been thinking of something you said to me earlier."

"Oh? What's that?"

"About God having a hand in bringing me to Edenford. Maybe I was brought here to rescue Thomas."

The curate thought for a moment. "Could be," he said. "But I have a feeling there's more to it than that."

Saturday the mystery regarding Drew's Bible was solved. The curate had borrowed it. Apparently, while preparing his sermon, he became curious about how the King James' translators had handled the passage. Drew was asleep and the curate didn't think Drew would mind if he borrowed the Bible. Of course, Drew didn't mind, but there was still the unanswered question regarding the note hidden in its pages. Had the curate read it or not?

All work ceased in Edenford at 3 o'clock in preparation for the Sabbath Day observances on Sunday. The evening meal consisted of vegetable soup. There was no bread or meat. Conversation during and after the dinner was low key. Shortly after 9:30 while the others were talking of bed, Drew announced that he had been sleeping too much lately, wasn't tired, and was feeling so good he thought he'd take a walk. He grabbed his walking cane and left. No one expressed undue alarm.

It was chilly outside. Halfway down High Street Drew thought about going back for a coat but decided against it. Considering how easy it was to slip out of the house, he didn't want to take any chances of complicating the matter. His shoeless foot was cold, but what could he do about it? He'd just have to manage somehow.

The dark cracks between the shuttered windows indicated that most of the families on High Street had retired for the night.

As he headed downhill toward Market Street, he had a sudden realization. Eliot said to meet him near the bridge, but he didn't say which bridge. Was he to meet him at the north bridge or at the south bridge by the mill?

At Market Street he had to decide. Which way? Left or right? He looked up and down the tree-lined street dimly lit by street lamps. A bulging row of shadows lined the road beneath the trees. Beyond the trees the village green and church could be seen clearly in the moonlight.

Suddenly, two figures emerged from beneath a tree midway down the road. Drew stepped into a shadow against the last house on High Street. Because of the moon's position, the shadow from the eaves didn't fully cover him. He pressed himself harder against the wall. Whispers and giggles came from the two figures. Holding hands they ran toward Chesterfield Road—away from him.

Drew chose the north bridge because that was the bridge he had crossed to enter Edenford and he assumed Eliot would come the same way. He hugged the right side of Market Street walking in the tree's shadows as the street rounded toward the main thoroughfare. Passing the church, he headed north on Bridge Street, which was lined with two-foot-high stone walls, and crossed the three-arched stone bridge. He looked for Eliot. No one. It didn't concern him; he was early.

Drew sat on the stone bridge wall and waited. In minutes he was shivering, as the cold penetrated his clothing. The trickling sound of the river below made him even colder, especially his toes. He tried folding his arms to keep warm, but his right arm still wouldn't bend far enough for that. To warm his toes he gingerly tucked them in the crease of the back of his right leg. He was beginning to wonder if he was at the right bridge. It was too dark to see the other bridge from here; he could barely make out the mill. Looking back at the village, he saw a few lights on some of the higher streets. What about the castle on the hill? No. Not a chance. It was too dark to be able to . . .

"Drew!"

Drew whirled around.

"Eliot?"

"Down here!" The voice came from the riverbank below the bridge. Drew looked down. It was Eliot, his hair sticking up like pickets.

Drew rounded the end of the bridge and slid down the slope to the river.

Eliot's eyes opened wide with surprise. "What the . . ? Are you blue?" He burst into laughter, his hyena laugh.

"Shh! Someone will hear you!" When that didn't work, "It was an accident!"

"No kiddin'! I thought ya did it on purpose!" Eliot fell to the ground, clutching his sides and laughing, rolling in the leaves along the bank. At times his laughter would taper off, then he'd take another look at Drew and start all over again.

Up to this point Drew had been so concerned with the noise of Eliot's laughing, that he hadn't taken a good look at him. Of the two, Drew looked the less strange. Eliot was dressed like a caveman, wearing nothing more than an animal skin loin covering. He was filthy and rolling in the muddy river bank only added a fresh coat of what was already there. All over his legs, arms, chest, and back were streaks of red. Scratches? Blood?

"Eliot, shut up! You'll wake the whole town!"

It took a while, but eventually Eliot's laughter digressed to an occasional snort. He got to his feet and stood opposite Drew, trying to keep from laughing.

"Your note said it was urgent. Is the bishop all right?"

"Got some great stuff for you, blue boy," Eliot chuckled.

"Is the bishop all right?"

"Sure. Why wouldn't he be?"

"I don't know. His last message to me was strange. Like he wasn't happy with me."

Eliot scoffed. "You really are stupid, aren't you? The guy loves you. Everything you do pleases him." Eliot stuck a finger in his ear and wiggled it vigorously as he spoke.

"So, why are you here?"

"Wait here." Eliot dug behind some bushes and pulled out a pouch. From the pouch he took a letter and a piece of paper. He handed Drew the letter first. Muddy finger marks were all over it. "From the bishop," he said.

Drew took the letter. The seal was broken. "It's been opened."

"Wanted to see if it was a love letter. What are all those numbers? Code, right? Why're you usin' code?"

"You shouldn't have opened my letter," Drew said, his voice rising.

A queer look crossed Eliot's face. He stepped back and raised his dirt-crusted fists. The other paper fluttered to the ground and landed at water's edge. "Want to beat it out of me? Come on! Try it! I bet you couldn't even land a blow." When Drew didn't respond, Eliot moved toward him, punching Drew's shoulder, slapping his face.

Drew winced, not so much from the blows, but from the pain on his burned flesh.

"Come on! Try an' hit me. Use the cane if you want!" Eliot taunted.

Drew shook his head. "Stop it, Eliot! What else do you have?"

When he saw Drew wasn't going to respond, Eliot lowered his fists. Facing Drew at all times he retrieved the paper from the water's edge. One corner was wet. "There was a raid at Peterborough," he said. "They was printin' Justin pamphlets. We found some of these. Pages of Justin's writing, in his own hand. The bishop wants you to match the writin' on this page with this curate's writin'."

"Christopher Matthews?"

"That's him. The bishop thinks this guy might be Justin. Maybe not. I took pages to a couple of other guys too. Same instructions."

Drew took the paper. "Tell the bishop I'll compare the writing."

"Tell him yourself!" Eliot spat. "In one of those number love letters!"

Drew tucked the letter and the writing sample in his shirt. He wanted to get out of there as quickly as he could. Eliot had always been strange, but Drew had never seen him this wild.

"I've got to get back," he said.

"What's the matter? Blue boy doesn't want to be seen with me?"

Drew planted the tip of his walking stick into the hillside and started up the slope.

"I'm not good enough for you? You can make love to a bishop, but not to me?" Eliot grabbed Drew's injured arm.

Drew stifled a yell and pushed him away.

"Hey! Does blue hurt?" Eliot came right back and began dancing around Drew, punching and squeezing every blue area he saw. Each contact brought fresh pain.

Drew tried to ward off the punches, but he had only one arm to defend himself. He took a wild swing with the stick, missing Eliot completely. The look in Eliot's eyes showed he was clearly enjoying Drew's pain.

Another swing and miss.

"You are slow, blue boy!" Eliot landed a couple of blows to prove his point.

Drew was getting angry. He tried again to go up the slope but Eliot jumped in his path. He tried to step around him and Eliot jumped in front of him.

"Eliot, I'm tired of your game. Let me pass."

"Try and get past me!" Eliot taunted. He stood on higher ground, hands on hips.

Drew looked around him. The river was too wide to attempt crossing it; immediately downstream the footing of the bridge blocked his way. The only way out of the river gorge was to climb the slope, the one blocked by Eliot Venner.

Drew moved straight at Eliot. Eliot pushed him back. A second attempt yielded the same results. On the third try, Drew lowered his left shoulder and tried to fake one way and slip past Eliot the other way. The fake worked, but Drew's burned foot slipped on some leaves and he fell with a thump. Eliot put a foot on Drew's back and let out an animal cry of victory.

Eliot's other foot was planted next to Drew's good arm. He saw his chance. Releasing the walking stick, Drew seized

Eliot's foot and yanked with all his might, sending the half-naked man plummeting to the ground on his backside. Drew tried to scramble to his feet; they failed him, and he went sliding down the slope.

Now Eliot was up, his eyes filled with fury and his dirt-covered cheeks puffing in and out with each exaggerated breath. Letting out a scream, he charged toward Drew who was still struggling to get up.

With hands held high, fingers extended like claws, Eliot charged. Drew did the only thing he could do. Having regained his balance, he stood in a crouched position, ready to take on his attacker. Eliot was hurtling straight toward him. At the last second, Drew dropped to the ground on his good shoulder and rolled into Eliot's legs. The charging Eliot flew over him, into the river.

Before Eliot could get out, Drew stood over him with a large boulder raised unsteadily over his head; his burned arm was stiff and weak, and did little more than steady the boulder.

"That's enough, Eliot!" Drew shouted.

Eliot spit water out of his mouth and shook his head. "I was only havin' a little fun."

"Go have fun somewhere else."

"I thought you were supposed to be some kinda knight or something." Eliot shook his head. "Knights are supposed to like fighting. Some knight you are!"

With the boulder still aimed at him, Eliot climbed out of the river, grabbed his pouch, and headed upstream.

Drew watched him go. He wasn't about to lower the rock or turn his back until he knew Eliot was gone. Just then he remembered something.

"Eliot!" he called in a forced whisper. "Eliot! He had to call several times before Eliot turned around.

"Shubal Elkins," Drew shouted. "Lord Chesterfield's

groundskeeper. Did you kill him?"

Eliot turned and walked upstream.

"Did you kill him?" Drew called after him.

Eliot Venner dropped his pouch. He raised both arms skyward and danced wildly in circles, around and around, howling like a wolf.

A hurt, exhausted Drew Morgan limped across the bridge into Edenford. He couldn't get over how much Eliot had changed. He'd always been crazy, but this Eliot was unstable and dangerous. Drew made a mental note to tell the bishop of his fight with Eliot tonight. Then he returned to the task at hand, the Justin manuscript. He always knew there was a possibility that Christopher Matthews was Justin, but Nell told him her father wasn't good at writing. Still, he'd have to check. That would mean finding a time he could sneak into the curate's study. He just hoped that it wasn't true.

"Master Morgan?"

Drew jumped at the unexpected voice. A tall thin figure emerged from the tree shadows in front of the church. The scarecrow. Ambrose Dudley.

"A little late for a stroll, don't you think?" the scarecrow asked.

Chapter 16

DREW was shaking. The bizarre evening had unnerved him. His toes were caked with mud and nearly frozen; his foot pounded with pain which gave him an intense headache; his bandaged right arm was stiff and he could barely move his fingers. He ached all over and wanted nothing more than to crumble onto his bedding in front of the fireplace.

He didn't want to think about his fight with Eliot. It disturbed him that his trainer turned on him like that. Why did Eliot want to hurt him?

Thinking of weird people, there was also Ambrose Dudley. Drew wasn't convinced the scrivener accepted his explanation of a late night walk and accidentally falling down the river embankment. But then why shouldn't Dudley believe him? He was out taking a stroll too!

Just then a frightening realization made Drew shiver. It was Dudley who had delivered Eliot's uncoded note! Had he read it? It would certainly explain his presence. Drew fought to remember if the note showed signs of having been opened. He couldn't remember any, but then he hadn't thought to check. It didn't matter. The fact was, Dudley was out there. Had he overheard Drew's conversation with Eliot? He had to have heard something. At least, the howling.

Drew nervously glanced behind him. The street was empty. The shadows were deep, though, deep enough to hide a skinny scrivener. Drew tried to walk casually, as casually as a blue man with frozen toes can walk. He took deep breaths to calm himself.

All right. Assume Dudley read the note and overheard my conversation with Eliot. Does that change anything? No. My plan can still work. To be safe, though, I will need to work quickly and get out of Edenford at the earliest possible moment.

Opening the Matthews' front door as quietly as he could, he stepped inside the dark room. A snoring sound came from the floor. Puzzled, Drew waited a moment for his eyes to adjust. After several blinks, the interior of the room came into view. The curate was asleep on the floor; Drew had assumed he would return to sleeping on the floor beginning tonight.

He stepped past the slumbering curate toward the staircase. A light at the top of the stairs guided his way up. The light came from the study where Nell was seated in her father's chair, bent over his desk. Drew couldn't see her face or what she was doing, and she couldn't see him. Considering his failure to explain his muddy appearance once tonight already, he decided to slip past the door and into his room.

His next step landed on a loose board that squealed under his weight.

"Oh!" Nell started, her left hand slapping her chest. "Drew Morgan! You scared me beyond Land's End!"

It was more than an expression. The horror on her face was real. Whoever she thought Drew was, it terrified her.

"Sorry," he said sheepishly. "I didn't mean to frighten you. You were busy and I didn't want to disturb you."

Nell turned some papers over on the desk. "Did you have . . ." She closed a ledger or journal of some sort before looking up. ". . . a nice . . . Drew Morgan! What in heaven's name happened to you? You look like you've been rolling in the mud! Have you been fighting?"

The sheepish look worked well with her moments before, so he stuck with it. "Well, yes and no. I haven't been fighting, but I have sort of been rolling in the mud. I guess I'm just naturally clumsy. I was walking along the river and fell down the bank."

"You look a mess. Not real smart, Master Morgan. You could have fallen in and drowned!"

He shrugged. "Maybe. It's just that I like the river at night, the way the moon reflects on it. It's peaceful; and I needed a place to think." He glanced at the papers she was hiding on the desk. "You're up late, aren't you?"

"Well . . . yes," she followed his glance. Satisfied that everything was covered up, she looked up again. "I do my best thinking at night. And journal writing." She tapped the cover of the book she had closed.

An uneasy silence hung between them. Nell fingered the edge of a piece of paper with one hand and adjusted her white cotton nightgown upward with the other. Drew wiggled his bandaged, mud-crusted blue toes.

"I guess I'll turn in," he said.

"Me too."

Drew went to his room, lit a candle, and closed the door.

Holding Bishop Laud's note so it faced the candle's flame, he scanned the neatly printed numbers: (41/3/18/2) (40/15/17/1-2) (10/2/21/6-16) (23/13/6/3-11) (18/6/8) (10/12/23/25-27) (42/1/23/8).

The first word was easy. His name. Huddled near the candle, he used his Bible to decode the rest of the message. *"Do not turn thee aside to thy right hand or to thy left. For the Day of the Lord is at hand. Oh, that I might have my request; and that God would grant me the thing that I long for! Return to me soon."*

Settling back in bed, resting his head on his good hand, Drew analyzed the message. It contained nothing new—hold your course, time is short, come home soon. There was, of course, the standard affectionate remark which made him think of what Eliot said . . . the bishop's lover. Eliot didn't really think that, did he? Drew shuddered at the thought and dismissed it.

Sitting up, he reached for the page of Justin's manuscript. It was crumpled and the lower left hand corner was torn off. Drew was confident it was in better condition when Eliot first received it. He smoothed out the wrinkles before studying it. The penmanship was careless and hurried, as if the author couldn't get his thoughts on paper fast enough. Then there were the letters themselves. The capital T began with a large loop that swooped across the top of the stem. The lower loops on both the g and y were pointed at the ends and the loops were so closed, so narrow, they were hardly loops at all. Drew hadn't seen enough of the curate's handwriting to tell just by looking at the manuscript if this was his. He would have to compare it with another writing sample. In the study he could probably find a letter or sermon notes.

Drew laughed at himself as he looked at the paper again. For the first time, words formed on the page. He had been so intent on analyzing the handwriting that he'd ignored the content of the page. It was the ideas behind the words that were throwing all England into turmoil. He smoothed the manuscript fragment again and began to read:

> *. . . leaders of our government follow the Lord? Should we, like them, forsake God too? Heaven forbid!*
>
> *And what should be our response if, in the name of the Lord, they move against us with the laws of England?*
>
> *Should we return hate for hate?*
>
> *Should our response to evil be evil?*
>
> *The Prophet Micah answers our questions.*

"He hath showed thee, O man, what is good, and what the Lord requireth of thee: surely to do justly, and to love mercy, and to humble thyself, to walk with thy God." (Micah chapter 6, verse 8)

Regardless of what evil men do to us, God's requirements of us remain unchanged.

Will we forsake justice simply because we are treated unjustly?

Will we abandon mercy because others are unmerciful?

Will we refuse to humble ourselves before God to follow in the footsteps of evil men? footsteps that lead to destruction?

"Alas!" Englishmen cry. "Unless we destroy the evil powers among us, surely they will destroy us!"

My response is, "Surely they will not!"

If there is one message in the Bible that rings clear and true, it is this: Evil men will ultimately fail; godly men will ultimately prevail.

Can you not see the truth in this?

If it seem unclear to you, use your eyes of faith and God will make it plain. The Ancients understood this truth. Though encompassed by evil men, they chose a life of faith.

By faith Abel offered a better sacrifice than Cain.

By faith Enoch pleased God.

By faith Noah condemned the world and became the heir of righteousness.

By faith Abraham obeyed God even though he did not know where he was going.

These men did not receive the things promised

From this point to the end of the page, words were missing, lost with the torn corner of the paper.

m from a distance. And they admitted they were
rims
    on the earth.
        rd us any less if we are as faithful as
            d not be dictated by our enemies,
                in the living God who will

Drew set the manuscript on the table and snuffed out the candle. He doubted seriously that Christopher Matthews was the notorious pamphleteer Justin. But he knew one thing about the curate and the unknown writer—the two men were cut from the same cloth.

A scream awakened him. Bolting upright, Drew's body jumped into action while his mind fumbled for details. It was a woman's scream. Now there was another sound. Laughter? No, not laughter. Sobbing. It was sobbing.

He jumped out of bed. Surrounded by darkness and still somewhat disoriented, he felt his way toward the door. His arm hit something. Crash! The candlestick. He could hear it rolling on the wooden floor. Shuffling his feet, he kicked it aside. He reached for the door and felt the latch.

Fully awake now, Drew stood in the hallway straining to hear more sounds that would give him direction. A sobbing came from Nell and Jenny's room. He stepped toward the door. Now he heard hushing sounds and a soothing voice whispering words of comfort.

"Just a dream," the voice said. "It's all right now. It was just a dream."

The voice was Jenny's.

By Sunday morning Drew was able to squeeze his blue toes into a shoe. It was painful and he walked with a limp, but it suited his purpose. He could endure the pain for a day.

Both Nell and Jenny were unusually somber as Drew walked with them to the church service. Drew concluded they were feeling the effects of Nell's nightmare. As was his custom, the curate had gone ahead to open the church building. The solemn trio ran into the Coopers at the town well. Little Thomas, still blue from head to toe, was carried to church in his father's arms as a thank offering to a merciful God. The boy was stiff and his eyes were barely open. He began crying halfway to the church from pain, but settled down once he was inside.

Since the disaster in Norwich when the Reverend Laslett publicly unmasked him in the Sunday morning service, Drew was cautious whenever he entered a church building. He always took a quick inventory of transgressions. If things were suddenly put right, he was in danger. The altar was not in the prescribed place, nor was it railed off. Good. The curate was standing in front. He was not wearing a surplice. Good. The litany began strictly according to the approved order of service. The people listened when they were supposed to listen, stood when they were supposed to stand, bowed and prayed when they were supposed to, all according to the dictates of the English Church. No cause for alarm yet. Then Matthews stood to preach. Would he read an approved sermon, or would he preach his own? The curate opened a book. It was his Bible. Good. When he spoke, he preached from notes. It was his own sermon, not an approved one. Good. Drew relaxed. There were no indications they were on to him.

For his sermon Matthews had chosen a Scripture passage from Deuteronomy that recorded Moses' final instructions to the people of Israel as they entered the Promised Land. Moses would not be joining them. For reasons that were unclear to Drew, this was the way God wanted it.

Drawing from the Scripture passage, the curate formulated

three admonitions for the townspeople of Edenford:

First, set your hearts on God's Word, he told them. For God's Word is a sure and constant guide for your life's journey. Second, command your children to observe God's ways. A nation is never more than one generation away from apostasy, he warned. Third, observing God's commands is not a vain thing; it is your life. He explained that this third admonition was the basis for true belief. Obedience to God's ways as taught in the Bible was the foundation for all of life.

Seated between Nell and Jenny, Drew pondered the words of Edenford's curate. When the preacher described the evils of the present godless generation, Drew buried his head in his hands. His shoulders shook. Jenny asked him if he was feeling ill. Drew didn't respond. As the curate expounded on his third point, Drew doubled over, his head and hands on his knees.

"The future of God's people in England is dark," the curate boomed. "Black, menacing forces muster on the horizon, building up strength to rain destruction upon us. But we are God's people. We are not without hope. In His graciousness, God has given me a vision of a promised land for His English people."

The curate had everyone's attention. Even those who had been dozing to this point listened intently. Their curate was offering them a glimpse into the future. No one wanted to miss it.

"God has shown me that His faithful people will prevail. More than prevail! God has shown me that His people will live in a land where people will set their hearts on the things of God, citizens and leaders alike. They will not crave power or riches, or the things of this world. In this land children will be taught to worship God and serve Him all the days of their lives. In this land men and women will live free from the fear of persecution. For the magistrates, the nobles, the common people, from the greatest to the least, will walk humbly before God. God has assured me it is not a vain thing to dream about such a land. This is God's will for us. The same God of Israel who led His people out of slavery and into the Promised Land will lead us from this land of persecution to a land flowing with milk and honey. No longer will we be the slaves of evil men, for we will live in a land of freedom."

His sermon concluded, the curate led the congregation in a prayer.

As she bowed to pray, Nell's eyes caught a verse from her Bible still open on her lap. "And the Lord spake unto Moses saying, 'Thou shalt therefore see the land before thee, but shalt not go thither, I mean, into the land which I give the Children of Israel.' "

Nell thought of the prophecy and her father, and she wept.

"May I say something?"

Drew stood and spoke loudly just as the service ended. Some of the children, anxious to get outside, had already made it to the aisle. Adults were gathering their belongings. The curate was standing to the side of the pulpit. Drew's words suspended all action.

"Do you wish to address the entire congregation?" the curate asked.

"Yes. May I come to the front?"

The curate nodded.

As Drew slipped past Nell and walked to the front, parents pulled restless children back to their seats.

Reaching the platform, Drew stood with eyes downcast, his hands folded in front. For a long time he just stood there, struggling for the right words. The longer he delayed, the more everyone's attention focused on him. He didn't say anything until all the rustling stopped.

"I was sent here to spy on you."

A collective gasp rose from the congregation. Drew looked up. The first face he saw was Jenny's. It registered shock. Next to her, Nell scowled. In the back David Cooper and James stood, huge hairy arms folded across their chests. Ambrose Dudley's face was gathered in a mass of wrinkles around his nose making him look like a weasel. There was one face Drew couldn't see since it was behind him—which was just as well. He didn't think he could bear to look at Edenford's curate right now.

"It's true," he continued. "Powerful men who hate Puritans taught me to believe you are evil, that you are a threat to England. I lied to you when I told you I was traveling to Plymouth. Edenford was my destination all along. My mission was to spy on your curate, Christopher Matthews, and to record any violations of Church of England procedures."

The congregation was becoming agitated. Drew hurried on, increasing his volume and intensity.

"I have noted several violations for which you can be prosecuted: The communion table is not set against the east wall, nor is it railed off; your curate doesn't wear a surplice when he officiates at church services; you do not bow at the name of Jesus; and you hold evening preaching services. All of these are in direct violation of English law."

The commotion grew even louder. Drew adjusted his volume upward again.

"Men have been tried, convicted, whipped, and disfigured for these offenses! I have witnessed these things personally!"

The congregation grew even louder. Drew had to shout to be heard.

"Please hear me out! For I have discovered one other vital fact!" He paused. The commotion subsided slightly. "I have learned that the men who hate you are wrong!"

Silence. This wasn't what they were expecting. Some, thinking they heard wrong, asked those sitting next to them to repeat what he said.

"They are wrong. You have proved that to me. You're not evil. You're not dangerous. It was wrong of me to spy on you. The very man I came to investigate welcomed me into his house as a guest. All of you have accepted me and loved me as one of your own. I never knew this kind of love existed."

Smiles of relief appeared.

"Through your actions you have shown me the true love of Jesus Christ. I am unworthy of you. My only request is that you forgive me. I will leave Edenford immediately and never trouble you again."

Head bowed, Drew stepped from the platform and limped toward the door.

"Drew! Wait!" the curate called after him.

Drew stopped mid-aisle.

"Let him go!" someone shouted. Several others echoed this sentiment.

Christopher Matthews went to Drew and put an arm around his shoulders. "You have heard his confession," the curate said, "and have witnessed his repentance. Isn't this the essence of everything we believe? Christ died to forgive our sin! Who among us came to Christ except through the forgiveness of sin? Who among us has not done something for which we are ashamed?"

The curate waited for an opposing opinion which he knew would not come.

Turning to Drew, the curate said, "Is this what you want? Do you want Jesus Christ to forgive your sin? Do you want to become one of His disciples?"

Drew looked into the curate's pleading eyes. The man's arm around his shoulder was warm yet firm. He glanced out at Jenny, her eyes were pleading, just like her father's. He couldn't see Nell's expression, her head was bowed, hiding her face behind a curtain of brown hair.

"If He will have me," Drew said softly.

Drew Morgan was baptized in the River Exe that afternoon.

To the children's delight, the celebration that followed canceled their Sunday afternoon catechism instruction. The people of Edenford ate, sang, and talked away the daylight hours. Without exception, every member of the town shook the new convert's hand. Their acceptance of Edenford's newest church member, however, was mixed.

Jenny gave Drew a hug, holding it a little longer than most of the women standing nearby deemed appropriate.

"My, aren't we full of surprises!" Nell said. She hugged Drew too, a brief hug around the shoulders.

Ambrose Dudley held out a bony hand which Drew found dry and cold. "Welcome, Master Morgan," he said. Leaning closer, he whispered, "By their fruits ye shall know them, Matthew chapter 7, verse 20."

That night Drew lay on his bedding in the darkness of the Matthews' sitting room. He stared at the ceiling beams and smiled.

Eliot, you're a genius! he thought. *You're weird, but a genius!*

The events of the day had unfolded just as Eliot said they would. The gambit worked to perfection. *"Begin by telling them the truth, that you're a spy."* Drew remembered laughing when Eliot first suggested the tactic. *"No foolin',"* Eliot insisted. *"It works! Tell 'em you're a spy and that you have the goods on them but you just can't go through with it. Tell 'em that they've won you over to the faith. That you've seen the light (that's an expression they like to hear) and that you've learned the error of your ways. The worse the scoundrel you make your-*

*self out to be, the more they'll want to forgive you. And then—
this is the best part—always tell 'em you're leaving, that you're
unworthy to be around 'em. They'll beg you to stay! Really! No
foolin'! They'll beg you to stay! And then they'll tell you every
secret in the church! They're suckers for the conversion trick. All
you have to do is look sincere and it'll work every time!"*

Ambrose Dudley was the real puzzle. Every indication was
that he suspected something; and surely he'd heard the yelling beside the river that night, if not the entire conversation.
Why hadn't he said something publicly? What was he waiting
for? Then again, maybe Drew was making too much of it.
Judging from the townspeople's reaction, he concluded he
had succeeded in looking sincere enough, because the plan
worked—to perfection.

After a full morning of business, it was Christopher Matthews who gave Drew the opportunity to sneak into his upstairs study.

"You look tired," he said. "That's not surprising. You had
a busy day yesterday and have been going strong all morning.
Why don't you go home and take a nap?"

Drew did his best to look sleepy-eyed. "I am tired," he
agreed. "But I have too much to learn and you need the help.
I'll be all right."

The curate insisted, as Drew knew he would, and it was
settled. Since he would be unable to sleep in the sitting room
while Nell and Jenny worked, he would have to go upstairs.
The curate would be gone and Nell and Jenny would be busy,
a perfect opportunity to get into the study.

Following a meager lunch of soup broth, Drew read Scripture to the girls as they worked. Then he yawned and climbed
the stairs for his nap. He pulled the bedroom door closed
from the outside, loud enough for the girls to hear it.

He didn't go to the study immediately, not until he was

convinced the conversation downstairs was continuing in a normal manner.

"You like him, don't you?" he heard Jenny ask.

"Drew? I don't know what you're talking about," Nell replied.

"What are you going to tell James?"

Nell didn't respond for what seemed a long time. Drew strained to hear something, anything.

"Well?" It was Jenny again.

"There's nothing to tell him," Nell said sharply.

When their conversation shifted to the bone lace, Drew concluded it was safe to move into the study. Remembering the creaking board that had scared Nell a few nights earlier, Drew took a large step over it into the study. His eyes darted around for loose papers.

The desk was neatly arranged with two stacks of books on the far right-hand corner. A quill pen and inkwell were situated center forward. There were no papers on the desk. Drew scanned the bookshelves above the desk. He spotted the curate's Bible and pulled it from the shelf. He flipped through the pages and found what he was looking for. Sermon notes from Sunday. Deuteronomy, Moses, the Israelites, and the Promised Land.

He pulled the page of Justin's manuscript from his pocket and laid the sermon notes and manuscript side by side. He looked for capital Ts, and lowercase letters with descenders — y, g, p. There were enough of them to make a valid comparison. He bit his lower lip and sighed. Satisfied, he put Justin's manuscript back in his pocket, the loose papers in the Bible, and placed the Bible back on the shelf.

Before leaving, he looked over the desk to make sure everything was as he found it. He was being overcautious. *Better to be sure than to get caught due to carelessness,* he reasoned. He checked the row of books on the shelf; some were pushed back farther than others. A random ordering. No one would notice any change. The inkwell and pen, undisturbed. The double stack of books on the corner. Just as they were when he came . . .

He noticed a familiar volume. It was on the bottom of the far right stack—the one Nell closed and hid from him the night he frightened her upon returning from his meeting with Eliot. Probably her journal. The temptation to take a quick look at it was irresistible.

Drew glanced at the doorway. He didn't expect to see anyone standing there—he would have heard them come up the stairs—but he looked to make sure. With deliberate slowness, he lifted the top books to one side and pulled the buried volume in front of him. He opened the cover. There was no name, no writing at all. There was, however, a finely crafted cross made of bone lace. A bookmark? He lifted it to examine it more closely. The strands were delicate and expertly woven, without flaw as far as he could tell. The cloth strands had a sweet, mild scent to them, reminding him of Nell. It was the same scent he smelled the day they walked arm-in-arm to the castle ruins. Holding the lace to his nose, he breathed in, savoring the scent and the memory.

Returning the lace cross to the front of the book, he flipped the pages randomly. It was Nell's journal. He read an entry. Lord Chesterfield was being unreasonable. He had demanded an impossible amount of lace in an unreasonable time. The crisis? A party at Theobalds. Nell was unsympathetic to his plight. In another entry, she and Jenny had had a fight. There were no details, but Nell was upset that Jenny was too trusting, too naive. Nell was afraid Jenny would some day get hurt. In another entry, Nell struggled with pride. She asked God to forgive her. And another, James was making advances. She asked God for wisdom in helping him mature.

This last entry infuriated Drew. A mental picture of that

hairy giant's hands on Nell incensed him. Then a thought struck him. *Does she say anything about me?* He flipped the pages toward the end of the book, looking for his name. There. Drew Morgan. . . .

The door downstairs opened and closed.

"Poppa!" He heard Jenny's childlike squeal. "What are you doing home?"

Hurriedly, Drew closed the journal and placed it back on the corner of the desk. Then, impulsively, he took the lace cross from inside the cover and thrust it in his pocket. Listening for steps on the staircase, he piled the other books back on top of Nell's journal. Still no sound of footsteps. The curate was explaining to Nell and Jenny that Cyrus Furman was suffering from loneliness. Since the Furmans didn't have a Bible, the curate had come to get his so he could comfort the watchman with Scripture.

Drew quickly tiptoed over the noisy floorboard, quietly worked the bedroom doorlatch, and slipped inside the room. He lay on the bed, his heart pounding. The heavy thud of the curate's boots fell on the stairs. A creaking floorboard indicated he reached the top landing. A few moments later, the floorboard sounded again followed by descending footsteps.

Drew lay on the bed for more than two hours, sleep far from him. In the darkness of the room, he took the lace cross from his pocket and gently caressed it. Raising it to his face, he inhaled Nell's scent and rubbed the lacework against his cheek.

The feelings that churned in him were troubling. He had never had such strong feelings for a woman. He had lusted after women before, many times, like Rosemary at Mile End Tavern. But once his lust had been satisfied, Rosemary disgusted him. He never wanted to see her again. It was true, he desired Nell strongly, but it was more than lust that attracted him to her. He wanted to be with her always. He wanted to make her happy. He wanted her to look at him with the respect he saw in her eyes when she looked at her father. He wanted so much to spend the rest of his life with her by his side. But how could he? She would never leave Edenford and her family. And his future was in London where fame and fortune awaited him.

In fact, everything he had dreamed of and craved all his life was now within his grasp. Notoriety. Praise. Maybe even knighthood. All these things would be his when he revealed to the world that Christopher Matthews was the notorious pamphleteer, Justin.

Chapter 17

As it turned out, Drew would not have had to sneak into Christopher Matthew's study to discover that the curate was Justin. He was told of the notorious pamphleteer's secret identity several nights later at a meeting.

Only a handful of men knew of these covert meetings that were held late at night in the back of the cobbler's shop. When he arrived with Matthews, Drew saw seven men squeezed into the cobbler's small back room among shoes, leather strips, and mounds of wooden heels. Drew recognized most of them: the cobbler David Cooper, of course; Charles Manly, the keeper of the inn; Cyrus Furman, and Ambrose Dudley. He had met two of the other men at church but couldn't remember their names; the third he had never seen before. Drew sat in the only vacant place left, next to the stranger who stared at him rather impolitely. Drew began to take offense and then remembered he was still tinted blue. The dye was fading, and everyone else in the village was used to his color. For the stranger, he was a new and unusual sight.

The curate thanked the men for attending the meeting and led them in a prayer, asking God to give them wisdom in the matters they would discuss.

Following the prayer, the curate looked around the room and chuckled at the close quarters. "Normally, we are six in number. Tonight, we are nine. Our two newest members don't need introduction. This is Ambrose Dudley's first meeting. We have known him for years, as he has distinguished himself as town scrivener. Welcome to the group, Ambrose."

Dudley acknowledged the curate's welcome.

"And you all know Drew Morgan, town hero and our most recent convert."

Drew smiled as everyone looked at him.

"The third gentleman here for the first time is a special guest. I have asked him to speak to us about a matter of utmost importance. He is a respected Puritan leader and a man after God's own heart, John Winthrop."

Drew looked at the guest sitting next to him. He sat erect, assured of himself with a slightly noble bearing. His dark brown hair was longer than that of most Puritan men, falling almost to his shoulders. His face looked even longer than it was because of his thin, straight nose, the line of which pointed past his mustache and down a beard that came to a neatly trimmed point.

The curate continued, "I have asked Master Winthrop to address a specific topic which I will announce shortly. First, we have some business to attend." He looked deliberately at Ambrose Dudley and Drew. Black smoke from the candles curled toward the ceiling, giving the room and the men a look of mystery to match their secrecy. "You two men were recruited after much prayer and are to be commended for coming tonight, even though you know nothing about our work and the reason for our secrecy. In faith, we ask you to join us and share our secret."

"If I may be so bold," Ambrose Dudley raised a thin straight arm, requesting to be recognized.

"Ambrose." The curate recognized him.

"Before any secret information is divulged, I must object to the presence of Master Drew Morgan."

For the second time that night, all eyes turned to Drew.

"I realize I have no right to speak out like this, since this is my first meeting. However, that is the very basis of my objection to him being here. You have known me for over three years. For two years I have served as your scrivener without a complaint lodged against me. Not a single complaint. Yet only now do you include me in your confidence. Master Morgan, on the other hand, has been here a matter of weeks. He arrived as a vagabond, despite the outcome of his trial, and is an admitted spy. I must confess it pains me to think it took me so long to earn your confidence, when a vagabond and spy is so readily admitted into your trust. If you ask me, you are making a mistake by opening yourselves to him so readily."

Ambrose Dudley took his seat.

"Maybe he's right," Charles Manly said.

"Gentlemen." All eyes turned to the curate. "I have defended this young man before and will not hesitate to defend him again. I believe there is no finer man in Edenford than Drew Morgan. It was I who recommended he join us. And I will not withdraw my recommendation now."

"Good enough for me," David Cooper said.

"Me too," said Cyrus Furman.

A chorus of assents followed.

Ambrose Dudley nodded toward the curate, conceding his defeat.

Christopher Matthews explained the covert operation to the newcomers. From John Winthrop's lack of reaction, Drew guessed he was already aware of the secret activities. The curate confessed to writing Puritan propaganda under the pen name, Justin. The manuscript pages were then hidden between layers in the soles of shoes and shipped to various sympathetic printers. An elaborate network of volunteers distributed the printed pamphlets. The new recruits would assist by delivering the special shoe orders from time to time.

Drew was surprised at the calm atmosphere of the meeting. They discussed their illegal operation with an attitude of somber resolve. For some reason he expected to see them wearing wicked grins as they plotted their sedition, the air charged with the anticipation of doing something for which they might get caught. None of these elements were present in the room. It was more like a planning meeting for a funeral than a covert operation.

One other element stood out in Drew's mind—these men were closer than brothers. He could see it in the way they looked at each other, an occasional hug or slap on the back, sometimes a gibe followed by friendly bantering back and forth. They were committed not only to their cause but to each other. Drew envied their closeness. He watched them from a distance, refusing to allow himself to be pulled in emotionally.

A new Justin manuscript was produced and hidden in a pair of shoes. The order was bound for a man named Whitely in Reigate. He would deliver the manuscript to an illegal press in London. It was decided that the bachelors, Charles Manly and Ambrose Dudley, would deliver the goods. Manly was obviously pleased to have his good friend as part of the secret society.

"God was pleased to bring John Winthrop into my life earlier this year," the curate said, as he introduced his guest. "The two of us have something in common. He does legally what I do illegally—writes pamphlets. I came upon his paper, 'Arguments for the Plantation of New England,' and on reading it was impressed with his logic and spiritual depth. I sought him out and have had several enjoyable discussions with him. Rather than relate secondhand information to you, I thought it best to invite him to speak to you directly. He may hold the key to the future of our village."

Matthews yielded the floor to their guest. When he stood he was taller than Drew imagined he would be.

Winthrop straightened his clothes and took an orator's stance before speaking, revealing his education and nobility. "On March 10 of this year of our Lord 1629, as you are well aware, the King of England dissolved parliament. Since that day, he has ruled England in dictatorial fashion, imposing ridiculous taxes—the notorious ship tax being one of them—to raise money without having to reconvene parliament. You yourselves have felt the sting of the king's policies. He taxes you while his bishop persecutes you.

"It is for these reasons that last September I joined eleven other God-fearing men in signing the Cambridge Agreement. We believe that our future lies elsewhere, in another land. We seek a charter that will allow us to emigrate to America.

"How can you leave England? I know the question is on your minds, I see it on your faces. I am persuaded that God will speedily bring heavy affliction upon this land. But be of good comfort. If the Lord sees it will be good for us, He will provide shelter and a hiding place for us and others. Evil times are coming when the church must fly into the wilderness.

"Think of the possibilities! It is our opportunity to provide a refuge for those whom God intends to save from the destruction that awaits us here. The intemperance of England is overwhelming our society. I fear for my children! The fountains of learning and religion are so corrupted that even the best minds and fairest hopes are perverted, corrupted, and utterly overthrown by the multitude of evil examples in the land. In America, we can raise our children to fear God and honor His ways.

"What can be a better work, a more honorable and worthy work, than to help raise and support a particular church while it is in its infancy and to join forces with such a company of faithful people? This new world adventure offers the possibility of joining with like-minded Puritans to plan and establish a pure church in a new land.

"England is crowded, and the poor are a great burden. Since the whole earth is the Lord's garden, why should we struggle here to live on a few acres, when we could have hundreds as good or better in New England?"

"But is it good land?" David Cooper asked.

John Winthrop welcomed the question. He pulled a printed pamphlet from inside his coat. "This was written by Reverend Francis Higginson who settled in New England earlier this year. Listen to what he writes about the land:

It is a land of diverse and sundry sorts all about Massachusetts Bay, and at the Charles River is as fat black earth as can be seen anywhere; and in other places you have a clay soil, in other gravel, in other sandy, as it is all about our plantation at Salem, for so our town is now named. The form of the earth here is neither too flat in the plains, nor too high in hills, but partakes of both in a mediocrity, and fit for pasture or for plow or meadow ground, as men please to employ it. Though all the country be, as it were, a thick wood for the general, yet in diverse places there is much ground cleared by the Indians, and especially about the plantation; and I am told that about three miles from us a man may stand on a little hilly place and see divers thousands of acres of ground as good as need to be, and not a tree in the same.

Winthrop lowered the pamphlet and continued, "Higginson goes on to say that corn grows in abundance—thirty, forty, sixty, a hundredfold is ordinary for a crop."

There were wide-eyed stares all around the room.

"He also describes a land where water is plentiful, with an

abundance of fish. As for wood, there is none better in the world—four kinds of oak, ash, elm, birch, juniper, cypress, cedar, pines, and fir. For beasts there are some bears, deer, wolves, foxes, beavers, otters, and great wild cats."

"What about Indians? Aren't they dangerous?" Charles Manly asked.

"There are Indians," Winthrop conceded. "You have all heard of the dangers from the Jamestown experiment. But I like to look on them as an opportunity for missionary work. They need to hear the Gospel of Christ.

"My task here is to tell you that I am forming an expedition to the New World. We will sail in the spring. And you are all welcome to join us."

"Women and children too?" David Cooper asked. "Isn't that exposing them to great risk?"

"It's true, there is risk. If we go, we may perish by hunger or the sword, and our families and friends come to misery because of us. But who can be sure of safety here? If the course be right, God will keep us from those evils, or enable us to bear them."

"Not me," said Ambrose Dudley. "I'm an Englishman. I'll always be an Englishman."

Winthrop smiled. "For myself," he said, "I have seen so much of the vanity of the world, that I esteem the diversities of countries as so many inns, whereof the traveler that has lodged in the best or in the meanest finds no difference when he comes to his journey's end. I shall call that my country where I may most glorify God and enjoy the presence of my dearest friends."

"What did you think of John Winthrop's proposal?"

Drew and Matthews walked the quiet streets of Edenford from the cobbler's shop to High Street. The meeting had ended soon after Winthrop finished speaking. No decision was expected or forthcoming. An invitation was extended. Now they would think about it and discuss it among themselves. The curate was asking Drew's opinion.

"It sounds exciting."

The curate smiled a knowing smile. "I thought you would think so. A far-off land, waiting to be tamed by adventurous spirits—*young*, adventurous spirits."

"Do you think anybody from Edenford will go with Master Winthrop?"

The curate shook his head. "No, their roots are too deep in Edenford. It would take something greater than a ship tax to dislodge them."

"Then why did you have Master Winthrop come all this way to speak to us?" Drew asked.

"God told me to."

Drew delayed sending a message to Bishop Laud. It wasn't because he was lacking any information. In fact, he had accomplished everything he set out to accomplish in Edenford—he had a list of violations against the curate, enough to put him out of circulation; and, more importantly, he had discovered Edenford's secret. A comparison of handwriting samples readily proved that Christopher Matthews was Justin; what's more, he had confessed the fact and Drew knew how the entire operation worked. So why did he hesitate when it came to informing the bishop of his findings?

If the truth were known, Drew didn't want his experience in Edenford to end. He had committed the ultimate sin for a spy—he had developed feelings for the people he spied on. He was accepted here. More than that, he was respected and loved. What was it the curate said of him at the meeting when Dudley challenged his presence? "I believe there is no finer man in Edenford than Drew Morgan." It was the best thing anyone had ever said about him.

Nell stood against the low stone wall of the ancient Saxon castle. Beyond her lay Edenford, basking in the lazy Sunday afternoon sun. The blue ribbon of the Exe River meandered slowly past the village in the background, studded with diamonds of sunbursts reflecting on its surface. Drew sat on the ground, reclining against a large granite block watching her. Her hands folded a leaf over and back, over and back in zigzag fashion. When she came to the edge of the leaf, she would unfold it, smooth out the creases and begin again. Drew couldn't remember ever seeing her hands still. They were always working on something. On this day of rest, her hands worked the leaf.

Trees stretched beside them and over them, encompassing them in their own private canopy. The light that filtered through the layers of leaves was soft and peaceful, making the sunlit village appear as a mural painted with bold strokes of brilliant green, yellow, and blue hues.

They had come to the castle ruins at Nell's suggestion. They talked of town events, the lack of food and money, and how various people were reacting to the hardship. Nell commented on Drew's improved physical condition. His skin had just a hint of blue, and he had regained full use of his right arm and left foot. She asked him how his apprenticeship with her father was going, and he replied that he was learning a lot about the woolen industry. Then they ran out of things to talk about and fell to silence. Nell had walked over to the wall and folded her leaf while Drew sat and watched her.

"James Cooper asked me to marry him."

"Oh?"

Nell had made her announcement matter-of-factly, without turning around to face him. Drew did his best to hold his voice steady in response. He hoped he didn't sound as startled as he felt.

Nell shook her head. "The night you were at that meeting

with Poppa, James came over and said he wanted to talk to me. We walked down to the village green and he asked me to be his wife."

"Congratulations."

Nell spun around. Her eyes flashed with anger and dismay. "Congratulations? Is that all you can say?"

Drew struggled to his feet. "What else should I say?"

Tears came to her eyes. She looked at him in disbelief. "I can't marry James!"

"Why not?"

"Uhhhh!" Nell turned away in disgust. She produced a handkerchief and furiously dabbed her eyes. "Well, for one thing, he's as dumb as a dirt clod. Then there's his ungodly temper. I'm not going to marry an immature child wearing a man's body simply because we were born at the same time and our fathers are best friends!"

"Do you really think your father expects you to?"

"That's another reason! Who's going to take care of Poppa? Jenny's of marrying age and the way she flirts with boys it won't be long before she gets married. Poppa will be all alone!"

Drew simply nodded. He wasn't about to disagree with her.

"And then, of course, there's the biggest reason."

"The biggest reason?"

Nell turned toward him. She looked at him in wonder. "You're incredible," she said. "You really don't know, do you?"

Drew's expression was blank.

"It's you, silly. How can I marry James when I love you?"

Drew didn't move. He looked for some sign that she was toying with him, but couldn't find any. Her cheeks were wet with tears and those sparkling brown eyes beckoned him to come to her. He took a hesitant step toward her. She flew into his arms, eagerly kissing him over and over again.

Her kisses were warm with tears as he pulled her closer. He embraced her with an intensity that frightened him. He had never experienced a sensation like this. It was as if their souls overlapped and each was now a part of the other. He never wanted to let her go. Nothing on heaven or earth could make him let her go. Nothing except Nell.

"This isn't right," she said pushing herself away.

With the greatest of efforts, he released her. "What do you mean?"

She took a deep breath. "It would be best if you just go." She stepped aside, clearing his way to the path leading down the mountain.

Drew lowered his head and walked toward the path.

"You would go, wouldn't you!"

Drew stopped.

"Isn't it enough that you're kind and caring and handsome? Must you be a gentleman too? Come here, my love!" She held her arms out to him.

Nell Matthews and Drew Morgan kissed each other until they were exhausted. With his blue-stained thumbs, Drew wiped the tears from her cheeks. He kissed one cheek, then the other, then the end of her nose, and eagerly sought her lips again.

After a while, they sat on the remnant of the castle wall overlooking Edenford at dusk. Nell leaned against Drew with her head on his shoulder.

"What are we going to do now?" Drew asked.

"What do you mean?"

"I mean what are we going to do about James? Your father? What are we going to do about us?"

Nell straightened herself and moved away from him slightly. "We're not going to do anything."

"But you said you loved me!"

"And I do. But nothing can come of it."

"How can you say that?" There was more than a touch of anger in Drew's voice.

"Nothing can come of it because we're too different. We come from different backgrounds and we have different futures." Drew attempted to interrupt her, but she wouldn't let him. "I don't care what you say, you will never be happy staying in Edenford. You can't fool me with this woolen industry apprentice game you're playing. You need challenges, adventure, excitement. The only excitement we've had in Edenford is what you've created since your arrival. If you stay, you'll be unhappy; and I could never leave Edenford. Don't look at me like that. Don't you know it breaks my heart to say this? This moment has been special to me. You don't know how I've longed for you to hold me. Until my dying day I will remember this place, your embrace, our kisses. But nothing can come of it."

Later that night Drew lay on top of his bedding and relived every moment, every sensation of the afternoon with Nell. Somehow, he would convince her to come away with him from Edenford. And if he could not, he would stay. For her, he could do it. He'd become a dirt farmer or a shepherd if it meant staying with Nell. She refused all his assurances that she was wrong. He'd have to prove it to her.

Sleep was far from him, but he didn't care. He didn't want to give up conscious control of his thoughts to random dreams, not when his waking dreams were sweeter than anything the land of slumber had ever given him.

He decided on his first step of proving his love to Nell. It would have to be secret for now, but someday he hoped to be able to tell her. Taking his Bible, he searched for the necessary phrases for his message to Bishop Laud. After much searching he found them, coded them, and wrote the code on a piece of paper. It read: (10/17/3/11-15) (42/24/6/1-4) (41/3/18/2). *"The man whom thou seekest, he is not here. Andrew."*

Drew looked for opportunities to be alone with Nell, but they were frustratingly few and far between. Once he asked her to take a walk with him after supper. Jenny and her father thought a walk sounded like a grand idea and the three of them strolled across the south bridge and back while Nell stayed at home and cleaned up the dishes. Another time Jenny was going to take a bowl of soup to Mrs. Everly, one of the town's widows who was under the weather. But the old lady got well and Jenny's assistance wasn't needed.

During this time Nell was distant and cool, showing no outward affection to Drew whenever someone was around. Occasionally, Drew would catch her at an unguarded moment looking at him. Once caught, she would turn her attention elsewhere as if he wasn't around. The Sunday following their rendezvous was the hardest for him. It was Nell's turn to help her father teach the children their catechism lessons. Drew tried to get her to trade off with Jenny, but she insisted in fulfilling her responsibilities. He spent an agonizingly slow Sunday with Jenny, thinking about Nell.

It wasn't until another full week had passed that it was Jenny's turn to help her father and Drew and Nell were alone. After lunch, while they were sitting under a tree on the village green, he suggested they climb the mountain to the castle ruins where they could be alone. She replied that it would be best if they remained on the green, where they wouldn't be tempted to start something that could have no satisfying conclusion.

"I just want to talk!" Drew insisted.

"We can talk here."

"You know what I mean."

"I know precisely what you mean, Master Morgan. That's why I think it best we stay here."

"Nell, if you love me . . ."

She shot him a warning glance that let him know he would get nowhere with that line of reasoning. He tried a different approach.

"I simply want to go some place where we can talk freely. That's all. You have my word that we'll do nothing that you don't want to do."

Nell's stony resolve melted as she lowered her eyes. "That's precisely my fear, Drew. I'm not afraid of you taking advantage of me. I'm afraid that once I'm alone with you, I'll not be able to control myself. I'm not sure you realize the depth of my love for you."

Drew's cheeks flushed. The thought of a woman like Nell having such feelings for him was more than he could handle.

He rose and extended his hand to her. "I will protect you against yourself."

Nell smiled sweetly. "That's like letting the fox guard the henhouse." But she took his hand and they walked up the hillside.

"Why won't you come away with me?"

Drew held Nell in his arms as they sat on an interior wall of the castle far under the tree cover. She was leaning back against him with her eyes closed. His arms were around her waist and her hands rested on his. They rocked gently back and forth.

Their passion had ignited within moments of reaching the castle ruins. They kissed feverishly, clinging to each other desperately as if they would never see each other again. With sighs and tears they expressed their love.

"I just can't go away with you. It wouldn't be fair to Poppa."

"Has he told you that?"

"No. Poppa would never tell me something like that. He'd tell me to go; whatever would make me happy, that's what he'd want. And I have a feeling he'd be very happy if I married you."

"Let's make your poppa happy."

Nell laughed. "You just don't understand. There are some things you just don't know."

"I know more than you think I know."

She craned her neck to look at him. "Oh, do you now?"

He nodded.

She turned forward and snuggled back against him. "You only know what we want you to know."

A loud commotion from the village rose over the crest of the hill. Shouts. Horses. Carts.

"What is going on down there?" Nell broke Drew's hold on her and walked to where she could see the village. Drew stayed where he was and watched her. How he loved to watch her move; the way she walked across a room, or used her arms and hands when she talked, and especially the way her slender fingers worked when she was making lace.

"Drew, come here! Something's wrong!"

Drew leaped to his feet and was by her side. Below them the little town of Edenford was in a state of pandemonium. Soldiers on horses were everywhere. Women were screaming, children dashing dangerously around the mounts; everywhere they looked people and animals jammed the narrow streets. The center of all the activity was the church building.

"Poppa!" Nell screamed, then covered her mouth with both hands.

Christopher Matthews could be seen between two burly soldiers as they dragged him from the church building. His hands were tied behind his back. Two lines of soldiers on foot held back the townspeople as they reached out to help the curate as he was loaded on a wooden cart.

"Come with me!"

Drew grabbed Nell by the wrist and pulled her through the stone doorway and down the hill. Several times she stumbled and he had to slow his pace.

"Go! Please save him!" Nell yelled, pushing him ahead.

Reluctantly, Drew left her behind and ran down the heavily rutted path. He pushed his way through the crowd of people lining Market Street just as the cart carrying Christopher Matthews passed by.

Four guards surrounded the curate in the back of the cart, two others sat in front. Soldiers lined the street, keeping the people back. Just as Drew reached the front of the line, a boy broke through the soldiers and ran into the street. The soldier immediately in front of Drew broke ranks to chase the boy.

Drew charged through the opening and leaped onto the back of the cart. The soldiers guarding the curate were ready for him. Drew's feet no sooner landed on the bed of the cart than one of the soldiers planted a foot in his stomach, sending him flying backward.

He hit the ground hard. Before he could get to his feet for a second attempt, two more soldiers had him by the arms. They dragged him behind the guard line and dumped him at Nell's feet.

There was nothing he could do.

"Where are they taking him?" Drew shouted to anyone who was listening.

Cyrus Furman was just off to their right. Tears streamed down the wrinkled ravines on his aged face. "He's been arrested," he said.

"By who? On what charge?"

"For seditious acts against the Crown."

"Who had him arrested?" Drew had to know where the order came from.

"Bishop Laud," the old watchman replied.

Drew held Nell Matthews in his arms as they watched Edenford's curate, Christopher Matthews, carted away across the north bridge to London.

Chapter 18

A S the last of the mounted soldiers crossed the bridge out of Edenford, the townspeople flocked to the meeting hall. The room filled quickly with animated, boisterous people who milled about like frightened sheep without a shepherd. Several men pushed a reluctant David Cooper to lead the emergency meeting. Drew stood near the front with his back against the wall. Nell was on one side, Jenny was on the other.

The beefy cobbler stood atop a wooden crate, his right arm wrapped around a support beam as he called for quiet.

"You all know what's happened," he shouted. "What are we going to do about it?"

Everyone began shouting at once. The cobbler waved them off with his black hairy arm. "One at a time! One at a time!" he shouted.

"We bring him back!" someone shouted.

"How? By ambushing the soldiers?" the cobbler replied. "Then what? Are we ready to fight the whole English army?"

"We can't just let them take him!" a woman yelled.

Somewhere from the back another man yelled, "I say our first order of business is to hang the spy responsible for his arrest! Hang Drew Morgan!"

The room exploded with shouts and curses, angry voices calling for Drew Morgan's death. The men who were closest to Drew pulled him away from the screaming, desperate clutches of the curate's daughters. His arms were twisted behind him. A large paw grabbed him by the hair and yanked his head backward. Drew found himself face to face with a raging red giant, James Cooper. Drew's screams of innocence were drowned out by the shouts for his death.

"Hold! Hold!" David Cooper yelled from his position above the crowd.

No one heard him.

Flinging himself into the crowd, the cobbler pushed his way toward Drew. "Let him go! Let him go!" he shouted over and over. When he reached the center of activity, he grabbed his son's arm which was now firmly around Drew's neck and pulled it away. "Let him go, James!"

The red giant's eyes spit anger at the one who dared break his hold on the traitor. It took both of the cobbler's arms to pull his son's right arm from around Drew's neck. For a moment it was a standoff. "I said to let him go!" the cobbler yelled.

Reluctantly, James obeyed his father.

"Listen to me!" he shouted to everyone in the room. "Would Drew Morgan be here right now if he was responsible for Christopher Matthews' arrest? Would he?"

The cobbler had injected an element of reasoning into the situation and the people didn't like it. They didn't want reason. They wanted revenge. They wanted action. They wanted their curate returned to them.

"I'll go to London myself!" the cobbler shouted. "I'm taking Drew Morgan with me. If he is who he claims to be, he knows where they've taken Christopher Matthews. I promise you, we'll bring the curate home! And if I find that Drew Morgan is responsible for the curate's arrest, I'll kill him myself!"

The people wanted more, but didn't know what else they

could do. It was agreed to send a delegation to Lord Chesterfield. They would beg him to go to London and seek their curate's release.

Having exhausted their scant resources, the people of Edenford filed out of the meeting hall with heads held low, comforting one another as best they could.

Following hasty preparations, David Cooper and Drew Morgan made the journey to London in three days. Along with his clothes and Bible, Drew packed his grandfather's cutlass for protection—from highway thieves, to be sure; but if things didn't go well, he imagined he would need it to protect him from the fury of a certain cobbler.

When they arrived in London they learned that Matthews was being held in the Tower, something of an honor for such a lowly curate. While Cooper tried to visit the curate, Drew went to London House to plead with Bishop Laud for Matthews' release.

The round cook welcomed him at the door with overly enthusiastic delight and ushered him into the library, even though the bishop was in a meeting. Bishop Laud was seated in a high-backed chair on the far side of the room, his chin resting on his hand when Drew entered the room. The bishop's guest was in a similar chair with his back to Drew. When the bishop saw Drew standing in the doorway, he jumped to his feet without apology to his guest and almost ran across the room. Drew found himself in a backslapping bear hug.

"Andrew, my boy! How good it is to see you!" The bishop stepped back and looked him up and down. "You're still a little blue. Oh, yes, I heard about that. Quite an act of bravery, I must say. My, how thin you are! We'll have to do something about that, won't we, cook?"

"Right away, sir!" the round cook bubbled over as he said it and went straight to his kitchen.

"Come in! Come in! I want to hear all about your adventure in Edenford!"

Drew motioned toward the visitor who had chosen to remain seated during the reunion between the bishop and his favorite operative. "I can come back later, if it's more convenient."

"Nonsense. In fact, he knows all about your work in Edenford. It's fortunate that I have you both here at the same time."

With his arm around Drew's shoulders, the bishop led Drew across the room.

"Introductions are hardly necessary," the bishop gushed. A tall, skinny form rose from the chair. He was so thin he looked like a scarecrow.

"Welcome to London, Master Morgan," said Ambrose Dudley.

"Fine job! Excellent work!" Bishop Laud praised his two Edenford operatives.

The three men sat in a circle facing each other. Ambrose Dudley wore a satisfied smirk on his face. The bishop was clearly relishing this victory with them.

"Ambrose and I are old colleagues from Cambridge," the bishop explained. "He used to be a poor excuse for a professor of antiquities before he became a first-rate spy. This was his first assignment," the bishop told Drew. "We hatched this scheme at Cambridge. We planted operatives in questionable small towns, knowing it would take them years to establish themselves as respected citizens."

"There are men planted in other towns?" Drew asked.

"Four others," the bishop said.

"Five," Dudley corrected him.

The bishop rolled his eyes toward the ceiling while he counted on his fingers. "I stand corrected. There are five."

"If you already had an operative in Edenford, why send me?"

The bishop sat forward on his seat. "That was my idea. And it worked, didn't it, Ambrose?" The bishop reached over and tapped Dudley on the knee. His friend's smirk grew larger. "I thought if we could stir things up, introduce a firebrand into the mix, it would accelerate things. And it did! Of course, I'd intended to send Eliot, but you did just as well, maybe better!"

"Why didn't you tell me about Dudley's role in Edenford?" Drew asked.

"An unneeded risk," Dudley answered him. "I had worked too long and too hard to have you jeopardize my cover. This way, if you failed, I would still be there. We would still have a foothold in Edenford." Dudley reached over and returned the tap he had received from the bishop. "I was really quite hard on the boy," he chuckled.

Drew was not amused. "You did your best to ruin me."

"That I did," Dudley replied. "And with good reason. If I was successful in discrediting you, it would make me look like a Puritan crusader and the people would trust me even more. As it turned out, you covered yourself well, and that too worked to our advantage."

The self-congratulations between the two college friends lasted about an hour longer. Then Ambrose Dudley excused himself. He said he was anxious to enjoy some of the luxuries of city life again.

When he was gone the bishop told Drew how pleased he was that he was not injured seriously in the dyeing vat incident. "There is one thing that disturbs me, though." The bishop walked to his desk, opened a drawer and produced a small slip of paper. He placed it on the desk, turned toward Drew so he could read it. Drew recognized his handwritten numbers and the bishop's translation below it: (10/17/3/11-

15) (42/24/6/1-4) (41/3/18/2). *"The man whom thou seekest, he is not here. Andrew."*

"I didn't tell Ambrose about your last message," the bishop said somberly. "Would you care to explain it?"

As Drew walked over to the chair he had been sitting in, he was searching for the right words to say. He knew this moment would come and he'd given some thought to his response, but now that the moment was here all his explanations sounded hollow. The bishop followed him over to the chairs, sat down and folded his hands in his lap, waiting for Drew's answer.

"Christopher Matthews is not an evil man," Drew began. "While I was there I got to know him, lived in his house, ate with him, worked with him. He's a good man with a good family. The townspeople love him. They respect him and need him, especially during these tough economic times."

Drew paused. But the bishop did not argue with him.

"I know you think he spreads dangerous ideas, but he's a fine decent man whom I've come to respect."

Bishop Laud looked at the floor as Drew finished. He said, "Matthews has two daughters, doesn't he?"

"Yes."

"Beautiful daughters, as I understand it."

"Yes. They're beautiful."

"Have you fallen in love with one of them?"

Drew didn't answer immediately. The bishop waited patiently.

"Yes, I have."

Taking a deep breath, Bishop Laud raised his head and looked squarely at Drew. "Andrew, there is always this danger whenever you go on a mission for a length of time. Do you remember Bedford? You fell in love with the minister's daughter there too. I believe her name was Abigail, wasn't it?"

Drew didn't respond.

"And in Colchester you allowed yourself to get too close to that young printer and his girlfriend we apprehended. That was why I was reluctant to send you to Edenford. The assignment was longer, which made the risk even greater. Don't you see, my boy, this has been your pattern. And in the same way that you have forgotten about these other people, you will forget about the villagers of Edenford."

Drew was not convinced.

"Andrew, listen to me, I know whereof I speak. Evil comes in many forms, oftentimes pleasing. Why, it is even taught that Lucifer himself masquerades as an angel of light. So let's not hear any more of this. In my mind, it is over and forgotten." He slapped his knees and stood. "Come! Cook has a delectable meal prepared for us. Let's celebrate our victory!"

The trial of Christopher Matthews was a macabre circus of ecclesiastical power with Bishop William Laud serving as keeper of the menagerie. The event was held in the notorious Star Chamber at the Palace of Westminster. It was a royal prerogative court, meaning that its authority rested on sovereign power and privilege. It was not bound by common law, and it did not depend on juries for either indictment or verdict. This allowed the king and his chief advisor, Bishop William Laud, to pursue their adversaries with a free hand.

The court was made up of the Privy Council, two chief justices, Laudian bishops, and, at his discretion, the king of England. When King James was alive, he attended Star Chamber trials regularly; he loved the debate and especially his royal privilege of announcing the verdict and passing sentence. His son, King Charles, did not share his father's fascination with things judicial, and rarely did he attend the Star Chamber proceedings. So when rumor circulated around London that the king would be at the trial of the notorious

Justin, people arrived as early as 3 o'clock on the morning of the trial for the privilege of standing to watch the event.

When Drew entered the packed chamber, he was immediately reminded how the court received its name; the ceiling was spangled with various representations of stars. Rows of chairs formed a U-shape around the small arena which was hardly bigger than a hallway. At the open end of the court were more rows of tables at which the various judges sat. Elevated above the tables and to one side was the king's chair.

Drew and Ambrose Dudley were ushered to their seats directly opposite the judges by an under sheriff. In accordance with chamber proceedings, the bishop had filed a petition against Matthews and depositions had been taken, including Drew's. To the chagrin of the bishop, his favorite operative proved to be an uncooperative witness. Drew's presence at the trial was unnecessary, but Bishop Laud requested he attend. The bishop intended not only to convince the court of Christopher Matthews' crimes, but to convince Drew as well. Drew went hoping to be given the opportunity to speak a good word on behalf of the accused.

From his seat he could see the curate in profile already seated on the lowest level in the chair of the accused, but Matthews didn't see him. As Drew scanned the crowd, he could see a black curly head bobbing in the back of the crowd that lined the walls of the court room. As tall as he was, Edenford's cobbler had to stand on his toes to see what was happening in the pit below him. *He must have waited half the night outside in the cold to get in,* Drew thought.

At precisely 9 A.M. the judges filed in and took their places behind the tables. Behind them, Bishop Laud strode confidently to the center of the court. In hushed anticipation, the court spectators looked in the direction of the king's chair. Their expectations were fulfilled when King Charles entered the court.

After a few required preliminaries, Laud addressed the judges. He spoke to them in the same way he would address an alumni reunion of old college friends. He began with a popular little poem that was currently circulating through the halls of Whitehall.

> A Puritan is such a monstrous thing
> That loves democracy and hates the king.

The bishop paused appropriately for the anticipated chuckles.

> A Puritan is he whose heart is bent
> To cross the king's designs in parliament.

Another pause and more chuckles. The bishop was clearly enjoying his prosecuting role in this particular trial.

> Where whilst the place of burgess he doth bear,
> He thinks he owes but small allegiance there.
> So that with wit and valor he doth try,
> How the prerogative he may deny!

"Your highness, my lords and colleagues, before you today is one of these monstrous Puritans, Christopher Matthews, curate of Edenford in Devonshire," Laud pointed to the accused. "I contend he is the worst of the lot. I say this because of his cowardly actions. This man is accused of spreading seeds of sedition in the village of Edenford, using his position of trust as curate. Endowed with the authority of the Church of England, this man has poisoned the minds of its faithful members! Not only that, he has scattered his ruinous seed throughout all England with his writings, while hiding behind a cloak of anonymity!"

A reading of the charges against Matthews followed:

"One, Christopher Matthews did willfully violate the laws of the Church of England to rail off the communion table. Witnesses have testified that they saw the table used for common purposes, including its use as a judicial bench wherein it was repeatedly pounded by the high constable.

"Two, Christopher Matthews did willfully violate the order of the Church of England that all duly appointed ministers wear a ministerial surplice in the performance of their worship service duties.

"Three, Christopher Matthews did willfully violate the directive prohibiting the lectureship of ill-educated ministers. He failed to use the old homilies assembled for that very purpose, choosing instead to use extemporaneous preaching not once, but twice each Sunday to spread his seditious lies.

"Four, Christopher Matthews did willfully write, publish, and distribute illegal and seditious literature under the name of Justin. In these writings he encouraged Englishmen to follow his example of disobedience to the Church of England and its leaders and to the English monarchy. This treason is the greatest crime of all."

At this point, the lord chancellor asked Christopher Matthews if he had anything to say in response to these charges.

Matthews rose with deliberate slowness. He looked at Laud and the assembled judges. "The good doctor," he nodded toward Laud as he addressed the judges, "saw fit to begin this hearing with a poem. I would respond with a prayer:

> From plague, pestilence, and famine,
> From bishops, priests, and deacons,
> Good Lord, deliver us."

Howls and hoots reverberated from the gallery. Color rose in the bishop's face until he was beet red. The lord chancellor pounded the bench for quiet.

For over an hour a succession of prosecutors read depositions, called on witnesses, and hammered away at Matthews as he faced his accusers. During the entire time Matthews stood tall, his head held high as his attackers swarmed around him, sometimes alone, sometimes in pairs. First one would attack, then another; when one got tired, a fresh prosecutor took his place, yelling, accusing, denouncing, charging, indicting the lonely curate.

Drew was reminded of the bearbaiting event he attended with Eliot. Christopher Matthews was the bear, dragged from his home, shackled in an arena, set upon by dogs to the amusement of the crowd. Like the bear he stood proudly, fending off the snarling mastiffs as they came at him, teeth bared, relentlessly tearing at him. And like the mastiffs at the bearbaiting, they weren't going to let up until the bear was dead.

Edenford's curate was visibly tired when the chief prosecutor rose to his feet. Christopher Matthews' eyes were red, his mouth dry, and his face drawn as the relaxed Bishop Laud approached him.

"What degree have you taken at a university?" the bishop asked.

"I have never taken a degree," Matthews replied.

"You have no degree at all?"

"None."

"Have you ever attended a university?"

"I have not."

"Not even a single class?"

"No."

"You do not have a degree, you have not attended a university, not even one class. Then tell me, sir, by what right do you preach and teach the things you do? What makes you qualified to discard the teachings of learned men — men who have devoted their lives to studies in our finest English universities—and substitute your own backwoods brand of theology?"

"It is only by the grace of God that I minister, sir."

Laud fell into a fit of rage. "You chattering fool! You think by that statement you can place yourself above all the godly men of England? Do you think that all learning is in your brain? That our universities stand for nothing? That ministers are best uneducated? That God cannot be found in England's halls of learning? What arrogance! What blasphemy!"

The bishop didn't give Matthews time to respond before asking him another question.

"How long have you been the curate in Edenford?"

"Upward of a dozen years."

"Who has maintained you all these years?"

"Lord Chesterfield has graciously supplied my living."

"And this is how you repay his graciousness? By tearing away at the foundation of his beloved country? By luring his villagers to revolt against him?"

"My sole intent was to meet the spiritual needs of the poor people of Edenford."

"Poor people? You made them a company of seditious, factious bedlams. And you prattle about calling them poor people? They organize and finance a countrywide publishing ring that secretly prints and distributes antimonarchy literature?"

"The people of Edenford are a good people . . ."

"Spare your breath, you prating coxcomb! I'll have no such fellows in my church who lead astray innocent people, using them for their own selfish ends."

For over two hours Bishop William Laud paced and ranted in front of the accused. His voice was high and harsh. His temper, which broke out frequently, was outrageous, and he threatened with passion. It was as though blood would have gushed from his face; he shook as if haunted by secret venom.

As the bishop's ranting slowed its pace, Drew stared in admiration at the man accused. Christopher Matthews was exhausted, yet unbowed. This angered his accuser even more.

"May God Almighty preserve England from devils such as you," the bishop concluded. "And He will. Rest assured, He will. For there are still those who desire England's glory, not her destruction. In the tradition of England they risk their lives to ensure that our land will forever be free from the clutches of scoundrels like you."

Drew could see what was coming. *No,* he prayed, *please no.*

"When you are punished, it is not enough for men and women to point to you and warn their children against a life of infamy."

No, no, no! Drew screamed over and over inside.

"They need someone they can point to and say, 'My children, there is a man of courage, a man who loves God and his country. Follow his example!' "

No!

"They'll point into the crowd, to the men who rescued England from the seditious lies of Edenford's scoundrel curate. And they'll say, 'Son, make me proud of you. Grow up to be like him!' " By now Bishop Laud's short, fat finger was leveled at his two Edenford operatives. "Grow up to be like Ambrose Dudley! Grow up to be like Drew Morgan! Crusaders of truth and justice who saved England from her greatest enemies."

Everyone in the Star Chamber stared at Dudley and Drew. But there were only one set of eyes that mattered to Drew. Edenford's curate turned his head toward Drew. Their eyes met. For Christopher Matthews, it was the final blow. His legs buckled as he crumbled into the chair. His head hung in defeat. The noble curate could take no more. There were too many attackers—snarling, snapping, biting—too many of them to fight. He was weary. Exhausted. The spectacle was over. There was no fight left in him.

Bishop Laud, the promoter and conductor of this Puritan-baiting, his face red and dripping with sweat, smiled in victory as the chamber erupted in applause for the brave men who had hunted and captured this wild and dangerous enemy of England.

"We have a precedent, lord chancellor," the bishop argued.

Christopher Matthews' guilt had been established by the court. The judges had rendered their verdicts. The consensus—normally announced by the lord chancellor—was read by King Charles. The bishop was now arguing the penalty. Punishments varied, depending on the severity of the crime, but the Court of the Star Chamber never condemned anyone to death. The bishop sought to make Christopher Matthews the first exception.

"Publishing without license has always been considered a high offense," he said, "deserving a proportionate punishment. Earlier monarchs set the standard. For example, Queen Elizabeth executed the Separatists Greenwood, Barrowe, and Penry for their secret printing. Can we do less and still uphold the law in England?"

It was soon evident that his plea was falling on deaf ears. To Drew's relief neither the king nor the judges desired to use this case to set a standard for the Star Chamber. Already the common courts were furious with the intrusion of the maverick Star Chamber into their territory. The resulting decision was a political one. The king didn't want to goad the out-of-session members of parliament needlessly.

So the sentence against Christopher Matthews was set and announced by the king. For his criminal activity he would be fined 10,000 pounds. It was a ridiculous sum, one he could never pay in his lifetime. So this part of his penalty would be shared by his village and heirs until paid in full. In addition, Matthews would be pilloried with one ear nailed to the pillory. His ear would be cut off when released. Also, his cheeks would be branded and his nose slit. In this way he would remain a living reminder of the punishment that awaited anyone who considered following his example.

Drew's eyes jumped back and forth between the curate and the bishop as the sentence was read. The curate's head was still bowed; he had hardly moved since he looked at Drew. But it was the bishop's reaction that disturbed Drew even more. The rotund cleric sat calmly in his chair as the verdict was read. It was unlike him to take a setback this calmly.

Just as the court was about to adjourn, a messenger ran into the chamber, handed a long cloth-covered bundle to the bishop, and whispered something in his ear. The bishop peeled back a layer of cloth and looked at the contents of the bundle. As he did, he grabbed his heart and fell back into his chair.

"Dr. Laud, is something the matter? Are you all right?" the lord chancellor asked.

"A moment, lord chancellor," the bishop said breathlessly. The room was deadly quiet as everyone waited on the bishop. His legs shook as he stood on unsteady feet. "Most disturbing," he said weakly. "This is horrible."

"Do you have something that concerns this court?" the lord chancellor asked.

"Not directly, my lord," said the bishop. "But it does have to do with Christopher Matthews."

"We would like to hear it."

"It's a civil matter, sir."

"Still, it won't hurt us to hear what you have to say."

"It has come to my attention," the bishop said in tones so low that people leaned forward to hear him, "that not only is this man guilty of sedition, but he is also guilty of the murder of Lord Chesterfield's son."

The words sent shock waves throughout the room.

"It's true!" the bishop shouted. "We have eyewitnesses! And . . ." the bishop unwrapped the bundle recently handed him, "we have the instrument of the boy's death!" He held an arrow over his head, the crossbow arrow Drew had extracted from the head of Lord Chesterfield's son. "It was a failed kidnap attempt! Matthews and his cohorts were attempting to extort money from the boy's wealthy father. When the boy proved too much for them to handle, their leader, Christopher Matthews, shot him through the eye with this! The boy's body lies in a shallow grave between two giant oak trees under the leaves of a bush. My informant can provide detailed directions as to where the sheriff will find the poor boy's broken body!"

Drew jumped to his feet. The word "liar" was on his lips, but never made it any further. Just as he began to shout there was an explosion of light and pain, then darkness.

Chapter 19

A bright light hammered his face. His head felt ready to explode. He turned to one side, then the other, but couldn't avoid the light. Lifting a hand up, he shielded his eyes. That was better, but the pain was still there.

It took him several minutes before he discovered where he was, not because the place was unfamiliar to him, but because it hurt him to keep his eyes open longer than a few seconds at a time. He was on his bed at London House. It was the morning sunlight that was falling heavily on his face.

With a groan he sat up. It wasn't a sure proposition that he would remain that way. His head was pounding and he felt dizzy and nauseous. He swallowed the pain as best he could and fought to hold on to his senses. Now that the sunlight was behind him, the greatest pain came from the back of his head. He reached there.

"OW!" he cried. That was a mistake. Instant pain.

Lowering his hand, a flash of gold caught his eye. At almost that same moment he felt an unusual weight on his finger. It was an enormous gold ring with large ruby stone setting.

Just beyond his window he could hear clipping in the bishop's garden. He balanced himself on unsteady feet and went to the garden to get some answers.

"I'm disappointed in you, Andrew," was the first thing the

bishop said to him. He had paused in his rosebush clipping and was kneeling on the lawn feeding a blade of grass to his pet tortoise.

Drew blinked at him, trying to keep everything in focus.

"I'm sorry we had to injure you."

"You did this?"

The bishop plucked another blade of grass and lowered it to the lipless mouth of the tortoise. His pet chomped the end of the blade appreciatively. "One of my men did. He was seated behind you in case he was needed. We had to protect you from yourself."

"Not a very subtle way of doing it. Weren't people a little suspicious?"

"Not at all. You see, he was arrested for attacking you. As they dragged him from the courtroom he screamed something to the effect that he was one of the curate's followers, that there were hundreds more like him who would willingly give their lives to free their leader, et cetera, et cetera. In truth, he's a common highwayman I use occasionally for little jobs. He was taken to Fleet Street Prison where he was promptly released. It looked good and served our purpose. People are more convinced than ever that Christopher Matthews is a serious threat to England. So you see, my dear boy, your misguided attack of conscience did the curate no good."

"What's to stop me from telling the truth now?"

The bishop was genuinely hurt. "Andrew," he said quietly, "I am the authority in England next to the king. God has ordained that Charles be king of England and that I serve as his spiritual advisor. *Together we are England.* Whatever we do is right because we do it for England and in the name of God." He resumed feeding his pet as he added, "If you spoke out now, you would only embarrass yourself. You see, while you were unconscious, you became England's most recent hero."

Drew looked puzzled.

Bishop Laud rose and brushed the grass from his knees. "Have you noticed the ring yet?"

Drew raised his hand and looked at the ruby ring.

"It's the first of King Charles' rewards for your efforts. Handsome, isn't it? You see, the king feels England needs a hero right now. Someone who will take the people's minds off his refusal to call parliament to order, the ship tax, and countless other petty controversies. Don't you see? You're the perfect answer! You're young, handsome, and have dedicated your life to serving crown and country. You just returned from a dangerous mission in which you were almost killed. You uncovered one of England's most notorious enemies. Then, you were almost killed again while testifying against the man in the Star Chamber! The king is quite impressed with you."

Now the bishop was standing directly in front of him. He held Drew's hand by the ends of his fingers, raising the ring closer to Drew's face.

"This is a token! King Charles has arranged a reception in your honor to be held one week hence. He wants to reward you publicly as a friend of the crown. Andrew, this is everything you have ever dreamed of! You are Lancelot, and King Arthur wants to honor his best knight!"

The week passed without incident. Drew rarely saw the bishop who was preoccupied with affairs of state. With London House all to himself, Drew agonized over his situation. To his dismay, the memories of Edenford dimmed with each passing day. Now that he was back in luxurious surroundings with comfortable bedding and rich food, he realized how much he had given up while at Edenford.

He couldn't get Christopher Matthews out of his mind, but what could he do? Besides, the curate was guilty of writing illegal pamphlets. Legally, Matthews was wrong. How could Drew fault himself for upholding the law of the land?

And speaking of the law of the land, the King of England was giving a reception in his honor! Just like Grandpa! The admiral had Queen Elizabeth; Drew had King Charles.

Drew's hands were cold from nervous anticipation as he dressed for his reception. He forced himself not to think of Christopher Matthews and Edenford and Nell.

Whitehall's banqueting house sparkled with lights and fashion and merriment. London's finest were in attendance — the powerful, the rich, the noble — all by special invitation of the king, all for one reason, to celebrate Drew Morgan, England's young hero.

They stood and applauded when he entered the room wearing the clothing of nobility and, by special permission, the cutlass that belonged to his famous grandfather.

They stood reverently when King Charles awarded him a medallion for courageous service. They laughed when they heard how he was dyed blue saving a boy's life. They stood in line to shake his hand. Young boys looked up to him as if he were a god.

His parents, Lord and Lady Morgan, journeyed to London to join London's elite in honoring their son, and they brought a jealous Philip with them. Lord Morgan sported a new suit of clothes and Lady Morgan wore a breathtaking diamond necklace purchased for the occasion. His parents gushed over him, telling everyone how they always knew he was destined for greatness. Drew saw genuine fear in their eyes as they looked at him, a silent plea not to spoil the illusion of a happy home they were creating. His success was their success, and if Drew knew his parents, they were sure to make the most of it.

Throughout the evening, Bishop William Laud stood near

Drew, acting like a proud father.

Drew had never before met most of those who stood in line to shake his hand. There was one man, however, whom he knew. He had traveled a great distance to be there. Lord Chesterfield offered Drew his hand but there was no smile to accompany it.

"It's with mixed feelings I congratulate you, young man," he said. "England's good fortune is my devastation; with a single blow you have uncovered my son's killer and deprived me of my town manager. I cannot replace the one and it will be difficult to replace the other. Interested in the position?"

The real killer of Lord Chesterfield's son stepped forward quickly, lest Drew be tempted to say something foolish. He grasped the lord by the hand and led him away. "I'm afraid you'll have to look elsewhere," the bishop said, with a wooden smile. "Andrew is too valuable to the king and me. We could never let him go."

Lord Chesterfield returned the bishop's smile kind for kind. "My dear bishop, there's no need to protect your protégé. My offer was in jest."

The bishop need not have been concerned. The thought of telling Lord Chesterfield the truth hadn't occurred to Drew. His mind was elsewhere, in a village four days journey west. It wasn't what Lord Chesterfield said that sent him there, but what he was wearing. A lace ruff. Lace cuffs. And an abundance of lace trim. Expertly crafted bone lace from Edenford, made by the skillful hands of two beautiful young women who lived on High Street. Who at this moment of Drew's glory were in their sparse sitting room mourning the absence of their father who was shut away in the Tower of London.

The thoughts of Edenford and Jenny and Nell overwhelmed him—their beauty, their laughter, morning breakfast with Christopher Matthews at the head of the table reading the Bible, praying for his daughters, then asking the same question he asked every day, "What are we going to do for God today?" The horseplay on the bowling green between the curate and his old friend, David Cooper, their good-natured joking, the solemn passion in their eyes as they met in secret, the displays of love shown the curate by the villagers for his selfless acts on their behalf.

The instant he saw Lord Chesterfield's lace, these thoughts welled up inside of Drew like a thermal spring. In comparison to the depth of life lived by the humble people of Edenford, the lights of Whitehall, the jewels, the wealth, the accolades, all the pretense of London's royalty was an empty vessel.

There was nothing for him here. Nothing the king could bestow upon him could compare to the wealth of emotion he felt in one Sunday afternoon alone with Nell Matthews.

He knew what he had to do. Drew Morgan would become a lone crusader. A man with a mission.

Shivering in the darkness, he sat at water's edge fingering the sheath of his cutlass, waiting for the prison barge. The curate's murder trial had gone as expected. The body of Lord Chesterfield's son was found exactly where Laud said it would be, the crossbow with it. Together with the crossbow arrow and Ambrose Dudley's eyewitness testimony (he described the late Shubal Elkins' point of view as told to him by the bishop), there was little for the judges to decide. They ruled that after Christopher Matthews endured the punishment as set forth by the Star Chamber, he would then be taken to Tower Hill where his head would be cut off. This too was an unusual form of punishment for a man of such low estate. Beheading was usually reserved for England's elite prisoners; the normal form of punishment was hanging. But Bishop Laud's passionate court arguments gave the case such widespread notoriety that the judges felt the circumstances warranted the more gruesome punishment.

Following sentencing at Westminster, the prisoner was moved to the Tower by barge on the River Thames. This was the safer route, since surface streets were narrow and had too many blind corners to insure a prisoner's safe passage. Christopher Matthews had been safely transported to the Tower two nights previous. Drew had watched discreetly from Upper Thames Street, noting the procedure and formulating an escape plan.

From the shadows of the bridge footing, Drew caught sight of the prison barge. It carried two guards and their hooded prisoner, a woman, if the rumor he heard was true. Drew scurried up the embankment to the street and ran as fast as he could along Upper Thames Street toward the Tower. The street was deserted except for two drunks leaning on each other as they walked. They shouted at him as he ran by, yelling something about reckless running. To his right Drew caught an occasional glimpse of the barge's progress between buildings and trees.

His heart pounded in his chest and his lungs burned. Ignoring the pain, he ran faster. Just before the street emptied onto the wharf, Drew left the road, sliding down a rutted embankment covered with wet, slippery leaves. He slid to the water's edge. His chest heaving, he crouched low, looking for the barge. It was darker near the river's edge and now that he was at water level, the slight mist on the surface obscured his view. He heard oars slapping the water before the barge appeared in the mist, with its three silhouetted figures.

Drew removed his shoes, flinging them aside, and slipped his sheathed cutlass down the back of his shirt. As soundlessly as he could, he waded into the river and launched himself into the river's current. He was well ahead of the barge's progress.

He swam to the stone wall at the edge of the wharf, staying close to the wall to avoid being seen by anyone on the wharf.

With deliberate speed he silently worked his way beneath the battery of four cannons positioned to salute incoming ships. Just beyond the cannons he stopped. There was an inset where the Queen's Stair descended from the wharf to the water's edge. He submerged until he was past the stone steps. He paused to locate the position of the barge—it was right where it should be. He had plenty of time.

Several feet beyond him, the stone wall took a sharp turn toward the castle. Drew followed it into a corner where the wall resumed its parallel course with the river. It was here he would temporarily lose sight of the barge. If the yeoman guards followed the same course as they did when transporting Matthews, they would keep distant from the wharf as long as possible. Then they would approach the Tower's water gate at a perpendicular angle. That would give him the time he needed. While he waited, he took deep breaths.

The sound of his heavy breathing echoed against the stones of the wall. Wiping water away from his eyes, he strained to focus on the center of the river. Nothing. *I should be able to see it by now*, Drew thought. He waited, but still no barge. His mind flashed the possibilities: *Someone or something alerted them to my presence; someone else intercepted them; they turned back or altered their course—but for what reason?*

Suddenly, an oar slapped the water and the bow of the barge appeared from around the corner just a few feet from him. It was so close he could see the white and gray whiskers of the yeoman jailer.

He nearly panicked. Leaning as far back into the shadow as he could, he looked for alternatives. The plan was to track the barge as it approached the water gate that led under the wharf, through Traitor's Gate, at the Tower walls. He would swim under it just as it reached the gate, letting it carry him in. The barge's altered course brought them dangerously close to him while it was still several yards from the gate. Drew's only chance was to swim under the barge now, but it was too far; he couldn't hold his breath that long.

Drew's determination overrode his good sense. He took a deep breath, submerged, and swam toward the barge. The water was dark and murky, and he couldn't see more than a few inches in front of his face. He swam forward. When he thought he'd gone far enough and still hadn't found the boat, he looked toward the surface.

Splash! An oar sliced into the water inches from his head. Drew ducked down as it swept passed him. With a strong kick he was under the barge, holding onto the edge as it pulled him toward the water gate of the Tower of London.

The barge entered the gate. Drew knew they had gone through because everything was darker now, pitch black actually, as the barge sailed beneath the wharf. The barge stopped. Drew's lungs were bursting, but he didn't dare surface yet. In the tunnel the slightest sound would give him away. He heard the muffled command of the yeoman guard. Almost time. He worked his way to the back of the boat, his lungs screaming for air. He wondered what it would feel like to gasp and, instead of air, feel nothing but liquid pour into his lungs. He heard the sound he was waiting for. Traitor's Gate creaked on its hinges. He could feel a swirling current as the gate moved through the water. He surfaced, hoping the movement of the gate would be enough to conceal any noise he might make. His face broke the water just inches away from the bulging backside of the paddling yeoman. Drew gasped silently for air then submerged under the barge again. He watched for signs that the yeoman heard him. To his relief the barge moved forward again.

The prison barge entered a chamber just inside the walls of St. Thomas' Tower. Still underwater, Drew heard muffled commands. The yeoman guard's oar hung in the water at a sharp angle, and the back of the barge slid sideways. There was a jolt as it hit the bottom step of a stone stairway. Drew waited for his chance to surface. The craft rocked back and forth a couple of times. Not yet. Then it dipped toward the steps. The prisoner was disembarking. Now! Drew surfaced on the far side of the barge. "Watch your step, m'lady," he heard a yeoman say. Drew submerged again; this time he swam down deep until he could feel the base of the stone steps. He followed the steps to the edge, then around a corner until he came to a wall. He continued along the wall until he reached the corner of the chamber. Cautiously he surfaced and gulped for needed air while he looked toward the steps. The guards were all business. One of the barge yeomen joined a Tower yeoman as they escorted the hooded prisoner up the steps. The other barge yeoman pushed off the steps and paddled the barge back the way it came. Traitor's Gate was closed behind him. Drew had made it into the Tower of London.

For several minutes he hid in the shadows of the watery corner, listening for sounds of movement. The only sound he heard was the gentle lapping of the water against the stone steps. He swam to the steps and climbed out of the water onto the first one. He pulled the cutlass from the back of his shirt and unsheathed it. He stood barefoot and dripping on the steps. Until now he hadn't thought about the fact that he would leave a wet trail wherever he went. He laid the cutlass down. Removing his shirt and pants, he wrung them out, wiping as much water as he could from his shivering skin. Clothed again, he shuffled as he ascended the stairs to dry the bottom of his feet. He still dripped, but only slightly.

Emerging into the open from St. Thomas' Tower, he glanced both ways for guards. An open expanse called the Water Lane separated St. Thomas' Tower on the outer wall and the other Tower structures. If anyone was on top of the Hall Tower, Bloody Tower, or the wall walk as he crossed the lane, they would see him. Drew inched his way along the wall toward the rectangular tower on the east end of St. Thomas' where it jutted out into the lane. Opposite the round Hall Tower, it was the shortest distance across the lane. He scanned the walls and towers opposite him. A guard on the wall walk was going the opposite direction. Drew sprinted across the lane with one hand holding the cutlass and the other holding the sheath. He followed the circumference of the Hall Tower and ducked under the gate into the Bloody Tower.

Christopher Matthews was imprisoned in Bloody Tower. "The same room as Sir Walter Raleigh," the bishop had boasted, as if that were an honor. Drew was determined that the room's current resident would not meet the same fate as its former famous occupant. King James had Sir Walter Raleigh beheaded.

A narrow circular staircase led upstairs. It looked like it was cut out of stone. There was room for only one person on the stairs. Drew stepped lightly on them, following their circular path, his cutlass leading the way.

The top emerged into a hallway with several heavy wooden doors. *Is the curate behind one of them? How can I find out?* It didn't seem like a good idea to start knocking on doors. There had to be guards with keys around someplace. That's why he brought the cutlass.

He started down the hallway when he heard footsteps behind him, not only footsteps but also the jangling sound of keys. Drew ran to the top of the stairway. Just then a yeoman appeared; he was thickset with a black beard and moved slowly. His head was down as he sorted the keys, choosing the one he needed. Drew smashed him in the face with the butt of the cutlass just as the guard looked up. The force of the blow sent the man's head pounding against the stone wall. He fell in a heap to the floor, bleeding profusely from a huge gash on his forehead. There were no signs of life.

Drew grabbed the keys but had no idea which door to try. He ran to the first door and tried several keys before one worked. He swung the door open gently. A wide-eyed woman stood on the far side of the room holding a bedsheet in front of her. The woman on the barge? Drew couldn't tell.

"Sorry to disturb you, ma'am," he said sheepishly.

He tried the next door. The last key he tried opened it. The room was dark. He called the curate's name several times. No one answered.

There's got to be a better way than this, Drew said to himself. He looked down the hallway at the yeoman who hadn't moved. Drew moved to the next door.

It swung open. Christopher Matthews sat behind a wooden desk in a high-backed wooden chair. An open Bible lay before him. Drew stepped into the room and closed the door.

"Drew!" the curate rose. He stared at a wet Drew Morgan carrying a sword and jailer's keys and said, "Oh, no."

"Hurry!" Drew motioned Matthews to follow him.

Matthews sat down. "Drew, what do you think you're doing?"

"Rescuing you! Follow me, we have to hurry!"

The curate didn't move. He looked at the fire crackling in the fireplace to the right of the desk. "No," he said. "I'm not going with you."

Drew was too dumbfounded to speak.

"Get out of here quickly, Drew. Save yourself."

"They're going to kill you!"

It was the curate's turn to remain silent.

"I can save you if you'll just follow me!"

Drew didn't realize it until later, but when he was old and reflected on this meeting, he came to realize that it was this single sentence that galvanized the curate's decision. Matthews was far too wise to trust a headstrong young man for his salvation.

"Drew, were you the one who handed me over to Bishop Laud?"

The words struck Drew like a blow. He had known this question would ultimately arise between them. At the moment he was focused on the rescue effort and the question caught him off guard.

"We don't have time for that now," he said. "Let's go!"

Christopher Matthews got up and walked toward him, a slow leisurely pace, not the pace of a man about to escape from England's famed prison Tower. Placing both hands on Drew's shoulders, he said, "That's all we have time for. You didn't turn me over to Bishop Laud, did you?"

There was no avoiding the question now. "That was my mission. I sneaked into your study and compared your handwriting to a Justin manuscript. Of course I knew after the meeting in the back of Master Cooper's shop. But I couldn't do it. I told the bishop you were not Justin."

Tears filled the curate's eyes. "During the trial in the Star Chamber when you were singled out as my accuser, I was devastated. Then when the man attacked you, I knew better. But I had to ask."

The curate turned away from Drew. "You were right when you told Bishop Laud that I am not Justin."

"*Not* Justin? You're *not* Justin?"

Matthews faced Drew and shook his head. "I'm not Justin."

"Then what . . . why?"

At that instant it was as if a light shone on Christopher Matthews' face. He raised his face heavenward and said, "Of course! Thank You, Lord!" Grabbing a dumbstruck Drew Morgan by the shoulder he pulled him toward a chair and shoved him in it. Pulling a chair opposite his rescuer he leaned toward Drew and said, "Listen carefully, we may not have much time. It all makes sense now." Again he raised his head, his lips moving silently forming the words, "Thank You, Lord." There was a steady flow of tears down his cheeks as he continued. "Drew, I'm going to tell you something that only three people know. You will be the fourth. Nell is Justin."

"But your handwriting . . . I compared your handwriting," Drew objected.

"Yes, that was my handwriting. A precaution in case something like this happened. I copied Nell's manuscripts before they were sent out, to protect her. No one except Jenny, Nell, and I know the true identity of Justin, and now, of course, you."

"Not even David Cooper?"

"David thinks I'm Justin."

Drew was beginning to understand. Christopher Matthews was willing to die to protect his daughter.

"But you can still escape!" Drew cried frantically. "You can assume another identity in a different city. Nell and Jenny could eventually join you. The secret would still be safe."

The curate smiled at him. His smile was odd for the situation. It was a relaxed smile, contented even. The kind of smile a proud father shares with his son when there is no one else around. The smile infuriated Drew. He was risking his life to save Matthews and Matthews was acting as if they were having an after-dinner conversation in his sitting room.

"I know why God sent you to Edenford," Matthews said.

"Laud sent me, not God!" Drew shouted.

"God sent you," the curate insisted with a quiet intensity. "I'm more sure of it now than ever before. But you're right in your feelings. You're in danger, and you must escape before you're captured."

"I'm taking you with me."

"I'm not going. I'm confident this is God's will for my life. Now, Drew Morgan, the time has come to find God's will for your life. Not your desires, not your hopes, not all the selfish things you've dreamed of all your life, but God's will, God's plan for you."

Matthews pulled Drew from the chair and pushed him toward the door.

"They're going to kill you!" Drew shouted.

"I'm sure they will. 'And fear ye not them which kill the body, but are not able to kill the soul; but rather fear him which is able to destroy both soul and body in hell.' "

"Is that from the Bible?"

"You'll have to look the reference for yourself. Drew, listen to me, you're the key to all of this. God knew all this would happen. He sent you to Edenford for one reason. You will protect Nell and Jenny after I'm gone. Through all of this, my only concern was for them, who would look after them if I died. Now I know! It's you. I place them in your hands."

"How can I protect them? The people will kill me if I go back to Edenford!"

"Don't you see, Drew? It all fits! Edenford must fly to the wilderness. England is no longer safe for them. They cannot survive the penalty my capture has placed on them. They cannot continue in a land that substitutes outward conformity for faith in God. Edenford must fly to the wilderness where they can build a new community, where they can worship God freely. My death is the best thing that could happen for Edenford; it will force them to flee. And you will go with them. Drew, I entrust my daughters into your hands. Keep my girls safe! Tell them their poppa loves them."

There was a commotion on the other side the door.

"You must escape!" the curate whispered. It was the first time Drew heard any note of panic in his voice.

Reluctantly, Drew reached for the doorlatch. He had to get out. How do you rescue someone who refuses to be rescued?

Christopher Matthews placed a hand on his shoulder. "God be with you, my son."

Drew swung the door open just wide enough to look out. He could see one way down the hall, the half that led to the narrow stairs. The yeoman's body was gone. *All right,* Drew reasoned, *the guards know something's up, but they don't know where I am. . . . I could be anywhere in the Tower compound. Still, half of the hallway is hidden from view. Only one way to find out.*

Swinging the door wide, Drew jumped into the hallway with sword drawn. It was empty! As he tiptoed to the stairway, his bare feet felt something wet . . . blood. He was standing in the yeoman guard's blood. He craned his neck to see down the corkscrew stairway. No sign of movement, no sound. He would have felt better if he could hear something, preferably distant sounds.

With his back to the stone wall, he inched his way down the stairs.

CLANG! The blade of a pike struck the stone wall, inches from Drew's nose. "Halt and surrender!" cried the yeoman warder.

Drew retreated backward up the stairs, guarding himself with his sword. The passage was too narrow for him to swing it. At the top of the stairs Drew slipped and fell. It was the yeoman warder's blood again.

CLANG! The pike struck. The only thing that kept him from being impaled was the circular stairs; the pike couldn't bend far enough around to reach him. Drew had an idea. Instead of getting up, he crawled down the stairs feet first as fast as he could. The yeoman warder saw him and raised his pike. Before he could bring it down, Drew planted a foot in his chest and sent the warder sprawling backward down the stairs.

Drew ran up the stairs, jumping over the bloody top step.

Two other yeoman warders were waiting for him at the end
of the hall, pikes leveled. He turned back to the stairs. His
stairway opponent had recovered and was coming up, pike
first. Drew stepped to the side away from the oncoming pike.
With one blow of his sword he knocked it to the ground;
with another, he swung at the yeoman warder. He missed.
His sword—the cutlass his grandfather had given him, the
one that had saved the seaman from countless Spaniards—
clanged against the stone and broke. Drew was left standing
helpless with the hilt of a broken cutlass in his hand as three
yeoman warder's pikes were leveled at him.

Bishop Laud was furious. When the yeoman warders
learned that Drew's residence was London House, the bishop
was notified. An hour later Drew was sitting in the bishop's
library while a scarlet-faced, ranting bishop screamed at him.

"I've given you everything!" he shouted. "What did you
have when you came to me?"

"Nothing."

"Nothing!" the bishop repeated. "I gave you a home. I fed
you. I gave you clothes." Then quietly but with no less intensity, "I gave you my love. What has bewitched you? What
could possibly make you do this to me?"

Drew didn't respond.

"Answer me!"

Still he said nothing.

The bishop seethed in fury. "I made you and I can break
you!" he yelled. "What were you thinking? What could make
you care so much for a spiritual heretic that you'd break into
the Tower of London and injure a yeoman warder?"

"He isn't dead?"

"Who?"

"The warder."

"No. You just split his forehead open."

"Thank God."

The words just hung there. They startled both Drew and the bishop. It was the first time either of them remembered Drew thanking God for anything.

"What has that curate done to you?"

Bishop Laud didn't return Drew to the Tower. Nor did he send him away immediately. Drew's punishment was that he would be forced to watch the execution of Christopher Matthews; then he would be set free. The bishop gave him a choice: return to London House in repentance within three days, or become an enemy to crown and country. If Drew did not come home to him in three days, Bishop Laud would have him hunted down and arrested for attempting to free Christopher Matthews. It was quite simple: Drew could choose to live as a fugitive or come home. But the bishop made it clear that if Drew was caught anywhere near the village of Edenford, he would suffer the same fate as Christopher Matthews.

The sky was menacing; its partner, a stiff north wind, planted a chill in everyone it touched. And on this execution day there were plenty of people for it to touch.

Tower Hill was so crowded with spectators it seemed to Drew that the entire countryside was there to watch the execution. People crammed onto elevated platforms constructed especially for events like this one. For the people of England, executions were considered free entertainment. They didn't have quite the excitement of bear or bullbaiting, but then the people weren't charged anything to attend.

Drew was escorted to the front of the scaffold by two mountains of flesh. He still hadn't given up on the idea of rescuing the curate. Several scenarios had played in his mind the night before the execution. Because of the crowd, all of them required assistance. One hope was that David Cooper was leading a rescue attempt and Drew could assist their efforts when they struck. Another idea was for him to break free from the guards, jump to the scaffold, overpower the executioner, grab his blade, fend off the sheriff and henchmen, free Matthews, and escape. It was the escaping part he hadn't figured out. He had no horse, no way to make a getaway through the crowd. He'd just have to trust his wits to figure out something when the time came.

He scanned the crowd of spectators, looking for familiar faces. He recognized no one. All he saw were faces of strangers wearing the same look of anticipation. They couldn't wait for the headsman to hold high the prisoner's head.

A cheering arose as the prisoner was escorted to the scaffold. In solemn procession came the headsman, the executioner carrying his ax, the bound prisoner escorted by the sheriff, and the chaplain. Bishop William Laud had reserved the role of chaplain for himself. The moment the procession came in sight, Drew was seized by big beefy paws on both sides of him. The two man-mountains were apparently following the bishop's orders to ensure that Drew watched the execution. He struggled to shake loose, halfheartedly at first to test their strength. Meaty grips clamped down on his arms. Now with full effort he yanked and pulled and he couldn't budge them. They weren't even knocked slightly off balance.

The headsman and executioner reached the top of the scaffold. As they moved aside Christopher Matthews came into view, the sheriff right behind him. Drew closed his eyes and shuddered, fighting back tears and bile. Since the night of the failed rescue attempt, the curate had received his Star Chamber punishment. There was a bloody stump where his left ear had been; his nose was slit open; and his cheeks were burned red and black, branded with the letters S.L. for "Seditious Libeler."

Bishop Laud was the last to reach the top of the scaffold. Everyone moved into place and the crowd quieted down. It was time for the festivities to begin.

The sheriff read the charges and the sentence. Then the prisoner was given an opportunity to speak the last words he would ever say in this life. On other occasions, preachers who had preceded Matthews to the scaffold had taken the opportunity to deliver a sermon, sometimes a rather long one, and thereby extend their lives a couple of hours. The curate of Edenford chose not to follow their example.

As Matthews stepped forward on the scaffold, it was evident he was in pain. He started to speak, then stopped, wincing from the fire on his cheeks and the fresh cut on his nose.

Drew kicked the mountain of flesh on the right at the same time he shoved the one on his left. His efforts were in vain. The grips on his arms tightened until he was lifted off the ground. His guards glared at him but said nothing, then dropped him to his feet again without relinquishing their vicelike grip.

Matthews straightened himself, raised his head and then his voice, "As God is my witness," his voice had a breathy, nasal quality to it, the effects of a slit nose, "I have lived my life in accordance to the dictates of His Holy Word. I stand here today because I have chosen to obey God rather than men."

The acting chaplain reacted to this verbal slap. Loud enough for all to hear, Laud said, "The voice of the holy Church of England is the voice of God!"

Matthews ignored him. "The throne of England and its church condemn me. But in a matter of minutes I will stand before the throne of God. And of this I am confident: Before His throne I am without fault. Thanks be to God through Jesus Christ my Lord."

A murmur went through the crowd. Then, on the platform there was a commotion. Shouts. *The rescue attempt!* Drew thought. He glanced at his two guards, then at the platform, then for the quickest way up the scaffold. The commotion died down as two men were hauled away. There was no rescue, only a common street fight.

The sheriff whispered something to Matthews. The curate continued, "With overwhelming sorrow in my heart, I can only conclude that those in control of England will no longer tolerate God-fearing men who speak their minds. To these merchants of hate who have the form of godliness, but not its power, I prophecy that you may win temporary victories, but you will ultimately fail. A great exodus is about to begin. For those who are faithful, God will provide a land of promise. And, just like Israel of old, a godly nation will rise out of a wilderness."

At this point the curate spotted Drew. Matthews' expression was one of compassion; his face grew wet with tears. He spoke the final words directly to Drew. "This new nation will not be founded on man's wisdom or by man's strength; the greatness of this nation will be that its foundation rests on the Word of God. 'Not by might, nor by power, but by My Spirit, saith the Lord of Hosts!' "

Christopher Matthews was led to the block.

Drew fought to pull himself free.

Matthews declined a blindfold when one was offered. He lay his head down on the block.

Bishop Laud approached the condemned man. He asked, "Do you not think you ought to be lying with your head facing east, for our Lord's rising?"

"When the heart is right," Matthews replied, "it matters not which way the head lieth."

With all his strength Drew Morgan struggled to free himself, kicking, yanking, screaming. He couldn't do it.

The executioner raised his ax.

"No!" Drew shouted.

WHACK!

A roar of cheers rose from the crowd.

The first blow didn't sever the curate's neck. So the executioner raised his ax again.

WHACK!

Another cheer.

The headsman indicated that there was still some skin attaching the head to the body.

WHACK!

The headsman jumped to his feet, holding the head of Christopher Matthews high for everyone to see. The crowd went wild.

Drew hung limp in his guard's arms.

Bishop Laud solemnly approached the body of the dead curate and said a prayer. Walking to the edge of the scaffold, he looked at Drew.

"Three days," he said. Then to the guards, "Give him his things and let him go."

Chapter 20

HE ran. As fast and as far as he could, he ran. Shoving his way through the sadistic crowd, blinded by rage, not caring where he was going as long as he got far away from the scaffold.

He ran through the city of the homeless living on the steps of St. Paul's Cathedral. He ran down Fleet Street past the ditch leading to the prison which bore its name. He ran down The Strand despising the people who transacted business as if it was just another day. *A good man . . . a godly man . . . died today! Doesn't anybody care?* He ran past Charing Cross, away from Whitehall and the king and the bishop. He ran across Knight's Bridge. He ran until his lungs were bursting and he could no longer see through his tears. And when he could run no longer, he collapsed into a ditch, buried his face in the dirt, and wept.

For hours he lay there. Horses with their riders passed by, as did carriages and travelers on foot who complained about long work hours, beastly managers, and skinflint employers. They all passed him by. No one asked if he were hurt.

It was night before he stirred from the ditch. The dark day had ushered in a black night. The wind blew with gale force, casting drops of rain like stones. Drew's head pounded as he stood up with pain so intense it nearly knocked him down. He stumbled onto the road, his limbs devoid of feeling, his face expressionless. His arms fell limp to his sides. He was barely aware that he was walking as one foot shuffled in front of the other carrying him back across Knight's Bridge and into London.

Aimlessly, he wandered the city's streets. Coachmen yelled at him to get out of their way. He tripped and fell into the open sewers which ran down the middle of the street. Prostitutes called to him from their windows. He ignored them all. Didn't they know? Couldn't they tell he was dead?

After a while he found himself standing opposite London House. There was a light coming from the bishop's library; two more lights beamed upstairs. A huge silhouette moved past one of the upstairs windows. It was so large it could belong only to the round cook. In his mind, Drew could see the interior of the house—his room, the bishop's bedroom where they used to lie awake and talk about knights and crusades, the library where he spent countless hours reading and relaxing far from the strife of home. The bishop was probably sitting at his desk in the library right now finishing up some business or writing a letter, but not in code. Only the two of them knew the code.

Without expression, Drew walked away from London House.

He was ambling down Mile End Road when the rain suddenly fell in sheets. It was a strong rain, driven so hard by the wind it traveled across the road. Shielding his face from the stinging drops, Drew fled to a familiar looking tavern.

"Close the door!" someone shouted as Drew entered.

He leaned against the door from the inside until he heard the latch fall. Then he stumbled to an empty table leaving a trail of water behind.

"Ale?" the tavernkeeper grunted. The man had bright red hair and a bulbous nose.

Drew stared at him with unfocused eyes.

"You deaf?" the tavernkeeper shouted.

Still no response.

Not one to pass up an opportunity to amuse his regulars, the tavernkeeper's next question was even louder, with a definite pause between each word. "Do . . . you . . . want . . . an . . . ale?" Then he basked in his reward of laughter.

Drew felt the outside of his pockets. "I don't know if I have any money," he mumbled.

The tavernkeeper cursed. "Get him outta here!" he yelled at a burly man propped in a chair in the far corner. The barrel-chested man grunted a response and came at Drew.

"Wait!" A heavily whiskered man with a tankard stood between Drew and the barrel. Squinting as he leaned closer to Drew, he said, "Ain't you Drew Morgan?"

Drew stared back at him and came up blank. He couldn't remember ever seeing those whiskers before.

"Sure it is!" The whiskered man beamed as he called to the other patrons. "This here's Drew Morgan!"

"You sure?" the tavernkeeper asked him.

"Sure I'm sure!" the whiskers said. "I was delivering meat to the palace during that royal reception when I sees him. I was in the kitchen when suddenly everyone in the banquet hall starts clappin' and yellin' and cheerin'. I pokes my head out the door to see what's the fuss. And it's him!" The whiskered man poked Drew in the chest, making his head bob back and forth. "It's him! Drew Morgan the spy!"

"Looks like a drunk to me."

"He's the spy, I tells ya! Ain't ya, son?" The whiskered man was inches from Drew's face.

Drew nodded into the whiskers.

Nearly a dozen chairs scraped the floor as everyone got up from their tables to look at Drew.

"Get the man an ale!" the tavernkeeper cried. To Drew, "No charge, Master Morgan. Ain't every day we get a hero in here. Drink all the ale you want."

"I sure do admire you, son," Whiskers said. "What's it like bein' a spy? Excitin' ain't it? Was there a time when ya thought ya'd get caught?"

An ale was slammed down in front of Drew. He took a sip, then nodded in reply to Whiskers' question.

Everyone cheered.

"What kinda trainin' ya have to do for undercover work?"

"Undercover work?" A woman with a half-open blouse pushed her way into the circle. "If we're talkin' about work under covers," she said, "I'm an expert."

Hoots and hollers testified to her boast.

The woman wormed her way onto Drew's lap.

"Rosemary's the best there is this side of London," the tavernkeeper said with a grin and a wink.

Drew looked into the face of the woman on his lap.

"Wait a minute!" she cried, "Wait just a minute! I know you! You came in here some time ago with that Venner guy, didn't you?" She looked at the men around the table and said, "That Venner kid is a real strange one, real strange!"

Drew wasn't sure what she meant, but her commentary on Eliot brought a roar of laughter.

"And you!" Rosemary turned her attention back to Drew. "I was your birthday present, wasn't I?"

Drew turned red. "Something like that," he said.

"That's right! And if I recall, you ran out on me!" With eyes and mouth opened wide with a surprised smile, she said, "How 'bout that, boys? I get a second chance with the hero!"

"Leave 'im alone, Rosemary!" It was the redheaded tavernkeeper. "You're embarrassin' him. Can't ya see he's had an awful day?"

"Don't see why," Whiskers said. "Should be a good day for 'im. The guy he spied on got whacked today!"

"That's right!" said the tavernkeeper.

"Didn't you go to Tower Hill, son?" Whiskers asked. "Musta been the whole city out there."

"Best execution I ever saw," one man said.

"You're blowin' beans," another man responded. "It took the executioner three strokes to do it. It was messy work."

"Dull blade," Whiskers said.

"That's what I liked about it!" replied the first man. "Three strokes—Whack! Whack! Whack!" The man hit the table with the edge of his hand for effect. "Single strokes are no fun, they're over too soon."

"I like to watch royal heads, myself," said Rosemary.

"Me? I like precision. Sharp blade. One stroke. Whack!"

"You're outa your mind! The more strokes, the better. Whack! Whack! Whack!"

Drew shoved himself away from the table. Rosemary fell on her backside with a thud. Throwing the door open he charged into the elements, wind and rain assaulting his face. He sloshed down the middle of the muddy road back toward the heart of London.

He had gone about half a mile when he thought he saw someone duck behind a tree trunk several feet in front of him and to the left. Slowing his pace, he altered his course toward the other side of the street. There was a sloshing behind him. He turned just in time to see a fist come flying at him. He fell to his knees in the mud. More sloshing sounds from behind him. Someone from behind grabbed him by the hair and yanked his head back. Through bleary eyes Drew recognized the man in front of him. He'd been in the tavern. Another fist came his way. Thud! Another. Thud! The man holding his hair let go and Drew fell face forward into the mud.

Barely conscious, he could feel himself being rolled over. Someone was searching his pockets and inside his shirt.

"He said he didn't have any money!" a voice whined.

"How did I know?" another voice, a raspy one, replied. "He's a hero. Heroes are rich."

Finding nothing, the robber with the raspy voice kicked Drew in the ribs.

"Leave 'im alone," said his partner.

"He deserved it," the raspy voice said. "Heroes are supposed to be rich."

Drew lay in the mud moaning, the rain beating down on him. Within minutes a little mud crater next to his cheek filled, the overflow pouring into Drew's nose and mouth. Choking and coughing, he rolled onto his back, rubbed his neck and struggled to his feet, slipping several times in the slick roadway.

Drew sloshed his way down Aldgate and then south toward the Thames. He made his way to Tower Hill and stood before the scaffold in the same place where he had watched the curate of Edenford die.

Just under the scaffold he saw his bundle. Laud's men must have left it there when he ran off. The first thing he noticed about it was the item that was conspicuously absent. The broken cutlass. Whenever he paused in his travels, he always leaned the cutlass against his bundle, but it wasn't there now. It had served his grandfather well, but it failed him. Just like he had failed Christopher Matthews.

He dropped to his knees to inventory what was inside the bundle. Clothes mostly. He found a pouch containing money. The bishop must have put it there. He counted it. A substantial amount. "Heroes are supposed to be rich," he laughed bitterly. At the bottom of the pack was his Bible ... the one Laud had given him ... the one the Puritans hated ... the one he read to Nell and Jenny as they made bone lace beside the open window on High Street.

He wept.

A weary Drew Morgan climbed the stairs of the scaffold and stood where the block was laid. The hard rain rolled off his face and hands; the wind made him shiver as the chill penetrated his skin and worked its way toward his heart. He welcomed it. He wanted the wind to freeze his heart and numb his mind so he wouldn't have to think anymore. So he wouldn't have to feel anymore.

He looked at the empty stands all around him. No one was cheering for him, no one applauding his courage. No one saluting his bravery for causing the death of a man who wanted nothing more than to love his family and serve his God.

As Drew dropped to his hands and knees, he saw blood-stains on the wood. Christopher Matthews' blood . . . Innocent blood . . . Spilled blood. It had soaked deep enough in the wood that the rain didn't wash it away. Drew rubbed the beams with his hands but the stains remained. He removed his shirt and scrubbed the boards furiously. The blood of Christopher Matthews was still there, an enduring testimony to Drew's guilt. There was no getting rid of it. He was forced to live with the stain.

What was wrong with him? Everything he had ever wanted in life was a few miles away. All he had to do was walk to London House and claim his heritage, embrace the bishop, acknowledge the applause, accept the rewards, be the hero of England that the bishop and the king wanted him to be. But now the thought of those things held no fascination for him, as if a spell had been broken and the gold he sought had turned into ashes.

Christopher Matthews had broken the spell. He had none of those things, yet he was the richest man Drew had ever met. Now Drew Morgan's gold had turned to ashes and now he had nothing. Nothing but taunting memories of what he could never have, cruel memories of mistakes he could never remedy, laughing memories of the boy who would be great:

Memories of Nell smiling coyly among the castle ruins . . .
Little blue-faced Thomas smiling at him . . .
Matthews defending him against Dudley's charges . . .
Jenny's sweet kisses under her canopy of hair . . .
Old Cyrus Furman holding his dead wife in his arms . . .
Eliot dancing half-naked beside the river . . .
Laud relentlessly pursuing his victim in Star Chamber . . .
The broken body of Lord Chesterfield's son . . .
Christopher Matthews in the Tower lifting his beaming face and saying, "Thank You, Lord!"

"I don't understand!" Drew shouted at the sky. "How could he do that? How could he be thankful when his enemy had triumphed? How could he rejoice when he was about to die?"

Drew sobbed and pounded the scaffold with his fists. Then the words came to him, the curate's words, *Edenford must fly to the wilderness. Keep my girls safe! Tell them their poppa loves them.*

Drew shook his head. "I can't do it!" he shouted.

"*Fly to the wilderness. Keep my girls safe.*"

"They won't listen to me!"

"*Fly to the wilderness.*"

"They'll kill me if I go back there!"

"*Not by might, nor by power, but by My Spirit, saith the Lord of hosts!*"

"No! It's not possible!"

"*Not by might, nor by power, but by My Spirit, saith the Lord of Hosts!*"

"No," he whimpered.

"*Fear not them which kill the body, but are not able to kill the soul; but rather fear him which is able to destroy both soul and body in hell.*"

"O God, help me!" Drew cried. "Forgive me for what I've done."

Drew Morgan fell prostrate on the scaffold. The heavy rain pounded the wooden boards.

"*Not by might.*"

"Lord, teach me to love."

"*Nor by power.*"

"Lord, give me strength."

"*But by My Spirit.*"

"Lord, take away my selfishness."

He talked to God until the sun rose.

Two deaths occurred that day. On the executioner's scaffold on Tower Hill, Christopher Matthews died and went to glory. Drew Morgan died to himself.

Chapter 21

AN invading conqueror couldn't have plundered Edenford any more than did the Star Chamber verdict. It killed their leader. It devastated their economy. It broke their spirit. Edenford's share of Christopher Matthews' sentence left the people absolutely no control over the affairs of their own village.

All businesses were now under control of the king. Shops, assets, equipment, everything had been seized. All these would remain confiscated until the village paid off Christopher Matthews' 10,000 pound fine. The businesses that were seized included David Cooper's cobbler shop, Nell and Jenny's lacemaking tools and materials, and Lord Chesterfield's woolen business—all of it, everything from the sheep to the stock of serges. Rents were increased, quotas were established, and penalties defined. The basis of all payment schedules was simple: The king got his money first—ship tax and payment on Christopher Matthews' fine. Lord Chesterfield got his rent money and limited profits second. (Chesterfield had argued passionately for a larger percentage of profit but to no avail. He was informed it was his penalty for selecting a Puritan as curate in the first place. Besides, the king wanted his money as quickly as possible.) The third and smallest portion of the village's income belonged to the villagers.

To manage his affairs in Edenford, the king appointed David Hoffman, the obese high constable, to be his representative. This was a logical choice since Hoffman was in charge of local law enforcement, which he readily employed to maintain the peace and his safety.

An Anglican bishop was given the Edenford living. It was one of three livings he held, the other two being Tiverton and Halberton. The new bishop promptly placed the communion table against the east wall and railed it off. Services were restricted to the format outlined in the Book of Common Prayer, nothing less and certainly nothing more. This meant there was no preaching and no evening service. Instead, people were encouraged to play on Sunday afternoons, in keeping with King James' *Book of Sports.*

Edenford wasn't the same village Drew Morgan had entered less than a year before. From his vantage point among the castle ruins, Drew noticed the difference immediately. Sitting in the shadows of the ancient Saxon's domain, he observed the people of Edenford going about their daily affairs. They walked with stooped shoulders. They greeted one another politely, but without warmth. The village had lost its sparkle, its hope, its will to live.

He contributed much of the depressed attitude to the presence of Edenford's newest residents—notably the waddling high constable who paraded about as if he were king, followed by his contingent of armed guards. Add to that the guards he posted throughout the village and one would get the impression that a foreign army had seized control of the village. Drew noticed one other new resident, Eliot Venner. He wasn't hard to identify. His wild hair and cocky strut stood in contrast to the conservative dress and depressed shuffle of the villagers. *At least he's wearing more than a loin cloth now,* Drew thought.

Eliot's presence raised a disturbing question. What did he

know about Drew's situation? Had he been in contact with
the bishop since the trial? With Eliot it was hard to tell. He
could have been on assignment or in the woods the entire
time. On the other hand, his assignment might be to locate
Drew.

It had been three months since Christopher Matthews'
death, since the night on the scaffold when Drew gave his life
to God. For the last three months he had traveled the back
roads of England from London to Edenford. Not a direct
route, but more like a meandering across England's countryside. As Drew walked he prayed. He'd stop and read his
Bible, primarily the Gospels. He'd meditate on what he read,
then get up and walk and pray some more. For those three
months Drew attended the school of the disciples. Jesus was
his teacher. Everything Jesus said to the twelve disciples,
Drew took to heart. Their lessons became his lessons; their
assignments, his assignments. When he read the words describing Jesus' death on a cross, he wept and thought of
another of the Lord's faithful disciples, Christopher Matthews. And when he read the commission of the resurrected
Lord, he remembered Matthews' commission to him,
"Edenford must fly to the wilderness. Keep my girls safe."

Drew Morgan was in Edenford to fulfill his commission.

He hid beside the house at the end of High Street, the end
that faced the bare cornfield which had once been Christopher Matthews' place of prayer. He poked his head around
the corner, looking down High Street. Jenny labored under
the load of two buckets of water. For the last four nights she
had performed the same chore at precisely the same time.
Setting the buckets down, she swung open the house door,
picked up the buckets, and went inside. Drew slipped around
the corner, followed her in, and closed the door behind him.

"Oh!" Jenny dropped the buckets, splashing water on her

dress and the floor. "You startled . . ." She swung around. "Drew!"

Nell appeared from upstairs. She stopped halfway down the steps, her hand on the railing. Her face was without expression, her eyes cold.

Jenny backed away from him, tripped on one of the buckets, and fell.

Just then, James Cooper appeared. He came from upstairs too. He was bigger and redder than Drew had remembered. "You!" he shouted, pointing a big beefy finger.

Nell held onto the railing with both hands as he pushed past her down the stairs.

Drew held up both hands. "Please, I didn't come here to cause trouble. I only want to talk to you."

"You got nothin' to say," the red giant said, closing fast.

"Give me one minute, that's all I . . ."

Drew's request was denied by a ferocious punch to his jaw. It sent him sailing against the door, where he hit his head. James dragged Drew outside and into the dirt field where he soundly thrashed him.

Drew remembered hearing a female voice; James' punches made it hard for him to distinguish whether it was Jenny or Nell yelling at the giant, telling him to stop before he killed Drew. Then everything went black.

When he opened his eyes, he saw a slow spinning motion that, together with the spinning in his head, made him sick to his stomach. He was on the far side of the south bridge. The spinning was the waterwheel of the fulling mill beside the river. Drew crawled to the edge of the river and vomited.

He sat under the bridge until it was night, then made his way back to the stone castle ruins.

Drew made camp on the far side of the castle's interior, the portion that had been reclaimed by the forest, offering enough cover to hide him from the village. There was only

one other person he knew of who ever came to the castle—
Nell. He wished she were with him now. If only he could talk
with her, he could make her understand.

In his mind he saw her standing on the staircase, James
behind her, coming from the bedroom. No, he didn't know
that for sure. But he came from upstairs. What was he doing
upstairs? Why was he even in the house? No matter how hard
Drew fought it, his heart filled with jealousy; anger caused it
to spill over into a curse. The thought of James being close to
Nell was too much for him. It hurt him far worse than the
beating James had given him.

"Lord, I need patience and I need it now," he prayed.
What if Nell never forgives me?

That possibility hadn't occurred to him before. He always
assumed she would forgive him if he had a chance to explain
to her. *What if she never forgives me?*

"I'll still love her," he said aloud. "I'll always love her."
Even if she marries James? Or is already married to him?

The thought pierced him. The dagger was invisible but the
pain was real. "I may not be able to have her, but nothing can
stop me from loving her," he said.

There was healing in his words. It didn't take the pain
away, but it lessened it. Drew Morgan took comfort in the
fact that no matter what James Cooper did, he could not strip
Drew of his love for Nell. No one could. Not even Nell
herself.

It was an exciting revelation for him. *Nothing Nell can say
or do can stop my love for her. She can hurt me. She can leave
me. But she can't stop me from loving her.*

Drew retired that night basking in the warmth of his love
for Nell Matthews.

"I need a Barnabas."

Drew was propped against the side of a stone wall. His

Bible in his lap was opened to the Acts of the Apostles, chapter 9. He read the verses again, "And when Saul was come to Jerusalem, he assayed to join himself to the disciples; but they were all afraid of him, and believed not that he was a disciple. But Barnabas took him, and brought him to the apostles."

"They were afraid of him . . . believed not he was a disciple. Lord, I need a Barnabas," he said again.

"Jenny!" It was a half-whisper, half-shout.

Brown hair swirled as Jenny's head snapped his direction. She was standing in front of her door, water buckets at her feet, reaching for the doorlatch when he called. Her face registered shock and she grabbed the latch.

"Jenny, please! I won't hurt you!"

She paused, her hand still on the latch.

"Meet me down by the river, next to the mill."

She shook her head no.

"Jenny, please trust me."

She didn't agree, but she was no longer shaking her head. Hand still on the latch, she stared at the base of the door while she considered his request.

"Please!" he pleaded. "As soon as you can. I'll be waiting for you there."

He didn't wait for an answer. As he left, she stood motionless in front of the door. He went to the river and waited. While he waited, he prayed.

The sun descended behind the western mountain, leaving the stream and grassy hillside in the twilight of evening. He didn't dare look over the ridge because someone might spot him, so he had to be content to scan the ridge every few seconds to see if Jenny would come. The twilight began to fade, giving way to night.

Like a fawn stepping into a clearing, Jenny Matthews appeared over the ridge. She stopped at the crest. Drew smiled and stepped toward her. She stepped back away from him.

"Thank you for coming," Drew said.

"Everyone knows you're here."

The smile on Drew's face vanished as he looked around him.

"No, I mean in Edenford. At least they know you were here yesterday. James told them."

"I guess I can't blame him," Drew said.

"Why?" Jenny asked. "Why did you come back?" Her voice quivered and tears filled her eyes. It hurt Drew to think he had caused her pain. She was the most beautiful woman he had ever known; her innocence only added to her charm.

"Your father sent me back."

"Father?" Her voice rose in expectation.

"I talked with him in London. He asked me to tell you that he loves you."

Jenny's hands rose to her cheeks, wiping away a steady stream of tears. "You saw my father in prison?"

Drew grinned. "Not exactly. I was trying to get him to escape."

"Escape?"

He nodded.

"I don't understand. What happened?"

"He refused to escape. Said it would endanger you, Nell, and the townspeople. He asked me to look after you."

"That sounds like Poppa," Jenny sniffed. "How did you get away?"

"I didn't. I was caught."

A puzzled look appeared on her face. It was almost dark.

"That doesn't matter right now," Drew said. "I need you to help me. To be my Barnabas."

The transition was too quick for her. She didn't catch the reference.

"You know, Barnabas trusted the Apostle Paul after his conversion, when nobody else would. Jenny, I need you to trust me."

"You sound like Poppa," she smiled, "always explaining things in biblical terms."

It was so good to see her smile. "Will you trust me?" he said.

Her smile faded and she looked down. "What do you want me to do?"

"All I want you to do is to help arrange meetings between me and some of the people in the village."

"Why do you need my help to do that?"

"Well, after yesterday's reception in your house, I don't think it would be wise for me to stroll down Marketplace Street at noon."

"I guess you're right," she said. There was a pause. Then, "Whom do you want to talk to? Master Cooper?"

"And Nell."

"Nell won't talk to you."

That hurt, but it was understandable. "Will you at least ask her?"

"I have to go now." Jenny turned and stepped away from the ridge. "I'll think about it," she said.

"Pray about it!"

She stopped and looked at him with appraising eyes. "All right, I'll pray about it."

He was reclining on one arm reading about Paul and Barnabas on Cyprus. Paul had just struck the sorcerer Elymas blind when Drew heard a twig snap. Someone was in the castle ruins! Drew rolled over on his belly and crawled behind the closest wall. How many were there? He glanced behind him and to both sides. No movement. Nothing but forest. Cautiously, he raised up and looked over the wall.

Nell Matthews stood in the open doorway of the castle ruins, the dappled sunlight shining around her. Her casual stroll indicated she was alone and didn't expect company. Deep in thought, she wandered slowly into the castle's large entryway. She was alone. Her dark brown hair rested gently on her white muslin blouse; a pair of scissors dangled from a ribbon around her waist against her dark skirt. Drew remembered fondly the times he'd watched her making lace. Those scissors were almost an extension of her right hand. She could grab them, snip a thread, and continue working the lace in one smooth motion.

Drew was surprised at how hungry his eyes were to see her. He was afraid to speak, afraid he might frighten her away. For several minutes he was content just to look at her, to satisfy his visual craving.

Nell walked to the center of the ruins and sat on the wall, the same place where she usually sat when she and Drew came to the ruins. Drew could see her face now. It was a somber face and her eyes were dull. She no longer had the confident set of her jaw, the look of smugness, that had intimidated and irritated Drew when they first met.

Quietly, he stood and climbed over the low stone wall. He was halfway to her before his movement caught the corner of her eye. She jumped from the wall with a start. When she recognized him, she ran toward the door opening. Drew had to vault one more low wall and sprint to catch her. He caught her by the arm just as she reached the doorway. Swinging her around, he grabbed her by the shoulders.

"I'll scream!" she warned him.

Instinctively Drew looked behind her, expecting to see a red giant lumbering up the hill.

"Nell! I have to talk to you!"

"What are you doing here?" she cried, as she struggled to pull herself free.

"Your father sent me."

She stopped struggling. "You expect me to believe that?" There was fire in her eyes, a blazing angry fire. With a quick sweeping motion she grabbed her scissors and pointed them at Drew's chest. "Let me go!"

Drew released his grip on her. She stumbled a few steps backward, then turned to run down the mountain.

"Why else would I come back?" he shouted after her.

He watched her run down the path, then lost sight of her as she passed behind the building which housed the looms. Sighing, he walked back into the ruins and sat on a large stone block. He didn't blame her. She was scared; who wouldn't be, given her situation? But how was he going to fulfill his promise to God and the curate if no one would talk to him?

"Why did you come back?"

The voice startled Drew. Nell was standing in the doorway. He started to get off the stone block.

"Stay right there!" Nell commanded. "Just answer my question."

"Is that why you came back?"

"It doesn't make sense. There's nothing for you here— nothing more you can take from us. So it doesn't make sense that you would come back."

"Or stay around, considering the reception James gave me yesterday," Drew added. He couldn't help feeling a little smug. She was perplexed and it bothered her.

"James was wrong to hurt you like that," she said.

"I was wrong to hurt you the way I did."

Nell fought a losing battle against her tears. "You still haven't answered my question," she said.

"Yes, I have. Your father sent me."

"I suppose he told you that during the Star Chamber trial? Or was it during his murder trial? You and Dudley certainly staged an impressive little drama."

Drew waited as she struggled to regain her composure.

"How could you?" she yelled at him. "He loved you!"

Now it was Drew's turn to fight back tears.

"I know," he said meekly.

They were silent for a long time.

"Well?" Nell demanded.

"All I can say is that I never intended things to turn out the way they did." The look of disgust on Nell's face told him she was obviously not convinced. He proceeded anyway. "I talked to your father in prison. He asked me to convey his love to you. He also asked me to take care of you."

He really lost her with that one. "I can take care of myself, thank you. Well, Master Morgan, it seems that since you have fulfilled your obligation to my father, you can be on your way now."

"Nell, I know you're not going to believe me, but I've changed. I've asked Jesus to be my Savior."

"We've heard that before, haven't we?" Sarcasm dripped from her words.

"What can I do to convince you?"

"There's nothing you can do to convince me, Master Morgan. You lied to us. You intentionally set out to deceive us. You killed my father and destroyed my village. I don't think you even talked to my father after his arrest. I don't think you'd have the gall to face him. And I think you came back here just to soothe your aching guilty conscience. Well, it's not that easy. You're just going to have to live with yourself. I may be a Christian, but I'm not a fool."

"Your father wasn't Justin. You are."

He just blurted it out. He was losing ground rapidly and it was the only thing that could save him. The moment he saw her reaction, he knew it was the wrong thing to do. Once before he'd seen that same look of horror on her face, the time he frightened her in her father's study after he returned from his river meeting with Eliot. At that moment, he also remembered her scream in the dark and the sounds of Jenny consoling her. She knew the price of being Justin and it scared her to death.

"There were only three people who knew the true secret," he said. "Your father, Jenny, and you. On the night your father forgave me and told me to take care of you, he told me the truth. He died to protect you."

Nell bolted down the hill, sobbing uncontrollably. Drew watched her and wondered if he'd done the right thing.

"Psssst!"

Jenny stood before her door again, water buckets at her feet. Brown hair swirled around her as she swung toward the now familiar sound. "Go away!" she hissed.

"Jenny! Please!"

She stomped toward Drew. "What have you done to my sister?"

"I can explain, but not here. Meet me by the river."

Jenny stomped back toward the buckets and shot him another angry glance.

"I can explain," he said again.

Hands on hips, she stood toe to toe with him by the river, much less tentative than at their previous meeting. "What did Nell tell you?" he asked.

"Nothing," Jenny said. "She just ran upstairs and shut the bedroom door. She won't talk to me."

"Then how did you know it was me?"

Jenny looked at him like he was the dumbest person on earth. "You're the only person who has ever had that kind of effect on her."

"I told her I knew she was Justin."

Jenny's face recorded her shock and fear.

"I'm sorry," Drew said. "It was the only way I could convince her that I'd talked with your father. Why would he tell me that if he didn't trust me?"

"You really are telling the truth, aren't you?"

Drew nodded.

"About everything?"

"Jenny, I never meant to hurt your father. I'd gladly give my life if it would bring him back."

"O Drew!" Jenny flung her arms around him and cried.

"Then you believe me?"

She answered him with a smile.

Closing his eyes, he raised his head heavenward. "Thank You, Lord!"

Despite Jenny's passionate pleas, David Cooper refused to meet with Drew. He warned Jenny to stay away from him, to run if ever he came near her again.

Drew refused to be discouraged by the setback. His spirits bolstered with his first convert, he was determined not to give up. He was confident there was an answer; all he had to do was discover the right question. He began quizzing Jenny, asking her to describe the townspeople's response to the new order of life in Edenford. They felt like they were living in a prison with guards watching them all the time, she said. They were disgusted with the church services and longed to hear some preaching. Some people stopped going to church all together, feeling God had deserted them. Of course, there was no longer any need for town meetings, since everything was decided for them.

"Meetings!" Drew exclaimed. "Are there any meetings at all?"

Jenny hesitated. It was the first sign of reluctance he had seen in her since she said she believed he was telling the truth.

"There were secret meetings before. About Justin pamphlets and things," Drew said. "Are the meetings secret? Is that why you're reluctant to tell me?"

Jenny nodded. "I'm not even supposed to know about them. But James Cooper has a big mouth."

A pang hit Drew at the mention of James. There was still the unanswered question of James' presence in the Matthews' house. But now was not the time. He let it pass.

"It's up to you," Drew said.

A select group of Edenford men met secretly in old Cyrus Furman's home. Among them were some of the veterans of the previous secret order—David Cooper, Charles Manley, and James Cooper as a recent addition. Since the curate's arrest and the resulting seizure of the cobbler shop, David Cooper's back room was no longer available to them. Jenny didn't know the subject of their meetings, but she knew that only faithful Puritans were invited. This was the remnant of believers in Edenford. The shades were pulled as ten men huddled around a single candle talking in low voices.

There was a soft knock on the door. Everyone froze.

"Relax, men," the elder Cooper said. "Armed guards don't usually knock softly before busting up a meeting." To the owner of the home he said, "Cyrus, answer the door."

The old man rambled over to the door. "Why, Miss Jenny, what brings you out so late at night?"

He opened the door. It swung wider than he'd planned when two people entered the room.

"You again?" James was on his feet, fists at the ready, charging at Drew.

Jenny stepped in front of Drew.

"James!" his father cried. "I'll take care of this!"

"I whipped him once for showin' his face, and I can do it again!"

The older Cooper grabbed his son around the waist, stopping his charge. "You beat him? You didn't tell me that. You only said you'd seen him." The cobbler took a good look at Drew. Even in the dim light, scrapes and bruises were still visible. "What do you want from us?" he said.

"I have a message for you."

"From?"

"From Christopher Matthews."

"I think you'd better leave," the cobbler said. He was restraining two people now, his son and himself.

"Listen to him!" Jenny cried. "He's telling the truth!"

"What have you been telling this girl?" The cobbler was seething.

"Master Cooper!" Jenny screamed. "I'll not have you talking about me as if I was some empty-headed mule! At first I didn't believe Drew either. But he told me something that could have come only from my father. I believe he's telling the truth."

"He probably got whatever it was by torturing the curate!" James said. "I've heard about them racks and the scavenger's daughter where they bind a man's neck and hands and feet with a piece of iron so he's pulled into a ball and can't straighten himself!"

"That's enough, James!"

"Jenny, are you sure he's telling the truth?" the cobbler asked.

Jenny looked at Drew. "Yes," she said. "I'm sure."

"What's the message you say you bring from Christopher Matthews?" the cobbler asked Drew.

" 'Fly to the wilderness.' "

For over an hour Drew told the men about his meeting and failed rescue attempt at the Tower of London. He told them of Bishop Laud's ultimatum and the deadline long since past.

"It's just another trick!" James Cooper cried. "We fell for it once. We're not gonna to fall for it again."

There was no other way to convince them. Drew took a chance. "Look," he said, "ask yourselves what I have to gain from being here. How can I hurt you any more than I already have? It doesn't make sense, does it?" The line of reasoning worked on Nell, he hoped the men in the meeting were equally logical. Then he took the chance. "Of all of us here right now, I have the most to lose."

He didn't expect them to believe him outright, and they didn't.

"You have another of Bishop Laud's spies in your village right now."

That got their attention.

"His name's Eliot Venner."

"No one in town by that name," Cyrus Furman said.

Drew described his former tutor — the wild hair, buggy eyes.

"Mitchell!" Cyrus said. The others agreed.

"Thomas Mitchell," Cyrus said.

"His name's Eliot Venner," Drew corrected. "and he's looking for me. If he catches me, he'll kill me. He killed Shubal Elkins."

"How do we know you're not just makin' this up?" It was James, of course.

"I'm making myself vulnerable, hoping you'll believe me. Anyone in this room at any time can have me killed. All you have to do is lead Eliot to me."

"Sounds like a good idea to me!" James laughed.

No one else laughed with him.

"Shut up, James," said his father. To Drew, "I'll check your story to see if you're telling the truth. If you're not, you'll have to answer to me."

Drew nodded.

For two days Drew hid in the castle ruins. He agreed not

to contact anyone in town during that time while the secret committee checked his story. Drew spent the time reading his Bible, praying, and dreaming of Nell. On the second night, he slipped into town and knocked on Cyrus Furman's door, not knowing what kind of reception to expect.

The door opened and he was ushered inside. The same men were there as before. James looked no friendlier and the other men were expressionless. The first clue to his fate came in David Cooper's first words.

"Have a seat, son," he said.

Son. It had a nice sound to it. A man doesn't use a term like that if he's about to kill you.

The cobbler described for Drew how he told Mitchell — or Eliot — that he thought he saw Drew Morgan loitering at the foot of the north bridge. "You should have seen that boy's eyes pop out," the cobbler laughed.

"They're always poppin' out!" Cyrus injected.

"Well, they was really poppin' out this time," the cobbler laughed. "He grabbed two guards and they went running down to the river like hound dogs after a coon."

Since Drew's vulnerability was confirmed, they told him the subject of their secret meetings. They were talking about the very thing Drew had encouraged them to do. They were planning to flee to the New World. The cobbler said they initially told Lord Chesterfield of their desire to join John Winthrop's expedition. He angrily refused and had the high constable post more guards in case they tried to leave. They were told they could not leave until the ship tax and fine were paid off.

"Just an excuse," the elder Cooper explained. "The king's determined to rule without parliament and so he has to find other ways to raise money. If it's not a ship tax or a fine, it will be something else. We can't take it anymore. Besides, we're dying spiritually. Matthews gave us a vision of a land where we can build a city based on our beliefs, free from the tyranny of tax and Anglican regulations. There are ten families all together. Somehow, God willing, we're going to the New World."

They told him what they had planned so far. John Winthrop had a fleet of eleven ships. Four would sail from Southampton in March. The other seven would follow a month later. The second fleet would sail from Southampton to Plymouth where it would pick up colonists from Devonshire and other western counties.

"Does Lord Chesterfield know when the ships are leaving?" Drew asked.

"Unfortunately, yes."

"That means he'll probably increase the guard in April."

"That's what we were thinking," the cobbler said.

"I think I know how to get you to the New World," Drew said.

"It's a trick," James warned.

"Let's hear your plan, son," the cobbler said, ignoring James.

"How many horses and wagons were you going to use to get you to Plymouth?"

"None. We're not a wealthy people, Drew."

"Can you get two horses and wagons on loan? We'll need skittish horses, horses that spook easily."

"We might be able to get some from Lord Chesterfield. We could tell him we need to transport a special shipment of serges to Exeter."

"Good. I know a special code that will come in handy. And I'll need James to help me do something dangerous."

"You're gonna do it too?" James asked.

"Yes."

"If you can do it, I can do it."

"I was counting on that," Drew said.

Drew outlined his plan to the men at the secret meeting. They thought it risky for a bunch of wool workers, but agreed it was their only hope.

They left Cyrus Furman's house one at a time at staggered intervals. Drew was the last one to go, besides David Cooper.

"I want you to know that I deeply regret my part in Christopher Matthews' death," Drew told the cobbler. "I know how much he loved you. I only hope that someday you will forgive me."

The burly black cobbler patted Drew on the back.

"One other thing. I didn't want to say this while everyone else was here. But the curate asked me to do one more thing."

"What's that?"

"He asked me to look after Nell and Jenny, to keep them safe."

Cooper put his arm around Drew's shoulders. "That's no longer your concern, son," he said. "They're no longer in Edenford. For their safety, I already sent them away."

"Where?"

The cobbler shook his head. "That's not your concern any longer, son. They're safe now."

"What's this?"

The oversized high constable held a crumpled slip of paper in his hand. A series of numbers were printed on it. Eliot Venner stood opposite him across the high constable's desk.

"That dim-witted cobbler's son was trying to hide it from me. I caught him translating it when I walked in on him at his shop."

The high constable rested both hands on his paunch, the note stretched between them. His belly roared. It was still two hours before lunch. He'd never make it that long.

The message on the paper read: (13/9/22/10/12/18/17/5)

(2/24/15/9/6/2/15) (17/5/24/11) (16/26/5/2/1/18/9/2/1)
(2/24/15/9/22) (24/13/15/6/9) (10/12/15/2) (9/24/17/2/15).

The number 3 had been printed and circled in the upper lefthand corner and there was a P under the first number of the coded message.

"That's James' writing." Eliot leaned over the desk and pointed to the circled 3 and the first letter. "And one more thing. Drew Morgan is part of this."

"Drew Morgan? He'd have to be out of his mind to come back here."

Eliot shrugged. "I recognize the code. He and the bishop used it to communicate with each other."

"Then you know how to translate it?"

Eliot shook his head. "The bishop didn't teach it to me. As far as I know, only him and Drew used it."

The high constable rubbed the middle of his three chins. This was proving to be an interesting morning, something to divert his attention until lunch time. "The numbers stand for letters," he said. "And number 13 is the letter P." He sat up. "I've got it!" he cried. "The number 1 is the letter A, two is B, and so on."

Fat fingers flew upward on his hand as he counted the alphabet to P. He slumped back down. "That doesn't work," he said. "P is the sixteenth letter of the alphabet, not the thirteenth."

"Like I said, James Cooper is a dimwit," said Eliot. "Maybe he got it wrong."

The idea sounded reasonable to the high constable. Fingers flew again as he began translating.

"What do you have?" Eliot asked when the first word was finished.

"M-I-V-J-L-R-Q-E" said the high constable. He fell against the back of his chair. "What does the circled 3 mean in the corner mean?"

"It could be James' code number," Eliot suggested. "Drew is 1, someone else is 2, James is 3 . . ."

"No. James wrote the 3, remember?"

"It has to be something easy. James ain't too bright."

"That's it!" the high constable bolted upward. "He wrote the number there because he's a dolt! It's a translation aid!"

Eliot wasn't following.

"P is number 13 on the note, right?"

Eliot nodded.

"When we counted, P was number 16 in the alphabet."

Another nod.

"Don't you see?" The high constable was relishing the fact that he had solved the mystery before Eliot. Which, in his mind, was not surprising. One of the things he disliked about his job was the continuous association with intellectual and cultural inferiors. "Let me make it easy for you," he said. "What's the difference between 16 and 13?"

"Three."

"Exactly!" A fat, stubby finger poked repeatedly at the circled 3 in the upper corner.

Eliot's eyebrows shot upward. He understood.

The high constable translated the first word again, this time adding three to each number before counting on his fingers. After the first word, he grinned the grin of a triumphant sleuth. When he was finished he read the note aloud. "Plymouth. Earlier than scheduled. Early April. More later."

"They're going to bolt!" Eliot cried.

"Not while I'm high constable. Send the chief guard to me. Come April, there will be more guards in this village than residents."

Chapter 22

FRIDAY, March 19, 1630. Ten o'clock at night. Two wagons rolled slowly down the road at the end of High Street, between the houses and the cornfield. Holding the reins and walking the horse of the first wagon was Drew Morgan; James Cooper held the reins of the other horse and wagon. A large sheet of canvas covered the cargo of both wagons. From beneath the canvas of Drew's wagon the bald head and scarred face of little Thomas Cooper stuck out. His father, David, sat on the back of the wagon to be driven by James. Drew and James worked to keep their skittish horses quiet. It was too early to make noise.

Drew patted his side pockets. They were heavily weighted with rocks. So far, everything was going according to plan. The high constable and Eliot had successfully translated the coded message. They didn't expect anything to happen until April. This was crucial to the success of the plan for three reasons: first, the number of guards would remain low in anticipation of the influx of additional troops in April; second, the timing would be a surprise; and third, the port of departure would be a surprise. The constable and Eliot expected the escape attempt to be made in April; it was taking place in March. They thought the port of departure would be Plymouth. It would be Southampton.

Drew led his horse past the house and out into the open

where the road intersected Market Street. Edenford's major artery stretched before him—to the left was the heart of the town, the village green, and the church building; to the right the south bridge led out of the village. Drew took one last look at the village that held so many memories for him. Then, he turned toward the south bridge. James followed close behind with the other wagon.

Drew's horse whinnied. This time he made no attempt to quiet him. They crept slowly toward the bridge. Drew looked back toward the village. *Where is he? They were almost to the bridge. This won't do! We're sneaking out of town and nobody notices!*

Just then, Eliot stumbled out of the town house at the far end of Market Street with a bottle in his hand. He shouted angrily at the people inside and slammed the door. *The Friday night cockfights. Right on time, Eliot.*

Eliot may have been on time, but he wasn't on course. He turned the wrong way and didn't see them.

Where's he going? His house is this way! As loud as he could, Drew coughed. As he did, he stood away from the horse so the staggering Eliot could get a good look at him.

Eliot turned and squinted his direction.

"They see us!" Drew shouted.

While Eliot stared at them, David Cooper counted to three, then disappeared under the canvas covering his wagon. Little Thomas lifted his canvas up, counted to three, then he ducked under too.

"Guards! Guards!" Eliot shouted. He ran unsteadily toward the wagons. "Drew Morgan," he shouted, "come back here!"

Drew shouted at the wagons. "Keep your heads down, everybody, it's going to be a rough ride!"

Drew and James jumped onto the wagons and urged the horses on. In a cloud of dust, the wagons quickly disappeared over the south bridge toward Exeter and Plymouth.

They traveled about half a mile before Drew reined the horses in. Little Thomas and his father jumped out of the backs of the wagons.

Drew joined them. "They should be close behind," he said. To Thomas, "Thanks, friend. Couldn't have done it without you."

Thomas smiled a big toothy smile. The burns had left him bald and scarred from head to toe. His joints were still stiff; he'd probably never have the flexibility in them he had before the accident. But tonight his spirits were high. He gave Drew a bearhug.

"He insisted on helping," said his father, "and riding in your wagon."

Drew returned Thomas' hug.

"God be with you, Drew." David Cooper hugged Drew too. To James, the cobbler said, "I'll see you in Honiton. Don't be late."

"I won't," James said.

Drew climbed back onto the wagon. It took an extra kick to compensate for the extra weight of stones he carried in his pockets. He watched little Thomas and his father disappear into the dark shadows of the woods. After Eliot and the guards passed by, they would return to Edenford and meet the other refugees on the far side of the north bridge. David Cooper would lead the band of fleeing Puritans north to Tiverton, east to Halberton, then south to the port at Southampton. It would not be an easy journey. The refugees would have to travel fast to join John Winthrop and the *Arbella* by March 29.

Drew shouted to James, "Remember, we don't want a high profile. Keep your head low!"

"I know what I'm supposed to do," James sneered. "You just get your wagon movin' and stay outta my way."

"Heeeyah!" Drew urged his horse on. James was right behind him. The two wagons picked up speed down the road toward Exeter.

Like waves on the sea the dirt highway rose up and down causing the drivers occasionally to lose sight of each other between swells. On one rise Drew looked behind him in the distance. The pursuit should be in sight by now, but they weren't. He urged the horses on, waiting to crest another rise. Still no one. Had something gone wrong? Had David Cooper and Thomas been discovered? Or possibly the larger group on the road north of town? Drew caught a glimpse of James who had just looked back too. The red giant was crouched low with a scowl on his face.

The wagons bounced dangerously from rut to rut, sometimes leaving the road surface entirely, sometimes skidding around curves in the road. It was difficult to drive the horses and stay low at the same time. Drew spread his legs further apart to balance himself. He looked back again. Still no one.

Just as he was about to pull back on the reins, he saw their pursuers cresting one of the hills in the road. Good. James saw them too. His scowl turned into a thin line of determination as the giant urged the horses on.

The pursuing horses were faster. Drew had counted on that. Eliot and the guards would gradually gain on them. Drew estimated there must have been ten guards in all. The ride was too rough to make an accurate count. He ducked back down and urged the horses on. They had to get further from Edenford. It was too soon for Eliot to discover the wagons were loaded with nothing but bound piles of serge scraps.

The ladies had spent a considerable number of evening hours bundling serges to populate the backs of the wagons. Each bundle had to be the approximate sitting height of one of the passengers. After working a while, the ladies got into the spirit of their deception. They named each of the bundles to represent a person in their group. Some of the bundles had physical characteristics drawn on them, others bore nicknames or pet names. One of the ladies sat a completed bundle in a chair, the one representing her husband, and told him things she'd been wanting to say to him for years.

On the night of the escape the bundles were loaded in the wagon in an upright position and covered with a sheet of canvas. During the beginning of the trip they remained upright, but now the reckless bouncing of the wagons had knocked them all over. It didn't matter. If the cargo had been real people, by now they would be piled on top of one another in the back of the wagon.

"Heeeyah!!!" Drew shouted at his horse.

The road leveled out. About a mile more and there would be a bend eastward, heading away from the River Exe. Another mile or so more and the road would turn slightly south and the gap between the road and the River Exe would continue to increase. Not until it crossed the Culm River would the road correct itself with a sharp turn west; the two would meet again just above the port city of Exeter. But Drew Morgan and James Cooper didn't plan to make it that far.

Drew checked behind him. Eliot was gaining too quickly. The features of the riders were becoming distinguishable.

The key to this part of the plan was keep low and get to the eastward bend. It was crucial that they reach the bend well ahead of their pursuit. For when Eliot and his men rounded that bend, it would be possible for them to keep the wagons in continuous sight until they finally caught up with them. That's why James and Drew had to keep low. They didn't plan on being on the wagons when Eliot caught up with them. If they kept low, it would take Eliot and the guards longer to realize the wagons no longer had drivers as they closed in. It would give James and Drew a greater chance to escape.

This was important, since getting caught was not part of the plan. These were not sacrificial lambs driving the wagons; they were two men who had something to live for—something in common, as a matter of fact. Or more precisely, someone in common. Nell Matthews.

Drew looked back and made eye contact with James. He saw the bend too. Drew urged his horse into the left turn. His wagon hit a rut, sending all four wheels into the air and nearly knocking Drew off the seat. The two right wheels came down as the wagon hit the bend. Drew leaned left and shouted at the horse again. The left two wheels hit with a jarring thud. Drew glanced back again just as some trees blocked out James and, further behind him, Eliot and the guards. Drew pulled on the reins, slowing the wagon.

James came skidding around the turn, the back of his wagon sliding sideways. Just past the bend, he pulled back too.

Drew jumped off his wagon while it was still rolling. He hit the horse's hindquarters. "Heeeyah! Get going! Heeeyah!" James did the same. The horses responded, but with reservation. They knew there were no drivers. Drew reached into his pockets for the rocks. Still yelling, he threw rocks at the horses. He was missing and the horses were getting out of range. He threw more rocks and missed again. He knew if he didn't hit the horses hard enough they would go a little way and stop. He threw again. Another miss. James was beside him throwing too.

"I can't throw any farther!" Drew said.

James puckered his lips which to Drew was an unusual expression for rock throwing. But it worked. One rock hit Drew's horse in the rear. Frightened, he took off. Three tries later, James hit his horse behind the ear. The second horse took off, almost catching up with the first.

Drew and James ran across a large open field toward the riverbank where there was a slope with reeds that would hide them. They had to make it to the river before Eliot and the guards rounded the bend and cleared the trees.

Smaller and faster, Drew outran the heavier James. As Drew sprinted across the grassy field, he looked up the road. A cloud of dust indicated their horses were still running. He looked the other way. The road was clear . . . for the moment.

Drew reached the edge of the bank and vaulted over some reeds. He hit the ground on his belly and climbed the short distance back up to the ridge. In the distance their horses continued to run; Drew thought they had even made up some of the distance lost when they stopped. James was puffing heavily as he ran for the riverbank, his arms churning as he pounded the soft earth.

Behind him Eliot and the guards emerged from the bend.

"Hurry!" Drew yelled.

The only response from the red giant was a heavy puffing sound and the thud, thud, thud of his boots hitting the ground. He was slowing.

Drew looked behind James. Eliot was pointing at the wagons and yelling something.

His chest heaving, James plodded toward the riverbank. He was still several feet away when Eliot turned his head to shout something to the guards behind him.

James fell over the embankment and into the reeds. He rolled halfway down the bank and came to a stop face up. His enormous chest gasped barrels full of air.

Had Eliot seen James? Drew held his breath as he watched the pursuers. No one slowed. No one turned to cross the field. Drew and James had done it!

"Come on, get up! This is no time to rest!" Drew knelt over his accomplice with a smile. He was half-jesting. It was urgent they get going, but the way Eliot and the guards were chasing after the unoccupied wagons, there was at least enough time for James to catch his breath. To his surprise, James took one more heave of air and stood.

The two men walked back to the forest where they had earlier hidden their separate bundles of goods. James' bundle was light; most of his things were with his family. Drew's bundle had his clothes, his Bible, and a treasured memento he discovered the day after his first conversion. Folded among his clothes was the lace cross he had taken from Nell's journal.

Drew held out his hand to James. This was where they would part ways. James would go back to the forest, then head west where he would meet up with the fleeing Puritan band just outside the village of Honiton. Drew didn't know where he was going. To the best of his ability he had completed his mission. Nell and Jenny were safe, at least according to David Cooper. And Drew had no reason to doubt the cobbler's words. The people of Edenford were on their way to the New World where they would be free from Bishop Laud and a money-hungry king. Everything Christopher Matthews had asked of him was accomplished. Drew's task now was to stay out of Laud's reach and discover what God had in store for his life.

Almost reluctantly James shook his hand. "Where you goin'?" he asked.

Drew shrugged. "I don't know."

They dropped hands and faced each other. An awkward silence grew between them.

Drew slapped James on the shoulder. "God be with you," he said. "Give my love to Thomas and your father."

James nodded. He turned north and walked into the forest. Drew Morgan crossed the river and walked west.

Drew spent Saturday alone. He wandered the roads of Devonshire north of Exeter avoiding Dartmoor, a large granite plateau with rocky peaks and shallow marshy valleys, thin soil, and coarse grasses. He preferred the promise of the central land. It was a fertile area with an exceedingly fair amount of corn, grass, and wood. In other words, it was more like Edenford.

While he walked, he prayed; when he rested, he read the Bible. That was all he had now—God and the Bible. He tried to tell himself that was enough. Maybe he was to be like the Apostle Paul, roaming from town to town, teaching and preaching, but never putting down roots. Having friends, but no family. No wife. At times he thought he could be satisfied with that kind of life, but often he wanted more. He wanted the kind of life Christopher Matthews had in Edenford— family, close friends, a fellowship of believers. . . . the kind of life the curate enjoyed until Drew Morgan came to town.

Drew followed the Creedy River into a little village called Crediton. It was Sunday morning and he went to church. Because it was a Puritan congregation, the communion table was not railed off, and the capable young minister preached his own message without wearing the mandatory surplice. During the sermon Drew's mind wandered. He was struck by the similarities between Crediton and Edenford. They were both small villages situated beside a river. The people were of Puritan persuasion. As the preacher spoke to them in familiar terms, it almost seemed a family gathering in the minister's sitting room. The difference between the towns was in their industry; while Edenford was a wool community, Crediton residents were farmers.

Following the service Drew met the minister who introduced him to Richard Tottel, a farmer and father of three daughters and a son. Tottel invited Drew home to share their Sunday meal.

The Tottels were a meaner sort of family, compared to the residents of Edenford; they were poor barley farmers. Richard was serious-minded and made of tough fiber, a man who was earnest in his walk, wise, sober, and grave. But then he had reason to be. Under the gray skies and cold drizzles of Crediton, he and his fathers had cleaned their ditches, repaired boundary walls, inserted new stones into their houses and barns, and plowed their fields with only moderate success. By denial and hard work over the generations, the family had added field to field and won a position among their neighbors.

Tottel's three daughters, the oldest two old enough to marry, hovered over Drew like flies over honey. They were comely enough with good black eyes, sharp-minded, and very neat. Every few minutes their father would shoo them away, but they would inevitably return.

Mrs. Tottel was Richard's third wife. He had seen the first two die in childbirth, along with child after child who yielded up their souls in convulsions or fever. However, it was evident to Drew these people did not pity themselves, did not bemoan their rank or position in life. They simply went on doing things as well as they knew how. Their daily life had given them a hardness that would not soon be broken.

While the Tottel girls stared at him, Drew had his first taste of a West Country tart, an apple pie with a custard on the top. And, since having company was a special occasion, the tart was topped with clotted cream—scalded cream and milk with a little sugar in it. The meal was delicious and Drew found himself entertaining thoughts of staying in Crediton for a few days. He couldn't see himself as a farmer, but maybe God had something in store for him here. At least that's what he was thinking during supper. After supper was a different story.

Following the meal the entire family gathered around the fire to talk and smoke. Drew came to learn it was a universal preoccupation in this part of the country. Tottel, his wife and daughters, even the younger children, lighted pipes of tobacco and puffed contentedly throughout the afternoon. The Tottels were offended that Drew did not join them. He left shortly after that and made his way down the road.

That night as he slept out in the open, he looked heavenward at the starry multitude, thinking and praying. Maybe he shouldn't have been so intolerant of the Tottels' use of tobacco. He was being unfair to them. He was hoping to find another Edenford, another Matthews family, another Jenny, another Nell. But Crediton wasn't Edenford and the Tottels weren't the Matthews.

He had been rereading Paul's journeys in the Acts of the Apostles and had come to the part where Paul and Barnabas were sent from Antioch on their first missionary journey. His blood was stirred afresh by the sailing references as they traveled first to Cyprus, then to Perga and Pamphylia. Before falling asleep, Drew decided to make his way to the coast.

Avoiding Plymouth and Exeter, he made his way eastward and reached the English Channel at Lyme Bay. He was in Charmouth for Easter Sunday. Finding no Puritan congregation, he attended a service at the Church of England, but left before it concluded. For some reason, everything the Bishop of Charmouth did reminded Drew that at that moment Bishop Laud was doing the same thing at St. Michael's in London.

The following day was March 29, when the first of John Winthrop's fleet would set sail for the New World. If all had gone well, David Cooper's family and the other Edenford refugees would be on board. Would Nell and Jenny be with them? Drew wished he knew. All the cobbler would tell him was that they were safe. But safe where? Would Cooper use that term to describe the hardships they would face on the rocky shore of a New World? Probably not. More likely, they were safe at the estate of a wealthy Puritan who took them in upon hearing of the heroic death of their father.

That afternoon Drew went to the seaside and scanned the waters. He didn't really expect to see them on their first day of sail, but he went anyway. Except for a bevy of small Flemish boats, there were no other ships to be seen.

On Tuesday and Wednesday he looked for them again and decided he had probably missed them in the night. The ships would sail with the wind, regardless of the time of day. Drew tried not to act disappointed as he continued his journey along the coast.

At Christchurch he took a small skiff to the Isle of Wight for no other reason than to get onto the water. Paul and Barnabas had their Cyprus; the Isle of Wight was Drew's English equivalent. He lodged at Yarmouth.

In his Bible reading he had concluded Paul and Barnabas' first missionary journey and was into their second one. His chest ached when he read of the disagreement between the two that caused them to go separate ways. They were friends, brothers in Christ. Why would they let a disagreement sever that relationship? The pain in Drew's chest grew heavier.

He fought back his rising emotions. *I'm just suffering from loneliness*, he reasoned. *This happens to people all the time.* To get his mind off the painful departing of friends, Drew read into chapter 16, about Paul at Troas. The apostle had a vision of a man standing on the other side of the sea calling to him to cross over and help.

On Monday Drew woke thinking about the excursion to the New World. They had set sail a week ago. By now they would be a little more than a fourth of the way to their new home. He dressed and walked to the wharf.

Frightened shouts split the air as the street he was walking emerged onto the wharf between two large buildings. Looking up at the wharf he could see an out-of-control carriage coming toward him, its driver slumped over to one side, and its solitary passenger—a man of great age—helplessly bouncing around in the carriage seat. A half dozen men trailed the carriage, all shouting at the horse to stop.

The horse was scared, its eyes wide with fright. Drew stepped into the horse's path, waving his arms wildly. The horse kept coming. Drew glanced quickly to both sides, in case he had to jump out of the way. Either way there was nothing to jump behind. If he didn't jump far enough, the carriage could run over him. Then a wild thought occurred to him. Change the direction of the horse's energies.

Drew removed his coat and charged the horse, yelling and waving. Then, as the horse drew near, he swooped his coat upward. The horse reared. He came down and reared a second time. Now Drew dropped his coat and with arms held high tried to soothe the frightened animal. The horse reared again. By now several of the pursuing men had caught up with the coach. They flanked the horse and one of them managed to catch the horse's bridle. The animal calmed down.

Shouting orders to the men, the elderly gentleman gave instructions regarding the care of the driver, but it was too late; the man was dead. He had suffered an attack and had just slumped over. It was still unclear exactly what had frightened the horse.

The elderly man approached Drew to thank him. He introduced himself as Captain Burleigh, captain of Yarmouth Castle. He was a grave but comely gentleman, and very old.

Drew responded by introducing himself.

"Morgan?" the old man said. "You wouldn't happen to be any relation to Admiral Amos Morgan, would you?"

"My grandfather." Drew smiled at the recollection. It had been too long since he'd thought of his grandfather.

"Of course, you are!" the captain seized Drew by the shoulders and looked him over. "Fine resemblance. And how is the old buzzard?" he asked.

"I'm sorry to say he died last year. We were very close."

"My condolences," the captain said. "Your grandfather and I had many adventures together."

Captain Burleigh invited Drew to stay with him at Yarmouth Castle. Drew drove the carriage as they retrieved his things from the inn where he was staying and went to the castle.

During a sumptuous meal of veal and beef, Captain Burleigh regaled Drew with stories of himself and Drew's grandfather; some Drew had heard before, others he hadn't. Drew learned that Burleigh had been taken prisoner at sea and was detained in Spain for three years. In 1610, he and his three sons accompanied Sir Thomas Roe on a voyage to Guiana.

Without going into detail, Drew explained that he had no desire to be a country gentleman like his father and was currently looking for some kind of direction in life. Either Captain Burleigh had not heard of Drew's recent reception with the king or chose not to bring it up. Either way, Drew was glad.

"If you're anything like your grandfather, you'll find your life on the sea," the captain said. "Why, if I were young again, that's what I'd do. Plenty of adventure on the sea, what with the Dunkirks. Blasted privateers! They raid our merchant ships and then scurry for their port in Flanders. If I had my way, we'd send a fleet of ships and steal the city away from the blasted Spanish. What with their continuous raids in the channel, we have every right. But then, who listens to an old sea dog like me? If fighting's not in your blood, there's always the merchant ships — trade in the Caribbean, slaving in Africa, transporting people to the new colonies in America . . . which reminds me! I've been invited to have breakfast with Captain Milbourne aboard his ship tomorrow. Peter Milbourne, a fine man under my command in Guiana. Come with me, boy! If you like it, I'll get you signed onto his crew! If not, what have you lost? At least you get breakfast."

Talking with Captain Burleigh brought to Drew's mind a thousand fond memories of his grandfather and adventurous tales of the sea. He agreed to join the captains for breakfast.

A low mist sat on the bay like a blanket, as the skiff bearing Captain Burleigh and Drew bobbed toward the ship. The air was dense and salty. Captain Burleigh sat erect, his back stiff as a board, as befitting a man of his position. There was no smile on his face, but Drew knew inside his blood was rushing at the opportunity to be on the sea again, even if the ship was in harbor.

Captain Peter Milbourne was a short man with a full brown beard. He was stern and unsmiling until his eyes met those of his former captain; then he brightened and his cheeks folded nicely in a grin. The two captains shook hands and Captain Burleigh introduced Drew as the grandson of Admiral Amos Morgan. Captain Milbourne was dutifully impressed and welcomed Drew aboard.

The captain of the ship escorted his two guests across the deck to the great cabin where they would dine. Drew turned to follow his host's lead and there, coming up the steps from below deck, was Nell Matthews.

Chapter 23

SEATED around Captain Milbourne's breakfast table were Drew, Captain Burleigh, Lady Arbella and her husband, Mr. Johnson, and John Winthrop. To Drew's surprise, he was aboard the *Arbella*, named after Lady Arbella, daughter of the Earl of Lincoln and one of the ship's most important passengers. The ship had sailed as scheduled on March 29, but unfavorable winds kept it from going any farther than Yarmouth.

Conversation was generally pleasant and varied, ranging from prospects of the wind shifting to the need for additional provisions since they were so long in port, to an occasional sea story featuring Captains Milbourne and Burleigh. Attention turned to Drew when Captain Burleigh told the breakfast group how the young man had rescued him on the wharf. It was then that Captain Burleigh offered Drew's services to Captain Milbourne.

"So you want to become a sailor?" the captain of the ship asked Drew.

"I've always had a fascination for the sea, but I think God wants me to go to the New World."

Captain Burleigh acted surprised. "Last night you didn't know which direction to turn. What persuaded you to become a colonist?"

The direction of the conversation peaked the interest of Winthrop. Drew was pretty sure Winthrop recognized him from the secret meeting in Edenford, but the appointed governor of the Massachusetts Bay Colony hadn't said anything. Now that they were talking about the colonies, he showed greater interest.

Drew wasn't about to tell them that his direction became clear the moment he saw Nell Matthews on deck. And in truth, that was only part of it—but a large part, to be sure. There was also the biblical account he had read of Paul at Troas. In the apostle's vision, Paul saw a man calling him from across the sea to teach the Gospel to the Macedonians. Drew was struck by the vision. It was as if God was using it to call him across the sea to America. His mission was to help build a city in the wilderness based on the Gospel of Christ. The presence of Nell Matthews on the *Arbella* merely confirmed the vision.

Drew told the breakfast gathering about the vision.

"We already have a full complement of seamen, fifty-two to be exact," said Captain Milbourne. "But since you're Amos Morgan's grandson, it's the least I can do to let you work for your passage. As for settling there, you'll have to talk to Winthrop here." The captain pointed at the governor with his knife. "Once you step on land, he's in charge."

"I'll gladly discuss it," Winthrop said in a polite tone that held absolutely no promise.

As the breakfast broke up, Drew stood with both captains as they said their good-byes. The other guests had left.

"I almost forgot!" the elderly captain tapped his forehead with two fingers. "I'm to relay a message to you from the navy. Bad news, actually. Word has it the Dunkirkers have ten sails in the Channel preying on English ships. They took the *Warwick* fourteen days ago. She came alone out of the Downs and has not been heard of since. She was a pretty ship too—eighty ton, only ten pieces of ordnance. Mason was her captain." The elderly captain moved for the door. "Watch the horizon and stick together," he advised.

Drew returned with Captain Burleigh to Yarmouth Castle to get his things. As they left the ship, Captain Milbourne gave the old seaman four shot out of the forecastle for a farewell. When Drew returned to the ship a few hours later, he was taken directly to the captain's cabin. An unsmiling Captain Milbourne greeted him.

In Drew's absence, Winthrop had spoken to the captain and filled him in on Drew's past activities leading to Christopher Matthews' execution. Winthrop also told the captain a young woman had approached him and strenuously voiced her objection to Drew being on board.

"Morgan, I make it a point not to ask sailors about their past," the captain said. "Most of them have a past they'd rather forget. And I don't care about politics and religion and Puritans and cavaliers. All I care about is this ship."

He stared hard at Drew, studying him like he would a sea chart. He wasn't sure it would be worth his effort to sail into these troubled waters.

Finally, he said, "Out of respect for your grandfather, if Winthrop will let you stay in Massachusetts, I'll sign you on for the crossing. Go talk to him in his cabin; then come tell me what he says."

John Winthrop was writing in his journal when Drew knocked. He listened intently as Drew described the events in Edenford that led to Christopher Matthews' death and his own conversion.

"David Cooper told me how you helped them escape," Winthrop added.

"Is his family on board the *Arbella* too?"

Winthrop shook his head. "They're on the *Talbot*," he said. "When the decision was made to flee Edenford, Cooper was concerned for the safety of Matthews' daughters and rightly so. He sent them to me. They've been with me ever since.

And they're the only ones from Edenford on board this ship."

Drew's heart was racing at the thought of being so close to Nell and Jenny again. "What can I do to convince you that I'm sincere in my desire to join you in your expedition?" Drew asked.

Winthrop ran a thin finger down his long straight nose as he thought. "You referred to Paul's Macedonian vision at breakfast and said you thought God was speaking to you through it. Do your truly believe that?"

Drew nodded. "The more I think of it, the clearer it becomes to me," he said. "One of the last sermons Christopher Matthews preached in Edenford was about Moses leading the people to the edge of the Promised Land. Then he invited you to speak to the secret meeting of leaders. I believe that had he lived, he was about to lead his town to the New World. He is unable to fulfill his vision for his people. The way I see it, it's my responsibility to fulfill his mission. It's the least I can do for the man who did so much for me."

"When I was a boy," Winthrop said, leaning back in his chair, a faraway look in his eyes, "I had little interest in religion. I was full of wickedness. At about age twelve I read some religious books and grew concerned about my wickedness. Afterward I wasn't as bad as before, but I was still wicked. In my middle teens when I was at Cambridge University, I became quite ill. I was far from home, isolated from everyone, and I turned to God. But that lasted only until I got better. Then, at age eighteen, not long after I got married, I came under the influence of Rev. Ezekiel Culverwell. Now there was a man of God, a great Puritan preacher. He was suspended for a time for not wearing a surplice. Then I read the writing of William Perkins who unsettled me. He convinced me that reprobates could do as much as I had done for God. His writings taught me that I had no occasion at all to consider myself saved. For a long time I remained very devout, but still very uncomfortable about my faith."

Winthrop closed his eyes as scenes from the past played in his head. He seemed to be choosing which one to describe to Drew next.

"Finally," he said, "at age thirty, I began to have a greater understanding of my complete unworthiness. My education, my family wealth, my relationships, were nothing. I was plunged to the depth of despair. And from this depth I was lifted up. And every promise I thought upon held forth Christ unto me, saying, 'I am thy salvation.' At that moment, a new man quickened in me."

Drew waited on Winthrop. It was a special remembrance and he didn't want to interrupt it.

"I had Ezekiel Culverwell. You had Christopher Matthews. It is by God's grace that the ministry of these two men brings us together. Who am I to stand in the way of a man who is seeking to find God's will for his life?"

Drew returned to the captain's quarters to report the governor's decision. The captain received the news without expression. "It will be a long voyage," he said. "If we get along well together, it will be a pleasant voyage; if we don't, this ship can be hell afloat. Your responsibilities are simple: Obey your orders and do your duty. That's all I've got to say. Go below to the seaman's quarters and report to Mr. Prudden."

The following day the Reverend John Cotton, a friend of Winthrop, came aboard the *Arbella* to preach a sermon to the colonists. The sermon, "God's Promise to His Plantation," was based on 2 Samuel 7:10: "Also I will appoint a place for My people Israel, and I will plant it, that they may dwell in a place of their own, and move no more."

Cotton emphasized the parallel between the Puritans and God's chosen people, claiming that it was God's will that they should inhabit the New World. He asked the question, "But how shall I know whether God has appointed me such a place?" Answering his own question, he said, "When there be evils to be avoided that may warrant removal: First, when some grievous sins overspread a country that threaten desolation. Second, if men be overburdened with debts and miseries. Third, in case of persecution.

"This may teach us all where we do now dwell, or where after we may dwell. Be sure you look at every place appointed to you, from the hand of God . . . but we must discern how God appoints us this place. There is poor comfort in sitting down in any place that you cannot say, 'This place is appointed me of God.' Can you say that God spied out this place for you, and there has settled you above all hindrances? Did you find that God made room for you either by lawful descent, or purchase, or gift, or other warrantable right? Why, then, this is the place God has appointed for you. Here He has made room for you."

Drew was attracted to the message and the polished eloquence of the speaker. But what he enjoyed most about the sermon was his view of Nell and Jenny Matthews on the far side of the deck. Jenny would look at him occasionally, but Nell never did. In fact, throughout the entire sermon Nell seldom looked up, as if she wasn't feeling well.

Following the sermon Drew made his way through the worshipers to where Nell and Jenny had been sitting. To his dismay, he watched as two women assisted Nell below deck. When she saw Drew coming, Jenny stayed on deck. She threw her arms around him.

"O Drew, thank God you're safe!" she cried. "I would have told you we were leaving Edenford if given the chance. But Nell and Mr. Cooper kept it from me until the moment we were leaving. Given the choice, I never would have left Edenford without saying good-bye."

Drew hugged her again. It felt good to be close to her again. "I know," he said. "You were the only one who believed in me. I'll never forget that."

"I still believe in you," she said, lowering her eyes.

They both became aware that they were attracting the stares of too many people. Reluctantly, they released each other and stood a respectable distance apart.

"Is Nell ill?" Drew asked.

"Ever since we left Edenford," Jenny replied. "At first we thought it was from all the anxiety and lack of sleep, but now we don't know. She hardly has any strength and spends most days in bed."

"I'll pray for her," Drew said.

Jenny stood opposite him and beamed.

"What?"

"It's just so good to hear you say things like that," she said. "You've changed since I first met you. You seem more confident, more mature. It's attractive."

At 6 o'clock in the morning on April 8, the wind rose from the east and north. A hoarse boatswain called, "Aaaaalllll haaaannnds! Up anchor, ahoy!" The entire crew was set into motion. Sails were loosed, the yards braced, and the anchor was heaved up from the depths of the harbor. The captain walked the deck barking orders, many of them unintelligible to Drew; others he heard clearly but had no idea how to respond. Not so with the other sailors. For them, the captain's orders were immediately executed with a furious hurrying about, a strange mixture of cries, and even stranger actions. In a few minutes the *Arbella* was under way. Drew could hear the noise of the water as the vessel leaned in response to the early morning breeze and headed for the narrow part of the Channel called The Needles.

Because the wind was so light, not all of the ships were able

to get out until the ebb. The *Arbella* passed through shortly
before 10 o'clock. The wind quickly died and the ship was
becalmed three or four leagues from The Needles. By 10
o'clock at night the wind came from the north, a good gale.
The ship weighed anchor again and sailed through the night.
By daylight they were opposite Portland.

"Aaaaalllll haaaandddss! Prepare for battle!"

Eight sails could be seen off the stern of the ship. Suppos-
ing they were Dunkirkers, the captain ordered the gun room
and gun decks to be cleared. All the hammocks were taken
down, the ordnance loaded, and the powder chests made
ready. Since this was where the landsmen were quartered,
they moved in with the seamen temporarily. Twenty-five
men, including Drew, were appointed for muskets.

The wind continued from the north. The eight ships proceeded toward the *Arbella*. They had more wind and were
closing the gap between the ships. By now the captain was
convinced they were Dunkirkers.

For an experiment the captain shot a ball of wildfire fastened to an arrow out of a crossbow. It burned in the water a
good time. Should it become necessary, the wildfire would
make a good weapon.

The women and children were removed to the lower deck
so that they might be out of danger. Once everything was in
place, all the men on the upper deck went to prayer. It was
encouraging to see how cheerful this made the company; not
a woman or child showed fear, though they were fully aware
of the danger. For there were eight ships closing against only
four ships in Winthrop's party; and the least of the
Dunkirkers' ships were reported to carry thirty brass pieces.
But the men of the *Arbella* put their trust in the Lord of
Hosts. That, and the courage of the captain, gave the colonists a peace and calm.

At about 1 o'clock, the eight ships had closed to within a

league of the *Arbella*. To show he was not afraid of them, Captain Milbourne tacked the ship about to face them. Should they choose to attack, he thought it best to settle the issue before night overtook them.

Drew and the other men with muskets lined the sides of the ship and prepared to open fire.

As the eight ships drew closer, they were identified as friends, not Dunkirkers. One ship was Dutch, another French, and three of them were English. All were bound for Canada and Newfoundland. When they drew near, the ships saluted one another, and fear and danger were turned into mirth and friendly entertainment.

Once the danger was over, the ships spotted two boats fishing in the Channel and bought a great store of excellent fish.

The next day they came over against Plymouth. The day after they passed the Isles of Scilly and were out in the open sea.

Drew went below to the seaman's quarters. Now that they were out of the Channel, sailing took on a whole new feel and he began to experience the discomforts of a seaman's life. He was exhausted. The day began early with a stiff gale north by west. The heavy sea beat against the bow of the ship with the sound and force of a blacksmith's hammer. Waves flew over the deck, drenching Drew and the other sailors. The topsail halyards had been let go and the great sails filled out; the wind whistled through the rigging; loose ropes flew about; men shouted orders and screamed replies as the *Arbella* plowed its way through the sea to the New World. Behind them followed the *Talbot*, the *Ambrose*, and the *Jewel*. Drew was beginning to realize that a sailor's life was not nearly as romantic as his grandfather had made it seem.

His legs were still unsteady and one sailor told him it

would take at least three days before he got his sea legs. Drew entered the steerage where he would bunk and found it filled with coils of rigging, spare sails, old junk, and ship stores that had not been put away. Everything had fallen together from the rolling of the ship. Drew's clothes, Bible, and minimal personal belongings were in there somewhere, probably at the bottom. Drew thought of the old sailor's adage, "Everything on top, nothing at hand."

There were no berths and there was no light, except that which managed to filter through the hatch. He would be allowed four hours sleep and then would be called for his first watch. Drew fell onto a sail and closed his eyes. From sheer exhaustion, he expected to be asleep instantly, but he wasn't. Just as he began to drift off, the initial symptoms of seasickness woke him rudely. For four hours he fought the alternating waves of slumber and nausea, as the ship rolled from side to side and the smells of the unsettled bilge water filled the steerage. Twice he ran to the deck and leaned over the leeward side to empty himself.

It was a wet, cold, exhausted sailor who gladly took his first watch on deck. At least the air was fresh, but the sloshing of his stomach made the waves seem calm in comparison.

And he wasn't suffering alone. Seasickness put the entire party out of sorts, so much so that there were no sermons on this Sunday.

The next day was fair weather and those who were sick and groaning in their cabins were brought on deck. A rope was stretched from the steerage to the mainmast and they were made to stand holding on to the rope. The warmth of the sun and the fresh air revived them so that most were soon feeling well and merry.

Drew had been ordered to slush the mainmast. He climbed the mast and applied the bucket of grease while rocking back and forth in extreme arcs to the movement of the ship. From his vantage point he watched as Jenny brought Nell on deck and led her to the rope. She shuffled slowly, her right arm bent across her waist, leaning heavily on Jenny. Her hand was unable to keep a grip on the rope; it would rest on top of it, then fall off. Jenny would place the hand on the rope again and a moment later it would fall off. While the others smiled and told each other how much better they were feeling, Jenny led an unrevived Nell back to the women's cabin.

As Drew finished slushing the mast, he prayed for Nell's health.

"No!" Captain Milbourne shouted in response to Drew's third request to see Nell. "It would invite trouble and I'll not have it on my ship! Good heavens, man, she's the one who didn't want you on this ship in the first place!"

"I know that," Drew said. "Still, it's important that I see her. I only want to pray with her."

"God can hear your prayers from the steerage," said the captain. Seeing the disappointment in Drew's face, he said, "Look, lad, there are plenty of women on board. There are more in the colonies. Why make yourself miserable over the one woman who doesn't want you? Let her go. Someone else will come along."

The call for the change in watch could be heard on deck.

"That's my watch," Drew said. "Thank you, sir, for your advice."

Drew walked on deck. The sea was calm and there was a light breeze, barely enough to drive the ship. They had made little headway that day. It was 11 o'clock at night and three other sailors were sharing his watch topside. One stood alone near the bow of the ship; the other two were at the stern. Drew walked to the starboard side and looked north. The sky was dark and clear, the stars shone brightly, as did the moon, which was much smaller than he had ever seen it in England.

The wind was brisk, as it had been the entire journey; everyone wore winter clothing.

"Good evening, sir."

The voice startled Drew. He swung in the direction of the soft voice. It was Jenny.

She giggled, pleased that she had startled him.

"Jenny! What are you doing up here?"

She pulled the shawl she was wearing tighter around her shoulders. "I was going to tell you I couldn't sleep, but that's not the truth."

Drew's response was a puzzled look.

"In truth, I asked one of the sailors when you stood watch. It was the only way we could be alone."

He looked at her soft features, highlighted by the gentle glow of the moon. The lesser lights of the sky reflected in her blue eyes. The corners of her mouth turned upward slightly, creating shallow dimples. Maybe it was the loneliness he'd been feeling. Maybe it was the fact that she accepted him while others still doubted. Standing before him was a woman who didn't reject him, who plotted to be alone with him. Whatever the reason, Drew had an urge to take her in his arms and smother her with the love he had been holding in for months, holding for someone who wanted nothing to do with him. It was with great effort that he restrained himself.

He looked down at his feet. He had to. If he looked at her any longer, he wouldn't be able to control himself. "I'm glad you came," he said. "How's your sister?"

His question disappointed her. Her lower lip protruded in a pout. She turned toward the sea and leaned against the railing. It seemed like whenever the two of them talked, it was about Nell or the people of the village or her father. They always talked about someone or something else, never about themselves. Yet, she shared his concern.

"Every day she's worse," Jenny said. "I'm really worried

about her." She blinked back tears as she looked out over the moonlit swells. "I was thirteen when Momma died. Poppa called it consumption. Nell is acting just like Momma did before she died. She's just wasting away, she has no energy, she barely breathes, and sometimes doesn't recognize me. Drew, I'm scared."

He put his arm around her. She turned toward him and they embraced. Jenny wept softly with her head buried against Drew's chest. He looked up in the direction of the watchmen on the stern. They were in animated discussion, oblivious to the fact that Drew was embracing a woman on watch. Nevertheless, Drew guided Jenny to a place out of their line of sight.

She lifted her head to him. With his thumbs, he wiped the tears from her cheeks. She placed her hands on his forearms and raised herself slowly toward him. Tilting her head slightly, she gently brushed her lips against his, pulled away, then brushed against him again. Drew's fingers followed the curve of her head, caressing her long brown hair as he pulled her to him. Her lips were soft and hot with tears. Jenny's arms encircled him as she stood on her toes and eagerly leaned into him.

"I love you," she whispered between kisses. "From the moment I saw you, I knew I would always love you."

A voice in his head told him to stop right now, before it went any further. But the voice was speaking reason, and reason had little authority over the emotions he felt at this moment. He desired Jenny. She was warm, full of life, and she loved him. She loved him!

I could bring myself to love her, couldn't I? If I could, it would make things so much easier. Why do I have to be in love with a woman who doesn't love me? Why can't I just accept the truth? Nell will never love me; Jenny does.

But he didn't love her. Not like this.

Drew gently pulled away. Jenny's eyes remained closed and her head tilted upward, eager for more.

"I'm on watch," he said. "There are other men around. If they see me, I could get in trouble."

She opened her eyes. The mention of reality had broken the romantic spell.

Drew held her hands in his. She was so beautiful. He was a fool.

"I asked the captain if I could go below and see Nell. He refused. I don't know what good it would do, anyway. Unless seeing me would make her so mad her blood would boil and kill the disease."

Jenny laughed.

"I could sneak you down right now. Everyone's asleep."

Drew shook his head. "It's too risky. If I was caught away from my post, I could be sentenced to death."

"When do you get off duty?"

"Four in the morning."

"Come to the women's cabin. I'll be waiting for you."

"No. You need your sleep."

Jenny smiled her pixie smile. "Believe me, I won't be doing any sleeping tonight anyway."

"I'll come as soon after 4 as I can."

Drew was relieved of his watch promptly at 4. He stretched and walked sleepily toward the hatch, but instead of going down to the steerage, he crept toward the women's cabin. He winced as he tapped lightly on the door. Immediately it swung open. Jenny was waiting for him. She took him by the hand, pulled him inside, and closed the door behind him. As he leaned forward, trying to adjust his eyes, she rose up on her toes and kissed him.

With a playful shrug and silent giggle, she pulled him by the hand across the room to the corner bunk where Nell was.

They had to choose their footing carefully—the cabin was crowded with sleeping women and children, many of them on the floor.

Jenny and Drew knelt beside Nell's bed. Her cheeks were hollow and a sheen of perspiration covered her face. She was motionless and Drew could barely detect her breathing. It hurt him to see her like this. She was so still and vulnerable, and he couldn't help but feel a measure of responsibility for her condition. If it weren't for him, she would be sitting in front of the window on High Street, crafting lace for the insatiable Lord Chesterfield; or applying her sharp wit and wisdom to paper, hoping to change her world. Instead, she lay before him dying.

"What are you doing in here?" the woman in the bunk who shared Nell's corner was up on one elbow. Her free hand pulled a blanket to her chin. Drew recognized her as the woman at the breakfast table, his first day aboard ship. "I'm calling the captain!" she said.

"Please don't, Lady Arbella!" Jenny pleaded. "He doesn't mean any harm. He's a friend. I brought him down here to pray for my sister."

Lady Arbella studied Drew. She seemed to note that he was on his knees.

"You may call the captain if you would like," Drew said, "but Jenny is telling the truth. I've come to pray for Nell."

Lady Arbella didn't soften. "All right, then. Pray."

Drew folded his hands, resting his arms against the side of the bed. "Dear God," he said, "I've not very experienced at praying to You, but please don't hold my inexperience against me, for I need Your help. I know I have no right to ask You for favors, especially when it comes to Nell. But I'm going to ask anyway, because there's nothing else I can do. Dear Lord, please heal her. She lies here because of my sin, not hers. All her life she has served You. She has taught children about

You. She has read the Bible and prayed and lived a holy life. She has risked her life trying to help her country see that it's wandered away from Your ways. She doesn't deserve to die. I do. If someone must have it, give me her disease. I'd gladly die so that she might live. Please let her live. Please. Amen."

Drew lingered a few moments before raising his head.

"Dear God in heaven," Lady Arbella prayed, "please answer this young man's prayer and heal Nell Matthews."

Drew looked at her. "Thank you," he said.

He took one more look at Nell before rising to his feet. Carefully he picked his footsteps leading toward the door. What he didn't see was a small hand partially covered by a blanket. When he stepped down, a child's scream split the silence. Drew froze as every woman in the cabin instantly sat up and glared at him.

Drew was sentenced to twenty lashes. He was openly whipped, put in bolts for a night, and given nothing but bread and water. Lady Arbella had argued in his defense to the captain, but to no avail. It didn't matter why he was in the women's cabin. Drew Morgan had directly disobeyed the captain, and for that he had to be punished.

Drew had never known such physical pain before; his back was a mess of red-ribboned flesh. But the thing that hurt him even more was the realization that Nell's condition wasn't improving. The amount of time she was awake and responsive grew less every day. It seemed as if God had turned a deaf ear to Drew's prayer.

On Tuesday, May 24, the captain steered the ship away from the wind allowing the sails to luff so that the mizzen shrouds could be straightened. The *Jewel* and the *Ambrose* approached to inquire if anything was amiss. They were relieved to hear nothing was wrong. Their presence gave the ships an opportunity to pass news back and forth. The company aboard the *Jewel* was in good health; but aboard the *Ambrose*, two passengers had died. They had the same symptoms as Nell Matthews.

When the first sounding was made on May 31, there were two men in foul moods aboard the *Arbella*—Captain Peter Milbourne and Drew Morgan. The captain was irritated that the sounding had no ground. But that was just a prick that aggravated a deeper wound. They had lost sight of the *Talbot* during the storm of April 21 and, despite several attempts, had not seen her since. The three remaining ships held course, but Captain Milbourne had left England with four ships and wanted to arrive with four. Drew shared his concern but for different reasons. The *Talbot* carried the Cooper family and most of the Edenford residents. Why would God help them escape from Edenford only to lead them to a watery grave? Is that the way God rewarded those who were faithful to Him?

And what about Nell? Her illness continued to exact its toll from her. According to reports from Jenny, she was nothing more than skin wrapped around bones. Drew didn't cease to pray for her, but his prayers were angry and filled with threats, should anything happen to Nell or the Coopers.

On Wednesday, June 2, the captain changed sails. He was sure they were near the northern coast, and knowing that the southern coast had dangerous shoals, he refitted the main mast with a strong, double mainsail. He didn't want to risk having old sails rip as he approached the rocky coast.

On Thursday morning, June 3, the captain ordered another sounding. No ground. A heavy fog and thick rain enveloped the ships. About 2 in the afternoon he ordered another sounding. Ground was struck at eighty fathoms. It was a fine, gray sand. The captain changed tack and fired a piece of ordnance to give notice to the other two ships.

Friday, June 4. About 4 in the morning the *Arbella* tacked

again. The fog was so thick they couldn't see more than a stone's throw. The captain ordered a sounding every two hours, but they had no ground.

Saturday, June 5. The fog dispersed and a handsome gale came from northeast, bringing rain with it. That night the captain ordered a sounding every half watch, but had no ground.

Sunday, June 6. God answered the colonists' prayers. Although it was still foggy and cold, a sounding was made at 2 o'clock in the afternoon. It had ground at eight fathoms. The mist began to break up and they saw shore to the north, about five or six leagues off. The captain supposed it to be Cape Sable.

Monday, June 7. A sounding at 4 o'clock revealed ground at thirty fathoms. Being a calm day, the captain suggested they do some fishing. In less than two hours, they took aboard sixty-seven codfish, most of them over a yard and a half long, and a yard in circumference. It was a timely catch; the store of salt fish on board was spent. The hungry colonists feasted on fish.

Tuesday, June 8. The weather was still cold. By 3 in the afternoon, land was sighted again. It proved to be Mount Mansell. A pleasant sweet air met them from the shore, a refreshing wind that some likened to the smell of a garden. Like Noah's ark, God sent the colonists a sign of his favor in the form of a wild pigeon that lighted on the ship.

Wednesday, June 9. The mainland lay off the starboard side all day. It was a land of many hills.

Thursday, June 10. The ship lost sight of land, regained it, then lost it again. About 4 in the afternoon, land was sighted again off the starboard bow. It was a ridge of three hills called Three Turks' Heads. Toward night, trees could be seen plainly.

Friday, June 11. Cape Ann was sighted. A ship was anchored near the Isles of Shoals. Five or six fishing shallops sailed along the coast.

Saturday, June 12. The *Arbella* was near port by 4 in the morning. The captain shot off two pieces of ordnance to signal their arrival. They passed through the narrow strait between Baker's Isle and Little Isle and came to anchor. About 2 o'clock in the afternoon, John Endecott, the governor of Salem, along with Mr. Skelton, the pastor, and Captain Levett came aboard to welcome the colonists to Massachusetts Bay.

Chapter 24

TO say the newly arrived colonists were disappointed when they saw the Salem settlement would be an understatement—like saying Bishop Laud didn't care for Puritans.

Drew's initial thought was that the pitiful collection of huts and shelters beside the bay had to be the remnant of an earlier encampment. The real colony must be hidden among the trees. But as he disembarked, the truth became evident. This was Salem. He tried to remember exactly what he had heard about the New World. Maybe he was expecting too much. But the looks on the faces of his fellow shipmates convinced him that they were just as shocked as he.

Governor Endecott and his replacement, John Winthrop, walked past Drew in animated discussion. Endecott had a round face and round eyes with heavy eyelids. He sported a long white mustache that flared at the ends and a long slim beard about two fingers wide that looked pasted to his chin. There was a stern set to his face and he spoke in a brash tone that displayed his quick temper.

Drew heard only part of Endecott's explanation to Winthrop, but it was enough to get a picture of a struggling settlement on the verge of failure. Of the two hundred settlers who had arrived the previous year, only eighty-five remained. More than eighty of them had died; the rest had returned to England. A general sickness had struck the colony in the winter, just as it had at Jamestown and Plymouth. The sickness ravaged the settlement. It was so severe that Endecott set aside his doctrinal differences with the Separatists and sent for Samuel Fuller at Plymouth. Doctor Fuller had an abundance of experience in cases of scurvy, fevers, and various illnesses that usually followed long sea voyages. If it hadn't been for the doctor's skills, the entire settlement might have been wiped out.

As the leaders moved out of range, Drew saw Jenny's shallop approach shore. He went to greet her and steer her clear of the two; he didn't want her to overhear what they were saying.

Jenny and Drew, along with most of the other new settlers, toured the settlement. Thatched huts of various sizes were scattered along the shore, separated only by mud and mire. The few children Drew and Jenny saw were dirty and wore ragged clothing. They were somber and quiet, with none of the excitement one would expect on the arrival of three new ships. The residents of Salem greeted the newcomers with genuine warmth; there was joy on their lips, but not in their eyes. The sunken and dark eyes of Salem revealed injured souls—they were tired of the hardships, tired from the lack of food, tired of attending the funerals of their friends. The people of Salem were beaten down and discouraged, and a shipload of fresh faces wasn't about to change that. Last year a similar shipload had arrived; most of them were now buried in the woods.

Jenny's face, normally innocent and cheerful, was white with shock. She looked as though she were walking through a graveyard and finding a headstone with her name on it. Drew tried to cheer her up, but with little success.

The only positive diversion of the day was the discovery of strawberry plants in full bloom. The fruit was large, red, and juicy. After so many days of salted meat, picking and eating the berries provided some festivity in an otherwise disappointing day. To get her mind off the condition of the settlement, Drew suggested that he and Jenny pick some berries for Nell and take them to her aboard ship to cheer her up.

That first night all the new arrivals slept on board ship, including Governor Winthrop and a native guest. The Indian chief, a friend of Endecott, was fascinated with the large sailing ship and asked if he could sleep aboard the *Arbella*. Permission was given and the Indian slept alone on the deck. On his last night of watch as a crewman, Drew studied the native while he slept. It was more than just curiosity, since Captain Milbourne had given specific instructions to the night watch to guard the Indian. He wanted no surprise guests joining the chief in the middle of the night. The Indian was dark and muscular, and his clothing of skins and shells reflected his habitat. When he first came on board, he was wide-eyed and all smiles. After a tour of the ship, he lay down on the deck and slept contentedly. And why shouldn't he? He wasn't the one who had just walked away from civilization to live in the wild.

Already, Drew had heard some of the colonists say they were returning to England with the ship. This was no New Jerusalem, it was Hades—the realm of the dead. Drew was quick to agree with them. Had he come alone, it would be one thing. But he wasn't alone—he was responsible for two women. He'd given his pledge to ensure the safety of Jenny and Nell. He knew Christopher Matthews had never intended for his daughters to live in this . . . this. . . The word came to mind and Drew didn't want to say it . . wilderness. This was a wilderness. He didn't want to use the word because it argued against him. Wasn't it the exact word the curate used? "It's time for God's people to fly to the *wilderness.*"

His instincts told him to take Jenny and Nell back to England for their own safety Yet he couldn't get the curate's words out of his mind. Did Christopher Matthews really think God's people belonged here?

As the new governor of Massachusetts Bay, John Winthrop called a meeting for one hour before noon the following day. Every ablebodied man and woman was ordered to attend. Only those who were needed to care for the sick were excused. Drew used this exclusion to insist that Jenny stay on board ship. It was better that she not hear some of the things that would be said.

Winthrop arrived wearing worn boots, breeches, and a soiled and frayed shirt. He looked more like a servant than a gentleman of breeding and wealth. He strode to the center of town, one of the muddier spots among the loosely situated huts, and addressed the people.

"I don't have to tell you that this is not exactly how we pictured life in the New World."

There were a few nervous chuckles. No one spoke up to dispute the statement.

"But by fall, each of you will have a proper dwelling and come summer of next year, we will turn this wilderness into a community. I'll not mislead you. Supplies are low, far below our expectations. We'll need to plant corn immediately and pray for a sufficient fall harvest. At the earliest possible date, we'll send a ship back to England for more supplies."

"And I'll be on it!" The man who spoke up wore a white shirt with a ruff and sported a sharply trimmed, fashionable beard. Drew didn't know much about him, only that he brought his wife and three sons with him and his name was Worthington.

"I pray you'll reconsider, Peter," Winthrop said.

"I didn't sign on to live in the mud like a pig," Worthington replied. "Nor did I bring my family all this way to bury them in the forest!"

Several other men voiced similar sentiments.

Winthrop raised both hands over his head to regain their attention. He didn't continue until everyone was quiet. Endecott was standing next to him. The new governor held out his hand and Endecott handed him several sheets of paper.

"While sailing here, I asked myself some questions about who we are and what we are attempting to do in this New World. I recorded my thoughts on these papers. Last night, just like you, I wondered whether we had made a mistake in leaving England. Then I reread my writing. Now more than ever, I believe God has a plan for us. And God's plan is for us to remain here, not to return to England. I read these thoughts to you hoping they will have the same effect on you that they had on me."

Winthrop lifted the papers and began reading. Drew looked around him at his fellow colonists. The folded arms, the set jaws, the tight lips all told him the governor was fighting a losing battle. Yet he continued. "I have titled my thoughts, 'A Model of Christian Charity.'"

Following a lengthy discussion of the scriptural basis of Christian love as it would apply to the new community, Winthrop proceeded to the application of the principles.

"Now to make some application of this discourse by the design, which gave the occasion of writing of it. Herein are four things to be propounded: first, the persons; secondly, the work; thirdly, the end; fourthly, the means.

"First, for the persons. We are a company professing ourselves fellow members of Christ . . . We ought to account ourselves knit together by this bond of love, and live in the exercise of it, if we would have comfort of our being in Christ. . . .

"Secondly, for the work we have in hand. It is by a

mutual consent through a special overvaluing providence and a more than ordinary appropriation of the
churches of Christ, to seek out a place of cohabitation
and consortship under a due form of government both
civil and ecclesiastical. . . .

"Thirdly, the end is to improve our lives to do more
service to the Lord; the comfort and encrease of the
body of Christ whereof we are members; that ourselves
and our posterity may be the better preserved from the
common corruptions of this evil world. . . .

"Fourthly . . . the work and end we aim at. These we
see are extraordinary; therefore we must not content
ourselves with usual ordinary means. Whatsoever we did
or ought to have done when we lived in England, the
same must we do, and more also, where we go. . . .

"But if we shall neglect the observation of these arti-
cles which are the ends we have propounded and, dis-
sembling with our God, shall fall to embrace this
present world and prosecute our carnal intentions, seeking great things for ourselves and our posterity, the
Lord will surely break out in wrath against us, be re-
venged of such a perjured people, and make us know the
price of the breach of such a covenant.

"Now the only way to avoid this shipwrack, and to
provide for our posterity, is to follow the counsel of
Micah, to do justly, to love mercy, to walk humbly with
our God. For this end, we must be knit together in this
work as one man. We must entertain each other in
brotherly affection; we must be willing to abridge ourselves of our superfluities, for the supply of others' ne-
cessities. We must uphold a familiar commerce together
in all meekness, gentleness, patience, and liberality. We
must delight in each other, make others' conditions our
own, rejoice together, mourn together, labor and suffer

together, always having before our eyes our commission and community in the work, our community as members of the same body.

"So shall we keep the unity of the Spirit in the bond of peace. The Lord will be our God, and delight to dwell among us as His own people, and will command a blessing upon us in all our ways, so that we shall see much more of His wisdom, power, goodness, and truth, than formerly we have been acquainted with. We shall find that the God of Israel is among us when ten of us shall be able to resist a thousand of our enemies; when He shall make us a praise and glory that men shall say of succeeding plantations, 'The Lord make it like that of New England.' For we must consider that we shall be as a city upon a hill. The eyes of all people are upon us."

Winthrop lowered the papers and continued.

"Our task is not an easy one," he said. "Winter is near at hand. And if Plymouth Plantation and last winter in Salem are any indication, some of us will not survive. But dying for a dream is not a vain thing. The sacrifice we make—whether that sacrifice comes through living or dying—will be the foundation of a new community. A community that will be a blessing to our children and our children's children for ages to come. Each family must decide for themselves. But as for me, I choose to live here and to send for my wife and family to join me at the earliest possible date. England holds nothing for me but persecution and the sword. I would rather battle the elements of the wilderness than to battle the bishops of England. For the glory has departed from old England; it is just beginning in New England."

Some were unmoved; they chose to return to England. However, John Winthrop won many converts that day. One of them was Drew Morgan.

The first order of business was to find a new site for the settlement. Salem lacked the resources to accommodate the numbers of people that were coming in the second wave of settlers. Scouting parties were sent up the Charles and Mystic Rivers in search of alternative locations. The reports that were brought back divided the party. They couldn't decide on a single location, but there wasn't time to debate. Crops had to be planted and houses had to be built. So, against John Winthrop's pleas, the colonists founded several community sites.

Sir Richard Saltonstall founded Watertown, four miles upstream on the Charles River; William Pynchon founded Roxbury; Mattapan was settled and renamed Dorchester by Roger Ludlow; Deputy Governor Dudley established Newtown; Increase Nowell presided over the base camp at Charleston; and John Winthrop established Boston.

Since survival was the order of the day, every person had a job. Some were appointed to provide fish for the community. These fishermen divided into teams and two shallops were kept on the waters at all times. Competition was encouraged between the fishing teams. The community would need to put up mounds of salted fish if they were going to survive the winter.

Other teams were formed to build shelters. Nothing fancy for the first year, just enough to get through the winter. The shelters to be built were called English wigwams, fashioned after the houses of the Pequot Indians. Tree limbs were stuck in the ground around a rectangular base. The tops of the limbs were then bent toward the center top of the structure and tied together. Horizontal limbs tied to the vertical studs provided stability. Each house had a door at one end and a fireplace at the other. The structure was covered with bark or thatches. Furniture consisted of a four-legged table and a bench made from the trunks of trees.

The women who were able did fieldwork in the mornings

and went to dig at the clambanks at low tide. The rest were appointed to nursing details under the direction of Mr. Skelton, the minister, who was also in charge of the food stores. It would be his responsibility to provide daily rations fairly.

Mr. Higginson, the other minister of the colony, was given the specific task of praying and preparing a strong word for Sundays, teaching the colonists what it meant to serve God and one another.

The colonists would meet every morning for daily work assignments, break at noon to eat, and work to four hours past noon. The rest of the day they were free to take care of the needs of their families.

Work was well underway when the *Talbot* finally reached port on July 2, twenty days after the *Arbella*. The first of the second wave of ships, the *Mayflower* and the *Whale*, had reached port July 1, and by July 6 all of the ships had safely arrived.

It didn't take long before Winthrop's prophecy of death for some colonists was fulfilled. On the day the *Talbot* arrived, Winthrop's second eldest son, Henry, was drowned in a fishing accident. And in August Lady Arbella fell ill and died; her husband, Isaac Johnson, died a month later. Their deaths had a profound effect on the colony.

Nell, on the other hand, began to show some improvement. She had been moved off the ship into one of several English wigwams built in Boston to house the sick. Her waking hours grew longer and the grayish cast to her skin gave way to a rosier tone. Jenny and Drew were at her side on the day the *Talbot* reached harbor. The doorway flew open and David and James Cooper crowded into the wigwam. They had heard Nell was close to death. They hadn't heard that Drew Morgan was in New England. The cobbler was dumbfounded; James was furious.

Drew stepped outside with the two Cooper men and related the events that brought him to the New World. When James ordered him to return to England with the *Lyon* when she sailed back for supplies, his father told him to calm down, that God had a purpose for everything and it was evidently God's plan that Drew come to Massachusetts. From his tone, Drew sensed the cobbler himself wasn't too pleased to find him in the colony, but there was nothing that could be done about it now. James was unconvinced.

Two other people weren't happy to see Drew Morgan as they disembarked—Marshall and Mary Ramsden. They were married now. When Drew knew them she was Mary Sedgewick and he an idealistic Puritan printing illegal pamphlets in Colchester. They still wore the brands on their cheeks. Marshall had let his hair grow so it was not as noticeable that his left ear was missing. When they saw Drew from a distance, their expression wasn't hostile, but then neither was it friendly. They turned and walked a different direction.

Drew was less angry with God now. It was as if God had repented and was now answering his prayers. Nell was regaining her health. The *Talbot* had safely deposited its cargo of Edenford folk on the shores of Massachusetts. And although the settlement was far inferior to what he had imagined, every day showed progress, and the more the people worked together, the closer in spirit most of them became.

Drew was one of the most diligent in the colony. He worked the various jobs he was assigned each day; then at 4 o'clock, while less industrious men spent time with their families or chatted under the meeting tree, he built a wigwam for Jenny and Nell, not waiting for the team of builders to get around to it. His industrious spirit drew the attention of the other men and became a source of amusement for several Pequot Indians.

Three of them regularly came to watch the colonists work.

They would stand on the outskirts of a large wooded area, pointing and laughing. And since Drew was always the last one working, he was often their sole entertainment. He tried not to mind that he was the center of attention for both the colonists and natives. He was aware of how the colonists felt about him — his reputation arrived with the *Talbot* — but he wondered what so amused the Indians. Were they entertained by his looks or manner of working? Or was he doing something wrong?

The structure of the house was built — the tree limbs were planted firmly in the earth, bent and tied securely together at the top. The front door frame was installed and he was almost finished with the fireplace, the hearth made of stones and the chimney built with sticks. The Indians were pointing and laughing at his handiwork. Palms down, they were making upward circular motions.

Drew had had enough. With stick in hand, he walked halfway to the Indians. They stopped laughing. He also had the attention of the men who had gathered under the meeting tree that day. One of them was Winthrop who talked with the men under the meeting tree to sound out the settlement's mood. As the men watched, Drew balanced the stick in an open palm and motioned with his free hand.

"Come on!" he said. "If I'm doing it wrong, show me how."

The Indians eyed him suspiciously.

Drew motioned again. "Show me how."

They didn't move.

Drew walked a few more steps forward. The Indians took a step backward toward the forest.

"Wait!" Drew said, holding his palm toward them. He balanced the stick in his open hand again and motioned toward them. "Help me. Show me how."

Drew walked slowly toward the Indians. One of the men

under the meeting tree spoke loud enough for him to hear, "Fool! He's gonna get hisself killed!" The men were on their feet.

Two of the Indians had retreated further into the forest when Drew reached them. One stood his ground. Drew held out the stick to him in an open palm.

The Indian looked at the stick, then at Drew. Then he reached out and took the stick. Drew smiled and nodded. Motioning to the wigwam he said, "Now show me how."

The Indian looked back at his companions. They stared at him, waiting to see what he would do.

Drew took several steps in the direction of the wigwam and motioned for the Indian with the stick to follow him. The Indian looked at the stick, then at the wigwam, and followed Drew.

When they reached the structure, Drew pointed to the stick, the chimney, then made the palms-down-and-upward sweeping motions that had so amused the Indians. The Indian with the stick nodded his head and chuckled; he pointed to the chimney, repeated the sweeping motion, and chuckled some more.

With palms upward, Drew shrugged. "What do I do?" he asked.

The Indian didn't respond.

Drew pointed to the stick, to the Indian, and, taking the Indian by the forearm, led him up to the structure. He seemed to understand. For several minutes the Indian circled the structure Drew had built, examining it. He grabbed the horizontal limbs and shook the structure. Then he walked to a different spot and did it again. A couple of Drew's ties came undone. The Indian tied them in a different manner, and shook the structure again. This time they held. Getting down on his hands and knees he stuck his head in the stone fireplace and looked up the chimney. He smiled, pulled his head out, and made the sweeping motions.

"Fire," Drew said. "The chimney will catch on fire."

This time it was the Indian who pulled Drew by the forearm. Taking him to the riverbank, they dug some clay and the Indian showed Drew how to daub it on the inside walls of the chimney. This wasn't unknown to the colonists, but it wasn't always done, and especially this thoroughly. The Indian helped Drew cover not only the interior walls, but the top and the exterior of the chimney as well.

The next day the Indian returned to helped Drew complete the job. The day after that, they began attaching the thatches together. Drew was no longer sole entertainer for the men under the meeting tree and the Indians by the woods. Now it was a two-man act, Drew and Sassacus.

Drew's Indian partner was particularly interested in the British insistence on doors for their wigwams. Although the English had patterned their wigwams after the Indians', there were two distinct European additions—the chimney and the swinging door with wooden hinges. The Indian huts used a hole in the ceiling of their huts to vent the smoke of their fires and a flap as a doorway. Sassacus seemed to take great pride that he had helped construct a chimney that wouldn't burn the hut down, and he watched carefully as Drew hung the door.

Nell and Jenny's wigwam had one other feature that was not common to the rest of the huts. One evening Sassacus pointed to the chimney, fluttered his fingers, let them fall on the thatch, then made the familiar upward sweeping motion. Drew understood. Ashes from the fire could rise from the chimney and ignite the thatches. It was a common problem for colonists and Indians alike. One night Drew came up with an answer.

He went to the *Arbella*, still in harbor, and bargained with Captain Milbourne to purchase the sails that had ripped during the crossing. He covered Nell and Jenny's hut with used canvas sails. Sassacus was impressed with the material.

Seeing that he was on to something, Drew returned to the ship and purchased more canvas, enough for his hut and for Sassacus. The Indian escorted Drew to the Pequot village and for two evenings the building team of Morgan and Sassacus entertained a different audience.

The Ramsdens didn't see him coming. Working hours were over, but a building team had just finished their wigwam and they were anxious to move in. Their new accommodations weren't much, but they were better than sharing a tent with several other families. Besides, it was home and a new start for them. The farthest thing from their minds was the pain and hatred they had known in England . . . until their unexpected guest arrived. His presence reminded them of everything they wanted to forget.

Marshall and Mary Ramsden had just deposited an armload of possessions in their hut and were coming back out for more when the door swung open and there stood Drew Morgan.

"Welcome to New England," Drew said.

Marshall stopped, blocking the entrance. Mary almost ran into him from behind.

"Who is it, Marshall?" she asked.

Marshall Ramsden didn't say anything at first. His face clouded and the brands on his cheeks turned bright red.

"Marshall?" It was the voice again. "Is something wrong, Marshall?"

Marshall stepped outside, allowing Mary to come face to face with their unexpected guest.

"Oh!" She clearly had not expected it to be Drew. One hand held on to the door latch, the other flew to her chest. Her look of shock gave way to concern as she looked at

Drew, her husband, and back to Drew.

"What are you doing here?" Marshall asked. It wasn't a friendly question; more like a line drawn in the dirt daring Drew to step over it.

"There is no reason you should believe anything I say," Drew began.

"At least we agree on something. Now you can leave." Marshall's words lashed at Drew like a whip.

Drew took the hit. He deserved it. He looked at Mary to see if she shared her husband's feelings. Her face was lined with frightened concern over her husband's anger and what he might do.

"I've come to ask you to forgive me."

There was no response. No softening.

"I was wrong. I hurt a lot of people. And the worst part was that I didn't even believe in the cause I represented. To put it simply, I wanted recognition and wealth and so I worked for the people who could give me those things."

Drew paused for a response. There was none. Marshall's arm's were folded tightly across his chest. A tight jaw indicated he was struggling to control himself. Mary looked at her husband in fear.

"Like I said, there's no reason you should believe me. But since we last saw each other, I've become a follower of Jesus Christ . . ."

"We've heard that story before," Marshall cut him off. "Our trust earned us these cheek adornments."

There was no use continuing. Not now anyway.

"I'm sorry," Drew said. With one last glance at Mary, he turned away.

"Drew." It was Mary's voice.

"Let him go!" Marshall yelled.

"Don't you yell at me, Marshall Ramsden!" Mary was indignant. She always did have a feisty spirit. She spoke again to

Drew, "You hurt us more than you're aware," she said.

Drew turned back.

"These were nothing," she held a hand up to the brands on her cheeks, "compared to the pain we felt when you silenced the voice of Justin."

The searing pain of Christopher Matthews' execution burned inside Drew as she spoke.

"We knew the risks when we printed his pamphlets," Mary continued. "But we also knew that even if we were caught, someone else would continue the printing. We were merely the distributors. You silenced the voice. During Christopher Matthews' trial, we prayed for a miracle. At Tower hill we prayed that God would send someone to rescue him." Tears came to her eyes. "And we heard about the reception the king gave you. It's hard for us to understand why God would let a godly man like Christopher Matthews die and let someone like you live."

Drew shared Mary's tears. "I've wondered the same thing," he said. "There is no defense for my actions. I don't deserve God's grace. All I can say is that through His grace I have been forgiven."

"A convenient grace, if you ask me." Marshall's anger had not dimmed.

"Not only has God forgiven me, but Christopher Matthews also forgave me."

"Do you find it easy to put words in a dead man's mouth?"

"And I have renounced my former desires. My only desire now is to continue the work of the man I killed. That's why I'm here. Why else would I be here? There is no wealth. There is no glory. Only wilderness, danger, hardship, and a chance to build a community based on the dictates of God's Word. As God is my witness, I have pledged my life to the success of this endeavor."

Drew could do no more. Mary left the doorway and stood

beside her husband. There would be no forgiveness today.

As he walked away, he looked over his shoulder twice. They remained in the same position as when he left them. Marshall's arms were folded, Mary by his side.

Several minutes later, Drew returned to the Ramsden's wigwam. They weren't there. Apparently, they had gone to get another load of their belongings. Drew went to work anyway.

"What are you doing to my house?" Marshall dropped the things he was carrying and ran at Drew.

Drew stretched the last of his canvas over the thatched hut. "This will protect the thatch from sparks from the chimney," he said while he worked. "Tomorrow, I'll finish your chimney. The builders don't usually clay all the way to the top, nor do they clay the outside. They're taking unnecessary shortcuts."

"You just stay away from my house!" Marshall shouted.

Mary grabbed her husband's arm. "What he says makes sense, Marshall!"

"No one else has canvas on their houses!" Marshall yelled.

"Nell and Jenny Matthews do."

"Matthews?" Mary asked.

"Christopher Matthews' daughters. They came over on the *Arbella.*"

The next day Drew finished putting clay on the Ramsdens' chimney.

Nell walked unassisted from the sick hut to her newly completed house. Actually she shuffled, and by the time she traveled the short distance she was winded. Still, considering the fact that many people didn't expect her to live, it was remarkable progress.

"Drew built it!" Jenny held the door open for her older sister, as Drew followed behind, ready to catch Nell if her strength gave out.

Nell steadied herself on the doorjamb, then moved to the crudely cut table and bench. Jenny and Drew patiently waited for her to catch her breath. Nell looked at the skeleton structure of tree limbs visible from the inside, at the rough wood fireplace, at the dirt floor covered with straw, and ran her hand along the top of the primitive table.

"It's nice," she said. Then she began to cry.

Drew wasn't expecting praise. A thank you would have been nice. He wasn't prepared for tears either. "Of course, this is just your winter quarters," he said. "Come spring and I'll build you a fine two-story frame house. Anywhere you want. You choose the location and I'll build it."

Nell fought back the tears. With a handkerchief she dabbed her eyes and wiped her nose. "Thank you, but no. I appreciate all you've done for us, Master Morgan, especially during my illness. But my strength is returning and Jenny and I will take care of ourselves from now on."

"Nell! How can you be so rude to Drew?" Jenny moved closer to his side.

"Drew, is it?" Nell said. "And when did you become so familiar with Master Morgan? What have the two of you been doing while I've been sick?"

"That's unfair," Drew said. "Jenny is devoted to you. She's been by your side constantly. I don't understand your bitter spirit."

"Bitter spirit? Why shouldn't I be bitter? Look around you! Because of you we are in this God-forsaken place, living in an animal shelter. I nearly died while crossing the sea. Who knows if I'll live through the winter? Dozens of people healthier than I haven't made it. You've killed the only male of our family."

"Nell, that's enough." Jenny moved toward her. "You're tired. You'll feel better after you've rested."

"Don't patronize me! I may be weak physically, but my

mind isn't feeble. Master Morgan said he didn't understand my attitude. Of course, he doesn't understand! It wasn't his father who was betrayed and murdered! It wasn't his family that was wrenched apart! It wasn't his life that was ruined!"

"Nell!"

Drew intervened. "Let her continue," he said. "She's wanted to say this for a long time."

"What are we going to do to earn a living?" Nell was weeping openly now. "How many fine folks of New England have a need for lace? There aren't even any looms on which to make cloth! How are we going to survive?"

"I'll take care of you," Drew said. "I promised your father I would."

"Did you? Did you promise him while his cheeks were being branded or while they were cutting off his ear?"

It was Drew's turn to get angry. "That's enough, Nell! I tried to steer Bishop Laud away from your father. I tried to rescue him after he was arrested. I've thrown away everything I've ever wanted in life in hope that someday I might be like him. As for this place," Drew motioned to the hut, "I agree it's not much. But it's temporary. I said you'll have a nice home by this time next year, and I mean it."

"What do you know about nice homes?" Nell said. "You built this one."

"I'll tell you what I know about nice homes," Drew said through clenched teeth. "In comparison to Morgan Hall, your house in Edenford had all the attraction of this wigwam!"

There was a pounding on the door that made the whole structure shake.

"Nell? Nell? Are you all right in there?" It was James Cooper.

The door flew open before Nell could answer.

"You again? What are you doing in here?"

"That's the same question I wanted to ask you in Edenford, when you came downstairs with Nell," Drew said.

The red giant seized Drew by his shirt and raised his fist.

"James Abel Cooper, let him go!" Nell's remaining strength was fading fast. Yelling at James winded her.

"I'll take care of him for you, Nell." James began pulling Drew outside.

"No!" Nell's voice wasn't loud, but James was familiar with the tone. He stopped and reluctantly let go of Drew. "Now listen to me," she said. "Both of you get out of my house. Don't ever come back."

"Nell, honey," James whined.

"If I have to, I'll get up from here and throw you both out!" Nell said.

"Nell Matthews, I've waited for you long enough," James said. "Your father's dead and you need a man, if you're going to survive here. I came to tell you it's time we get married."

"Not now, James," Nell said. "Get out."

James Cooper cocked a huge hairy red finger in Nell's direction. "I'm serious, Nell. I'm tired of waiting for you. Either we get married soon or you can forget about me. If I walk out that door, it's over."

"That's all I ask," Nell said wearily. "I want it to be over. Walk out the door."

James looked at her dumbfounded. Seeing she was serious, he slammed the door with an open palm. It flew open and banged against the side of the hut, breaking the top wooden hinge. He stalked out.

"You too," Nell said to Drew.

"You can't mean that!" Jenny cried. "I can understand James, but not Drew."

"I mean it."

"This is my house too! And Drew can come here whenever he wants!"

"Not while I'm alive." The way she looked, that wouldn't be long. Pale and shaking, she laid her head on the table.

Jenny looked at Drew. "Wait for me outside," she said. "I'll spread out a blanket for her to rest on."

His anger was gone. The sight of her on the table took it away. She had said some things to hurt him, but she was tired, sick, and frightened. He wished he would have remembered that before he said some of the things he did.

Drew went outside and maneuvered the broken door closed.

"I'm sorry," Jenny said, as she took Drew by the arm. "Nell didn't mean the things she said."

"Yes, she did. But she's ill and frightened. And she's right."

Jenny snuggled up to him. "Let's walk to the woods."

It was early October and the leaves were turning. The sun lowered itself onto the horizon, but not before setting the forest ablaze with color. There wasn't much activity in the settlement other than routine chores—drawing water from the river, borrowing fire from a neighbor if the coals accidentally went out, minor repairs on the wigwams. After several months, the routine of daily life had provided a small measure of security. There were undoubtedly several men sitting under the meeting tree watching Drew and Jenny walk arm in arm. But then with news in short supply, there was little else to talk about than one another.

"You did a fine job on the wigwam," Jenny said.

"It really isn't much," Drew said. "It's sort of funny... I've always admired my grandfather and wanted to be like him. He built Morgan Hall and I built a wigwam. Hardly something to brag about."

"Drew Morgan, you stop talking like that! Was your grandfather in danger for his life when he built Morgan Hall? Did he build it for someone else while he slept in a old tent?"

"Well, no."

"If you had his resources, I daresay you could build a house much more grand than Morgan Hall. And if he had what little resources you have to work with here, I doubt if he could have built anything finer!"

"Kind thoughts. Thank you."

They were just inside the wooded area when Jenny pulled Drew behind a tree. "No, Master Morgan," she said. "Thank *you!*" She threw her arms around his neck and kissed him passionately.

Drew didn't know what was wrong with him. He loved Jenny, but he loved Nell more. It was wrong for him to bring Jenny here. Wrong for him not to break away from her immediately. But she felt so good pressed against him. She was warm and eager for his embrace. She gasped for air.

"Drew darling, I've wanted to thank you like this for days, but there just hasn't been time when we could get away."

She came at him again.

"Jenny," Drew tried to stop her.

She grabbed the back of his head and pulled with all her might. Though he resisted, his mouth smashed against her teeth.

"Jenny, no!" he managed to say, their lips still pressed against each other. She didn't listen. Reaching behind his head, he grabbed her hands and freed himself. "No! This isn't right!"

In his desire to be firm, he may have spoken a little too harshly. Jenny stood in front of him with a hurt look on her face.

"What do you mean, 'no'?" she demanded.

"This isn't right. We shouldn't be doing this."

A playful look crossed her face. "Well, Master Morgan," she purred, "aren't you the shy one?" She reached for his shirt and played with the collar. "You surprise me. I didn't think you would be so prim and proper."

Drew took her hands in his. "It's not that," he said.

"Good!" Her eyes lit up and she leaned into him.

"Jenny! Listen to me. Please!" He held her at a distance.

She shook free; a pouting lower lip appeared. There was anger in her eyes.

"It can't be like this," he explained. "We can't be like this."

He knew he was getting through because she was backing away. Tears welled in her eyes. Her lower lip quivered.

"Jenny, I don't want to hurt you. You're the only friend I have left in the world."

"Friend?" She shouted the word.

Drew nodded. "You're my dearest friend. You trusted me when nobody else would and I'll never forget that. I love you as a friend, and I always will. But my heart belongs to Nell."

Tears turned to sobs.

"Jenny . . ." Drew reached out to her.

"Don't touch me!" she slapped his hand away.

"Jenny, please understand."

She backed away from him like she would a wild bear. Her back hit a tree and she winced from the impact. She was sobbing uncontrollably now. Her legs began to buckle and she slid down the trunk of the tree.

"Jenny. I didn't mean to hurt you, but I don't know what else to say." He took another step toward her.

Her eyes flew wide open and she stretched out her hand like it was a claw. Inching her way back up the tree, she said, "I know exactly what you can say."

Drew waited for her to continue.

"You can say good-bye to your last friend on earth!" She bolted from the woods. Drew could hear her sobs all the way across the compound. With the hinge broken on the door it took her several tries to get it open, then several more to close it. Drew could no longer hear her sobbing.

Chapter 25

BOSTON Colony's town meetings and church services were held under a tree, since there were no buildings large enough to hold everyone. Drew would arrive early, a carry-over from Edenford. He would greet people as they arrived. They were polite in their response, but not warm. When it came time for the service to begin, Drew would inevitably be sitting by himself. Nell and Jenny made it a point to arrive late. This way Drew was already seated and they could sit on the opposite side of the congregation. Although David Cooper seemed friendly enough, he never invited Drew to join him and his family, which was just as well. Drew didn't know if he could keep his mind on the church service if he sat next to James Cooper. It was his impression that it might be difficult to think worshipful thoughts knowing the person sitting next to you wanted to rip you apart. Inevitably, there would be an empty zone surrounding Drew Morgan when the service began.

Reverend Higginson preached quality sermons. They were well structured, biblical, and profitable, but they weren't the sermons of Christopher Matthews. They lacked passion.

When the church services were over, everyone went their own way. They shook Drew's hand, smiled their Sunday morning smiles, and walked away. Sunday was the loneliest day of the week for Drew. At least on other days, by sheer necessity, the men were forced to work next to him.

On the last Sunday of October, Drew Morgan brought a friend with him to church, the Pequot Indian named Sassacus. The presence of the dark, nearly naked visitor threw the congregation into a turmoil. The people of Boston had not yet determined what they thought of the Indians. Most agreed that the Indians needed to hear about Jesus Christ, but that's what missionaries were for. Taking the Gospel to the Indians was one thing; bringing Indians to church was something else.

The issue was settled when John Winthrop welcomed Sassacus to God's church under the tree and invited the Indian and Drew to sit with him. Drew shared his Bible with the Pequot and pointed to the words, even though the Indian couldn't read English. The Indian held up the lace cross in the Bible, the one that had belonged to Nell. Drew pressed it tenderly against his chest to show the Indian that it was one of his dearest treasures. Whenever it was time to pray, Drew would motion for Sassacus to bow his head and close his eyes. Inevitably Drew would peek to see if Sassacus' eyes were closed. They weren't. Sassacus would jab him good-naturedly for peeking.

The Pequot Indian became Drew's regular Sunday guest, as they attended services and then spent the afternoon together. Drew did his best to explain the Gospel message to the Indian, even though he knew little English. In the process, Drew learned some Algonquin words and phrases.

"Master Morgan, may I have a moment of your time?"

It was after working hours and Drew was laying thatches against his wigwam, one of the last to be built in the settlement. He looked to see who was addressing him. It was John Winthrop.

"Yes, governor. What can I do for you?"

The governor of the colony wore a serious expression. This wasn't going to be a casual conversation. Drew couldn't help but wonder about the topic. Did it have to do with Nell and Jenny? Or was he going to be asked not to bring Sassacus to the services any more?

"Supplies are low," the governor said. Drew breathed more easily. It was a serious topic, but not a personal one. "We won't make it through the winter." It was a pronouncement. Not a guess or an estimate but a statement. People would die for lack of food this winter.

"What can I do to help?" Drew asked.

"I need someone to talk to the Pequots, to persuade them to sell us more corn. They've already sold us some, but we need more, much more." Winthrop leaned closer. "You've developed a friendship with Sassacus. Do you think he would help us buy more corn from his tribe?"

"He's a good friend," Drew said. "We can ask him to help."

Sassacus agreed to help. He, Drew, and Winthrop bartered with the Pequot leaders for more corn. The Indians kept only enough to get them through the winter. But still the colonists didn't have what they needed.

So the governor dispatched Drew by ship to the Narragansetts to trade for additional supplies of corn. Drew invited Sassacus to join him, thinking it would be to his advantage, since both tribes spoke Algonquin. Sassacus recoiled at the mention of the Narragansetts and Drew chose not to press the point. To the cheers of the colonists, Drew returned with 100 bushels of corn. They had enough food to survive the winter, provided the *Lyon* returned as scheduled.

"Can I help you?"

Marshall Ramsden stood, hands on hips, as Drew lifted the door to his wigwam into place. Mary stood behind her husband. She was smiling.

"I'd welcome your help!"

The two men fit the door in the frame with wooden hinges.

"Is the claying all done on the chimney?" Marshall asked.

"Finished yesterday."

"What about the canvas? I see you don't have it on yet."

"There isn't any more."

"You didn't keep enough for yourself?"

"I gave you mine."

Marshall stood opposite Drew and looked at him a long time. A half-smile stretched to one side of his face as he shook his head and rubbed his chin. Drew was a puzzle he couldn't figure out. "I was wrong about you," he said.

"You were right about me. I played the fool and hurt a lot of good people, like you and Mary. It's something I'll always regret."

"But you've changed."

"By the grace of God."

"Pity," Marshall said. "I was kind of fond of the old Drew Morgan." A puzzled expression crossed Drew's face. It was just what Marshall was after. "But I've come to admire and respect the new Drew Morgan. And I'd like to be his friend."

"Me too." Mary added.

The three of them hugged at the door of Drew's newly completed house. The first house he ever owned. That night they shared a meal and filled in the gaps since their carefree days in Colchester.

Drew learned that the brands on Marshall and Mary's cheeks had opened many doors for them. Although the general populace of England regarded the marks of Laud a disgrace, some wealthy Puritans saw them as a badge of honor and courage. One was a wealthy Oxford Puritan who convinced them to come to the New World. He was an old man who was unable to make the journey himself, but wanted to have a part in founding a community where God was king. He told the Ramsdens he couldn't think of a better way to do that than to invest in a young couple. He would provide the funds and supplies, if they would supply the work and the babies.

"He really said you were to supply babies?" Drew asked with a laugh.

Marshall nodded with a wide-eyed smile. Mary grinned and blushed.

"He's been extremely generous," Marshall added. "He has agreed to help me set up a printing press as soon as there is a need for one in Boston."

"Your own press?"

A look of boyish excitement on Marshall's face revealed his delight.

"Until then," Mary said, "he wants us to send him descriptions of life in the colony. He'll print and distribute them throughout England to encourage others to come to the colonies."

"I send him my accounts, but they're really not good." Marshall said. "I'm a printer, not a writer. And I feel like I'm letting a good man down."

Drew lifted his face upward. "Thank You, Lord," he said.

Mary and Marshall looked puzzled. "You're thanking God that Marshall isn't a writer?"

Drew nodded. "Yes, because I know exactly where you can find one."

"You're a writer?" Mary asked. "Please say yes; we're desperate."

"No, I'm not. But I know where you can find one. Right here in the colony."

Snow didn't come to the colony until late November, when it arrived with a fury, far more severe than anything the colonists had experienced in England. With the cold weather came sickness and death. Supplies were rationed and began to run low. The *Lyon* wasn't expected until December. Drew knew that Governor Winthrop had sent the ship back with a long list of vital supplies, but he had never given it any thought as to who was paying for the supplies. It was in confidence that he learned that Winthrop himself was supporting the colony with his own money. Never once did he hear the governor make the slightest complaint, even when the colonists began to blame him for not doing enough to stem the tide of hunger and disease.

When the cold weather struck, Nell's health held steady. Although she had never fully regained her strength, to Drew's relief she didn't regress. It was Jenny who concerned him now. Ever since she ran from him in the woods, she had changed. Her expression was always sober, nothing like the pixie flightiness she was known for. Rarely did she smile; rarer still did she laugh.

"What did you do to my sister?" Nell whispered. She stood in the snow with a heavy wool shawl wrapped around her shoulders as Drew worked.

Drew had stopped by to repair the outside of their wigwam. The canvas had slipped in places. It was late afternoon and Jenny was taking a nap.

"You're in no condition to be standing out here," Drew said. "Go back inside."

"I'm not going inside until you tell me what you did to her!"

And you're stubborn enough to stay out here too, Drew said to himself.

Nell continued, "All day long she mopes around. And she won't tell me what happened! Drew, she's all I have left! What did you do to her?"

"I told her I didn't love her."

"Of all the inconsiderate things to say! She's only a child! Why would you even say something like that?"

Drew yanked hard on a rope. The hut shuddered.

Nell folded her arms and stared at him. She wasn't going to leave until this was resolved.

He faced her directly. "Jenny was hoping there could be more between us. I have deep feelings for her, and I told her so, but not romantic feelings."

"You told an impressionable young girl you have deep feelings for her? And then you tell her you don't love her?"

"Am I on trial here?"

"I just can't understand how you can be so brilliant one minute and so insensitive the next!"

"You think I'm brilliant?"

"No, I think you're insensitive."

"Nell, I didn't want to hurt her."

"For someone who doesn't want to hurt people, you seem to be quite good at it."

Drew swallowed the anger that was rising in his throat. This wasn't the most pleasant conversation he'd had recently, but at least it was a conversation with Nell. And they were coming few and farther in between.

Drew's words were measured and deliberate. "Like I said, I tried not to hurt her. Tell me, how should a man tell a woman he doesn't love her, in a way that won't hurt?"

Nell didn't have a ready answer for him.

"That's only half the problem, though," he said.

"Oh? What's the other half?"

"Not only is she upset that I don't love her; she's also upset because I told her I love you."

Nell rolled her eyes. "Why would you tell her that?"

"Because I do."

"Anything that was between us once is gone. It died with my father."

"It can be resurrected through our Lord."

Nell's mouth fell open. "Drew Morgan! You have the nerve! Is nothing too low for you? You would use God to manipulate me?"

"Of course not! I pray for you and Jenny every night, no manipulation intended. My prayers and desires are sincere."

"It would be more profitable if you would confine your prayers to yourself."

"I find time to do that too."

"And since we're talking about your unwanted intrusion into our lives . . ."

"I thought we were talking about my love for you."

Nell let the comment pass. ". . . I'll have you know we no longer need your help. We are perfectly capable of supporting ourselves."

"Doing what?"

"It just so happens that I have been asked to record colony experiences for publication in England. Master Ramsden and his wife, Mary, live on the other side of the meeting tree by the forest. He has employed me to write descriptions of colonial life for which I will be paid. Quite handsomely, I would add. So it seems that God has chosen to take care of us poor, helpless Matthews girls without your help."

"Congratulations, Nell! I couldn't be happier for you."

The *Lyon* didn't arrive in December as scheduled. Nor did it come in January. The corn supply was exhausted. The clambanks had been stripped clean. There were no more ground nuts to scavenge. The colonists in Massachusetts Bay prayed that God would extend their meal and oil like He did for the poor widow in the Old Testament. However, they didn't have a prophet like Elijah; they had only a governor who feared that the *Lyon* had met disaster on the sea. Governor Winthrop sought council from the two resident ministers, John Endecott, and other leaders of the colony, including Drew Morgan. Some suggested sending relief expeditions to Plymouth Colony seeking help; others thought they should approach the Indians again and take by force what they needed, if the Indians wouldn't barter for it. Winthrop listened to all the suggestions and carefully weighed them. His conclusion was to declare a day of fasting for February 6. On that day they would place themselves at God's mercy as they never had done before.

On February 4, the governor distributed the last handful of meal in the community barrel to a poor man on the verge of starvation. Parents gave their last bit of food to their children while they went to bed hungry. It looked like by sheer lack of food the day of fasting would begin a day earlier than announced.

February 5 dawned cold and without promise. As the colonists prepared themselves for the worst, the *Lyon* sailed into harbor laden with provisions! On her way back to England she had come across a dismasted ship. She had towed the crippled ship to port, which accounted for the delay in her return to the colony. The *Lyon's* hold was filled with wheat, meal, peas, oatmeal, beef, pork, cheese, butter, suet, and casks of lemon juice for those who suffered from scurvy. Governor Winthrop canceled the day of fasting and ordered a day of thanksgiving. It was a sign from God! He had answered the prayers of His people and provided for their needs, just like the Israelites in the wilderness!

It was a day of dancing and hugging and merriment as the colonists celebrated God's provision. For generations afterward men would sit before the family fires and tell their children of the goodness of God and how He poured out His blessings on the Massachusetts Bay Colony. Twenty-six additional colonists from England joined the festivities. Among them was the highly respected minister Roger Williams.

Drew celebrated as joyously as the rest of the colony, laughing and carrying on, until something happened to cut his celebration short. While all around him people were dancing and singing, Drew saw something that chilled his heart. In Boston's bay a shallop bobbed up and down as it approached shore. It was one of many that day. All the others brought provisions and supplies and renewed life for the people. Not so this shallop. On board this one was the unmistakable profile of death. Drew watched with mounting fear as the shallop carrying Eliot Venner touched the shore.

Chapter 26

THE colony's festive mood stretched into the spring and summer months. As the days grew warmer and the ground dried, a fresh determination and stern resolve permeated the colony. The completion of new building projects added to the sense of anticipation. Each frame structure was a confirmation that a town was being carved out of the wilderness. Families would live in homes, not thatched huts. Businesses would be erected where men could ply the trades which required skill and training. Ever since their arrival everyone was a common laborer with a single task—survival. But now, cobblers could be cobblers and blacksmiths could be blacksmiths. Until now the colonists hadn't realized how much of their personal identities were tied to their trades.

Nell Matthews realized this truth as much as any other skilled worker. Writing vignettes of colony life for the Ramsdens' benefactor was a rejuvenating tonic. She wrote every morning, recording significant dates and events, people's impressions and feelings, and compiling quotes. In the afternoon she traveled from house to house, business to business, interviewing people. She wanted to know everyone's thoughts from the time they decided to leave England to the present moment. At night, she would arrange her notes for the next morning's work.

She interviewed everyone in town once and some of them

twice. Everyone except Drew Morgan. She even did her best to interview Sassacus before talking to Drew.

Drew was content to wait. He knew it was just a matter of time before she would come to him. Yes, she was stubborn, but she was also meticulous. It would be a struggle of monumental proportion, but Nell would never be content with an incomplete record of colony events. She would come to him.

In the meantime, Drew built a two-story frame house. He had volunteered his labor to help a carpenter build a house for his family of seven. In exchange, the carpenter would teach Drew how to build. The carpenter was an honest man who respected Drew's willingness to exchange work for knowledge—unlike some of the other craftsmen. Now that the threat of starvation was over, many of the tradesmen charged exorbitant prices for their services, some of them so much that they needed to work only one or two days a week to make a handsome living.

The house that Drew built was large enough for a family. The entryway led into a spacious room with a large brick fireplace. It served as both sitting room and kitchen. Just inside the front door to the right, a stairway led up to the second story which had two bedrooms. As Drew promised, he built the house for Nell and Jenny. He would continue living in his wigwam until he could build another house for himself. But when he offered it to the Matthews girls, they refused to move into it. David Cooper had offered to share his house with them, but it was already crowded. Besides, Nell couldn't see herself living under the same roof as James, even though he hadn't bothered her, or even attempted to talk to her since she ordered him out of the wigwam. The Ramsdens offered to let Nell and Jenny live with them in their house until another house could be built, but workers were scarce and the months were quickly slipping away. Winter was coming when no one would be able to build. Nell didn't want to intrude on the Ramsdens for an entire winter.

It was Governor Winthrop who persuaded Nell and Jenny to move into the house. He argued that it was only for the winter. Come spring he would personally help them build a house of their own. But he was responsible for the well-being of every colonist and it was poor stewardship for them to live in a hut when there was a house available to them. Not wanting to be a poor steward, Nell agreed to move into the house Drew had built.

There was a note stuck to the door of Drew's hut that Saturday afternoon. As usual, all work ceased at 3 o'clock in preparation for the Lord's Day. Drew had just returned home from the bayside. He carried a musket, the first one he ever owned. He had bought it from the first mate of the ship *Hopewell*. Though there were occasional rumors of Indian trouble, Drew had never felt the need for a firearm . . . until Eliot Venner came to town.

The note was from Nell. After all the things he'd been through, he was surprised at how deeply his emotions were stirred at the mere sight of her handwriting, especially when the writing spelled his name. The note invited him to join her for lunch on Sunday. She had questions she wanted to ask him to complete her chronicle of the colony.

Sunday afternoon Drew stood at the door of the house he built. It was situated at the top of a small rise, and the bay spread out before it like a restless carpet. It was late summer and the leaves rustled in the brisk breeze. He knocked.

"Master Morgan." Nell was formal and polite as she opened the door.

Drew followed her into the sitting room.

"Where's Jenny?" he asked.

"She's with friends," Nell replied. "She won't be joining us." Then, lest he think this had been her arrangement, she added hastily, "Following the service she was invited to take a walk down by the bay. I'm glad for her. As you know, she's kept to herself for too long. This will be the first time she's been out with friends her age since we've been here. Frankly, I was surprised she agreed to go. Maybe it was because she knew you were coming over."

Nell was cutting slices of bread on the pantry shelf. She glanced up at Drew, looking for a reaction. He was sitting at the table, tracing the pattern of the wood grain with his finger. If the statement bothered him, he didn't show it.

"Anyway," she continued, "that will give us uninterrupted time to finish this, and then you can be on your way."

"I'm in no hurry."

"Well, it just isn't good for you to be here alone with me. It doesn't look right. You know how people talk. If I would have known that Jenny wasn't going to be here, I would have invited the Ramsdens to join us." Nell was nervous. It wasn't like her to babble.

Nell served the cold venison and bread. They prayed and ate a silent meal.

While Drew had a second helping, Nell asked him his impressions of the colony upon his arrival. Prompted by her questions, Drew described life as he saw it—his initial disappointment in the condition of the colony, his reaction to living in a thatched wigwam after having been raised in Morgan Hall, his unexpected friendship with Sassacus, and his official excursions to the Pequots and Narragansetts to barter for food.

He tried not to stare at her during the meal and interview, but he found it difficult. It was the first civil discussion they'd had since before her father died. He didn't remember eating anything; he was too busy savoring her presence. He still felt intimidated by her intelligence and self-confidence—that hadn't changed from the first time they had met—and she still excited him. His chest pounded. His blood raced.

Nell laid her quill pen across the paper, a signal that the interview was over. It was too soon. Drew thought about asking for another helping just so he could stay longer.

Nell leaned forward. Placing her elbows on the table, she rested her chin on her hands. "This is a lovely house," she said. "I haven't thanked you for letting us stay in it. Thank you."

"I promised you I'd build you one."

She shook her head. "This is your house. We'll move out in the spring."

Drew didn't want to argue with her. It was too nice an afternoon to spoil.

"It seems I have something else to thank you for," she said. "I've been talking with Mary Ramsden."

The name on Nell's lips made Drew uncomfortable. How much had they shared with each other? The last thing Drew wanted was for them to be comparing notes about his previous covert actions. "The Ramsdens are a nice couple," he said. "I like them."

"From what I hear, you know them from Colchester."

"What did she tell you?"

"Nothing much, really. Only that they met you in Colchester."

"What does that have to do with thanking me for something?"

Nell smiled that intimidating smile of hers. "Part of your mysterious past? Or should I say notorious past?"

"You'd only hate me more if I told you," he said.

Nell's smile faded. "I'm sorry," she said. "I really intended to thank you." She sat up straight, laying her still folded hands on top of the paper and quill. "Mary told me that you recommended me for this job."

Drew shrugged. "Marshall needed a writer. I happened to know a good one."

"Do they know that I'm Justin?" There was a tremor in her voice as she asked.

"Of course not! I would never tell them that."

"I know," she said, her head lowered. "It's just that I had to ask."

There was a silent interval. Drew thought hard for something, anything, that would keep the conversation going. He didn't want the afternoon to be over.

He thought of something. "I didn't thank you for the meal. It was great."

She told him it was her pleasure.

"And for interviewing me. Thanks for including me in the chronicle."

"You're welcome."

Another long silence.

"I've missed these times," he said.

"What times?"

"Sunday afternoons together, the afternoons we spent together at the old Saxon ruins overlooking Edenford."

Mistake. He'd crossed the line. The look of insult on Nell's face indicated he'd been caught on forbidden ground. Well, since he was already here, he might as well forge ahead.

"Nell! What must I do to earn your forgiveness?" he cried.

"It's not a matter of forgiveness," she said. "I forgive you. I just can't love you. Not after what you've done."

"I don't believe you," he said.

"I don't care what you believe."

"I learned a lot of things from your father," Drew said. "And one of the most significant lessons he taught me was that love never gives up."

"And look what it got him."

"You don't believe that."

Nell took out a handkerchief and wiped her nose. "Now you're telling me what I believe?"

"You're much like your father," he said, "but you've been hurt and are afraid that if you love you'll get hurt again."

"I think it's time you left, Master Morgan."

"I think you're right, Mistress Matthews." Drew looked for a way to end their conversation on a civil note. "Do you have any final interview questions for me?"

Nell looked at her paper with blurry eyes. "There is one question I haven't asked you that I asked everyone else. When the *Lyon* sailed into harbor on February 5, what were your thoughts?" Nell waited with quill poised.

When he didn't answer, she looked up.

"What's wrong?" she asked.

"Do you remember . . . let me see now," Drew closed his eyes and tried to remember the name Eliot used in Edenford. "Thomas Mitchell! Do you remember a man who came to Edenford after I left, by the name of Thomas Mitchell?"

Nell shook her head. "I don't know anyone by that name."

"Wild hair, bulging eyes, pockmarked face."

She shook her head again.

"He's one of Laud's men. He trained me."

The mention of the bishop's name brought a trace of horror to her face. "Drew, what are you trying to tell me?"

"He's here in the colony. I saw him disembark from the *Lyon*."

"What's he doing here?" There was panic in her voice.

"He said he came to settle in Roxbury. That he had broken with Laud."

"Do you think he's telling the truth?"

"No."

"Then what is he doing here?" Nell was beginning to cry. The fear she thought she'd left in England had caught up with her.

"I don't know," Drew said. "I haven't seen him since the day he arrived."

Nell was shaking. Drew wished he hadn't told her.

"What did you say his name was? Mitchell?"

"That's the name he used in Edenford," Drew said. "His real name is Eliot. Eliot Venner."

Nell gasped. "That's who Jenny's with!" she cried. "She said she was going to the bay with the Billingtons and a young man by the name of Eliot Venner!"

"The Billingtons?"

"A family at church. He's a fisherman. They have a daughter Jenny's age."

Drew raced out the door and scanned the bay.

"Good afternoon, Master Morgan." The voice came from his right. Jenny was walking up the hill. She was alone.

"Are you all right?" he shouted.

"And why shouldn't I be?" There was no mistaking the indifference she had for him in the tone of her voice.

"Jenny!" Nell stood in the doorway.

"What's going on?" Jenny asked.

"We were just concerned about you," Nell replied. "Is everything all right?"

"Fine!" Jenny replied. "I had a wonderful afternoon."

"With Eliot Venner?" Drew asked.

"Your teacher!" she replied.

"He told you that?"

"He told me a lot of things. We spent the afternoon together. He really is a sweet man."

Drew pointed a stern finger at Jenny. "Stay away from him, Jenny. He's dangerous."

"And since when did you start caring about me?" Jenny shot back at him. She stomped into the house and went straight upstairs.

"I'll talk with her," Nell said, as she closed the door.

From everything Drew was able to find out, Eliot had been

a model colonist since the moment he stepped off the ship. He asked around until he learned where the Billingtons lived. They were a crude-mouthed family of five with two sons and a daughter who had met Eliot several months previous. Eliot was visiting and took a liking to Jenny, so they introduced him to her and invited her to join the family for the afternoon. According to the Billingtons, Eliot was a gentleman the whole time.

Drew informed David Cooper of Eliot's presence. The cobbler had seen Eliot from afar, not long after the February festival, but didn't seem all that concerned. "Of course, he chased us. It was his job. Do you think the high constable was going to do it?" Cooper bulged his cheeks and held his hands out wide as he described the high constable. "Besides, what can he do to us here? Ship us all back to the Star Chamber?"

Governor Winthrop was equally unconcerned. The governor was talking to Reverend Roger Williams when Drew called on him. Williams spoke highly of Eliot, having become acquainted with him on the voyage over. The minister likened him to John the Baptist, lacking social appeal but deeply spiritual.

"People change," the governor said. "You of all people should know that."

Drew wasn't convinced. He knew Eliot and Eliot's methods. He had to find out why he was in the colony, and then stop him from doing what he came to do.

"Eliot!"

Drew saw him about to enter a wigwam down by the bay. His arms were full of clothes and miscellaneous household items. He was alone.

"Drew!" Eliot returned the call. "Be right back." He disappeared into the hut and reappeared moments later. "Drew!

Good to see you again!" He extended his hand in greeting. Drew folded his arms. "What are you doing here?"

"Didn't like Roxbury, and they didn't like me; Boston's better." Pointing to the wigwam he said, "The Billingtons told me I could use their hut since they have a house now."

There was something different about Eliot. This wasn't the same Eliot who took Drew to the bearbaiting, or who sat in the bishop's study, and definitely not the same Eliot who attacked him beside the Exe River. He seemed calmer, more mature, more sure of himself. His language seemed improved. Had Eliot grown up or was it an act? Even his hair was brushed down more than usual.

"What are you doing in Massachusetts Bay Colony?" Drew clarified.

"We went over this once already, didn't we?"

"Let's go over it again. Why are you here?"

Eliot folded his arms to match Drew. He smiled a big smile. It wasn't devious or malicious, but combined with those eyes it was still unsettling. "Why can't you accept me for who I say I am?"

"Because I know you."

"And you know how I work, my techniques, my roles."

"Exactly."

"And there's no room in that oversized Christian heart of yours for the possibility that God could save me?"

"Is that what you want me to believe? That you've been saved?" Drew asked.

"That's what you want everyone to believe about you, isn't it?"

"Tell me about your conversion experience."

"All right." Eliot rolled his bulging eyes skyward. He spoke in rapid monotone. "Not long after Christopher Matthews was executed, I started doubting my role in Bishop Laud's scheme of things. How could the bishop kill such a good man? If anyone deserved to die, it was me. I was the sinner, not Matthews. Life was miserable. I couldn't find peace. In utter despair I turned to the only One who could save me, Jesus Christ. I asked Jesus to cleanse me of my sinfulness and come into my heart. He did and has been doing a wondrous work even to this day. There. Satisfied?"

"You're mocking me," Drew said.

"Of course I am."

Drew's anger rose. He could feel his face getting hot.

Eliot laughed. "Your testimony, my testimony, what's the difference? They're all the same."

"What are you doing here, Eliot? Have you come for me?"

"I haven't decided yet."

"What does that mean?"

"The bishop doesn't want me to hurt you directly," Eliot snorted. "The fool! I've never understood what he sees in you. But he does want me to destroy the colony."

"How? By getting the charter revoked?"

"Now, Drew, I can't tell you all my secrets. Actually, I haven't decided yet. You know, you're a bigger fool than he is, Morgan. Why didn't you just take all the gold and honor he wanted to give you? You're stupid, Morgan! What do you have here?"

"I have more than Bishop Laud could ever give me," Drew answered.

Eliot let out a loud, long snort. "Have it your way," he said. "Anyway, the bishop wants to hurt you by hurting the people you chose instead of him. He's left the specifics up to me."

Jenny! That's why Eliot went after Jenny! Drew made a fist. "You stay away from Jenny Matthews!"

"She's a pretty little doe, isn't she?" Eliot's grin turned wicked.

"I'm warning you, Eliot, stay away from her!"

"Or what? You'll hit me? You would hit your brother in the Lord? And how would you explain it to all your fine Christian neighbors? They think I'm wonderful."

Drew began to back away. "I'll find a way to stop you," he said.

"You can't stop me," Eliot laughed. "You know that. Christians want to believe the best in a person. They want to believe that their precious God can save someone like me! You know how the plan works. That's the beauty of it! It works every time and there's nothing you can do about it."

"I'll find a way!" Drew shouted. "And stay away from Nell and Jenny. I mean it, Eliot. Stay away!"

"And blessings on you too, my brother in Christ!" Eliot shouted after him.

Drew remained awake all night. He had to think of a way to expose Eliot Venner. He reviewed everything Eliot taught him about infiltrating Puritan communities. Somehow he had to beat his teacher at his own game. The problem was that the colonists didn't know Eliot like he did. They would believe Eliot until it was too late. *How can I warn them? How can I stop people from believing something they want to believe?*

Drew prayed for wisdom. He prayed for Nell and Jenny's safety. He prayed his longest prayer for Eliot. Drew had concluded there were only two sure ways of stopping Eliot: God would have to change him or Drew would have to kill him.

The Reverend Higginson preached an exceptional sermon the following Sunday morning about God's unrelenting love, using Hosea as his text. He explained that even though the prophet's wife had played the harlot and been unfaithful, Hosea ransomed her from destruction. Higginson concluded that Hosea loved his wife in the same way that God loves His church.

Drew barely heard any of it. He stood in the back of the congregation and kept an eye on Eliot who was sitting near the front. Drew prayed that somehow God would reach him, but that didn't seem likely. Several times he saw Eliot stare back at Jenny Matthews. When their eyes met, he would smile and wink. Jenny would smile and wrinkle her nose back at him. It infuriated Drew. He remembered when Jenny looked at him that way. Eliot was giving him no choice.

Drew had come to the service prepared to expose Eliot as the murderer of Shubal Elkins. He could have gone to Winthrop and made the charge privately. Of course, Eliot would deny it. It would take almost six months for correspondence to travel back and forth to England confirming Drew's allegations. In the meantime, Eliot would be free to work his evil. Drew couldn't let him have that much time. However, if the accusation was made publicly, even though Eliot would still be given the benefit of the doubt, everyone would have been warned. They would be more cautious in any dealings with him.

The Reverend Higginson was about to conclude the service. It was time for Drew to expose his former teacher.

"Reverend, may I say something?"

Eliot beat him to it. Smoothing down his uncontrollable red hair, Eliot stood before the congregation.

"Is it something that would be profitable for everyone?" the pastor asked.

"I have a confession to make," Eliot said. "There's something you should know about me, since I'm living among you now."

"And what's that?"

"I'm a murderer," Eliot said.

The congregation gasped. Just like Eliot told Drew they would during his training. Get their attention by confessing the worst thing you can think of.

"I killed a man last year on the road from Tiverton to Edenford. I didn't mean to kill him. He attacked me and I defended myself. No one knows I did it." Eliot began to weep. Real tears.

"If I may!" David Cooper was on his feet. "I'm from Edenford. I knew the man who was killed. And the killing was brutal, sadistic. Certainly not an act of self-defense."

Eliot looked horrified. His bulging eyes were white with fear. He looked as if he was about to lose control. "I don't know anything about that! Honest, I don't!" He was weeping profusely now. "He came at me with a knife and knocked me to the ground. Just as he was about to stab me, I hit him in the face with a rock. No one else was around! I left him there in the middle of the road. You've got to believe me!"

John Winthrop stood in front now. He addressed David Cooper, "Could someone else have brutalized the body?"

Cooper shook his head. "I don't know. Elkins, the man who was killed, had been dead for several days when his body was found."

Winthrop: "Is there any evidence of which you are aware that would discredit this man's testimony? Was this Elkins known as a highwayman?"

Cooper: "He was a groundskeeper for Lord Chesterfield."

Winthrop: "Can you attest to the good character of the man?"

Cooper: "No. He was a crude, disreputable man."

Winthrop to Eliot: "If no one knew this, why tell us now?"

There were several moments of sniffing and nose-wiping before Eliot could continue. "Dreams of that horrible day have been haunting me."

The Reverend Higginson entered the public conversation. "Have you confessed this to God?"

Eliot smiled weakly and wiped his nose again. "Oh, yes," he said. "In fact, if there was anything good to come from that day, it was my salvation." At this point Eliot deliberately looked toward the back of the congregation, directly at Drew. "He was my inspiration."

All eyes turned to Drew Morgan.

"You see, both of us were Laud's boys," Eliot continued. "I saw how the execution of Christopher Matthews changed Drew. He had everything the king and the bishop could offer him laid at his feet. And he threw it all away! I couldn't understand it! Then I saw the change in Drew Morgan's life and I knew I wanted to be just like him. I asked Jesus Christ to be my Savior too. I renounced the bishop and ran away. Even now the bishop is hunting me. If he finds me, he'll kill me. All I want out of life now is to find a place where I can live in peace and serve my Lord. But I can see now that this isn't the place. I've killed a man. I'm not worthy to live among good people like you. I'll go back to England on the next ship and trust God to protect me from Bishop Laud."

Drew was seething. This was textbook procedure. Confess to them, then tell them you're not worthy to live with them, promise to leave, and they'll beg you to stay. And that's exactly what was going to happen. Drew could see it in the eyes of the congregation.

"He's lying!" Drew shouted. "He murdered Shubal Elkins in cold blood. He's still working with Bishop Laud. And he's here to destroy the colony!"

No sooner were the words out of his mouth than Drew knew he'd made a mistake. He'd played right into Eliot's hands. "*Once you confess, they'll defend you,*" Eliot had told him. "*They'll defend you to the death.*"

Winthrop: "Do you have any evidence to support your claims, Master Morgan?"

Drew: "Eliot told me himself, just yesterday, that he'd come to destroy the colony."

Eliot: "Drew, why are you doing this? Why would you say

something untrue like that? I thought you were my friend. I'm a Christian today because of you!"

Winthrop: "Did anyone else hear your conversation?"

Drew: "No."

Eliot: "As God is my witness, I don't know why Drew would falsely accuse me. Drew, have I injured you in some way? Is it because I've been seeing Miss Jenny Matthews? If it hurts you, I'll stop seeing her."

Winthrop: "The question remains, what are we to do with Master Venner until we can verify his innocence?"

Roger Williams stood. "I've done it once privately, now I'll do it publicly. I can attest to Master Venner's spirituality. Having journeyed with him aboard the *Lyon* to the colony, I found him to be a decent fellow with a deep interest in spiritual things. In my opinion, unless there is someone who can accuse Master Venner of wrongdoing here in the colonies, it would be unjust for us to detain him during the time it would take to verify his story. And even if we discover the worst, what then? Look at the man!"

The congregation saw a humbled, broken Eliot Venner standing before them.

"This wouldn't be the first time God took a rascal and changed him into a godly man. Have we forgotten our Bible lessons? Moses was a murderer, yet God used him to lead the Israelites to the Promised Land. King David was not only a murderer but an adulterer as well; yet the most precious of the psalms flowed from his pen and he was called a man after God's own heart! I say we should let the grace of God do its work in this man, and when we get the facts from England, then we can deal with any outstanding criminal issues."

The congregation chose to follow Williams' advice. Since no one brought charge of misconduct against Eliot, he was allowed to remain free. Upon dismissal, the congregation flocked to him. They told him how they admired his courage for making his confession and urged him to stay in Boston. They promised to pray with him for Drew, that God would forgive his jealous spirit. Jenny Matthews stood by Eliot's side, holding his hand.

There were side conversations that drifted in Drew's direction. Some of the men who sat daily under the meeting tree recalled seeing Drew and the Matthews girl walk into the woods together. They commented on how she was always seen hanging on him since they arrived and how he built a house for her and her sister. No wonder he hated Eliot, now that the Matthews girl turned her attention to Eliot.

Drew stood alone. Those who were crowded around Eliot steered a wide course around Drew as they left. As he turned to leave, he heard his name called.

Leading an entourage, Eliot Venner approached him. Arms widespread, he embraced Drew. "I forgive you, brother," he said. "I only pray that we can be close friends." Leaning close to Drew's ear, he whispered, "You can't stop me."

Someone matched his stride. Drew looked up and saw the familiar face of David Cooper.

"A familiar performance," he said. "Seems like I witnessed a similar one in Edenford not long ago."

"Step by step, just like he taught me." Drew looked at the cobbler. "You don't believe him?"

"Let's just say I've learned to trust you."

Drew stopped. "Thank you," he said. "That means a lot to me."

"And Eliot told you he came here to destroy the colony?"

"Yesterday, when I told him to stay away from Jenny."

"What's his plan?"

"I don't know."

The cobbler let out a big sigh. "We've got a problem."

"There's one thing I'm counting on," Drew said.

"What's that?"

"Eliot is wild. It strains him to act like a good Christian. He can't do it for long. There comes a point when he has to drink and go wild. He goes after women and..." Drew paused. "... he kills things. He likes to kill things."

"Shubal Elkins," the cobbler said.

Drew nodded. "Shubal Elkins."

As Drew expected, Jenny was furious with him.

"How could you stand there and say things like that against him?" Jenny screamed.

It was the afternoon of Eliot's "confession." This discussion couldn't be avoided. So Drew walked up the hill to Nell and Jenny's house. Somehow he had to convince Jenny to stay away from Eliot.

"You don't know him like I do!" Drew insisted. He was standing by the hearth. Jenny was standing opposite him, angry and close to tears. Nell sat on the table bench facing toward them with her back to the table.

"You're talking about the old Eliot! He's changed!"

"Jenny, I'm asking you to believe me. Eliot told me he only wants to hurt you to get back at me. That's what he's here for. His confession, his behavior, it's all a performance! He's a dangerous man!"

Jenny began weeping. "He's a good, gentle man," she said softly. "All his life he's been mistreated because he was poor, because of the way he looks; but none of that matters now. The old has gone. This is a new Eliot."

"Nothing's changed! It's an act!" Drew shouted.

"That's exactly what everyone in Edenford said about you!" Jenny shouted back at him. "I was the only one who believed in you! And now I feel the same way about Eliot You're wrong about him and I'll prove it to you!"

Drew was stymied. How could he argue with her? If it

weren't for her faith in him, he would never have regained the trust of the Edenford Puritans. But she was wrong about Eliot. Dangerously wrong.

Memories of Jenny and Edenford flashed in his mind. The first time he saw her she flew down the stairs and leaped into her father's arms, peeking at him from around her father's shoulder with that pixie grin of hers; the way she giggled to the point of tears when he read aloud the Song of Solomon; her tender kiss under the canopy of hair when he was recuperating; her fierce commitment to Nell's well-being on the voyage over. She was so full of life, so caring. She deserved happiness. Drew ached for her. There had to be some way to save her from her own innocence.

"I agree with Drew," Nell said. She rose from the bench, her hands folded delicately in front of her. The tone of her voice was low, motherly. "It wouldn't hurt to stay away from him for a while. If what Drew says is true, it will become evident soon enough."

Jenny recoiled. Her chin quivered and she began to weep. "Stop treating me like a child! All these years," she cried, "all these years I've loved you, listened to you, supported you. When everyone expected you to marry James, I was there for you! When Poppa was arrested and you had nightmares every night, I was there to comfort you!" Her tears flowed freely. Her voice trembled, at times failing her. "Of all people, I thought at least you . . . at least you would know what it was like . . . for no one . . . to understand."

Nell was crying with her now. "Jenny, I only want the best for you. I don't want you to get hurt!"

"You just don't want me to be happy!" Jenny screamed.

"That's not true!"

"It is true! You will always have Drew! Who do I have?"

Drew couldn't help but take pleasure in Jenny's statement, even if only for an instant. *You will always have Drew.* She could only be referring to Drew's devotion to Nell, but then again, she could be revealing a bit of confidence passed between two sisters. *Does Jenny know something I don't?*

"Jenny, dear. We have each other. We always will."

Jenny laughed mockingly. "Well, that's great for you! You have me and you have Drew and what am I supposed to do? Stand to the side and be content while the two of you finally admit you love each other, get married, and have children? Well, that's not good enough! I want a husband and a family too! And if the man I marry doesn't measure up to your standards, so be it! It's my decision, not yours!"

Jenny ran from the house. Nell looked hopelessly at Drew, then ran upstairs. Drew found himself alone in the sitting room. For a long time he waited, hoping Nell would come back downstairs. She didn't, so he went home.

Eliot's boast haunted him: *"There's nothing you can do to stop me!"*

The next day Drew began tracking Eliot's activities. On the second day, Drew lost him. Eliot had disappeared.

For two weeks Eliot Venner was seen by no one in Boston. When he returned, he was buried under a load of furs and pelts. He'd been out trapping, he said. He sold his catch and went back out for more. He brought back good quality furs and fast gained a reputation for being one of the best trappers in the colony. Of course, traders loved him—he became one of their regular suppliers. Together the traders and Eliot were getting rich.

Sassacus and Drew sat in Drew's wigwam. So many people in the colony were still upset with Drew for the way he'd treated Eliot that it was good to spend an evening with someone who accepted him as a friend. They'd eaten a meal of clams that Sassacus brought and Drew cooked.

After the meal, Sassacus told Drew that there was dissension in the Pequot tribe. Some were unhappy with the British settlers—each year more colonists came wanting more land. Already the Pequots were squeezed between Narragansett Bay and the Connecticut River. Now the colonists were squeezing them from the east. Also there was unrest between the Pequots and the Mohegans. For years they had lived under joint rule, but a faction among the Mohegans wanted independence.

"These are troubled times," he concluded.

"For us too," Drew added.

"And for the forest animals," said Sassacus. "A demon haunts the forest. Our braves have found rabbits and raccoons and other animals staked to trees, their bellies slit, their eyes gouged out."

"What else have you seen or heard?"

"I have seen only the animals, but others have talked to Dutch and French traders. Someone is killing their trappers, stealing their furs and pelts. They blame us, but we don't do it."

Eliot. It strains him to conform. He has to run wild. He likes to kill.

The report from Sassacus explained Eliot's absences, and how a London city boy could become a successful trapper in such a short time. Drew sighed a heavy sigh. There was no consolation in being right when no one would listen to him. Eliot was loose. The killing had begun.

Chapter 27

ELIOT Venner and Jenny Matthews were married on the second week of November, two weeks before the first heavy snow of the season.

The wedding was held under the meeting tree. The bride and groom were all smiles as they exchanged vows. Rings were not exchanged. It was a papist symbol and they no longer had to live under the invisible hand of Catholic influence.

Nell stood beside her little sister. Throughout the ceremony, they glanced at each other frequently, smiling, sharing the moment. It was as it should be, the two of them together. They'd spent countless hours together in front of the window which opened out to High Street making lace, talking, gossiping, praying. They were a close family, always supportive of one another. It wouldn't have been right for Jenny to get married without Nell at her side. And Nell did her best not to do anything that would tarnish her sister's wedding. But there were unguarded moments—moments Jenny never saw—when a look of fear would cross Nell's face, as if she was having a premonition of danger.

For the Boston colony the wedding was a reason to celebrate, to give thanks, and to look to the future. Eliot and Jenny's children would be the first of a new generation to be born in the colony.

Drew couldn't share their excitement. He was feeling much the same way he had felt standing at the foot of the scaffold on Tower Hill. There, it was Bishop Laud and Christopher Matthews, the victor and the vanquished; here, it was Eliot Venner and Jenny Matthews, the beast and his prey. *And it is my fault. It was my pride, my thirst for glory, my cursed vanity that led the predators to the home of the Matthews.*

For a moment, Drew wished he wasn't a Christian. The solution would have been easy then; he could have killed Eliot and this wouldn't be happening now! He clenched his teeth and fists, wanting to curse. *Just for a minute, Lord,* he prayed, *let me play by their rules. I can fix this! The only reason Eliot is getting away with this is because he knows my Christian faith won't let me come after him! Lord, free me from my commitment to You for one minute, that's all I ask!*

God's answer to his prayer entered Drew's mind in the form of a familiar Scripture passage, "Not by might, nor by power, but by My Spirit, saith the Lord of Hosts!" It was the passage Jenny's father had quoted when the men of Edenford wanted to use force against Laud; Matthews used it again on the scaffold before he died. *Christopher Matthews lived, and died believing the verse. So must I.* Drew unclenched his fists.

Following the ceremony, Jenny moved away from the well-wishers and came to where Drew was standing off to the side. Her long brown hair swished from side to side as she approached and flashes of light sparkled in her eyes. She wore her pixieish smile and Drew was dismayed at how it still stirred him.

"Drew! I'm so glad you came to my wedding!" She wrapped her arms around him and squeezed tenderly.

Her hair smelled fresh, her warmth against him was almost more than he could bear. Leaning his cheek against her forehead, he held her close.

"Eliot and I are going to be so happy!" Jenny said. "You'll

see, Drew, he's a good man. And we'll invite you and Nell for dinner." She broke away from the embrace to look up at him. "She does love you, Drew."

"Jenny, I never wanted to hurt you," Drew said.

"I know that now." She smiled at him, her eyes moist. "And it worked out for the best! You have Nell. I have Eliot."

Drew pulled her close to him. *He can't have her. He can't have her.* Drew said over and over to himself. *If I don't let go . . .*

"Jenny!" It was Eliot. "Jenny, come here a minute. I want you to see something."

Jenny Venner pulled away from Drew to go to her husband.

"God be with you, Jenny," Drew said.

For the second time in as many months Drew climbed the small hill to the house he built for Nell and Jenny, where Nell now was living alone. It was Sunday afternoon and Nell had invited him to dinner. Because of her chronicles of the colony, he'd anticipated the previous invitation. This one came as a surprise.

The bay stretched lazily toward the horizon. The trees were bare now. It was late October. Drew hoped the afternoon would be uncomplicated. A ridiculous hope, considering the history of their relationship. It was a selfish wish; he just didn't need any more aggravation right now.

He and David Cooper had gone to Winthrop and expressed their concerns to the governor regarding Sassacus' "demon." The cobbler went along to verify the grisly details of the Edenford killing. As Drew was relaying the information, he wished he'd brought Sassacus with him too, since his report was secondhand information. As it turned out, the governor had already heard about the bizarre mutilations from other Indians and trappers. Winthrop acknowledged the incidents were similar and found it coincidental that the events both occurred when Eliot was in the territory. But there was nothing he could do without direct evidence. When Drew pressed the point, the governor retorted that Drew was in the vicinity of both incidents too. For all he knew, Drew was the one doing the killings. Another attempt to stop Eliot, another failure.

Please, Lord, Drew prayed as he neared Nell's house, *all I'm asking for is a pleasant afternoon.*

Just then, the door to the house opened and a redheaded giant emerged. James Cooper. Nell was right behind him. Neither of them saw Drew. James turned to say good-bye and Nell hugged him. The giant returned her hug with his big paws, too tightly for Drew's taste.

"Thank you," Nell said, smiling. "That's very sweet."

It wasn't until James turned to leave that they noticed Drew. James didn't say anything as he passed by; he just smiled a goofy grin and raised his bushy red eyebrows.

"Come in, Master Morgan!" Nell smiled sweetly.

"What was he doing here?" Drew demanded.

Her eyes flashed anger. "Since when do I have to ask your permission to see anyone?"

Not a good start, Drew, he said to himself. To Nell, "You're right. I'm sorry. Please forgive me, my emotions are on edge. . . ." He didn't say the rest of the sentence out loud, but he thought, *especially when it concerns you.*

"Apology accepted," she said. Her words forgave him, but her tone was icy.

The sitting room was empty when he entered. "Who else will be joining us?" he asked.

"No one. Just us."

He thought of reminding her of several things she'd said the last time they were alone in this room together. Things like, "*It wouldn't be fitting if the neighbors knew we were alone,*" and, "*I would have invited the Ramsdens if I had known Jenny wouldn't be here.*" But he said nothing. He wanted it to be a pleasant afternoon.

The meal was tasty. Baked cod, bread, corn. Nell was cordial, even warm to him. Drew was perplexed, but he was enjoying himself.

"I suppose you want to interview me some more for your journal," he said.

She was clearing the table. He was looking for something to do with his hands.

"No," she said.

"Oh," he said. He picked up a spoon and tapped it rhythmically on the tabletop. She took the spoon from him and placed it with the rest of the dishes. Their backs were to each other; she at the dishes, he at the table.

"I'm thinking about returning to England," she said.

"You can't mean it!" Drew jumped to his feet.

Nell kept her back to him. "That's why James was here," she said. "He's going back in the spring. He doesn't like it here. I could go with him."

"But you told me you don't love him!" Drew cried.

"I *don't* love him!" Nell swung around and looked at Drew like he was a dunce. "I'm not going back so I can be with James! We would just sail together, as friends."

"I can't believe you want to go back to England!" Drew shouted. "What about Bishop Laud?"

"What can he do to me that can't happen to me in this wretched place?" she shouted. The more she spoke, the more she lost emotional control. "If you're right about Eliot, what difference does it make where I live? He can kill me here or in England! Besides, if he doesn't kill me, the Indians will, or I'll starve to death, or die from disease!" She wept uncontrollably. "There's nothing for me here!" she shouted. "Nothing but pain and suffering and death! I have no family. . . . I've lost Jenny. . . . Eliot's going to hurt her, Drew! I know it—I can sense it. I can't stand by and watch that happen. . . . It will kill me to see her hurt. . . . It will kill me!"

She fell into his arms, sobbing.

As he held her, the only sound in the room was that of her sobbing.

"If you go back to England," he said softly, "I'll go with you."

She pulled away and looked into his eyes. Her face was drenched from the tears. She didn't say anything, she just looked and looked.

"I've been thinking a lot about Edenford," she said. She found a handkerchief and sat at the table.

Drew sat beside her. He chuckled.

"What?"

"I just remembered the time you asked me to describe God."

"I asked you to tell me what you believed in," she corrected, enjoying the recollection. "And you said God lived in the trees!"

"I was pointing toward heaven!" Drew protested.

They both laughed.

"And I'll never forget the look on your face when you started reading the Song of Solomon out loud to Jenny and me," she said.

"You tricked me into reading it!"

"Only because you wanted to force that awful King James translation on us!"

They both stared at the table in silence, lost in thoughts of Edenford.

"I remember the time you told me you would never leave Edenford," Drew said.

"I never wanted to," she said softly.

There was an uneasy pause between them. Nell scratched the end of one fingernail with another. Drew pushed a crumb around the table with his finger.

"Drew, I'm so afraid here," she said.

"I know."

"You'd really go back to England with me?"

"If you left, there would be nothing to keep me here."

"But I can go back safely. No one there knows I'm really Justin. If you go back, Laud will surely try to kill you!"

"I know."

"And you'd still go back?"

Drew nodded.

Nell focused on a fingernail as she spoke. "I remember the look on your face when I told you James asked me to marry him."

"I was devastated," Drew said.

"If I remember correctly, you congratulated me!"

"What else could I do?"

"You could have forbidden me to marry him."

Drew laughed. "Would you have obeyed me?"

"No." Nell laughed.

Drew pushed the bread crumb on the table. "I remember when you told me you loved me," he said.

For the longest time Nell studied her fingernail. She began to weep softly. Raising her head, she brushed away a tear. "I still do," she whispered.

Drew couldn't believe he heard right. He was struck dumb.

Nell began laughing, then covered her mouth with her hand. "You should see your face right now, Master Morgan!"

"You love me?"

"Yes, Drew. My dear Drew."

He took her in his arms, kissing her feverishly, holding her with all his strength for fear that something or someone would separate them.

"Drew, my dear Drew, can you ever forgive me?" Nell cried between kisses.

"Shhh. It's all right!"

"I hated you when Father died. I blamed you."

Drew stroked her hair. "That doesn't matter now."

"I didn't want to forgive you, but I always loved you."

"Nothing," he swore, "nothing will ever separate us again!"

It was late when Drew strolled down the hill from Nell's house toward his hut. He wanted to shout. He wanted to sing. He wanted to tell someone, anyone, that Nell Matthews loved him. Then he started laughing. Halfway down the hill, he stood with his hands on his hips and looked heavenward. "You're incredible!" he shouted heavenward. "All I asked for was a pleasant afternoon!"

Sassacus joined Drew and Nell the following Sunday during the morning worship service and for dinner afterward. The Indian had shown thoughtful interest in the God of the British settlers. He had become a regular at the worship services so that he knew when to stand and when to sit, was beginning to try some of the songs. He followed the Bible reading and sermon intently even though he still understood less than half what was being said, and closed his eyes through the entire prayer (after a while Drew stopped checking).

On this particular Sunday, Sassacus was mightily distracted. Everything was fine as the service began. Reverend Higginson prayed the invocation and they had just finished singing the first hymn. Eliot and Jenny hadn't arrived yet, but it wasn't unusual for the two of them to come late. When the hymn was finished and the people began to sit down, Jenny and Eliot arrived. With them was another Indian.

Pleased looks passed through the congregation as the people glanced back and forth from Drew, Nell, and their Indian friend to Eliot, Jenny, and their Indian friend. Eliot had given the community every reason to be proud of him. He made an excellent living as a trapper, had bought a home from a wealthy family who had returned to England, married one of the respected Matthews girls, attended all church and social functions when he was home, and now was following Drew's example in developing friendly relationships with the Indians. The people of Boston couldn't understand why Drew wasn't as proud of Eliot as they were.

In their Sunday morning pride they failed to notice the reaction of Sassacus to the arrival of the trio. Drew's friend tensed the moment he saw the other Indian and for the remainder of the service was on edge. During the service Drew leaned over toward him and asked what was wrong. "Later," Sassacus replied. Yet he remained so agitated that Drew doubted he heard any of the sermon. The Indian wasn't even aware that the service had ended until people rose to leave.

"Drew! Nell!" Eliot motioned for them to join him. Jenny hung on his arm, but from the look on her face it wasn't from devotion. She kept her head lowered, blinking rapidly. Her chin quivered.

Uncas, surrounded by church members, was nervously preoccupied with the swarm of people who wanted to grab his hand and pump it.

Sassacus stood by himself off to the side. When Drew motioned for him to join them, he refused, preferring to keep a distance, rigid and watchful.

"I'd like you to meet someone," Eliot said, as Drew and Nell approached.

Drew hated it. Eliot flaunted his position. Like a smiling vulture, he took every opportunity to mock his prey. Overtly warm and cheerful to him in public, with Jenny always by his side, Drew didn't miss Eliot's hidden message: *There's nothing you can do to stop me.*

"I'd like you to meet a friend of mine," Eliot gushed. "Drew Morgan, this is Uncas. Uncas is a Mohegan."

Drew extended his hand. The unsmiling Indian squeezed until Drew showed a hint of pain. Nell didn't offer her hand. The cold eyes of the Mohegan slid over to her. The Indian studied her with a look that made her feel uncomfortable.

"Maybe you and I ought to become missionaries to these Indians!" Eliot said loud enough for other people to hear.

While Eliot watched for the expected favorable response, Uncas eyed Sassacus standing far off. The Mohegan's eyes were rock.

Drew turned his attention to Jenny. "How are you doing?"

"We couldn't be happier!" Eliot answered for her, patting her hand on his arm. "She's a terrific woman!"

Jenny didn't say anything. When she looked up, Drew saw a bruise under one eye. It was all he could do to keep from slugging Eliot.

As it turned out, it wasn't a good day to have company for dinner. Drew and Nell desperately needed to talk about Jenny's abuse. The unspoken topic preoccupied their thoughts the entire meal. Sassacus was noticeably quiet too. Drew had always known him to be a pensive man, more comfortable with listening and observing than with speaking. But today he hardly said a word after they entered the house.

"You don't like Uncas, do you?" Drew asked as they ate.

"Not a good man."

"Do you think he is interested in learning about God?" Nell asked.

"Uncas interested only in Uncas."

"Then why do you think he came to church?" Nell asked.

Sassacus stared at his plate. "Don't know," he said.

Several times during dinner the three of them unsuccessfully tried to initiate happier conversation. They offered opinions about when they thought first snowfall would arrive, since it came late the previous year. Sassacus seemed pleased to hear that the colony was in much better shape to survive the winter. Drew and Nell smiled as Sassacus told them he had his eye on a certain Indian maiden. He expected to be sharing his hut with her by next winter.

Between the failed attempts to sustain pleasant conversation, Drew and Nell learned that Uncas was a sub-chief of the council and the leader of the disgruntled Mohegan faction that wanted to break the Pequot-Mohegan alliance. There were rumors of an armed uprising. Sassacus took the rumors seriously, based on Uncas' reputation. He was known as a warrior with no heart. He was unfeeling and ruthless, and worst of all, ambitious. Uncas wanted to be sole chief of the Mohegans.

Sassacus didn't stay long after dinner. He graciously thanked his hosts and returned to the woods.

"Drew, I'm frightened! What are we going to do?" Nell asked.

As they sat before the fire, Drew buried his head in her hair.

"Me too," he said. "We'll just have to leave it in God's hands and wait for an opportunity."

"But he hit her!"

"I know," he said softly. "I know."

"Can't we do something?"

"A lot of men hit their wives," Drew said. "It's not a crime."

Flames crackled in front of them, a cozy warm fire that kept the outside chill at a distance. Inside the house, in front of the fire, in each other's arms, this was the only place they felt secure. It was here that they had made the decision to remain in the colony. They were not safe, no matter where they lived, so they might as well stay here. At least they had each other; of that they were finally sure.

"Do you think he'll kill her?" Nell asked.

"It's his nature to hurt people."

"You didn't answer my question."

Maybe it was wishful thinking, but Drew didn't think Eliot would kill Jenny. His scheme was bigger than Jenny. "No, I don't think so. But we've got to find a way for her to communicate with us if she needs our help."

Nell turned around to face him, eager to do something, anything besides sit around helplessly.

"We need to do this right away," Drew said, "because eventually, Eliot's going to shut Jenny away from us."

"Why?"

"She's the closest to him. Already she's beginning to see who he really is. That's a threat to him. He can't risk letting her talk to anyone."

Nell nodded in understanding.

Drew explained to Nell the Bible code he and the bishop had used.

"It won't work," Nell said immediately.

"Why not?"

"We don't have the same translations," she said. "Jenny and I have the Geneva Bible. You have that *other* translation."

Drew ignored the obvious slur on his translation. "Then she'll have to send the message only to you, or use entire verses or something like that. If we're aware of the problem, we can work around it."

Next, he showed her how a message looked when coded.

"So that's what that paper was in your Bible!"

Drew looked at her. "You saw the coded message in my Bible?"

She nodded. "When Poppa left it in his study. I didn't

know what it was and I didn't care."

"Did you see the message from Eliot too?"

"Are you implying I was snooping through your private things, Master Morgan? I found the coded message by accident."

His tone became exaggerated, playful. "You were reading the notorious, forbidden, scandalous King James version of the Bible secretly in your father's study?"

"I was curious!" she defended herself.

They interrupted their planning with a few kisses.

Then Drew outlined the dangers of the note plan. Eliot would be suspicious if he saw Jenny passing a note to Drew or Nell. They needed someone neutral. They couldn't use the Coopers because there was an Edenford connection. They needed someone they could trust who had no connection with Edenford. The Ramsdens. Perfect. As far as they knew, Eliot was not aware of any connection between them and the Ramsdens.

"Eliot must not be allowed to see a coded message!" Drew warned. "Although he couldn't translate it, he's seen the code before and would immediately associate it with me!"

"We'll just have to pray that God will blind his eyes!" Nell said.

The air was biting as Drew made his way down the hillside toward his hut. It wouldn't be long before the first snow of winter fell. The sky was clear and a half-moon shone overhead. Drew couldn't get over how small the moon looked in Boston. It was so much larger in England.

Something was wrong at his wigwam. Was someone standing by it? He couldn't quite make out a figure. He quickened his step, straining his eyes toward the hut. Then he ran. It was a person. Not standing, but leaning against the hut. Leaning backward. He ran faster.

"O Lord, please, no!" he cried.

Sassacus was tied to the outside of Drew's wigwam. He was stretched against the side, legs and arms spread apart wide. There was no movement.

As Drew got closer, the grisly sight unfolded. Stripped of all clothing, his flesh was cut all over. Muscles, normally hidden beneath the skin, were exposed to open air. Hundreds of wounds seeped with blood. Shallow breaths made his slit cheek flutter, showing his teeth and making him look like a fish on the ground trying to breath through its gills.

There were so many wounds and so little sign of life that Drew didn't know where to begin. He fought to untie a hand.

"Sassacus! Hold on! I'll get help!"

Eyes blinked open. His back arched against the hut, he looked straight ahead at the stars.

"Unnn . . . nnksss."

Drew could barely hear him. "I'll have you down in a minute." But he was lying. The sight of his friend had unnerved him. Drew's hands were fiddling with the leather tongs, but he was making absolutely no progress untying them.

"Unn . . . kassss," Sassacus said again.

"Uncas? Uncas did this to you?"

The Indian nodded.

"Anyone else?"

Another nod.

"Sassacus, did Eliot Venner do this to you?"

The Indian nodded again.

"Paaa . . . fff . . . me."

"Hold on, Sassacus," Drew cried, as he fought the knot.

"Praaa . . . fo . . . me."

"Pray for you?"

Sassacus nodded. His head slumped to the side. Drew's friend was dead.

Out of his mind with rage, Drew ran the length of the settlement to Eliot's house. He pounded on the door, shouting Eliot's name, challenging him to come out. No one answered. He ran around the house banging on the shuttered windows. No response. Tearing a limb from a tree, Drew used it as battering ram to force his way through the front door. The house was completely dark. He ran from room to room, shouting Eliot's name.

The Venners weren't home.

Chapter 28

WHEN Eliot returned to the colony a week later, he was loaded down with pelts. Said he'd been out trapping and took his wife with him to show her what he did when he went away. Part of the time she stayed with the Pequots. When told of the murder of Sassacus, he performed a remarkably believable role of a shocked and grieving friend. Real enough to satisfy most everyone in the colony. Said he wasn't surprised that Uncas had a part in it. The two had parted ways. According to Eliot, the Indian was crazy and dangerous.

Despite Drew's objections, Governor Winthrop could find no reason to charge Eliot with the death of Sassacus. According to Drew's testimony, the Indian never spoke Eliot's name when he died. A nod from an Indian in obvious agony was hardly enough evidence to try a man for murder.

Under the pretense of taking Jenny sewing materials to make samplers, Nell visited the Venner house. Eliot didn't want Nell to come into the house and he said he'd give the materials to Jenny. Nell insisted on seeing her sister. Although she made it into the house, Eliot stayed in the sitting room with them. Nell took her time demonstrating new stitches and sewing techniques to her sister. Eliot was obviously bored, but stayed nearby nonetheless. He interrupted the ladies once, demanding that Jenny pour him an ale. She jumped at his command, stopping herself midsentence to get her husband his drink. Eliot finished his tankard of ale while the ladies talked. Nell suggested Jenny get her husband another one, and soon after that another.

Nell told her sister about the code when Eliot went outside to relieve himself.

"How did she look?" Drew asked.

Nell's hands were shaking. She fought back tears. "She's scared to death of him, Drew. You would hardly recognize her. She's thin and pale. She flinches every time he speaks or comes near her. She never smiles. There's no life in her eyes. She told me that Eliot will hurt her because I came to visit her." Nell could hold back the tears no longer. "I'm just glad Poppa isn't alive to see her like this!"

The winter of 1631 was a difficult one. During January and most of February, the snow was heavy. Women were rarely seen outside the home; their duties were inside, cooking and nursing the sick. There were few social occasions, so Jenny Venner's absence stirred little concern among the colonists.

Drew and Nell didn't see Jenny again until the first Sunday of March at a church service. She and Eliot arrived late. If it wasn't for the fact that she came with Eliot, Nell wouldn't have recognized her sister. She was white and drawn, her cheeks were hollow, and a dark gray shade surrounded her sunken eyes. She wore her right arm in a sling; an accident, Eliot explained; she slipped on the stairs and broke it when she tried to stop her fall. During the entire service, Jenny never looked up, never smiled.

In the spring Eliot went trapping, though it wasn't his usual two- or three-week stints. This spring he limited his trips to a day, two days at the most.

On one occasion Nell watched him head into the woods, waited an hour, then ran to the house to see Jenny. The door was bolted shut from the outside and the latch was tied with strips of leather. All the window shutters were nailed shut. Nell knocked and identified herself. Jenny answered weakly from behind the door. She sounded ill. Her voice was hoarse, she sniffed loudly and couldn't complete a sentence without coughing violently. Her cough made a deep rattling sound in her chest. When Nell said she was going to untie the door and come in. Jenny flew into hysterics. She pleaded with Nell to leave. When Nell refused, Jenny became so distraught that at times her language was unintelligible. She said that if Eliot learned Nell had been there, he'd kill both her and Drew. Jenny begged Nell to leave. The only way Nell could get Jenny to calm down was by promising to leave.

When Nell returned home she was so angry, she cried the rest of the day. Drew attempted to see Jenny too, but with similar results.

It was Mary Ramsden who eventually succeeded. She convinced Jenny to allow her to pry open a shutter and pass in food and medicine. When Eliot came home and discovered that the shutter had been pried open, he beat his wife.

For a month and a half no one in the colony saw Jenny. During that time Nell made it a point to walk by the Venner house every day that Eliot was gone. She paused just long enough at a side shutter to slip a piece of paper through the crack. Every day there was a different message and a Scripture verse. She told her sister how much she loved her, and reminded her of God's love. Most of the Scripture passages were words of comfort from the Psalms, like, "Yea, though I should walk through the valley of the shadow of death, I will fear no evil: for Thou art with me: Thy rod and Thy staff, they comfort me." Nell only hoped her sister would think to burn the messages after reading them so that Eliot wouldn't find them.

One day, while she was stuffing the paper through the crack, she heard a weak voice from the other side.

"Nell?"

"O Jenny! It's so good to hear you! How are you, darling?"

"I saw Poppa last night, Nell."

"Poppa?"

"He was calling to me. He said it would be all right, Nell. Poppa said it would be all right."

"Yes, Jenny. It will be all right."

"Nell?"

"Yes, Jenny?"

"He told me he loved me."

"Yes, Jenny. Poppa loves you. And so do I."

Boston colony was booming. It was the building season and everyone was busily making their mark on the town's expanding profile. The days were longer and the colonists began to shed their winter clothing. The town was filled with promise. The people of Massachusetts Bay were fulfilling their dream of turning the wilderness into God's city.

Drew emerged from his hut and stretched his aching muscles. It was dusk and he was hungry. It had been an interesting day, a good one. His muscles ached from hauling wood for David Cooper's new cobbler store. The beefy black-haired cobbler was positively giddy about having his own shop. Drew had offered to share his limited construction knowledge with Cooper, since the cobbler couldn't afford to hire one of the overpriced professionals. Then, in the middle of the working day, John Winthrop and Alex Hutchinson, a member of the colonial council, pulled Drew aside, and told him the people of Boston were impressed with him. The two men wanted Drew to consider becoming a member of the council. Drew could hardly wait to get over to Nell's for dinner and tell her the news.

'Drew! Drew!" Mary Ramsden ran toward him with a picture frame of some kind in her hand. She could hardly speak for lack of breath.

"Jenny..." she said.

Drew grabbed Mary by the shoulders. "What about Jenny?" he shouted.

Mary gasped for air. "... gave me this." She held up a framed sampler. It was a picture of a house with sun and clouds overhead.

Between gasps Mary said, "I was walking by the house... she motioned to me from a window... handed me this. Then Eliot appeared behind her... she was scared... so scared." Mary took a deep breath. "She said it was for me, a thank you for helping her when she was sick." Another deep breath. "But I think there's a coded message in it."

"What makes you think that?"

"She said she was particularly proud of the border. Said it twice. She was scared, Drew. Real scared."

Drew searched the border. It was a series of Xs in brown, yellow, and orange thread. A seemingly random pattern. Nothing special that he could see across the top, down the right side, across the bott... there! On the bottom. Three numbers—40, 21, 35.

Drew handed the sampler to Mary. "Wait right here!" He ducked into his hut. A moment later he emerged with his Bible.

"What was the first number?"

Mary studied the bottom of the sampler. "Forty."

Drew counted down the books in the index. "Forty! Matthew. Next number."

"Twenty-one."

Drew turned to Matthew, chapter 21. "Next number!"

"Thirty-five."

He found Matthew 21:35 and read aloud, "And the husbandmen took his servants, and beat one, and killed another, and stoned another."

"God help us!" Mary cried.

"Mary, go get Marshall. Tell him to go to Nell's house. Tell him to take a gun." Mary nodded grimly and ran toward home.

Drew got his musket and loaded it. His hands shook as he filled the pan with powder and loaded the ball. Then he ran toward the Coopers' house.

Little Thomas was playing in a field near the home with friends. It was nearly dark, but it was easy to pick him out from among the other boys by the stiff way he moved. It was doubtful he'd ever fully recover from the vat incident.

"Thomas! Come here quickly!"

"Master Morgan!" The boy ran to greet him.

"Listen to me, Thomas, listen carefully." Drew's tone and serious expression had the boy's immediate attention. "Go home and get your father and James . . ."

"But James is sailing for England tomorrow," the boy interrupted.

"This is more important. Tell them to go to Nell's house. Tell them to take their guns. Tell them Nell needs help. Hurry!"

Thomas ran as quickly as his stiff legs would carry him.

Jenny's message warned only of danger; it didn't say where or when. But for Drew it no longer mattered if Eliot was planning something for tonight, tomorrow night, or next month. This matter was going to be settled tonight.

His first act was to protect Nell. Marshall and the Coopers would do that. He was going to Eliot's house. Jenny wasn't going to spend another night with that man.

The house was dark when he approached it. He circled the house from a distance, looking for any bit of light from between the cracks of the shutters. There wasn't any. He used the tree in front of the house as cover for his approach, holding his musket in front of him with sweaty hands.

He sneaked quietly to the door. It was unlatched and cracked open.

Crash!

He slammed the door open with his shoulder, charging past the stairs into the sitting room. It was so dark he could barely see. He looked for movement of any kind. There was none. No one was there.

His chest was heaving from the strain. Drew waited for his eyes to adjust more fully to the darkness. He tried to wet his lips, but his mouth was dry. There was an eeriness about being in someone else's house in the dark, an eeriness that was compounded knowing it was Eliot Venner's house.

When his eyes adjusted to the details of the room, what he saw made him sick. Dead animals were everywhere . . . lying on the table with their entrails falling to the floor, raccoons, rabbits, squirrels were nailed to the walls as if they'd been crucified.

"Eliot!" he shouted.

Fighting back the rising sickness, Drew charged up the stairway. The upstairs rooms looked like the rest of the house. Stands were toppled. Clothes were thrown everywhere. Drawers hung halfway from their dressers like tongues from a mouth, mocking him. There were mutilated animals everywhere, some of them dressed in Jenny's clothes.

Drew had to steady himself against the wall as he fled downstairs and out of the house.

The fresh air did little to calm him. He had never been more grateful to get out of a house in his life. The only thing to do now was to join the others at Nell's house. They could help him figure out what to do next.

To get to Nell's house, he had to walk back toward his hut near the edge of the forest to reach the road that led up the hill. The town was quiet, as if nothing was wrong, just another peaceful evening in the new world.

He heard a scream from the woods. Jenny!

"Drew, run! He'll kill you!" Jenny at the edge of the woods. Alone. Unable to stand unassisted, she propped herself against a tree with one hand.

Drew ran toward her.

"No!" she screamed. "Run, Drew, run!"

An instant later a heavy hand bolted from behind a tree, striking her to the ground. Jenny let out a whimper as she crumpled to the ground.

To reach her, Drew had to cross a small field.

Eliot Venner appeared. Even from this distance Drew could see the enormous sea of white surrounding his eyes. He was covered with only a breechcloth. He had streaks of paint all over his chest and arms and legs. He grabbed Jenny by the hair and yanked her to her feet. He laughed his hyena laugh as he pulled Jenny into the woods.

"Eliot!" Drew shouted as he ran.

He charged into the woods, looking past trees and bushes listening for a movement that would indicate their direction. There! Eliot was dragging Jenny, his hand across her mouth. Drew could hear her muffled cry.

Keep fighting him, Jenny, and I can catch up with you.

Three strides. A vine pulled taut in front of him caught Drew's foot, sending him flying to the ground, his musket flying even further. Instantly, Indians appeared from around trees. Five. Ten.

Thhhuuuump! Thhhuuuump!

They hit him with clubs. Again and again.

Thhhuuuump! Thhhuuuump! Thhhuuuump!

A crushing blow hit the back of his head; he hovered between conscious thought and unconsciousness. He was aware that his face was in the dirt, everything else was unclear. There were rustling sounds around him. Then sounds. Voices.

Jenny? Jenny crying?

Words he couldn't understand. Different. Men's voices.

"No!"

More rustling.

"First the woman in the house."

Everything went black.

He tasted dirt; pieces of leaves and dirt in a dry mouth. The back of his head felt like it was split open, the front of his head throbbed. The forest. He was still in the forest. But for how long? It was dark and damp. Gunshots. Were those gunshots he heard, just as his senses returned to him?

Crack!

Gunshot! Jenny! No, Nell! The woman in the house!

Drew struggled to his hands and knees. His head hung low like deadweight on the end of a rope. He forced himself to blink back the pain, the nausea that tried to knock him to the ground again. Using his arms he worked himself up the side of a tree. He made it to his feet, with the tree as a support.

His mind screamed at his body to move. *Nell needs me. I promised I would take care of her. She needs me now.*

The musket. He looked around him on the ground. It was gone. His musket was gone!

Drew pushed himself from the tree, half stumbling, half running. He crossed the grassy field toward the scattered English wigwams. Thin wisps of smoke curled upward from the chimneys into a clear sky. Some of the wigwams were dark as he passed them, the people inside asleep. They hadn't heard the shots. Other colonists stood in front of their wigwams, doors open, men holding their wives close to them, all of them staring in the direction of Nell's house. They'd heard the sound but couldn't see anything; a peninsula of trees from the forest blocked their view.

Drew startled the onlookers as he ran past. They wanted to know what was happening. He didn't answer.

He reached the road. It began its incline toward the hill and Nell's house. Faster. He must move faster. His lungs burned. His head pounded. He pushed harder, driven by one thought: *Save Nell. Got to save Nell.*

As he cleared the obstructing tip of the forest, Nell's house came into view. It was dark. The shutters were closed. Tiny slits of light in the cracks of the shutters were the only indication of life. Drew stopped. It looked peaceful enough.

He started forward again. A slow run. His eyes darted back and forth, looking for danger, sudden movement. As he ascended the slope leading to the house, the bay came into his view on the right. It lay tranquil, highlighted by white sparkles of moonlight. The house was still a good distance in front of him. To his left a large field separated the house from the edge of the forest. Nothing moved.

As he got closer, he noticed dark areas on the field. A little closer. Forms, human forms. They were men lying face down. Dead men. One. Two. Three of them. Three dead Indians.

A wild inhuman cry split the air. From the black interior of the forest a charging horse emerged followed by dozens of running Indians. Eliot! His wild red hair flew backward in the wind as he came at Drew.

"Run, boy! Run!"

David Cooper shouted at Drew from the doorway of Nell's house, musket in one hand, his free hand waving, motioning for Drew to run for the house.

Eliot's eyes bulged with rage surrounded by an unholy sea of white; a hideous look of laughter twisted his face. His scream sounded like that of a wounded animal.

Drew ran for the open door, urging his weary legs into motion; his head pounded with each footfall. It was too far. Eliot was coming too fast. He'd never make it. Drew's heart and lungs were on fire as if they would burn through his chest. The Indians were right behind Eliot. All running at him, weapons raised. Eyes of hate fixed on him, yelling. Almost halfway there. They were coming too fast. He couldn't make it.

The shutters on the house flew open.

Blam! Blam!

Muskets spit fire and smoke from the windows of the house.

Dirt kicked up in front of Eliot's horse. One Indian fell to the ground and rolled.

Blam! Blam! Blam!

Eliot's horse crumpled beneath him, sending him sprawling over its head. Another Indian fell.

Fffffthump! An arrow flew in front of Drew, striking a tuft of grass near his feet. He stumbled. Another arrow whizzed past his head.

Drew ducked his head and ran up the steep incline to the porch.

Fffffthump!

He charged past the burly cobbler and into the house. The door slammed behind him. Shutters followed. He'd made it!

Nell flew into his arms. "O Drew, you're safe! Thank God!"

He fought for breath. Nell was choking, almost suffocating him with her hugs. There were smiles all around. The cobbler. Marshall Ramsden. Even James was grinning.

"Thought they had you, son," the cobbler said.

The celebration didn't last long.

Marshall peeked through the crack in the shutters. "They're heading back for the woods," he said.

While Nell doctored Drew's head, they told him about the first attack. Eliot and the Indians crept across the field and were surprised to find an armed welcoming party. Drew told them about the ambush, using Jenny as bait.

"Has anyone seen her?" Drew asked.

They hadn't.

"Why is Eliot doing this?" Marshall asked.

"Eliot's orders are to hurt the people I love," he said.

"Orders?" the cobbler asked.

"Laud. He hasn't forgiven me for choosing Nell and Jenny over him."

The pious cobbler cursed the prelate.

"Drew Morgan!"

The voice came from outside.

"It's Eliot!" Marshall cried, looking through the crack between the shutters. "He's got Jenny!"

Drew ran to the window. Marshall cracked the shutter open wider so Drew could see. Eliot stood at the edge of the forest. He held Jenny in front of him, a knife at her throat.

"I'll kill her!" Eliot shouted. "I'll kill her unless you come out!"

Drew closed the shutter.

"What are you going to do?" the cobbler asked him.

"I have to go out there."

"No!" Nell cried. "No, Drew, please. I don't want to lose you too."

"She's right," said the cobbler. "If you go out there, they'll kill both you and Jenny."

"I've got to try," Drew said. "I promised her father I'd protect her. I've got to try!"

Drew looked at Nell. She didn't have to say anything; he'd studied her face too long—sometimes secretly, sometimes not so secretly—not to know what she was thinking. The resolute look in her steely brown eyes, the way her lips pressed together in a firm line, these things told him she agreed with his decision. He pulled her to him and held her close. It had taken so long for them to get together. He didn't want it to end now. *Please, God, don't let it end now.*

He broke the embrace and headed for the door.

"At least take a weapon!" Marshall cried.

Drew shook his head. "They won't let me get close to her, if I'm carrying a weapon."

"Here. Take this." James thrust a pistol at him.

Drew refused it.

"You can hide it back here," the cobbler said, grabbing the gun. He turned Drew around and stuck it in Drew's waistband at the small of his back.

The wood and metal pistol was bulky and pulled his waistband tight, making it uncomfortable for Drew to walk. He had no idea how he was going to reach for the gun, especially if he needed it in a hurry.

"David had five stones when he went out to meet Goliath," the cobbler said. "You've got only one ball. Make it a good one."

"As I recall, David only needed one stone," Drew said. He opened the door and stepped out. The last thing he saw was Nell on her knees, weeping and praying, as he closed the door behind him.

"We're praying for you, Drew!" The voice startled him. He whirled around. There, lining the edge of the road and facing the forest was a band of colonists, all of them armed.

"We heard the gunfire," John Winthrop explained. Beside the governor were the Reverends Higginson and Williams.

Drew thanked them for their presence and prayers.

The eyes of all the colonists were fixed on him as Drew walked toward the field. As he walked, he surveyed the situation. Eliot stood in front of the trees, shielding himself with Jenny, a knife at her throat. Behind him, an undetermined number of Indians hid behind trees and bushes.

Drew walked to the middle of the field and stopped. His heart almost failed him when he got a closer look at Jenny. Her face and arms were black with dirt and dried blood. Her dress was ripped, her beautiful brown hair matted with dirt and leaves and twigs. Eliot was using her long hair to hold her up, his left hand wrapped around it like a sailor would wrap his hand around a rope. His right hand held a knife against her throat. There were already several red lines across her neck where she'd been cut. Jenny's eyes were wide with fear as she stared out the corners at her captor.

Drew could see some of the Indians better now. He recognized one of them. Uncas.

"Keep coming!" Eliot shouted at Drew.

"No!" Jenny screamed. "Run, Drew!"

Eliot yanked her head back savagely. "Shut up!"

Instinctively, Drew started toward Jenny. Just behind Eliot, several Indians readied their bows Drew stopped. "Let her go, Eliot!"

"Come here or I'll kill her!" Eliot's eyes bulged wider, his cheeks puffed with each breath, sweat dripped from his chin.

"You don't want her! You want me," Drew shouted.

Uncas said something. Drew couldn't make it out. But Eliot did. He whipped his head toward the Indian, causing the knife to cut into Jenny's neck.

"This is my hunt!" he shouted at the Indian.

Jenny whimpered and her legs gave way. Eliot jerked her upright, demanding that she stand. Somehow she found enough strength to obey him.

Drew felt helpless. He had to do something to resolve this now. "Eliot! This is between you and me now!" Drew screamed. "But you'll have to come out here to get me!"

"All right, blue boy," Eliot hissed.

Drew had seen the look before, Eliot always used it to his

advantage, to intimidate, to frighten people. He opened his
bulging white eyes as wide as possible and added a toothy,
wicked grin. He looked like an animal possessed by demons.
With halting steps, Eliot shoved Jenny toward Drew in the
middle of the field until he was just a few feet shy of his
former pupil.

"Drew, I'm so sorry," Jenny whimpered.

Eliot mimicked her voice. "Yes, Drew, we're so sorry.
Soooooo sorry!"

"It's over, Eliot! Let her go!" Drew shouted.

"Over?" Eliot cooed. "It's not over; the fun is just beginning!" He snapped Jenny's head back. Her sharp cry was
followed by a whimpering sound which Eliot obviously
enjoyed.

"You're wrong, Eliot. It's over! Look over there!" Drew
pointed to the armed colonists. "You can't hurt them now.
They know what you are!"

"But I can hurt this one!" Eliot pulled the knife against
Jenny's throat, another fresh red line appeared. A drop of
blood trickled down the blade. For a moment Eliot was mes-
merized by the drop's trek across the shiny blade.

"You've had plenty of chances to kill her and didn't!"
Drew shouted.

Eliot glared at him.

"You didn't kill her because you want me," Drew said.

Eliot grinned. It was a hideous grin. His bulging eyes grew
even wider. "I'd like to let her go!" he said in a singsong
voice. "Can't. Promised Uncas he could have her after I killed
you! Seems only right, doesn't it? I gave you Rosemary. I
give him Jenny." His grin grew larger. "I was right about
Rosemary, wasn't I?"

Drew began circling to his right. "It's either Jenny or me,
Eliot! You can't kill us both. If you want me, you're going to
have to let her go."

Eliot stepped to the side, countering Drew's movement. He jerked the blade. Another trickle of red appeared.

Drew stopped. To his left was the house and the colonists. To the right, the forest and Indians. If he could get Eliot to release Jenny, maybe the colonists could cover her while she ran to the house.

"You failed, Eliot! You could have destroyed the colony, but not now. You could have killed both Jenny and Nell, but not now!" Drew laughed at him. "Think of it, Eliot—all that wasted time, all that time trying to control yourself, trying to act like a decent person. All those wasted months trying to convince people to trust you. And what do you have to show for it? Nothing! You couldn't do it! Bishop Laud's famous infiltrator couldn't act good long enough to complete his mission! You've gained nothing because I outsmarted you! Poor Eliot Venner, the crafty whelp from the streets of London—outsmarted by the son of a rich nobleman!"

Eliot began making animal noises.

Drew laughed again. "You know, you're even more stupid than that fat bishop who plucked you from the streets!" he cried. "Laud thinks he killed Justin! He didn't! Justin escaped. Over there in that house!"

Eliot glanced behind Drew at the house.

"Poor stupid bishop and his inept operative! You killed the wrong person! Christopher Matthews isn't Justin! Nell is Justin!"

Eliot let out an unearthly scream and shoved Jenny at Drew.

Her momentum knocked Drew backward to the ground as Eliot lunged at them with the knife, the gun in Drew's waistband gouged him in the back as he hit the ground hard; Jenny's weight pressed against him as the wild-eyed, dripping face of Eliot Venner plunged toward them. Mustering all his strength Drew rolled Jenny to one side just as the blade plunged into the ground beside his head. The guttural scream of a hunter who hates missing his mark rang in Drew's ears. As Eliot pulled the knife out of the earth for a second attempt, Drew smashed him in the temple with his elbow, knocking him aside.

Jenny. Get her to the house. I've got to get Jenny to the house. Drew scrambled to his feet at the same time as his attacker and positioned himself between Eliot and Jenny; she was still on the ground, groggy, moving slowly; Eliot grinned his yellow-toothed grin as he flashed the knife back and forth while Drew reached down behind him and, without turning his back on Eliot, helped Jenny to her feet. She was weak, so weak, drained of energy; she used Drew to pull herself up, steadying herself against him, clutching his clothes and almost knocking him off balance. Drew wanted to turn and help her, but he couldn't; he had to keep his eyes on Eliot, hold their attacker off with his eyes until Jenny was on her feet, so she could run, run to the house. She was steady now and her hand was against his back. She felt the pistol.

"No!" he shouted at her. "Run! Run for the house!"

Jenny didn't hear; she grabbed the butt of the musket. Drew pushed her hand away. The pistol tumbled to the ground.

"Run for the house!" he shouted. She didn't move; he shouted again.

Ffffffthump! Drew's right leg collapsed under him, he fell to one knee, the shaft of an arrow buried in his thigh, pain burned in his leg, crippling pain, spreading to his hip; he fought to steady himself, to keep himself from falling over. *Fall over now and I die. Got to save Jenny, save Nell, got to stop Eliot.*

Ffffffthump! A scream. Distant. Nell. Nell's scream. Drew knew if he turned his head Eliot would be on top of him, but Nell was screaming! Why? Drew shot a quick glance to the house. Nell was screaming something about Jenny; Jenny was face forward on the ground, an arrow protruded from her back.

"No!" The scream welled up from inside Drew, exploding from within.

Blam! Blam! Blam! Blam!

Musket shot whizzed past him, peppering the trees along the edge of the forest, bark and wood chips flying everywhere, driving the Indians back into the woods. Two of them hit the ground, the others fled, running to the safety of the woods and the darkness.

Just as Drew turned back, Eliot jumped toward him, savagely slashing with the knife; Drew leaned back, dodging the blade. Once. Twice. Eliot threw himself on Drew, knocking him backward, slamming him to the ground; the painted, sweaty chest of his attacker pinned his head against the dirt and rocks and thistles of the field. He tried to push Eliot off, his hands slipped, couldn't get a grip, too wet. At least, this close Eliot couldn't strike, too close, too high up on him, he'd have to lift himself up to strike. Drew wasn't able to stop him—his wounded leg screamed with pain, Eliot was too heavy, too strong. Drew thought of Nell and Jenny and Christopher Matthews, how he'd failed them, hurt them. He'd tried to make up for it, but he'd caused too much pain, there wasn't enough time to make up for all the pain, not enough time and now it was over.

The painted chest of Eliot Venner lifted up as he prepared to ram his blade into his victim; Drew blocked his arm, but Eliot was too strong; he couldn't hold back the blade much longer; it would find its mark. Drew thought of his grandfather, for some reason; he'd always thought he'd die like his grandfather, die old, not like this. Eliot repositioned himself to add his weight to his strength, to force the knife down, and as he did, his knee kicked the arrow in Drew's thigh.

Drew screamed from the pain; Eliot liked the sound and kicked the arrow again. Like a hot poker, the arrow twisted in Drew's leg, and he shrieked in agony. Now Eliot was laughing his hyena laugh. Drew felt unconsciousness begin to creep over his eyes like a dark mist, his arms were giving way; the laughing London savage kicked the arrow again.

Blam!

It was a loud sound, loud enough to startle Drew's failing senses awake, the sound of a musket very close. Drew's attacker bolted upright, his arms fell limp, the knife dropped from his grasp, falling to the dirt, the wild eyes of Eliot Venner stared sightlessly ahead, the right side of his head black with gunpowder as he fell forward on top of his prey.

Fighting back the pain, Drew struggled to free himself from the weight of his attacker's limp body; shoving Eliot aside, Drew raised himself up to see who had fired the shot, who had saved his life.

Propped up on one elbow, the smoking gun fell from her hand. Their eyes met for only a second. But in that second, the dying eyes of Jenny Matthews told Drew she would always love him.

EPILOGUE

Nell approached her husband from behind and tenderly put her arms around his neck. "Reminiscing?" she asked.

Drew nodded.

"They're waiting for us," she said.

"Just give me a moment."

Drew Morgan sat at the table in the sitting room of the house he built overlooking Boston's bay. In front of him were two books, the Bible he'd brought over with him from England and his journal. Twenty-two years had passed since he penned his first entry in the journal:

May 16, 1632. Jenny was buried today. She's with her father now. I pray he'll forgive me; I failed in my promise to keep her safe. My only comfort is in knowing she's in a place where no one can ever hurt her again.

Nell sat beside her husband and caressed his arm. "I'm glad we didn't go back to England. God's been good to us here."

Drew nodded his agreement as he flipped the pages of the journal. One place was marked with an envelope.

February 26, 1645. Received word from England today. Bishop William Laud, Archbishop of Canterbury, was executed on January 10 of this year. He was held in the Tower of London during his trial and then was beheaded.

The account of his death had two quotes in it.

Nehemiah Wallington rejoiced, "His little grace, that great enemy of God, his head cut off."

John Dod wrote, "The Little Firework of Canterbury was extinguished on Tower Hill."

I can't help but have mixed feelings. Bishop Laud was a wicked, hateful man. But he was always good to me.

"Did I ever tell you your father was a prophet?" Drew asked.

Nell smiled. "What are you talking about?"

"When he had charge of me in Edenford, he took me bowling with David Cooper. After the game, we sat by the river and your father told us a story about a poor man who attempted to rob a thief. The thief scolded him, telling the poor man he was going about it all wrong, and then proceeded to teach him the correct way to rob someone, whereupon the poor man robbed the thief the correct way."

Nell laughed. "That sounds like one of my father's stories."

"Anyway, after the story your father likened the thief to Bishop Laud, claiming the bishop was teaching England to hate and kill, and that his teaching would be his own undoing. According to the reports I read of Laud's trial, the man who fiercely prosecuted the bishop was previously one of Laud's victims in the Star Chamber. Bishop Laud's prosecutor had no ears and wore brands on his cheeks."

Nell pointed to the envelope. "Why do you keep that?"

"I don't know. Does it disturb you that I keep it?"

"A little."

It was a letter from Archbishop Laud, written from London's Tower just days before his execution. Drew didn't receive it until well after the archbishop's death. In the letter the archbishop wrote that no one had ever hurt him as much as Drew. He said he had no remorse for his actions. There was no mention of Eliot. At the bottom of the letter the bishop had written: (6/1/17/20-23) (40/5/14/13) (5/1/7/5-6) (22/5/4/1-2). *"God be with thee on thy journey. My beloved."*

It was the identical message Laud used when he taught Drew the code.

Nell reached over and closed the journal. "I just don't want to think about Archbishop Laud today," she said. "This is a special day and I don't want him ruining it."

"Like it or not," Drew replied, "we never would have met if it weren't for him."

"I still don't want to think about him today." She pointed to the Bible resting next to the journal, "And I still don't like that version of the Bible." She squeezed his arm and gave him a peck on the cheek. "Come on, it's time to go."

Drew and Nell Morgan walked down the hill toward the old meeting tree, long since abandoned as the location for services once the church building had been erected.

Waiting for them was their family. Christopher, their eldest son, was twenty years old. Lucy, nineteen, was standing next to her intended, William Sinclair, a schoolmaster. And Roger, sixteen, resembled his father at that age.

Drew stood tall before them, a proud father.

Christopher had associated himself with Reverend John Eliot, the former pastor of Roxbury, in missionary activities among the Indians. Together with his mentor, Christopher was learning Indian dialects and assisting the missionary in founding thirteen colonies of "Praying Indians," comprised of over 1,000 members.

Lucy was a headstrong young woman who always favored the abused, neglected, and the outcasts. Her outspokenness had gotten her into trouble on more than one occasion. Yet, she was a woman of conviction; and although her father didn't always agree with her, he was proud of her spirit of determination.

Roger was still an unknown. He spent his days daydreaming of pioneers and tales of the western country. Drew had little doubt that the boy would be an adventurer.

"A Morgan family tradition begins today." Drew addressed his family with the tone of fatherly authority. "A tradition that will be passed from generation to generation of Morgans until the Day of Jesus Christ our Savior."

He looked at each child separately. Christopher had his mother's brown eyes; Lucy resembled Jenny, the aunt she never knew, with her beautiful, long straight hair; Roger was fidgety, restless.

"The tradition that we begin today is the passing of our family's spiritual heritage on to the next generation." Drew held up his Bible. "This is the symbol of our heritage, the Bible I brought with me from England. Inside . . ." Drew opened the Bible and pulled out a cloth cross, ". . . is a cross made of lace. This is your mother's contribution to the family legacy."

He replaced the cross and closed the Bible. "The person who holds this book has a twofold obligation. First, it will be his responsibility to ensure that the spiritual heritage of the Morgan family is passed to the next generation; Second, it will be his responsibility to choose a person from the generation following him to succeed him. In a family ceremony like this one, he will deliver this Bible, this cross, and the admonition to the candidate to remain faithful to God and His Word."

Nell scowled at Roger. He was drawing something in the dirt with his shoe and not paying attention. The boy caught his mother's glance, sighed, and looked at his father.

"In the front of the Bible," Drew opened the cover, "there will be a list of each person who has been entrusted with the care of the Morgan spiritual heritage. The list begins with my name. He read aloud:

"*Drew Morgan, 1630, Zechariah 4:6.*

"Below that, I have written:

"*Christopher Morgan, 1654, Matthew 28:19.*"

Christopher smiled. He liked his father's choice of verse. "The Scripture reference that accompanies my name was given to me by my spiritual father, your grandfather, Christopher Matthews. It has become my life's verse. As Christopher's father, I have chosen a life verse for him: "Go ye, therefore, and teach all nations, baptizing them in the name of the Father, and of the Son, and of the Holy Ghost."

Drew Morgan handed the Bible to his eldest son. "As the head of the Morgan family, I proudly entrust to your keeping the responsibility of carrying on the Morgan family faith. My prayer for you is that God will bless you with a son, and that one day you will hand this Bible to him with a similar charge. I also pray that you will be as proud of him as I am of you."

Drew hugged his son; Nell kissed him on the cheek.

"Before God, I promise do my best to make you proud of me," Christopher said.

"We're already proud of you, son."

For the remainder of the afternoon, the Morgan family and William Sinclair sat beneath the meeting tree, reminiscing about growing up in Boston colony, and telling various family tales, many of them having been stretched beyond believability. The highlight of the afternoon came when Drew Morgan told his family the story of the beginning of the Morgan family faith.

"The story begins at Windsor Castle," he said, "the day I met Bishop Laud. For it was on that day my life began its downward direction."

AFTERWORD

Historical fiction is the weaving together of two colorful strands—historical fact and imaginative fiction; the finished product, if the author is successful, is a narrative tapestry depicting scenes of life from a previous age. In this type of work the question inevitably arises as to how much of each strand the author used. How much of the tale is fact and how much is fiction? Of course, the amount of each strand and its placement in the overall tapestry is the creative task of the author. For those who are interested in this author's use of these two strands, I offer the following paragraphs.

In general, the life and times of the men and women in seventeenth-century England is based on historical research. From this research, I attempted to re-create the physical, emotional, and spiritual setting of the era. Then, having identified the paramount conflicts and interests of that day, I chose characters that would portray the various sides, som historical and some fictional.

Historically, I selected Bishop William Laud, King Charles I, and John Winthrop to portray interests on each side of the conflict. Other historical characters making minor appearances include Rev. John Cotton, Roger Williams, Rev. Francis Higginson, Rev. Skelton, and Governor Endecott. The fam-

ilies Morgan, Matthews, Cooper, and Chesterfield are fictitious as are Eliot Venner, and Marshall and Mary Ramsden.
The story is carried along by the fictitious Drew Morgan.
Through his eyes we see the controlling desires of the English
church and crown, the awakening evangelical faith of the Puritans, the emptiness of the vast wealth of the class of country gentlemen, and the riches of spiritual life through Jesus
Christ in the midst of persecution and poverty.

Actual settings — Windsor Castle, the city of London, the
Tower of London, Winchester, Cambridge, and Massachusetts Bay Colony — were depicted using information from historical documents. Maps, drawings, journals, and records of
these places were employed in an attempt to re-create how
they appeared to the people living at that time.

The conflict between Bishop Laud and the Puritans is based
on fact. Laud's relentless determination to force the Puritans
to conform to the authority of the church is a matter of
history. His consuming hatred, persecution, and punishment
of Puritan ministers and pamphleteers is based on fact, as is
his insistence on the positioning and railing off of the altar,
the wearing of the surplice, and his opposition to preaching.

Laud's personality is sketched from his own writings as
well as descriptions of him by various primary sources. I
made two notable exceptions to his recorded personality, in
that I gave him a sense of humor and a desire for a close
confidant. From all accounts Bishop Laud was a humorless
man who had no close friends. He despised women — he
would not allow women in his London residence — preferring
male companionship. His journal implies agonizing struggles
with homosexual tendencies, so I imply them also. He was
also a man driven to make the entire realm subservient to the
Church of England. In this he underestimated his opposition
both in England and in Scotland. As history records, he was
tried and beheaded.

The sea battle of 1588, resulting in the defeat of the great Spanish Armada and the battle of San Juan de Ulua, are based on historical accounts. John Hawkins, Sir Francis Drake, the *Minion* and the *Judith* are historical, as is Hawkins' redesign of the English fighting ship. Amos Morgan's part in the refit is fictitious.

Morgan Hall is a sixteenth- seventeenth-century country home. The King Alfred Inn is based on inns and inn customs of the time. The Matthews' house is a typical example of living quarters in small towns in Devonshire.

The writings of the pamphleteer Justin for the most part are mine. In some of the writing I used the dichotomous form of pamphleteer Peter Ramus and some phrases from Thomas Cartwright. I refrained from using the vitriolic personal attack on Bishop Laud, a common practice among pamphleteers, notably William Prynne. The sermons of Christopher Matthews are the product of my pen.

Bearbaiting was a popular event in the seventeenth century, not only for commoners but for King James I as well. The king enjoyed throwing dogs to wild animals at the Tower of London's menagerie. The people of that day were crude and bloodthirsty as reflected in their gruesome entertainment. Public executions were regarded as midweek holidays.

Lord Chesterfield's hunt is based on the account of a royal hunting party and hunting procedures as described in Tubervile's *Booke of Hunting* printed in 1576.

The accidental death of Lord Chesterfield's son and Laud's use of it to frame Christopher Matthews is fiction. In this event I portrayed Bishop Laud's machiavellian approach to his work. He was a man driven to employ anything at his disposal to achieve his desired end. One note in his defense: I'm convinced that despite his ruthless methods, he sincerely believed he was doing the best for England, the church, and God.

The use of the Bible to transmit coded messages is my own invention.

The town of Edenford is also fictional. If you travel to County Devon today, you will not find it on the west side of the Exe River south of Tiverton. However, in creating Edenford, I drew heavily upon accounts of the region for that general time period. One especially helpful source in this regard was *Early Tours in Devon and Cornwall,* R. Pearse Chope, ed., Newton Abbot (Devon): David and Charles, 1967, which published the journal entries of Devonshire travelers in 1540 and 1695.

Drew's entrance into Edenford and his subsequent arrest are based on a true account of the period: *History of the Life of Thomas Ellwood* by his own hand, 1661. And Christopher Matthews' parable about the downfall of Bishop Laud is a historical tale recorded in Abraham de la Pryme's *Diary* of that same period. Both accounts portray the danger of traveling in England in those days.

King James' *Book of Sports* which not only authorized but promoted recreational activities on the Sabbath is history. Laws were passed by King James I and his son Charles I forcing Puritans to read the book aloud from the pulpit.

The Puritans' preference for the Geneva Bible over the King James Version is fact. Actually, the Puritans preferred two Bibles—the Geneva Bible and the Bishops' Bible. The king's response was to license the printing of his version only, which hastened its acceptance among Bible-reading Englishmen. The Scripture passages used by Nell and Christopher Matthews are quotes from The Geneva Bible, a facsimile of the 1560 edition; I modernized the spelling for easier reading.

The wool industry and the methods of producing serges are based on historical descriptions, as is the production and popularity of *punto a groppo,* bone lace.

Bishop Laud's free use of the Star Chamber to advance his

personal agenda is a matter of record. After the death of the Duke of Buckingham, Laud was without doubt the second most powerful man in the kingdom and King Charles' closest advisor. The Star Chamber punishments described in this work are based on court records. The death penalty was not an option for a Star Chamber trial; that sentence had to come from a common-law court.

The names of the ships sailing to America and most of the highlights of the crossing are based on real events as recorded in John Winthrop's journal—the delay in sailing, the breakfast on board the *Arbella* with Captain Burleigh of Yarmouth Castle, Winthrop's personal testimony, the presence of Lady Arbella, the feared attack by the Dunkirkers, the ships' order of arrival and the dates they arrived, the frequent soundings as they neared their destination, the first impressions of the newly arrived colonists, and the first dwelling places are all based on his firsthand account.

Rev. John Cotton's sermon to the departing settlers is a condensation, a mixture of direct quote and paraphrase arranged to give the gist of the message in a short space. When John Winthrop addresses the disgruntled, newly arrived settlers by reading paragraphs of his thoughts while crossing the Atlantic, I'm quoting portions of his work, "A Model of Christian Charity." Winthrop actually shared these thoughts with the settlers while they were still at sea. I imagined he would have used many of the same thoughts during his attempt to convince them to stay, so I placed the reading of the text later than it actually occured in history.

The early difficulties with the Pequot Indians are based on fact. The Pequot tribe grew increasingly concerned over the rapid growth of the colonies and the settlers' burgeoning intrusion upon their territory. Tensions escalated when a Boston trader was murdered in 1636, presumably by a Pequot Indian. A punitive expedition of settlers was sent to avenge the killing. The result was the destruction of the Pequot settlement. Between 500 and 600 Indians were killed or burned to death in the fires, effectively destroying the entire tribe. This was one of the first major conflicts between the bay settlers and native Americans.

Jack Cavanaugh
San Diego, California
1993